SPECIAL E

The shrieking of metal against metal caused Jake to open his eyes. The metallic scream sounded more like the New York City subway than an aboveground rail. The ceiling lights went off and failed to come back on, although sunlight streaming through the wide windows illuminated the interior.

Something did not feel right to Jake. He heard a door slide open and recoil behind him, and as he forced himself to turn around once more, he heard a woman's piercing scream.

Three Indian men had entered the car. At least he thought they were Indian. But there was no doubt in his mind that they brandished semiautomatic rifles. And as he narrowed his eyes, he saw that the emaciated-looking men wore blank expressions, their eyes unblinking. His body turned numb, except for the pain in his back.

They're looking for me!

Without warning, the lead dead thing lowered his AK-47 and triggered a burst of gunfire that decimated a woman's torso like canned tomatoes.

No!

Screams filled the car, and a passenger stood up. The second man fired a burst from his weapon, causing the passenger to dance with his arms spread wide before he dropped to the floor like a slaughtered cow.

Jake reached inside his jacket for the reassuring grip of his Glock, only to realize he had left it at the office on doctor's orders.

Shit out of luck . . .

THE JAKE HELMAN FILES
DESPERATE SOULS

GREGORY LAMBERSON

MEDALLION
P R E S S

Medallion Press, Inc.
Printed in USA

PREVIOUS ACCOLADES FOR
GREGORY LAMBERSON'S *PERSONAL DEMONS*

DESPERATE SOULS

GREGORY LAMBERSON

DEDICATION

To my mentors in storytelling:
William F. Nolan, Frank Henenlotter, and Roy Frumkes

Published 2010 by Medallion Press, Inc.

The MEDALLION PRESS LOGO
is a registered trademark of Medallion Press, Inc.

Names, characters, places, and incidents are the products of the author's imagination or are used fictionally. Any resemblance to actual events, locales, or persons, living or dead, is entirely coincidental.

Typeset in Adobe Garamond Pro
Printed in the United States of America

ISBN: 978-160542170-4

10 9 8 7 6 5 4 3 2 1
First Edition

ACKNOWLEDGMENTS

Writing *Desperate Souls* was a different experience for me. Although it is a sequel to *Personal Demons*, it is the first novel I've written that was not based on one of my screenplays. Like *The Frenzy Way*, it combines police procedural, noir, and horror in what I like to call "action horror."

I wish to acknowledge my two police consultants, retired NYC detective Chris Aiello, aka "Chris the cop," and fellow author Joe McKinney, a San Antonio homicide detective.

I also wish to thank my advance readers, Chris Hedges and Jeff Strand, and all the supportive people at Medallion Press, especially Helen Rosburg, Adam Mock, Ali DeGray, Heather Lewis, Paul Ohlson, and Lorie Popp. It's great to be part of such a special team.

If you do not give me the Bull of Heaven,

    I will knock down the Gates of the Netherworld,

    I will smash the doorposts, and leave the doors flat down,

    and will let the dead go up to eat the living!

And the dead will outnumber the living!

—Ishtar in *The Epic of Gilgamesh*

ONE

Avenue in Brooklyn. Returning from church, where she served on a committee dedicated to serving the poor, she had stopped for milk at a corner bodega, where she had spent too much time discussing the sorry state of the neighborhood with the proprietor, Miguel Ruiz.

Now she found herself hurrying home and scanning shadowy door-ways for signs of danger. After the Great Recession, New York City had seen its most dramatic crime increase since the crack cocaine epidemic of the 1980s. Lucile remembered those days well, and in her opinion, the current environment posed a far greater threat to senior citizens like herself. At sixty-seven, she had begun to give serious consideration to her sister's invitation for Lucile to move in with her in Florida.

With swollen ankles and creaking knees, the retired bookkeeper crossed the street, passing a blockade constructed of graffiti-covered plywood. The plywood obstructed the entrance to a subway station that city officials had closed in a desperate attempt to help stave off impending financial disaster. A homeless couple covered in filth slept sitting up with their backs pressed against the blockade.

Cut the services and the cops, Lucile thought as she passed beneath the construction awning that ran the length of the block. *You might as well cut our throats.* After Governor Raymond Santucci's recent cutbacks, Mayor Myron Madigan had been forced to lay off thousands of police officers, which contributed to the crime wave, especially in downtrodden neighborhoods. Lucile had watched Flatbush Avenue rise and fall and rise and fall again.

A scarecrow, tall and gaunt, stood at the far corner, silhouetted by the dying light. Drawing closer to him, she discerned emaciated gray features. Dark, bulbous eyes that reminded her of a frog's locked on her from within sunken sockets. She did not recall seeing him before, but the scarecrows all looked the same, regardless of race. Dangerous new drugs had created a dangerous new breed of criminal, driven to brutal acts by the all-consuming need to get high.

Pulling her purse tight against her bosom, Lucile stepped closer to the metal framework supporting the awning at the sidewalk's edge. The scarecrow's dull eyes followed her, although the addict's head did not move. Lucile slipped her right hand inside her purse and closed her fingers around the cool metal of the tear gas canister.

Just try it, she thought. *I'm ready for you.*

She had been mugged three times in the last six months—once at gunpoint, once at knifepoint, and once with no weapon at all, just three wild-eyed young men with pallid skin and darkened eyes.

Never again.

Lucile would welcome death before allowing another one of these fiends to rob her dignity, let alone what little money she carried on her person. She kept her cash in a secret pocket on her dress, not in her purse. If the fiends demanded her money, she would surprise them with a gas blast from the canister, which she had purchased from a sympathetic pawnshop owner. It didn't matter that automobiles traversed the busy avenue beside her; none of the drivers would stop for an old woman taking a beating. And any people with sense had already gone inside and locked their doors.

As she reached her block, her instincts told her to look over her shoulder. Sure enough, the scarecrow lumbered across the street behind her. Quickening her gait, she increased the distance separating them and reached her building's entrance. Inside the vestibule, she withdrew her keys, making it harder to grasp the canister if she needed it, and jammed the longest one into the lock. Her heart thumped from her panicked rush inside, and she almost dropped the keys. If the fiend cornered her in the foyer before she opened the door, she didn't stand a chance.

Entering the lobby, she closed the inside door behind her, making sure the latch clicked into place. The scarecrow stopped outside the front door and turned in her direction. She couldn't tell if he saw her through both doors or not. Then he opened the outside door and entered the vestibule.

You ugly, godless son of a bitch!

The scarecrow crossed the tiled floor, and the first door closed behind him. Praying he didn't have keys, Lucile stepped back as his shadow fell over her. The scarecrow pressed his face against the glass, his eyes locating hers.

He's half dead. She had seen this look many times.

The doorknob turned and she caught her breath, but the door didn't open. Fearing the scarecrow might punch his fist through the glass, she climbed the stairs as fast as her beleaguered joints permitted. At the top, she glanced over her shoulder.

The scarecrow remained at the door but had stopped turning its knob. Stepping back, he turned and stood looking at the front door.

That one isn't locked, Lucile thought, willing the scarecrow to leave. She turned back just in time to see another figure bounding toward her from the shadows. With her heart jumping in her chest, her mind absorbed the teenage boy's appearance: Hispanic, hair cropped close beneath a red hooded sweatshirt, hungry eyes blazing within sunken sockets. *Another scarecrow!*

She heard the echo of his sneakers slapping the floor as he raced toward her, then saw him raise a pipe high over his head. In that instant, she forgot all about the tear gas in her purse. Instead, she wondered whether or not she would fall all the way down the stairs after he hit her.

He brought the pipe down onto her skull, and she never learned the answer.

Hearing the old woman's scraping footsteps on the stairs, Louis Rodriguez slid the lead pipe from his belt and gripped it in his right hand. He had been about ready to give up on this building when he'd heard the downstairs door open and close. Now the woman stopped one step below the floor where he hid, and he couldn't control his need for drugs anymore. Emerging around the hallway corner, he saw that she had stopped to glance over her shoulder at the lobby below. She turned toward him, her eyes registering his presence, and looked up as he raised the pipe over his head.

Louis had never killed anyone before, but he found it easy enough to brain the old woman. As the pipe split her skull open, he felt no remorse, only gratitude that she did not scream as she toppled backwards. He watched with perverse fascination as her head struck the stair six feet below and her feet rose into the air. Her body executed a half flip and slid down the remaining stairs feetfirst, her face smashing against each edge on the way down.

Ignoring the blood that erupted from beneath her wig like lava from a volcano, he snatched her purse and dumped its contents on the floor. Lipstick, tissues, compact, keys, metal canister . . .

No money.

Louis frisked her body, turning her pockets inside out until he found what he wanted: six folded twenty-dollar bills.

Yes!

Still clutching the pipe, he ran outside, breathed in fresh air as he stepped around a fellow junkie loitering out front, and broke into a run. He did not run out of fear of getting caught but out of pure anticipation. He tried to contain his elation, so the other scarecrows on the street wouldn't suspect he had come into cash.

Shit like that gets you killed these days.

7

Louis ran along blocks occupied by fortified buildings until he reached the empty space where the old car wash had been. He had scored coke from a worker there back in the day, but the White Lady was hard to find now. Staring across the rubble at the Dumpster behind the shuttered pizzeria next door, his heart sank.

Too soon.

He glanced at the darkening sky.

Relax. Relax. It won't be long. They only come out at night.

Shifting his weight from foot to foot—the junkie's dance—he dug his fingers into his palms and chewed the inside of his mouth to dull the pain seizing his belly. The shadows in the empty lot lengthened, and his breathing took on a deep, anticipatory rhythm.

A shadow moved along the restaurant's brick wall. It hadn't been there a few minutes ago. A second shadow appeared and then a third. The shadows stopped elongating as their sources stepped into the glare of a streetlight, and at last the things revealed themselves to him. They wore common street clothes—oversized sneakers, baggy jeans, and hoodies like Louis's, their hands stuffed into their pockets.

Louis couldn't discern the things' features, but he knew without question that his connections had arrived. He moved forward, feeling an odd mixture of desperation and dread despite the pipe in his hand. He wished he could score from someone else, but the only other dealers around were the same as these: dead to the world.

The dealers turned their heads in Louis's direction but showed no

8

sign of recognition, even though Louis had been a steady customer for weeks. Standing before the dead things—boys roughly his own age— Louis swallowed. The thing standing in the middle tipped its head back, revealing taut, almost skeletal, features. It didn't blink because it had no eyelids, and its dull, flat black pupils focused on Louis, causing him to shudder. The creature waited.

"I need some Magic," Louis said, holding up his newfound cash. "Three bags."

The creature on the left removed a bony hand covered with leathery skin from one pocket. Opening its coarse fist, it revealed three plastic bags filled with black powder in its palm. The thing on the right took Louis's money and pocketed it.

Louis snatched the Black Magic and fled, as anxious to escape the dead things as he was to snort Magic.

Louis ran three blocks to the abandoned apartment building he called home. His family lived a few blocks west, but he could not remember the last time he had seen his grandmother or younger brother. He put them out of his mind just like the old bird he had just snuffed. Racing up the grimy cement stairs, he leapt onto the window ledge and pushed the plywood there. The wood bowed inward, allowing him to slip inside, and he heard the board snap back into place as his sneakers touched the rotted linoleum floor.

The haunted eyes of scarecrows loitering in the lobby followed him up the stairs. Once these wretches had been cokeheads, crackheads, and heroin addicts; now they craved Black Magic. Some, like Louis, snorted it. Others smoked it, injected it, or mixed it into their favorite cocktails. They lived for Black Magic. They robbed for Black Magic. And, Louis now understood, they killed for Black Magic. Their DNA demanded it.

Hurrying along the second-floor hallway to the deserted apartment he occupied, he thought of nothing else. He pushed the front door open and entered the one-bedroom flat: no real furniture, just milk crates he had stolen from outside a Korean deli and a coffee table he had hauled upstairs from the sidewalk. Not even a mattress. A layer of soot on the living room windows served as the only curtains he needed, and the streetlight outside provided gray light.

Closing the door, which no longer had a lock, he ran to the coffee table and kneeled before it. He unclenched his fist and dropped the bags of Magic on the table, opened one with trembling fingers, and emptied its contents, like fine black sand, onto the table's chipped wooden surface. He stopped blinking, and his nasal passages opened and closed like the gills of a fish. Taking a half straw from his pocket, he snorted Black Magic without bothering to separate it into lines.

Oh yeah, he thought as his bloodstream absorbed the black powder. *Heaven. This is what it's all about.* The old woman he had murdered never entered his thoughts again.

Lost in a world of fantasy, Louis spent the next six hours snorting

Black Magic and playing with himself. His mind fabricated the perfect woman, statuesque with a sculpted physique, her smooth flesh as dark as the drug consuming his life. Every time he pictured her, his hand groped for his penis, which he stroked to painful orgasm. Then he snorted more Magic, and the cycle started anew. He ignored the pain from the bleeding fissures on his erection for as long as he could, then dulled the agony with even more Magic.

Finally, when his hand and imagination had given him more joy than any real woman could have, the room spun around him even though he lay on his back. His heart tightened, and he sucked in his breath—

Oh no!

—and pain stabbed his heart, which exploded in his chest and ceased to beat.

Oh, God, please no!

There were so many things he still wanted to do in his life. He wanted to get high, and he wanted to get high again after that.

Too late . . .

But even as his body cooled and evacuated its bowels and bladder, Louis's mind continued to formulate thoughts. Lying dead of an overdose on the floor of an abandoned building, covered in his own feces and urine, he experienced shame and despair. He knew that he had met the inevitable and disgraceful fate of a junkie, and yet his consciousness remained intact, trapped within his disgusting corpse.

Oh, Jesus, what's happening to me?

He wondered if he would spend eternity trapped in this filthy shell or if he would pass on to some other form of existence. He had no hope of reaching heaven but held out for purgatory over hell.

Murderers go to hell.

The sudden beating of his ruptured heart caused hope to rise from the bowels of his corpse. Looking inside himself, he saw that this was impossible: the organ in the center of his chest remained a hopeless and unmoving mess.

Then what—?

Thrum-thrum-thrum . . .

He heard it, loud and clear, like a great machine reverberating through water.

Thrum-thrum-thrum . . .

Drumbeats!

His mind catalogued the building's tenants. One or two of them might have been musicians at one time but no longer. They were all addicts, like him. If any of them had arrived with musical instruments, they had long since pawned them to buy drugs. No, the more he thought about it, the more certain he became that the drumming existed only in his head. Was his brain liquefying already? What further degradation must he endure?

The answer came in the form of movement within his body: muscles drew tight, and his view rolled over from the ceiling to the floor.

WHAT THE HELL?

He saw his hands flat on the floor. Then his left knee came into view, and he stood erect. But this was impossible! Not only had his dead body risen from the floor, but it had done so of its own volition, without any input or desire from him.

Thrum-thrum-thrum . . .

Someone or some*thing* had seized control of his body.

Dozens of thoughts crisscrossed his overstimulated brain all at once. Perhaps he could make this work for him. Maybe he could adapt to this new situation. All he wanted to do was get high . . .

His naked body pulled on his dirty clothes and crossed the room.

Wait a minute. What's happening? I don't want to go outside like this! I want to clean myself up!

His body ignored him. It reached for the doorknob and opened the door.

You can't do this! You need *me!*

His body stepped out into the dark hallway, following the drumbeat he heard in his head.

Little more than a subconscious thought pattern, Louis screamed.

TWO

"Jake, over here!"

Jake feinted left as Edgar barreled toward him, then danced beneath his former partner's outstretched arms and passed the orange ball to the boy who had maneuvered beneath the chain-link basket.

Grasping the ball in both hands, Martin twisted his body and leapt straight into the air.

Edgar charged at him, but the ball rattled through the basket and struck the asphalt.

"Score!" Jake raised both arms over his head and grinned as Martin's sneakers touched ground.

Edgar roped a muscular arm around his twelve-year-old son and staggered to a halt. The boy beamed at him.

"This isn't fair anymore," Edgar said, wiping sweat from his forehead. "You're getting too big." He glanced at Jake. "And you're in too good of shape."

"Eleven months without a cigarette," Jake said, giving Martin a high five.

"Yeah, well, this two-on-one thing ain't cutting it anymore. I need help. Maybe I should ask Vasquez to join us and even things up."

"You would invite a woman to come along on Guys' Day Out?" Jake winked at Martin. This wasn't the first time Edgar had introduced his current partner, Maria Vasquez, into a conversation. Jake appreciated his friend's intention, but he had no interest in dating. Sheryl had been dead just under one year, murdered by the serial killer called the Cipher. Jake still carried a piece of his wife's soul inside him.

"You're just afraid she'll dance circles around your ass."

"Used to be you didn't need any help. You beat me and Martin without breaking a sweat. What's wrong? You feeling your age?"

"I don't get to make my own schedule the way you do. I have a *real* job. Responsibilities."

Cracking his neck, Jake observed a medical helicopter crossing the cloudless blue sky. "So quit and come into practice with me."

Martin's eyes widened. "Yeah!"

Edgar snorted. "What, give up my pension to play private eye with you? I don't think so."

"Imagine how the bad guys would tremble in their underwear if they knew Helman and Hopkins were working the street together again."

"Bad guys? What bad guys? The only bad guys you tangle with are cheating spouses and deadbeat dads."

Jake shrugged. "I've had my share of scrapes. And I don't get to call for backup. I'm a lone wolf."

"You're supposed to call in backup anytime you get in a jam, *lone wolf.* That's what makes you 'private' and me 'professional.'" Edgar nodded to his son. "You gonna stand there listening to this man's nonsense or are you going to run a few laps? Give me half a mile."

"All right," Martin said. "Don't leave until I get back, Jake."

"You know it, partner."

Martin took off, all legs and arms and enthusiasm, and circled the track.

"I can't believe how big he's gotten," Jake said, meaning it.

"Tell me about it. We can't keep him in the same clothes for more than a season."

"I remember when he was only half as tall. Seems like just last year."

"I think time speeds up the closer we get to our own deaths."

Jake glanced at his friend. "Aren't you the morbid one?"

"Not at all. I live each day like it's my last. How about you?"

Jake returned his attention to Martin, who had circled half the track. "I'm working things out. But I think I've got a pretty positive attitude considering . . ."

Considering he had resigned from the department in disgrace rather than submit to a mandatory drug test after killing two bad guys during a tavern robbery he had foiled. *Considering* Sheryl had given him his walking papers after discovering he had been on the take to support his cocaine habit. And *considering* the love of his life had been murdered by his enemies. Then there were the considerations Edgar didn't even know about.

Edgar clasped his shoulder. "You're doing well."

Martin passed them and increased his pace.

Knowing he would never have a son or a daughter of his own with Sheryl made Jake love the boy even more. "To be that young again, with that kind of energy . . ."

"I think the same thing every time I see him." Edgar chuckled.

"He's a great kid. You've done a good job with him."

Edgar shrugged. "His mother deserves the lion's share of the credit. She's the one who's there for him every day. I'm just a weekend father and only then if the job doesn't get in the way."

As partners, Jake and Edgar swung by the Jackson Heights house where Joyce and Martin lived whenever their caseload permitted it. Joyce and Edgar had never been married and maintained a friendly enough relationship for Martin's sake. "You've set a good example for him."

"I hope so." Edgar's voice cooled. "Check that out."

Jake followed Edgar's sight line. An emaciated Caucasian man lurked on the other side of the chain-link fence, scanning the field for a victim. Filthy rags hung off his skeletal frame.

"Goddamned scarecrows are everywhere. The other day an old lady in Brooklyn got murdered in her own building. Some son of a bitch caved her skull in with a pipe. I just know it was a scarecrow. Black Magic is everywhere. That's the kind of thing that drives a parent crazy."

Jake nodded. He had never witnessed anything like the drug epidemic sweeping the city.

"If I catch those things anywhere near Martin . . ." He sighed. "The city just laid off another two thousand cops—can you believe it? We've already got our hands full with these Machete Massacres."

Jake had read in the newspapers that the corpses of several drug dealers had turned up, theirs limbs dismembered by machetes. As members of the Special Homicide Task Force, Edgar and Maria had their hands full. Jake did not miss that kind of action.

"We're still on for dinner, right?" Edgar said.

"Of course. I wouldn't miss meeting this new woman in your life for the world. Has Martin met her?"

"Nah. I don't think it's a good idea yet."

"Why? He's met your girlfriends before."

"*Lady* friends. Dawn is different, though. She's special. I don't know if he's ready yet."

Jake burst into laughter.

Edgar shot him a look. "What?"

"I never thought I'd see the day. Edgar Hopkins, murder police extraordinaire and eternal bachelor, head over heels in love."

Edgar looked away. "Fuck you." Then he laughed, too.

Jake took the R train to the Twenty-third Street stop in Manhattan, where he merged with a hundred other bodies exiting the dark subway station. Unemployment had skyrocketed, and more people used public transportation because fewer could afford taxis. On the sidewalk, he ignored panhandlers' outstretched hands. Homeless people sat shoulder to shoulder with their backs against storefronts. Jake felt lucky to have a roof over his head.

As usual, he passed through the cool dark shadow of the Tower, the high-tech office building he had protected as director of security for the reclusive billionaire Nicholas Tower and his company, Tower

International. The high-paying job had been a short-lived assignment: when Jake discovered that Tower was manufacturing illegal genetic hybrids and had been responsible for the murders committed by the Cipher, he had fled. Old Nick then ordered the Cipher to murder Sheryl.

Now the Cipher and Old Nick were both dead by Jake's hand. So was Kira Thorn, Tower's executive assistant, who had attempted to murder Jake in the apartment he had lived in with Sheryl. He had moved out soon after that, but first he mailed evidence of the company's genetic experiments and illegal activities to the heads of the ACCL: the Anti-Cloning Creationist League. The grassroots organization had posted the evidence online, but government agencies dismissed the images and video footage as a hoax.

A modern urban legend was born, and Tower International's reputation died almost overnight. The government filed an antitrust case, which resulted in the megacorporation being broken into several smaller companies, and Tower International's stranglehold on the genetics industry was broken. Every day brought a new scandal involving the company and saw a new Tower subsidiary fold.

But the company still existed, with the Tower still its headquarters. Names and faces that meant nothing to Jake had assumed control of the corporation's remaining assets. He did not trust them. If the government wouldn't ensure that Tower International never again engaged in scientific skullduggery, Jake intended to do that himself. That was why he had set up his shop as a private investigator on the fourth floor of a small building on Twenty-third Street, where he kept an eye on the Tower. So far, he had observed nothing suspicious.

Other unforeseen complications had arisen, though. Jake had underestimated Tower's importance to the global economy. The company's tentacles reached out to every industrialized nation on Earth, and when the government stepped in, their intervention helped cause the collapse of the global economy. Banks, manufacturing, medical advances, airlines, investments—virtually any institution in which Tower owned a stake—self-destructed. Jake had succeeded in bringing the old man's company to its figurative knees but in so doing had wreaked untold damage on the entire world.

He passed the Cajun restaurant, where he often ate and sometimes met clients, next to the building where he lived and worked and the storefront where a psychic worked. He had glimpsed the attractive woman who worked there through her front window but had not introduced himself because he never saw her outside. Inside the building's vestibule, he punched his personal security code into a keypad and entered the building's sparse lobby. No doorman, just several security cameras and alarms that Jake had installed as "security consultant" in exchange for reduced rent on his office. He had never met the landlord and made his monthly check out to Eden, Inc.

Jake chose to take the building's wide stairs over its confined elevator whenever possible. Although he had played basketball with Edgar and Martin for an hour, he liked any exercise he could incorporate into his daily routine. The stairs opened up onto each floor, allowing him to see the closed doors of his neighbors. On the fourth floor, next to a plain steel door, a simple nameplate off to one side read Helman Investigations and Security.

He unlocked the door, entered the office, and pressed the keys on another security pad. The front room served as a receptionist area, even though he had no real receptionist. The suite had an old-fashioned railroad apartment layout, with each room directly behind the other. He passed through a kitchenette with a narrow bathroom, then his own office, which overlooked Twenty-third Street and afforded him a view of the Flatiron Building, the Woolworth Building, and the Tower. It was illegal for individuals to maintain residences in office buildings, of course, but he had the run of the place after hours and an understanding with the building's agent.

Entering his bedroom behind the office, he stripped off his damp T-shirt, shorts, and underwear and stepped inside the shower stall, a narrow construct with an opaque glass door facing his bed. He missed having an actual bathtub, not to mention a toilet in the same room as his shower, but he could not argue with the rent he paid.

His signing bonus from Tower and Sheryl's life insurance policy had enabled him to set up shop here. Contrary to what Edgar thought, Jake's business did not thrive on divorce cases. He took his share of them but only when they met the same criteria as his other cases: he had to know that in some small way, his efforts helped someone. Although he had killed Kira in self-defense, he had executed the Cipher and Old Nick in cold blood and felt compelled to atone for his actions.

Showered and shaved, Jake dressed in comfortable slacks, a blue shirt, and a tie. He typically worked in jeans and casual shirts, but since he had made plans to meet Edgar and his girlfriend for dinner, he decided to dress up a little.

When the front door buzzed, he looked up at the security monitors above his office sofa and saw a thick Hispanic woman and a boy standing in the building's vestibule. He buzzed them in, then waited in the suite's doorway. As they got off the elevator, he saw that the woman was in her early fifties. Her footsteps echoed in the corridor, her weight shifting with each slow step.

"Mrs. Rodriguez? I'm Jake Helman."

"Hello." Dressed head to toe in black, the woman gestured at the boy standing beside her. "My grandson Victor."

Measuring the boy by Martin's height, Jake estimated his age to be nine. "Hello, Victor."

The boy regarded him with sad eyes. "Hi."

Jake stepped back from the door, allowing them to enter. "Can I get you some water?"

Carmen Rodriguez surveyed the office. "Yes, please."

"What about you, Victor?"

Keeping his eyes on Jake, Victor shook his head.

"How about a Cherry Coke?"

The boy shrugged. "'Kay."

Jake led them into his office, where they sat on the leather sofa, and served them refreshments. He wheeled his chair around his desk and sat facing them with his legs crossed. "Why don't you tell me how I can help you?"

Carmen sat with her hands folded on her lap. "Do you have children,

Mr. Helman?"

"I'm afraid not."

She scrutinized him as if trying to determine his character. "I have two daughters. One lives in Puerto Rico, the other in North Carolina. I used to have three daughters, but Rosario died when she was twenty-eight. Rosario was Victor's mother. She died of a heroin overdose."

Jake glanced at Victor. The boy sipped his Cherry Coke.

"I hide nothing from the boy. He needs to know the truth. I raised him and his brother like they were my own. Now Victor's brother, Louis, is dead, too."

The black dress, Jake thought. *She's in mourning.* "I'm sorry."

"Louis was six years older than Victor. Fifteen. Very independent that one, always getting into trouble."

"May I ask how he died?"

Carmen's face seemed to change shape. "I don't know."

"But you know that he's dead?"

"*Si.* I've seen him with my own eyes."

Jake suppressed a frown. "I don't understand."

"Louis used drugs. This Black Magic. When I found out, I gave him an ultimatum: give up the drug or give up your family. That same day, he moved out. That was three weeks ago. Three days ago, Victor came to me and said, 'Grandma, I saw Louis. He's selling drugs on the corner.' These days in this economy, it's hard for a young man to find honest work. Boys are likely to do stupid things for money.

"I went to this corner, and sure enough, there was Louis, with two other boys. Victor was right; they were selling drugs. I've lived in

Brooklyn all my life. I'm no fool. A young man starts slinging, there's little chance of saving him. He's headed for prison or the morgue or both. I went up to my grandson and called his name. When he turned to me, I wanted to scream. *Estaba muerto.* He was dead."

Jake felt an odd sensation in his body, as if the temperature of his blood had just cooled. "You mean he looked like death?"

"No, I mean he *was* dead. He stood there like a functioning human being, doing the devil's work. But he didn't blink. He didn't speak. He was dead. So were the other boys."

Jake tried not to exhibit any reaction. After all, he had seen things he never would have imagined possible, things that had sent him spiraling toward the brink of insanity. Phantoms searching for their souls. Angels and demons. Monsters. He knew that impossible beings walked the earth in different forms. "Mrs. Rodriguez, I've seen Black Magic junkies. We all have. They look very unhealthy."

Carmen fixed him with an appraising stare. "You have to be alive or only half dead to be a junkie. These boys were as dead as dead gets. A junkie is standing at death's door, only he doesn't know it. These boys crossed over and don't care."

"What did they do next?"

"They just stared at me with their awful eyes. They didn't say anything. They didn't do anything. Louis's expression was no different than the others'. There was no spark of life or recognition in it."

"What did you do?"

"I did what anyone would do. I got the hell away from that corner. I went there intending to drag Louis home, but I ran away to save my own life. I still have one living grandson, and I aim to keep it that way. We avoid that corner. Louis is still out there, selling that drug."

Jake glanced at Victor. The boy had stared at the floor during his grandmother's entire account, his expression never changing. *Now for the million-dollar question.* "Why did you come to me with this problem?"

"What else could I do, call 911? 'Hello, my grandson is dead and selling drugs down the block. Can you make him stop?' I came to you because Miss Laurel sent me. She says you can help me."

"Miss Laurel?" Jake had difficulty maintaining his poker face. Only one person on Earth knew anything about his unusual experiences: Bill Russel, the former CIA spook who had become an operative for Nicholas Tower and Kira Thorn. But Russel had fled the country, choosing to remain in the shadows rather than deal with the fallout of Tower International's collapse.

"The psychic downstairs."

Jake's heart skipped a beat. He supposed there was nothing strange about a fellow tenant in the building referring a client to a private investigator, but for Miss Laurel to claim she had knowledge of his experiences sent chills down his vertebrae. *What does she know?* He intended to find out. "It was kind of Miss Laurel to refer you to me. I'll have to thank her in person. Do you have a photograph of Louis?"

"Right here." Carmen opened her purse and took out a glossy school portrait of Louis. "This was taken at his school six months ago."

Jake studied the photo. Louis had been a good-looking kid with short hair and an infectious smile. "And the corner where he slings?"

"Montclair and Caton, near Flatbush Avenue."

The heart of Brooklyn, Jake thought, picturing the 70th Precinct neighborhood. *Rough turf.* "Do you know what time he works?"

"They only come out at night. What are you going to do?"

Jake shrugged. "I'm going to go there and see what's what. Then I'll get back to you."

Carmen appeared relieved that Jake seemed to believe her, but her voice grew tentative. "If you don't mind me asking . . ."

"I don't know what I can do for you, Mrs. Rodriguez. Maybe nothing. But I will look into this"—he raised Louis's photo—"and I'll let you know what I think. If I can help you, we'll work something out regarding my fee. But it won't cost you anything for me to see for myself what's happened to Louis."

"I understand." She got to her feet. "God bless you."

THREE

The door closed behind Jake, jingling bells announcing his arrival, and he stood alone at the top of two steps leading down into the parlor. He didn't know what to expect but saw no crystal ball, no tarot cards, no hint of the occult, just a round table with a red tablecloth in the room's center and a sofa on the far wall. Hearing the aggressive voices of political pundits on a cable TV news show in a back room, he suspected that Miss Laurel lived on the premises as well.

Miss Laurel emerged from a side doorway wearing a tight charcoal gray dress. Long sandy brown hair framed her high cheekbones in waves. She stopped for a moment, registering Jake's presence with her bright blue eyes, then stepped forward.

Not exactly a gypsy, Jake thought, his eyes finding their way to her full breasts.

"Hello, Mr. Helman," she said, offering her hand.

Jake measured her crystalline eyes and then her hand before he shook it. "Miss Laurel, I presume?"

"Laurel Doniger. It's nice to finally meet you. I've heard a lot about you from Jackie Krebbs."

Jackie was Jake's contact with Eden, Inc. "You don't look surprised to see me."

Her smile revealed perfect white teeth. "You're not here to borrow a cup of sugar. I knew you'd be stopping by after your appointment with Carmen."

"Thanks for the referral."

"You're welcome."

"How did I earn such a neighborly gesture?"

"Like a lot of people who come to me, Carmen needs help. I offer advice, not physical assistance. She needs action, and she obviously can't turn to the police. I hear you're good at what you do."

"Did Jackie tell you that?"

Nodding, she gestured to the sofa. "Would you like to sit down?"

"No, thanks. I don't think I'll be staying long. Carmen said you told her I had experience in matters like hers. Did Jackie tell you that, too?"

This time she shook her head. "No, that's just my impression of you."

"And yet we've never met until today . . ."

She smiled, a sparkle in her eyes.

"Oh, that's right." Jake snapped his fingers. "You're psychic, aren't you?"

Still smiling, Laurel said, "I'm sensitive to other people's energy. I don't pretend to know the future. I only read my clients' energy and help them see things more clearly."

"And you read my energy, without me ever setting foot in here before?"

"You've occupied your office upstairs for almost a year now. I know you live there, I feel your vibrations around the clock."

Jackie told her I sleep in my office, Jake thought. "What else do you know about me?"

"I know you're a good man who's had some very bad experiences. I know you've suffered a terrible loss, which you blame on yourself. And I know you genuinely want to help people."

Jake narrowed his eyes. *She's drawing conclusions from readily available data. The papers called me a hero after my gunfight in that bar, and it was a big deal when the Cipher killed Sheryl. I was big news for about a week.* "Someone's been busy online."

"You do your background searches on the Internet, not me."

"That's part of my job description."

"And knowing things about people that I couldn't possibly know is part of mine."

"You haven't done a very good job of convincing me so far."

"I didn't realize I needed to. But I've learned a lot more about you since you walked through that door." She offered her hand as evidence. "Touch is very important in my profession."

Jake's smile tightened. "Can you read my mind right now?"

"No. I don't read minds. I read energy."

"Fine. Can you—?"

"You're wondering if Carmen and I are running some sort of elaborate scam on you. We aren't. She's a client of mine, and her distress is real. If any man in this city can help her, it's you."

"I'll give you this much: your instincts are good."

"Call it whatever you like. Hopefully Carmen will be our mutual client soon."

Jake's voice softened. "I'm an ex-cop and a private investigator, not some kind of occult detective. You've got me all wrong."

"My specialty is helping people see the truth about themselves."

"What's in this for you?"

"I like to help people, too."

"For a fee."

"Not always. Sometime I do pro bono work. Just like you."

"We'll see about that. In the meantime, I just might discover a thing or two about you and Carmen as well."

Laurel bowed her head. "I'm sure you'll do whatever you think is necessary."

A woman of mystery. But a con woman all the same, just like all psychics and mediums. Lady, you've picked the wrong mark.

He thought her smile returned, wider.

Jake drove to Sylvia's on Lenox Avenue in Harlem. The restaurant took up nearly the entire block. He gave Edgar's name to the hostess, who escorted him between the crowded tables to one against the far wall. He zeroed in on the most beautiful woman in the restaurant, and when her eyes made contact with his, he knew she was Edgar's date. Then Edgar, sitting with his back to him, turned in his seat. He and the woman rose at the same time, and Jake saw that Dawn stood almost six feet in heels. She wore her long straightened hair parted on one side, and her flame red, strapless dress resembled lipstick on her creamy coffee-colored skin.

"Here he is," Edgar said. "The man of the hour."

"I'm flattered," Jake said. "But only for an hour? Fame is fleeting."

"Jake Helman, Dawn Du Pre."

"Hi," Dawn said, extending one hand. "It's nice to finally meet you."

Jake shook her hand. "Same here. Edgar won't shut up about you."

"As a publicist, I appreciate that."

Jake waited for Dawn to sit, then did likewise. Scanning the tabletop, he saw a fourth place setting. "My spider sense is tingling. Is someone joining us?"

The look in Dawn's eyes confirmed he had been set up.

Edgar's voice took on the sound of manufactured innocence. "Well, Vasquez wasn't doing anything tonight, so I asked her to sit in. You don't want to be a third wheel, do you?"

Jake focused his attention on Dawn. "It's a good thing he's a cop, because he'd make a lousy criminal."

Dawn clasped Edgar's hand. "That's what I love about him."

Uh-oh, Jake thought. *This is for real.*

"Girls like bad boys, but a smart woman needs a good man."

"I hear that," said another woman, in a higher pitched voice than Dawn's.

Looking up, Jake saw Detective Maria Vasquez, his replacement as Edgar's partner in Special Homicide. Since Sheryl's funeral, Jake had seen her a few times in Edgar's company when they were working. She always managed to appear fashionable, even when standing knee deep in a case, but nothing could have prepared Jake for the image she presented now. Her tight green dress, which accentuated her compact figure, matched her eyes, and her curly brown hair spilled over her shoulders. Rising once more, Jake tried to wipe the surprise from his face.

"Hi," Maria said, looking into his eyes. "Good to see you again."

"Same here, Vas—Maria." He held out the unoccupied chair beside him.

"Thank you. It's nice to be around a man with manners for a change." Winking at Dawn, she said, "I'm stuck driving around with this one all day."

"You're tougher than me," Edgar said.

"You got that right." Maria turned to Jake. "So what do you think?"

Jake looked around the table. "I just met her, and I already think she's too good for him."

"I can see this is going to be a long night," Edgar said, and laughter circled the table.

A waiter with gray hair came over to the table and smiled at Maria, then Jake. "May I get you something to drink?"

"What are you all having?" Maria said.

"A Manhattan," Dawn said, gesturing to her half-full glass.

"Martini," Edgar said.

Maria turned to her right. "Jake?"

"Uh, I'll just have a lemon-lime soda."

"I'll have the same." Maria smiled at the waiter.

"No, don't hold back on my account," Jake said.

"It's okay—"

"No, I insist. I want you to enjoy yourself."

"Okay, in that case I'll have a Scotch on the rocks."

"Very good," the waiter said and left the table.

"I've never met a private eye before," Dawn said to Jake. "It sounds awfully exciting and romantic."

"It's neither. No femme fatale has ever walked into my office, and I have yet to stumble over a murder or a conspiracy while shadowing an unfaithful spouse. My job involves a lot of boring surveillance, nothing like what you see on TV or in the movies."

"He's just being honest," Edgar said in a deadpan voice.

"Do you have a card?" Dawn said.

Jake fished for his wallet and took out a business card, which he handed to Dawn.

"'Helman Investigations and Security,'" she read. "May I?"

"By all means. Would anyone else like a card? I need all the business I can get."

"Sure," Maria said, and Jake handed one to her.

"I'll pass," Edgar said with a dismissive smile.

The waiter returned with their drinks.

"To Edgar and Dawn," Jake said, raising his glass.

"To two beautiful women," Edgar said.

The four of them touched their glasses.

"Mm, I love soul food," Maria said to Jake. "Don't you?"

"Absolutely."

"This is delicious," Dawn said. "But I grew up in Louisiana. I love Creole cooking."

"There's a great Cajun place next to my office on Twenty-third Street," Jake said. "You should try it sometime."

"How about next week?" Edgar said. "We could make it a foursome again."

An embarrassed silence hung in the air.

"Subtle," Maria said, staring at her plate.

Beneath the table, Edgar swung his knee against Jake's.

"Why not?" Jake said. "The three of you coordinate your schedules and let me know what night works best. If we can't manage it, we'll do it for sure the following week."

"Then it's settled," Edgar said before turning to Jake. "Hey, Maria and I are working with a couple of your other ex-partners."

Jake cocked his right eyebrow. "Oh?"

"Here we go," Dawn said to Maria.

Edgar swallowed his food. "Yeah, Brown and Beck from Narcotics. The bosses think our Machete Massacres are related to Black Magic, so they've combined our investigations, sort of an unofficial task force because they don't have the manpower to spread around. I'm in charge."

Jake felt his gut tighten. He had worked with Gary Brown and Frank Beck for three years in SNAP—the Street Narcotics Apprehension Program—based in Alphabet City. Because of his time in the HERCULES Counterterrorism Unit after 9/11, he had found a path into Homicide, whereas Brown and Beck never made it out of Narcotics. The two men had become detectives just like Jake, but after so many years in Narcotics, they would never escape that unit.

"Congratulations," Jake said. "But I'd watch your step around Gary and Frank."

"You saying they're bad apples?" Maria said.

"No, I'm not saying that," Jake said. "I never had any problems with them. Just watch your backs is all."

"Narcotics is a bad place to be," Edgar said, as if explaining anything Brown and Beck might have done in the past.

"True that," Jake said.

Dawn set down her fork. "I'm done. I want to save room for dessert."

"I hear you," Maria said. "Something with chocolate and nuts."

A cell phone chimed at the table, and Edgar took out his phone. Frowning, he answered the call. "Hopkins." As he listened, his expression turned grim. "Okay, we'll be there as soon as we can." Hanging up, he turned to Maria. "No dessert for us. We got a bad one across 110th Street." He lowered his voice. "Another Machete Massacre."

Maria smacked her lips. "I'm on a diet anyway."

Edgar turned to Jake. "Hey, do you mind driving Dawn home?"

Dawn said, "Oh, that isn't necessary . . ."

"I don't mind," Jake said. "Order your dessert."

"I'm driving," Edgar said to Maria.

"Good," she said, gulping her drink before rising.

"You want to stop at your place first, so you can change?"

Maria looked at her dress. "After I went through all the trouble of fixing myself up? Not on your life." She and Jake traded smiles. "See you around, right?"

Jake stood. "Count on it."

"Good night, Dawn."

"See you, Maria."

Leaning across the table, Edgar kissed Dawn on the lips. "See you later?"

"I'll wait up," she said.

Edgar squeezed Jake's shoulders. "Dinner's on me next time."

"Suuuuuuuure . . ."

Edgar and Maria headed out of the restaurant together.

"There go two of the best dressed cops in Homicide," Jake said, and Dawn laughed.

"Nice car," Dawn said as Jake drove his Chevy Malibu down Second Avenue. The sun had set, and young people loitered outside the bars.

"I think you're being sarcastic," Jake said. "I wanted a hybrid, but I couldn't afford it."

"It gets you where you need to go, right?"

"It does more than that. I spend a lot of time in this car on stakeout. It's like a second office."

"And your office is your home," Dawn said, running the middle finger of her right hand over the Malibu's armrest.

"Edgar told you about that, huh?"

Dawn nodded. "Don't be mad at him. I think it's sweet that you didn't want to live in your old apartment without your wife."

Jake did not feel like discussing Sheryl with Dawn. "I'll get a new apartment eventually, but the rent on that office is high, even with deductions. For now, while I get my life back together, the office suits my needs fine. When you own your own business and have to put in long hours, it makes sense."

"I know," Dawn said in an agreeable voice.

"What sort of publicity do you do?"

She shrugged. "Where's Old Nick?"

Jake's blood chilled. Even after almost a year, the phrase elicited fear in him.

Dawn grinned, oblivious to his sudden discomfort. "You name it: authors, athletes, musicians. Anyone who can afford to hire someone to help make them famous. I divide my time between here and L.A., but I have a few clients in Chicago as well."

"Edgar told me you got box seats for the Knicks at the Garden."

"Say the word and I can get them for you, too."

"Thanks. I appreciate that. I'll let you know. You said you were raised in Louisiana. What led you into publicity?"

"Getting out of Louisiana," she said, laughing. "I was born here in the city, so I guess I've always been a city girl at heart. I'm damned good at what I do."

"Edgar thinks you can do no wrong."

"That's my man."

Jake slowed down as they passed 105th Street.

"On the right," Dawn said.

Jake pulled over to a six-story apartment building next to a construction site. "Nice location."

"It's an up-and-coming neighborhood, as they say."

"Doorman?"

"Uh-huh."

"Good."

"What I really want is to live on the top floor of that building when it's finished."

Jake looked beyond the plywood fence surrounding the construction site at the skeletal frame of the high-rise in the making. "Looks like twenty floors."

"They're already taking applications. I submitted mine."

Jake offered her a supportive smile. "Steep."

"I'm working hard for it." She grinned. "Listen to me, broadcasting my ambitions."

"That's okay. It's refreshing when someone knows what they want and goes after it. So many people just talk about what they want out of life."

"How about you? Do you know what *you* want?"

He thought about it. "Not anymore. My life's changed, and it can never go back to what it was. I'm just trying to find my way."

"Well, it was very nice meeting you." She offered her hand. "I know you'll figure things out."

He shook her hand. "Thanks, Dawn." He watched her get out and enter her building, walking with confidence. Edgar had done all right for himself.

Time for work, he thought, gazing at the night sky.

FOUR

"You seem happy," Maria said, watching Edgar from the corner of her eye.

"Life is good," Edgar said as they rolled down Broadway in the unmarked Dodge Charger he had signed out from the motor pool for the night, one of the perks of being on call for task force business.

"Speak for yourself. You aren't a woman pushing thirty. Dawn got her hands on you just in time."

"You're only twenty-eight."

"My clock is ticking, partner. You know what it is to be a Puerto Rican woman with no kids at my age?"

"Hey, you made certain choices and sacrifices. You've got a lot to show for your hard work: you're the youngest detective in Special Homicide and the only female."

"Still . . ."

"You're right where you want to be, so stop pretending to feel sorry for yourself."

"You think your boy likes me?"

"Martin? Sure."

She clucked her tongue. "Don't play yourself. Jake."

"Oh, Jake. Jake is complicated. He likes you, but . . ."

"But what?"

"He's still in mourning."

"It's been a year . . ."

"Eleven months. He's still hurting inside, and he isn't ready."

"Yeah, you're right."

"You don't want to be his rebound tail anyway."

"Like I ever *would* be. Now you're being stupid." She looked out the window at the emaciated bodies walking the sidewalks. "Look at all these scarecrows. It's like one of those old newsreels of the concentration camp survivors."

"It's night. Time for them to score."

"Is this what the crack epidemic was like in the eighties?"

"How old do you think I am? I wasn't a cop in the eighties."

"You were *alive*, weren't you? Because I was like five years old."

"Yeah, I was alive. It wasn't exactly a prosperous time in the black community during the Reagan years. I don't know what did more damage, the Man or the drug."

"Yo, Edgar, you're my rabbi, right? I mean, you taught me damn near everything I know about being a murder police."

"Yeah, sure. I'm your Obi-Wan Kenobi, and you're my Grasshopper."

"Why didn't you tell me you took the sergeant's exam?"

He glanced in her direction. "How'd you know about that?"

"You think you're the only one in this car who's got sources! I've got sources."

He shook his head. "You haven't got sources."

"I got *sources.*"

"Get the fuck outta here."

"I figured it out, okay? I *am* a detective. I got the gold shield and everything. You just happened to take a personal day when the test was taken."

Edgar chuckled.

"So why didn't you tell me?"

"I didn't see any reason to."

"You didn't see any *reason*?"

"Yeah, that's right. I don't know how I did yet, so I didn't see any reason to have this discussion."

"Well, we're having it now—understand? We're partners. If you're going to mess that up, I think I deserve to know."

"Look, I'm forty-three. I got eighteen years on the job, eight of them in Homicide. I got something good going on with Dawn, and I'm ready for a change."

"You want to give up the street?" Maria sounded incredulous.

"I want a promotion and the raise that goes with it."

"You gonna retire when you reach your twenty, too?"

"Who knows? Even if I scored high enough to make the grade, I still have to wait for a slot to open up. You're stuck with me for a while yet."

"You know they won't keep you in Homicide."

"I do know that . . ."

"You could get stuck in some shit detail like Narcotics or the K-9 Unit."

Edgar said nothing.

"Would you have done this if Jake was still your partner?"

"Hell, yes. He was a bigger pain in my ass than you are. Now can we drop this?"

She didn't say anything for at least five seconds. "I got *mad* sources."

Edgar parked outside the bakery on 110th. Three RMP cars lined the curb, their strobes throwing red and blue light on the faces of the spectators standing alongside the yellow crime scene tape. Maria hung her badge on a chain around her neck, they each pulled latex gloves on, and they got out. Crossing the sidewalk, they gave their names to the uniformed recorder stationed outside the bakery.

Inside, they saw the other uniforms milling about the glass display counter. A wide archway behind the counter led into the kitchen area, where camera flashes went off at intervals. Circling the counter, they entered the kitchen. As they did, Maria felt self-conscious, imagining the eyes of every uniformed officer on her ass.

Serves you right, she thought.

Crime Scene Unit specialists and Detective Area Task Force detectives swarmed the space, measuring blood spatters and photographing bodies. Maria saw a woman's naked legs on the floor, protruding from behind an aluminum rack. Flour and blood spotted her thighs. The headless trunk of a man lay on a marble-topped table. His arms had been hacked off like his head. The mixture of blood and flour made it appear as though someone had strewn cotton candy all over the bakery.

"Another Machete Massacre," Maria said. *Obviously.*

Edgar said nothing.

They passed the decapitated corpse of a woman slumped against a slop sink. Blood drenched her breasts.

"The supercops are here," said a familiar and sarcastic voice.

They turned to see Gary Brown walking toward them, followed by Frank Beck. Brown chewed gum on one side of his mouth. His blond hair made it difficult to see the gray that had started to come in. Beck, thicker and shorter, wore a permanent sneer on his face.

Gary looked her up and down. "Looking good, Maria."

"It's Vasquez," Maria said, recalling what Jake had implied about the Narcotics detectives.

"Whatever you say."

"We got six DOAs," Frank said. "Five of them naked, all of them headless."

"The heads are here," Gary said. "In the refrigerator, the oven, the mixing bowl . . ."

Frank gestured to a wooden table where a powdery substance had been spattered with blood. The resulting mixture had congealed into something nasty. "There's at least two keys of coke here and a thousand empty vials. A real pharmacy."

"Are the vics all black?" Edgar said.

Gary flashed his teeth. "Every one of them, right down to the overseer.

Makes sense, doesn't it? Russians, Dominicans, Puerto Ricans, Columbians, Koreans, Chinese. The new power players in town don't want to just take over; they want to wipe out the competition. And they're doing a pretty good job, if you ask me. From what I see, the Italians are sitting this war out."

"I saw a surveillance camera in the front," Maria said.

"It's just a live feed, no recorder," Gary said. "They used it for security, not playback."

"Let's get started on a chain of title," Edgar said. "Whoever owns this bakery allowed it to be used for a front. If nothing else, they can identify this gang for us."

"Already in motion," Gary said.

A fifth detective joined the party. "Did I hear someone mention 'gang'?" Bernie Reinhardt from Gang Prevention slid into the conversation with his hands in the pockets of his khaki slacks and the ends of his mustache drooping like tired tree limbs.

"Didn't see you there, Bernie."

Mustering a smile, Bernie pushed his glasses up his nose. "That's because I'm as quiet and unobtrusive as a cat."

Maria stifled a laugh. Bernie's sense of humor could be as dry as a desert.

"This is the seventh attack we've seen like this," Bernie said, gesturing at the gore. "The machete screams Haitian to me, but from what I hear, the Haitians are more afraid of this than anyone else."

"Maybe that's the point," Maria said.

"Lovely dress. Of course it's the point. Whoever's hacking these people apart wants to spread fear as much as they want to move drugs. There's something primal and ritualistic about these murders. They could have used guns, but guns are too *clean*."

"Guns are too *noisy*," Edgar said.

"You've heard of silencers?" Before Edgar could answer, Bernie continued, "Trust me, these people made as much noise screaming as a gun would have made. Machetes are an instrument from another time. They inspire fear of the old country and of old ways."

"Are you afraid of the old country, Bernie?"

"Brighton Beach? Sure, I'm afraid of my mother."

Maria giggled. "You're too much."

"You got that right," Gary said.

"You don't think my insight has merit, Brown?"

"What insight? You haven't *said* anything. No wonder the gangs are running roughshod over this city: you guys in Gang Prevention can't stop them."

"Indeed we can't. Our budget has been cut as much as yours, our manpower's as depleted. And we can't stop gang activity until you stop narcotics activity. How's that coming?"

Gary's face reddened. "Swell," he said before stalking off with Frank at his heels.

"Isn't he too short to be a cop?" Bernie said once Frank was out of earshot.

Edgar snickered.

"Come here," Bernie said to both of them. "I want to show you something that will stop your laughter in its tracks."

They followed him over to a ceramic-tiled wall not far from the body of a naked pregnant woman. "See that?" He pointed at what appeared to be flesh clinging to one tile. "It's human flesh."

"You sure about that?" Edgar said. "It looks kind of gray."

"That's because it's dead. Very dead. And it's not alone. There are pieces of tissue dripping from corners and tables all over this kitchen."

Maria cocked one eyebrow. "What are you trying to say?"

Bernie led them over to the clothed corpse of the overseer. The man's dismembered hand still clutched a Glock. "Look at the shell casings on the floor. The overseer went down fighting. He fired at least six shots." He gestured at the wall with the dead skin.

"You saying the dead skin belonged to our perps?"

"It would certainly seem that way, Detective Hopkins. The collateral flesh doesn't match that of any of the vics. Now I've done you a solid. How about you do one for me and shut down some gangs this week?"

FIVE

Jake sat in the Malibu's front seat, sipping coffee from a thermos. After dropping Dawn off at her building, he had driven downtown to his office and changed into all black clothing, then parked on Montclair, with the corner of Caton in view, without drawing any unwanted attention. The car's dents and wear and tear had appealed to his desire for anonymity, and he had spray-painted the vehicle charcoal gray to render it nearly invisible on nighttime stakeouts like this. By parking as far from a streetlight as possible, he was able to blend into the darkness while observing his surroundings.

In the distance, six-story concrete buildings rose into the sky along Flatbush Avenue, towering above the darkened four-story buildings before him. Several storefronts and apartment buildings had been boarded up, minimizing the amount of available light. Half a block ahead, three figures stood motionless in front of an abandoned church. Two of them wore hoodies, the third a do-rag. All three wore baggy jeans and stylish sneakers. Lean bodies and hard faces.

Hoppers.

Corner boys.

Jake had busted young men like this while serving in SNAP and had shaken them down for drugs and cash during darker times as a homicide detective. He pushed the memories back into his mind but did not shut them out. It was important to remember his actions. That was the best way to atone for his crimes.

He had taped a photocopied enlargement of Louis's photo to the dashboard. Raising his high-definition camera so that it rested on the steering wheel, he activated the night vision feature, and the LCD screen blossomed with bright green light. He trained the camera on the drug dealers and zoomed in on them. Two of the boys were black, the third—one of the two wearing hoodies—appeared to have light skin.

That could be Louis, he thought, but it was impossible to match the glowing eyes and shallow cheeks to the image hanging from the dashboard. He needed to approach the boys up close, a feat he did not relish. Over the last hour, he had witnessed at least two dozen addicts purchase drugs from the boys. He had also watched the same ugly hookers walk back and forth on Montclair and had not seen even one RMP or patrolman. The darkness felt heavy, the neighborhood deserted except for the dealers. Anything could happen to him on these streets, and no one would know a thing about it.

He reflected on dinner that evening. Dawn had been charming, and he should not have been surprised that Edgar had invited Vasquez to join them. He liked Maria: the attractive woman had style and moxie, and because she worked Homicide, they had a lot in common.

Still, he had no desire to enter into a relationship, physical or otherwise, with another woman. He still loved Sheryl and hoped to be reunited with her one day.

Before he could dwell on this matter further, his stomach tightened, his senses warning him that someone lurked nearby. Turning to his left, he came face-to-face with a ghostly countenance pressed against his window, bulbous and unblinking eyes staring at him from leathery gray skin.

He jumped in his seat. *Jesus!*

As a cop in SNAP he had seen many drug addicts up close, and as a homicide detective he had seen murder victims even closer. The emaciated woman standing before him fell somewhere between the two. The look in her eyes was a mixture of fear and desperate drug lust. Her hot pants and belly shirt hung like rags on her bony frame.

Jake could not roll down his window without starting the engine and alerting the corner boys to his presence, so, with his heart still beating fast and his eyes locked on the woman leaning over him, he switched off the dome light, then opened the door a crack.

"Yeah?" he said in an impatient tone. He knew better than to show any weakness to a creature like this, who was a predator as much as she was a victim.

"You want a blow job?" she said in a raspy voice.

Jake's nostrils flared, and he gagged as her stench enveloped him. He did not know the exact source of the foul odor and had no desire to learn it. "No. But I'll give you twenty bucks to walk away and forget you saw me."

She looked him up and down. She reminded him of a life-sized puppet more than a human being.

He pulled a twenty-dollar bill from the empty second cup holder by the stick shift, and he slid it up the window.

Her eyes dilated into wide black saucers, and when the twenty came within her reach, she snatched it with the speed of a bird. Then she scampered toward the corner.

Closing the door again, Jake raised the camera and zoomed out wide enough to capture the wretched prostitute in the frame, then followed her progress to the boys.

The dealers formed a triangular pattern facing her, with Do-Rag on point and the Hoodies flanking him. She gesticulated with the twenty, and Do-Rag nodded. The Hoodie on the left took a step forward, grabbed the twenty from her, and returned to his position. Then the Hoodie Jake suspected might be Louis walked forward, reached into his jacket pocket, and took out something too small to see, which he deposited in the hooker's open palm. Even before he returned to his spot, she hurried down the sidewalk, moving in and out of the pools of light provided by the streetlights, and disappeared around a high wooden fence.

My cover's safe until her high wears off, Jake thought. Not that it mattered: he had already decided to introduce himself to his subjects of investigation.

He took a roll of black gaffer's tape from the glove compartment, tore two strips from it, and secured the camera to the dashboard. He adjusted the camera so it recorded the corner from a wide angle. Then he opened the car door, stepped out into the night, and shut the door hard enough that the sound carried across the street. Reassured by the feeling of his Glock in its shoulder holster pressed against the left side of his rib cage, he followed the pothole-riddled pavement toward the corner, walking neither fast nor slow but with deliberate purpose.

The three young men turned to him in unison, their hands at their sides. Do-rag had a deep scar on the right side of his face, and a milky sheen covered his eyes. At first Jake thought the dealer suffered from blindness, but those sickening orbs locked onto him and did not waver.

Jake's own eyes shifted to the Hoodie on the left, who also seemed to be plagued by cataracts, and then to the Hoodie on the right, whose face did indeed resemble that of the boy in the photo Carmen had given him. Something was *off* about all three figures, no doubt about it. They stood as still as statues, and when they did move, it was with machinelike efficiency. He felt their eyes on him, which caused his blood to curdle.

What's wrong with these guys?

Focusing his attention on The Boy Who Might Be Louis, he said, "Louis Rodriguez?"

The boy's sunken eyes did not blink, but his cracked lips parted.

It is him. No surprise there. Just means that Carmen was right on that score.

And as Jake studied Do-rag's taut chest beneath his black vest, he realized what troubled him about all three drug dealers.

They're not breathing. That's why they're so still. But that's not possible . . .

All three of the corner boys were dead on their feet. Functioning. Selling drugs.

Black Magic.

Jake wanted to flee for his life, but with lightninglike speed, Do-rag reached behind him, pulled a Glock from his waistband, and extended his arm straight out with the barrel turned sideways a foot shy of Jake's face.

Fuck me! Jake raised both hands level with his head and took an automatic step back.

"Whoa, whoa, *whoa . . .*"

Dead or alive, Do-rag had moves. And now he moved toward Jake, keeping the distance between them consistent as Jake stepped off the sidewalk and backed into the street. Hoodie One and Louis followed, maintaining their triangular formation.

"Okay, fellas, take it easy. I'm not a cop, and I'm not looking for trouble. I was just hoping to score a little Magic, but if you don't want to help me out, that's okay. I'll just get into my car back there and be on my way."

If I could just reach my gun—

Not a chance. Do-rag increased his gait, forcing Jake to walk backwards even faster. Jake wanted to look over his shoulder to locate his car, but he feared that any deviation from this new routine would provoke Do-rag into firing a round into his brain. And if he turned and ran, he could take a bullet in the back. Fear kept his eyes trained on the gun before him. Now where the hell was his car?

As if on cue, his left leg struck metal. Steadying himself with his right hand, he stepped over the curb onto the sidewalk and moved to the driver's-side door. His focus kept switching from the barrel in his face to the countenance of the dead thing gripping the gun.

"I have to take out my keys, okay?"

Do-rag and his thugs stopped advancing, and Jake reached into his pocket and took out his keys. Using his remote control, he unlocked the car door and opened it. His heart skipped a beat when he spotted the glowing LCD screen of the camera taped to the dashboard. Praying this would not lead to more trouble, he slid behind the wheel, his movements slow and controlled. He felt completely at their mercy, which he doubted they had possessed even when they had been alive. Why should they have any now?

With sweat forming on his brow and his heart gaining speed, he closed the door. Resisting the irrational desire to lock it—what good would it do?—he inserted his car key into the ignition and started the engine. He wanted to see what his aggressors were doing, even though he suspected they continued to stand motionless, but once again, the pervasive fear he felt dictated his actions.

Instead, he steered the Malibu out of its parking space, pulled into the street, and sped toward the corner. Glancing at his rearview mirror, he saw the three figures walk lockstep into the middle of the street.

Fuck this and fuck you!

Jerking the wheel to his left, he executed a U-turn, and the Malibu's front right wheel jumped the curb. As the car bounced back into the street, the corner boys stopped walking and stood frozen, except that Do-rag raised the Glock in both hands, aiming it at Jake, who swept the camera off the dashboard with his right hand, knocking it onto the seat beside him.

There's no need to create evidence that can be used against me.

Then he stepped on the gas, and the car rocketed forward. Do-rag's

Glock issued a muzzle flash, and a splintery white spiderweb appeared in the windshield even as Jake heard the gunfire. He steered left, avoiding the next shot, then right, slamming against a parked sedan in a shower of sparks. Then he plowed straight into the corner boys.

Hoodie One threw himself against a parked car and Louis dove onto the sidewalk, both of them dodging Jake's trajectory. But the Malibu smashed into Do-rag, and the drug dealer disappeared beneath the car.

Jake stomped on the brake and searched his rearview mirror for signs of movement. He saw Do-rag lying on his back in the street. The drug dealer rolled over, planted his palms on the asphalt, and raised his head, staring at Jake's car.

Oh no you don't! Jake's temples throbbed. He refused to get tangled up in this kind of shit again.

Do-rag did a single push-up, which allowed him to stand. He still held the Glock, and as Hoodie One and Louis joined him in their triangular pattern, he raised the gun and fired it. The rear windshield turned into a pattern of white cracks.

Jake shifted the car into reverse, glanced at his side mirror, and floored the gas. The car lurched backwards, and the three figures grew larger in the side mirror. Jake heard a series of bangs against the rear bumper and trunk and saw Hoodie One roll clear across the street until his body collided with the curb. Then Do-rag came into view, lying once more on his back, his chest torn open and his rib cage winking at the moon, no blood glistening on the bone. Out of the corner of his eye, Jake glimpsed Louis crouching behind the sedan he had smashed against. Stepping on the brake, Jake waited.

Do-rag got to his feet and turned around, his ruptured torso grinning at Jake like a jack-o'-lantern. His legs buckled, and his shattered left arm swung at his side like a pendulum. Hoodie One stood as well.

"FUCK YOU!"

Shifting gears again, Jake sped forward even as Do-rag's grunts lumbered toward him. Do-rag raised his Glock, but Jake smashed into him. This time the gun went flying. As the gangbanger disappeared beneath the car once more, Jake stomped the brake pedal. He didn't wait to see Do-rag rise again; instead, he shifted the car into reverse and backed up at full speed. The car shook, and he heard a loud snapping sound.

Stopping the car, he glared at the crumpled heap on the street. Bones jutted out from pulverized flesh, and way too many joints undulated. Shifting the gear again, Jake revved the engine. Then the thing on the ground turned its faceless head toward him. Jake sped forward, aiming the front left wheel for the grisly mass perched between the thing's shoulders.

Do-rag disappeared from view, and Jake heard a loud crunch as the Malibu shook. A sudden flash of light coming from beneath the car caused Jake to believe that Do-rag had fired his Glock one more time. But Jake had seen the dead dealer discard the weapon!

What in the world—?

As Jake sped away from the carnage, he looked into the side mirror. A sphere of tarnished light rose from the broken body in the street.

No no no no NO!

As Do-rag's soul rose into the night sky, it darkened into a pustulant gray mass and disappeared.

Jake stopped the car again, jumped out, and gazed at the sky. He saw no sign of Do-rag's soul, which had no doubt begun its journey to its ultimate destination. Jake's knees wobbled. He had not witnessed such a light show since the demon Cain had claimed Old Nick's soul in the Tower. The entire episode had left him wondering if he would continue to see souls leaving the bodies of those killed in front of him. Now he knew the answer.

Hoodie One and Louis approached Do-rag's shell from opposite directions, and Jake turned to get back into his Malibu. The squealing of tires made him look up just as a black Escalade raced around the corner ahead of him, its headlights forcing him to squint. He dove into the front seat and shifted the gear without even reaching for the door. The Escalade bore down on him. Stepping on the gas, he spun the steering wheel right. The Malibu jumped out of the Escalade's path, but the SUV tore the open door from its hinges and flung it sparking across the street.

Steering his car into the proper lane, Jake craned his neck and watched the Escalade smash into Hoodie One and Louis, hurling them aside like department store mannequins. Jake stopped the car long enough to fasten his seat belt and glimpse the Escalade turning around. Then he saw Louis and Hoodie One return to their station as he sped away.

Jake raced northwest on Flatbush Avenue toward Schermerhorn Street, with the Escalade in hot pursuit. Drawing stares and laughter from pedestrians who noticed he had no door, he maneuvered around the traffic, and the Escalade did the same thing. Wind resistance filled the car through the open space, leaving him exposed and feeling helpless despite the seat belt and shoulder strap.

He made a sudden turn onto Schermerhorn, locked his eyes on the side mirror, and saw the Escalade follow. He had never been in a car chase, either as the lead vehicle or the pursuer. Checking the speedometer, he saw he was doing seventy-five in a forty, and the Escalade had no trouble keeping up. He made a right onto Adams Street, and the Brooklyn Bridge, outlined in lights, rose into the night a mile ahead.

Almost there, he thought.

The Escalade picked up speed, moving to cut him off.

Who's in that vehicle? he wondered as he accelerated to eighty-five miles per hour. *More of those things? Damned good drivers.* He weaved around cars and trucks making late night deliveries. The Escalade lost ground but remained within sight. Jake cursed Do-rag for rendering his back window impossible to see through.

Ahead, the lights at the top of the suspension bridge were too high for him to see. With no toll required, he sped onto the massive bridge that connected Manhattan and Brooklyn. Like a salmon swimming upstream to spawn and die, Jake felt compelled to cross the East River and reach his home turf, the island called Manhattan. Below, a garbage boat smashed through the choppy waters. Noting the camera on the seat beside him, Jake reached over and ejected its high-definition video card, which he stuffed into his pants pocket.

With the Malibu's engine roaring and wind whipping his face, he thought he heard a pop behind him. Concentrating, he heard a second pop. And then the back window shattered, and he heard a third pop.

They're shooting at me! He ducked. *Son of a bitch!*

Horns honked around him, and the Escalade pulled up beside the Malibu in the next lane, like an unstoppable shark. The SUV's rear window lowered, and Jake glimpsed the eyes of a dead man just a few feet beyond his front passenger window. He was older than the corner boys but just as dead. The dead man aimed a sawed-off shotgun at him.

Jake drew his Glock from its spring-loaded shoulder holster. The dead man fired the shotgun, blasting out the Malibu's passenger-side window. Jake jerked the steering wheel left and then straight, fighting to regain control of the car's trajectory, and fired three rounds from his Glock through the now empty window space.

At least one round struck the dead man in the forehead. His corpse convulsed like a marionette controlled by a puppeteer with multiple sclerosis, and his soul escaped through the bullet wound.

Head shots do the trick, Jake thought. He decelerated the Malibu, falling behind the Escalade, then moved over two lanes to his right. Speeding up, he pulled alongside the Escalade on its right-hand side and opened fire, his right hand laying the gun over his left arm for balance. His Glock's ammunition punched holes in the Escalade's doors and ricocheted off the tinted windows.

Bulletproof glass, he thought as Manhattan beckoned to him like a display case filled with diamonds. *I gotta get me some of that if I survive the night.*

The front and rear windows of the Escalade lowered on the passenger side, revealing two armed dead men staring at Jake. One held a handgun, the other an Uzi.

We definitely need stricter gun laws in this country, Jake thought as he depressed his Glock's trigger and held it in the firing position. The close muzzle fire caused him to lean back in his seat as the reports struck the Escalade and its passengers. Their bodies rocked from side to side, but this did not prevent them from aiming their weapons at Jake with calm detachment.

The muzzle fire stopped, and Jake realized he had spent his ammunition. There was no way for him to reload while steering his car at eighty-five miles per hour with one hand, so he accelerated to ninety-five as heavy gunfire erupted from the Escalade, blowing out the window behind him. Jamming the hot metal gun back into its shoulder holster, he continued to increase his speed until it reached one hundred. He whipped around the cars ahead of him, switching lanes like a NASCAR driver.

Drivers honked their frustration at him, then slowed down or moved out of the way as the Escalade passed them with guns blazing.

Behind him, he heard a siren.

RMP, he thought. *About time and way too late.*

Looking over his shoulder, he spotted red and blue strobe lights streaking toward the Escalade.

They'll never be in time to settle this situation.

A thousand lights from Chinatown and the Lower East Side illuminated Jake's path as he neared the end of the bridge. Most of the other traffic had either stopped or moved aside, giving the Escalade ample space to catch up to him. Jake sped onto the street, praying nothing would cause him to slow down before he reached his target.

Come on! Come on!

Turning onto Park Row, he saw the thirteen-floor building in the distance across the street from City Hall, the Malibu's headlights illuminating wooden police barricades. Only one entrance and one exit existed, both protected by giant steel plates and a tollbooth manned by uniformed officers, making an assault by vehicle impossible. The street had been closed to civilian traffic since 9/11, causing calamity with the traffic around Chinatown. Beyond the barricades and before the security booth, concrete barriers blocked the way.

Jake plowed through the barricade, splintering wood flying around his vehicle. The Escalade stayed on his tail, gunfire issuing from its interior. The RMP appeared behind the Escalade.

Damn it, Jake thought as concrete barriers came into view ahead of him. *This security is going to kill me!* If he stopped or slowed down, the Escalade's occupants would kill him for sure; if he struck the concrete barrier head-on, he'd be crushed.

With no time left to spare, he stomped on the brake and jerked the steering wheel left. The Malibu spun sideways, its right side smashing into the barrier. The impact rolled the car *over* the barrier, and the Malibu spun side over side through the air. Gripping the steering wheel in both hands, Jake extended his arms, pressing his back into his seat.

The spinning car struck the asphalt on its passenger side. It rolled yet again, and Jake feared his body would absorb the impact through the gaping hole beside him. Instead, the car landed on its passenger side again, sparks flying from its metal skin. Then it rolled onto its roof, and as the passenger side caved in, Jake glimpsed the giant steel plate that protected the security booth speeding toward him.

An instant later, the expanding air bag obscured his vision and hurled him into darkness.

SIX

Jake heard liquid sloshing onto the ground as hands eased him from the car, his back sliding over the sidewalk. Gasoline fumes filled his nostrils, and his eyes snapped open, taking in the panicked expressions of two men towering above him. The younger of the two men wore a police uniform, the older one a sports jacket and a tie.

Detective, Jake thought. He heard a car door slam somewhere beyond his field of vision, followed by footsteps.

"Is he okay?" a woman shouted.

"He'll live." The detective sounded displeased by Jake's survival chances.

"I've got to pursue that Escalade! Will you call it in?"

The male policeman said, "Get going. I'll take care of it!"

Raising his head, Jake saw the PW running from behind. Short but fast. She ducked into her waiting unit and took off, siren wailing.

The PO stepped out of Jake's sight and spoke into his hand radio, calling for backup.

Jake stared at the mangled wreckage of his Malibu. The vehicle lay upside down on the asphalt, roof partially caved in, right side flattened, riddled with bullet holes. Gasoline poured out of the car's ruptured tank.

So much for my second office.

"Can you stand?" the detective said in a gravelly voice.

Jake nodded. "I think so."

"So impress me."

Hard ass. Jake climbed to his feet. His left knee burned with pain, and his shoulder on that side ached. His head tingled and he felt nauseous. White powder from the deflated air bag covered his clothes.

"You need medical treatment?" said the broad-shouldered detective, who wore his hair in a military cut and looked about fifty.

Jake shook his head. He just wanted this night to end.

"You sure? It's no big deal to have an ambulance check you out. Probably a good idea in case there's a lawsuit down the line."

"Don't want one."

"Suit yourself. Lieutenant Geoghegan, Major Crimes Unit. You just crashed your car into One Police Plaza."

That was the idea, Jake thought. "Jake Helman." He knew Teddy Geoghegan by his reputation: pure by-the-book NYPD.

"Who were those guys?"

"Beats the hell out of me."

"Really? Huh. Well, the officer over here is technically first officer on the scene, which makes me the investigating detective. If I don't sound too happy about that, it's because I was on my way out of here after pulling a twelve-hour shift. This sounds good for at least three hours' worth of grief."

Great . . .

Geoghegan gestured to the gate next to the security booth. "Since you're refusing medical treatment and you wanted to drop in so badly, shall we get on with this?"

Sighing, Jake accompanied the detective past the booth and into Park Row. They walked to the center of police power together. A dozen men and women had already gathered outside the building, half of them in uniforms.

Sitting in the bull pen on the fifth floor, Jake fed his story to a civilian typist who helped him fill out his police report.

Good practice for my car insurance company, he thought.

Then he cooled his heels for half an hour before Geoghegan took him into his office. The detective sat behind his desk, his back to the window, and Jake sat opposite him.

"Enlighten me."

Pompous ass, Jake thought. "I'm a PI—"

"I know who you are," he said, making little effort to mask his contempt.

I bet you do. You knew who I was the minute you laid eyes on me.

"Big hero homicide cop drops two skells in a bar, then resigns the next day. Go figure."

"I had enough of killing," Jake said.

"You wanted a piece of the quiet life, eh?"

"I want to make an honest living without dealing with any bureaucratic bullshit or departmental politics."

Geoghegan smiled. "The red tape was too much for you, huh?"

"Some people like that shit, like pigs in swill. It wasn't for me."

"So you think you're better than the rest of us because you won't eat shit?"

Jake shrugged. "I didn't say that."

"The way I hear it, you aren't better than anybody."

Here it comes. "I never said I was."

But Geoghegan didn't bring up the controversy that surrounded Jake's resignation from the force. "You gonna tell me what the hell happened out there?"

Jake took a breath before speaking. *Don't let him throw you off.* "A client hired me to track down her grandson, who she thinks might be slinging over on Flatbush Avenue. I went looking for the kid but didn't find him. I must have stumbled into the wrong neighborhood or something, because this black Escalade came out of nowhere, guns blazing. I got the hell out of there as fast as I could, but they followed me over the bridge."

"So you led them here?"

"It seemed like the safest place I could reach."

"When you say you must have stumbled into the wrong neighborhood, did you get out of your vehicle?"

Jake held the detective's gaze. "Yes."

"How come?"

Careful. He had to cop to getting out of the Malibu to explain its missing door. "Like I said, I was looking for the kid, but I didn't see him. Then the Escalade came ripping around the corner and tried to mow me down. I dove into my car, and the Escalade took off my door."

"You fire your weapon?"

Jake saw no point in lying. Ballistics would only screw him up. "Wouldn't you? It was self-defense."

"You hit anyone?"

"No. We were going too fast."

Geoghegan tore a sheet of paper from a pad and handed it to Jake with a pen. "Client's name and the name of her grandson, with any relevant contact info."

Jake wrote down Carmen and Louis Rodriguez's names, then took out his cell phone and located Carmen's telephone number.

Geoghegan looked at the information on the paper when Jake handed it back to him. "How do I know you didn't just go over there looking to score some dope?"

Jake stared at the detective. "I'm clean."

"I hear maybe you had a habit."

"That's one story."

"And everyone knows how cocaine cops pay for their stash."

"That's another story."

"Way I remember it, you were after the Cipher, and the Cipher killed your wife after you resigned. And what happened to the Cipher?" He snapped his fingers. "Oh, right—some *unidentified vigilante* managed to whack him without leaving any evidence. A real pro, who never had reason to strike again. We could use a guy like that now, what with all these layoffs."

Jake felt his jaw tightening. "My wife's got nothing to do with what happened to me tonight."

"Now if the wife of a straight-up cop had been murdered and the scumbag who did it turned up dead, I'd say, 'Good riddance' and sleep well at night. But when I think about the Cipher buying it in his own apartment, for some reason I don't feel so good. Something just doesn't feel right about that."

Major Crimes Unit, Jake reminded himself. "Forgive me if I sound unconcerned about your feelings, but three men tried to kill me tonight, and I don't know why."

The shit-eating grin on Geoghegan's face widened. "How do you know there were three of them? PW Cassidy reports the vehicle had tinted windows."

Jake's pulse quickened. *Damn it! Why did I have to be such a wiseass? He's right.* "Because they pulled up beside me and lowered their windows to shoot, and I got a good look inside before they opened fire. What happened to them, anyway?"

Geoghegan sat back in his chair. "They got away."

Jake actually felt relieved by the news. The last thing he wanted was to be connected to living dead hit men. "They circled the area and went back to Brooklyn."

"You seem to know their moves pretty well for an innocent bystander."

"I led those gangbangers to your doorstep. They'd have been crazy to stay in Manhattan."

"One could say the same thing about you, if you're lying and they know who you are."

"They don't."

"Good thing for you." Geoghegan stood.

"Am I free to go?"

"Not just yet. Someone else wants to talk to you."

Now this *is fucked up*, Jake thought, sitting in the interview room. *Who the hell wants to talk to me so bad that they kept me here an extra forty minutes already?*

He got his answer when the door opened and a figure from his past entered: Gary Brown from Narcotics, his former partner in SNAP. Jake hadn't seen him since Sheryl's funeral.

Now this is a coincidence. Maybe there's something to all this psychic hooey.

"Hey, Jake," Gary said, closing the interview room door.

Jake looked his former partner up and down. The detective wore fashionable Italian slacks, a button-down shirt, and a designer tie. He also appeared to have aged ten years in the span of one. "Looks like you're moving up in the world, Gary."

Gary sat down. "Eh. It's good to be a detective, but I'm still in Narcotics. It's a real shit hole down there, partner. I'd rather be where you're sitting."

Jake looked around the interview room. "Really?"

"Working for myself? Hell, yeah."

I thought you were working for yourself. Rumors had Gary and his partner, Frank Beck, working overtime for any drug lord looking for muscle. "What, and forego your pension?"

"Maybe you're right. I just get restless doing the same thing year in and year out. Hey, did you hear I'm working with your *other* ex-partner?"

He's feeling me out. "Edgar? No, I hadn't heard. He's a good man."

"Yeah, how about that? Two of your former colleagues pitching for the same team. It's a small world. You should see the number who's working with him now. Latin chick, real fine."

Now Jake had to play along, even if Gary knew better. "What are you guys working together on?"

"Task force on these Machete Murders, only now they have us on Black Magic, too. No telling if anything will come of it. But that's why I'm here now: gangbangers try to shoot up a citizen; the call goes out to the Task Force to decide whether or not to investigate. I'm on call, and when I saw your name, I just had to see what was doing. Weird, thinking of you as a civilian, pal. You're still one of us at heart, always will be."

What, a dirty cop? Jake had witnessed Gary and Frank in action. They always knew who worked for whom on the street, and they always had their hands out. Jake had managed to steer clear of their operations, but once he'd joined Homicide and started using coke himself, he found himself resorting to their tactics to pay for his habit. In a way, Gary had been his mentor. "I don't think I can give you much assistance." Jake repeated the story he had told Geoghegan and the civilian typist.

Chuckling, Gary shook his head. "Come on. Who do you think

you're shitting? I'm onto you, brother. No way in hell Jake Helman is going to get chased by gangbangers from one borough to the next and not know why."

Jake's gaze drifted to the two-way mirror opposite him.

"There's nobody there, and the recorder's off. It's just you and me in here, breaking bread."

"Like I told Geoghegan—"

"Theodore? The man doesn't know shit. And that's what his opinion is worth. I know what time of day it is without looking at my watch. You know that. Do me a solid on this, and I'll remember it."

Jake interlaced his fingers. "I got nothing to share with you, cousin."

Gary leaned closer, his eyes intense and jittery. "I need to deliver these cocksuckers."

Wired, Jake thought. "Sorry. I don't know anything about these machete killings."

"Your client hired you to find her grandson, right? What gang does the kid run with? That's a good place to start."

Jake maintained his innocent expression. "I don't know that he is with a gang. His grandmother just suspects he's slinging. He could be getting laid for all I know."

Gary relaxed his features from his mouth up. His jaw remained coke tight. "You'll call me if you hear anything about this?"

"Sure."

He reached into his pocket and tossed a card onto the table. "We could work this thing together on the side, just like old times. There could be something extra in it for each one of us."

"I'm not interested in collaring perps anymore. Those days are behind me."

Drumming his fingers on the table, Gary said, "Yeah, I guess so."

As Gary exited the interview room, Geoghegan walked in.

"Am I good to go?" Jake said.

"I'm afraid not." The detective gestured to someone Jake could not see, and then a balding man in a crisp suit entered, briefcase in hand.

FBI, Jake guessed.

"When someone attempts to ram One PP, it raises eyebrows outside the department," Geoghegan said in a mock sympathetic tone. "Allow me to introduce Agent Riley from Homeland Security."

Fuck me, Jake thought.

"I'll try not to keep you too late, Mr. Helman," Riley said as he set his briefcase on the table and sat down.

"That's a relief," Jake said in a deadpan voice.

"The district attorney is sending an ADA over to take a statement, too," Geoghegan said. Stepping outside the interview room, he closed the door.

When they finally released him, Jake pretended to be afraid to go home because the gangbangers might still be out there, waiting for him. For all he knew, they really were. But he had another reason for coaxing a ride to his office in the backseat of the RPM, and as the squad car pulled out of Park Row, he stared at the reporters gathered outside. Camera strobes and video lights spotlighted the wreckage of his former car. He'd managed to keep his picture out of the paper, which was always a good thing.

As the car drove uptown, the uniformed driver oblivious to what had occurred, Jake catalogued the night's incidents. His would-be assassin's soul had risen from his body. Did that mean it had been trapped inside the cadaver? He experienced a sick feeling of déjà vu, and yet this latest brush with the impossible seemed entirely different from those he had endured in the Tower and completely unrelated.

When the PO dropped him off on Twenty-third Street and drove away, Jake cast his eyes upward at the imposing, self-illuminated structure that haunted his dreams. Unlocking the front glass door, he entered the lit lobby, unlocked the alarm box on the wall with a key, punched in his code, and locked the door from the inside. Bypassing the stairs this time, he took the elevator to the fourth floor. With his footsteps echoing in the hallway, he glanced over his shoulder as he approached his office door, spooked for the first time since he had moved in.

I'm all alone, he thought. *Except maybe for Laurel on the first floor.* But he considered the storefront a separate building.

Flicking on the overhead light in his office, he closed and locked the door. He entered the kitchenette, removed a Diet Coke from the miniature refrigerator, and entered his office. He popped the tab on the can, sipped the soda, then set the can down on his desk and stepped over to the immense safe in the far corner. The iron cube was two and a half feet by two and a half feet. Too large and heavy to move without a hydraulic lift, it came with the office and remained a permanent fixture. Jake had hired three different locksmiths to install three combination locks, with none of them knowing the other combinations.

Crouching on one knee, he dialed the combinations and twisted the heavy brass levers. The safe door swung open with a metallic groan, and Jake gazed inside at the safe's contents. On a shelf that divided the safe's height in half, a DVD-R in a jewel case lay upon a laptop, which rested beside a file folder. Jake removed the jewel case and the laptop, then closed the safe door but left it unlocked. Then he sat behind his desk and affixed a fully charged battery pack to the laptop. Ignoring the flat-screen monitor on his desk, he inserted the DVD-R into the laptop.

He did not have a wireless router for the laptop or an Internet hookup. The compact computer existed solely for the DVD-R. Jake made sure that no one could ever hack into this isolated system. He needed to ensure that the DVD-R's contents were known only to him. When the disc loaded, he downloaded the program and waited.

Afterlife, he thought.

An animated globe rotated into view on the monitor. A DNA strand enveloped it. Then gleaming gold text filled the screen: Tower International—Building Better Life. Jake hadn't seen these images since the week he spent working as Nicholas Tower's director of security at the Tower. He had been too frightened to view the contents of the download again. When the animated introduction ended, a main page appeared. The table of contents was so long that it more resembled an index found in the back of a research book. Jake went straight to the search engine and typed in a single word: *zombie.*

A moment later, a section of the dense file opened, one of several hundred reports Tower had commissioned on the supernatural during his quest for immortality. The names of four researchers appeared at the top of the report: Dr. Donna Bidel, Ramera Evans, Professor Blake Carlton, and Javier Soueza. Jake copied the names down on a notepad, then scrolled through the 112-page document, including photos, illustrations, a glossary, and a bibliography. Sipping his Diet Coke for an infusion of caffeine, he returned to the beginning of the section and read it straight through to the end.

Zombies, or reanimated human corpses, exist in the Afro-Caribbean spiritual belief system of vodou, which depicts living people enslaved by powerful sorcerers. The word *zombie* entered English usage sometime in 1871. The beliefs that zombies eat human flesh and that they can be destroyed only by destroying their brains are cinematic devices created by George A. Romero and his co-screenwriter, John Russo, in the 1968 film *Night of the Living Dead* and have no basis in true vodou. A more accurate portrayal of zombies appeared decades earlier in the 1932 film *White Zombie*, which starred Bela Lugosi as "Murder" Legendre, a mill owner with an undead labor force.

Jake scanned a glossary of terms related to the research data.

Bokor: a vodou sorcerer or sorceress who revives a dead person as an enslaved zonbi.

Jumbie: West Indian for "ghost."

Nzambi: Kongo term meaning "the spirit of a dead person."

Nzúmbe: the Kimbundu ghost.

Zonbi: Louisiana Creole or Haitian Creole; a person who has died and has been resurrected without the power of speech or free will.

Zonbi astral: a human soul captured by a bokor to increase the bokor's power.

Jake continued reading into the night, digesting terms and dates and geographic locations related to zombies. Finally, he rubbed his eyes and uninstalled the program from the laptop's hard drive. Having processed the file's information, he wondered if Tower had been taken for a fool by his research team. Although Jake had found the dozens of cases of modern zombies around the world interesting, nothing he read had persuaded him that the creatures existed. Still, the hair on the back of his neck had prickled at the mention of bokors capturing human souls for their own nefarious purposes.

Soul catchers, Jake thought. The term alone sent an icy chill through his core.

Then the lights went out.

SEVEN

A beam of light shot up behind Jake. It came from the high-intensity emergency flashlight that he kept plugged into the outlet behind his chair.

Power's out, he thought as he swiveled around and stood up. But he did not snatch the flashlight from the outlet. The blinds over the window to his right glowed from the city lights outside, and as he peeked through the slats, he saw lit windows in the buildings on either side of him. Only the power in *this* building had been cut.

Three . . . two . . . one . . .

The lights came on again as he expected, juiced by the emergency generator that he had recommended Eden, Inc. install in the basement. As he watched the security monitors on the far wall flare back to life, he unfastened his cell phone from his belt.

When the phone rang in his hand, he answered it. "Jake Helman." Scanning the security monitors, he studied each floor. No sign of intruders yet.

"Mr. Helman, this is Central Alarm Station. What is your—?"

"Evolution." With his password given, he added, "I'm on-site. There's nothing to worry about. Thank you." He powered down the laptop.

"Have a good night, sir."

"You, too." Seizing the laptop in both hands, he ran it over to the safe, set it on its designated shelf, closed the iron door, and spun the combination dials.

His mind raced. The power lines had been cut in the back of the building, which was where the intruders would have to break in. Even as he formulated this scenario, he saw on one monitor the black metal door in the rear of the lobby swing open and a figure lumber forward: tall, shaved head, Chinese. His eyes resembled black pits. Three men followed him. One appeared Hispanic, one African American, and one Caucasian.

A regular United Nations envoy, Jake thought, watching the men move with mechanical precision. They wore identical expressions: flat, impassive, dead. He wrinkled his eyebrows. *These aren't the corner boys or the Escalade hit men.* Then who?

His heart skipped a beat.

All four men had something else in common. They carried gleaming weapons.

Machetes.

The bald Chinese man thumbed the elevator call button, and the door opened seconds later. Without speaking to his fellow assassins, he boarded the elevator, and the door closed. The black and Hispanic men headed toward the stairway, while the Caucasian stood guard in the lobby

Covering their bases, Jake thought as he stepped onto the leather sofa. *But so am I.*

Grasping the frame around the painting mounted on the wall, a black-and-white depiction of Manhattan when the Twin Towers still dominated the sky, he removed the canvas, revealing a niche where he stashed his secret arsenal. Lifting a Beretta from its compartment, he screwed a silencer into its barrel and slapped a magazine into its grip. He had learned his lesson after taking out the Cipher, and the Beretta was one of several untraceable—and illegal—weapons he owned. The silencer was also illegal. He took a second magazine and an additional silencer for the Glock in case he needed it, returned the picture to its rightful place, and hopped off the sofa. With no police response to the alarm, he could handle this situation his own way.

Whatever the hell that *is.*

On the lobby monitor, he saw the black man climb the stairs and the Hispanic man twist the knob on the door leading to the basement. When the knob did not turn, the man stepped back, raised the machete high over his head, and brought it down in a powerful swing that produced sparks and sent the knob rolling across the tiled floor. He pushed the door open and descended the stairs.

Jake ran to the window, raised the blinds, and threw the latch. The window ground open, and he looked outside. He saw plenty of traffic in the street and on the sidewalks despite the late hour. Reaching the sidewalk posed no problem; the green fire escape provided an easy exit. But he didn't want to escape. He wanted to sneak into one of the neighboring suites and take the intruders by surprise. A six-inch stone ledge ran the building's length, but the nearest windows contained air conditioners.

Screw that.

He closed the window and its blinds, then sprinted through the office to his front door and turned the locks as quietly as possible. The echoing squeak that the door issued as he opened it made him shudder. The elevator hadn't reached the fourth floor yet, but he knew the noise had been heard by the assassin ascending the stairs.

Stepping into the hall, he discerned the stairway at the opposite end thanks to an opaque window laced with wire through which city lights shone. As he closed the door and locked it, he heard the elevator and ran down the hall to the dark stairway. Throwing himself around the corner of the stairway leading to the roof, he pressed his back against the wall and gripped the Beretta in both hands. He stared down the stairs at the third floor, which he had climbed every day for nine months. The building had felt safe to him. He should have known better.

The floor and stairs vibrated as the elevator reached its destination. Jake listened to the elevator door slide open and held his breath. Then he heard footsteps walking away from him toward his office.

I can't believe this is happening again.

Sharp banging echoed through the hall.

He's banging on the door with the machete's handle.

Jake sprang from his hiding place as silent as a jungle cat, gun raised in both hands, and moved forward.

Oblivious, the Chinese man continued to bang on Jake's office door. Then he stepped back and raised the machete in both hands.

Jake saw his shadow fall over the man's gray skin. "Looking for me?"

The Chinese man spun around and glared at Jake. A milky white sheen covered his black eyes.

He's dead all right.

Jake squeezed the Beretta's trigger three times. Muzzle fire flared through the silencer in the dim lighting, and the Chinese man's body jerked as each round tore into his torso, but no blood flowed from his wounds. Instead, little puffs of discharge, like sawdust, clouded the space before him.

Without so much as looking at the bullet holes, he charged at Jake, who backpedaled in surprise. The Chinese man brought his machete down in a powerful arc, and Jake leapt backwards to avoid the blade, which struck the floor seconds before Jake's back did the same. Staggering forward, the Chinese man raised the machete again.

Jake leveled the Beretta, took careful aim, and fired again. This time his shot penetrated the Chinese man's forehead, and liquefied brain burbled through the hole. The Chinese man dropped his machete and toppled to the floor. Then his flickering soul shot through his cratered head, blinding Jake before fading from view.

I should have tried that first, Jake thought. But he had wanted to find out what would work against these things and what wouldn't.

Scrambling to his feet, he ran over to the corpse and examined it. He set his gun on the floor and searched the Chinese man's pockets. No identification. No money. Nothing to suggest who he had been or where he came from.

Or why he wanted to kill me.

They had gone through an awful lot of trouble on short notice to come after him.

Jake sensed that the black man had reached the fourth floor even before he turned around. To his horror, the dead thing stood only a few paces behind him. *How the hell did it get up here so fast?* he wondered as his heart thudded in his chest.

The black corpse raised its machete as the first one had.

Jake reached for the Beretta on the floor, but the machete whistled through the air, and he snatched his hand back just as the blade struck the gun.

Son of a bitch!

With his survival instincts kicking in, Jake leapt over the Chinese man's body and rolled across the floor. He came up in a crouch, his back against his office door.

The black man stared into his eyes from ten feet away.

Does he even see me? Jake's chest rose and fell.

The black man slid his machete into his belt at an angle, then reached behind him and pulled a Glock from his waistband.

Make up your mind!

As the dead man raised his gun and held it sideways, gangsta style, Jake whipped his own Glock from its shoulder holster and fired. The round missed the black man and shattered a portion of the wired window at the far end of the hall.

Goddamn it! He had hoped not to leave any evidence of the battle.

The corpse fired its gun, the ensuing shot deafening. The round flattened against the office door.

Jake returned fire, and the dead thing's face disintegrated into pulp. It collapsed onto the floor, and Jake waited for it to rise again. It did so, on its hands and knees, and stared at Jake with one eye.

Jake rushed forward, pressed the silencer against the thing's head, and squeezed the trigger. A hole the size of a baseball opened up in the dead flesh, and the corpse struck the floor. The black man's soul rose from the wound and faded.

That leaves two.

Scooping up his Beretta, he headed downstairs.

As Jake stepped onto the second-floor landing, he encountered the third zombie on its way upstairs.

Shifting his machete from his right hand into his left, the Hispanic man reached inside his shirt and drew out a gleaming .45.

Jake froze with one foot planted on the stair below him. Even as he brought up his Beretta to fire, confusion rained down on him. He had seen the Hispanic man go into the basement and had expected to run into the Caucasian man next. Had the white zombie remained in the lobby?

His answer came in the form of a shuddering groan from a spring as a door opened behind him. Spinning on one heel, Jake saw the Caucasian emerging from the garbage chute room. They had laid a trap for him!

Holding the machete in its right hand, the white-faced zombie wrapped its arms around Jake in a bear hug. With their faces only inches apart, Jake smelled fetid flesh and putrid breath. Staring into Jake's eyes, the thing tilted its head back, opened its jaws, and jerked its head forward, clamping its mouth over Jake's neck. Envisioning his flesh tearing, Jake opened his own mouth to scream, then realized he felt very little pain. The zombie raised its head, and through its still moving jaws, Jake saw purplish black gums but no teeth.

A gummer!

Jake struggled in the thing's iron grip to no avail, then tried to aim each of his handguns at the creature's head. No such luck, and a random shot could just as easily blow out his own brains. So he jammed both barrels against the zombie's midsection and squeezed the triggers repeatedly. Over the sounds of the muffled gunfire, he heard rounds tearing through solid matter. As he filled his attacker with lead, the thing remained stone-faced.

Jake stopped firing when he heard the empty Beretta clicking. Realizing that he needed to save the ammunition in his Glock, he looked over his shoulder at the Hispanic zombie, which had almost reached them. That assailant still had not raised either of its weapons.

The Caucasian squeezed Jake's torso harder, forcing the air from his lungs. With his breathing halted, Jake heard his heart hammering that much clearer. Bending his legs at the knees, he raised his feet off the floor, throwing the Caucasian zombie off balance. As the creature teetered forward because of the extra weight in its arms, Jake planted his feet back on the floor and kicked backwards with all his strength. This propelled him and the Caucasian zombie straight back into the Hispanic zombie, and all three of them tumbled down the stairs.

Holding on to both guns for dear life, Jake heard metal clattering down the stairs, but he couldn't tell which weapons had been dropped. Halfway down, the Caucasian zombie released Jake, who rolled across the lobby floor.

Leaping to his feet in the bright lobby, Jake glanced out the front glass doors as the zombies rolled onto the lobby floor. Reflections in the glass made it impossible to see the Manhattan nightlife outside, so he had no idea if any passersby had witnessed the sudden arrival of him and his attackers.

As the zombies climbed to their feet, he stepped into the alcove leading to the basement door, out of sight of anyone who might be watching. The zombies' eyes seemed to focus on him at the same time, like identical digital cameras, and they gathered up their weapons and lumbered toward him in unison. Jamming the empty Beretta into his waistband, he raised the Glock in both hands and squeezed off a shot.

The round tore into the dead center of the Caucasian zombie's forehead, and the creature fell backwards and splayed across the stairs, out of public view except for one foot. The man's flickering soul rose from the head wound and faded.

Damn good shot, Jake thought with pride as he trained his Glock on the Hispanic zombie's head and squeezed the trigger. The barrel locked back in plain sight, the gun out of ammunition.

Shit!

The Hispanic zombie charged at Jake, who seized the thing's wrists and forced the weapons away from where they could do him harm. The dead thing head butted him, and he saw spots before his eyes as his forehead turned numb. They grappled in the corner; then Jake lunged for the edge of the narrow stairway leading to the basement. Hurling the zombie into the space below, he made sure it didn't take him along for the ride.

The zombie struck the stairs face-first and flipped heels over head on its way down. As Jake raced after it, he heard metal scraping cement. The zombie hit the floor and rolled, then stood before Jake could reach him. Its face had collapsed into a mostly unrecognizable mass of bone and tissue.

Glimpsing the .45 on the floor ten feet behind its owner and the machete in the dead thing's right hand, Jake leapt into the air with his legs before him. *I hope he doesn't cut my feet off . . .*

The zombie took the impact full in its chest and spiraled backwards, the machete flying from its hand. Ready for action as he landed on the floor, Jake sprang to his feet. The zombie rose, made eye contact with Jake, then looked from left to right, calculating the distance to each weapon.

Go for the machete, Monte. Go for the machete.

It went for the .45.

Panic drove Jake scrambling for the machete. Out of the corner of his left eye, he glimpsed the zombie hunching over for the gun. Jake's hands closed around the machete's handle. The zombie turned toward him, swinging the .45 in his direction. Jake had no choice but to leave himself fully exposed as he cocked the machete with both hands, bringing his arms behind his head. It took all his willpower to ignore the gun's barrel and concentrate on the zombie's crown as he brought the machete down with all the force he could muster.

An instant later, the machete cleaved the creature's head, coming to a stop between its eyes. Gray fluid containing chunks of pink spurted out of the wound. Jake waited for the gun to fire, but instead, it slipped from the Hispanic man's hand, and a moment later, the zombie joined it in a heap on the floor.

With his chest rising and falling, Jake watched the man's flickering soul rise and fade.

Jake seized the .45 and ran upstairs to the lobby. Concealing the gun from the glass doors behind him, he raced to the black metal door and flung it open. He switched on the overhead light and scanned the storage area for any more of the damned dead things. Satisfied that he was alone, he crossed the cluttered space to a wide metal door in the back. As expected, the locks on the door had been broken. If he had not answered the call from the alarm company, the dispatcher would have called the police, and some unsuspecting uniforms would have been in store for four big surprises.

They wouldn't have come here if I hadn't, he reasoned. *They must have followed me from One PP.*

This begged the question: how large was this network of dead things? He had seen three of them dealing drugs on Flatbush Avenue, four had chased him over the Brooklyn Bridge, and four more had invaded the little office building. That made eleven that he had encountered in one night.

And I cut that number in half, give or take a head.

On his way up the stairs to the fourth floor, Jake collected the various weapons that his assailants had dropped. He estimated that he had only two hours remaining before sunrise, which left him little time to accomplish what needed to be done. Entering the slop sink room on his floor, he opened the garbage chute and deposited the guns and two of the machetes, which banged and echoed their way down to the basement trash compactor.

Inside his office, he set the two remaining machetes on top of his safe for further inspection later and fetched a digital still camera, an ink pad, and several sheets of blank paper. He photographed each of the dead things from several angles, working his way down to the basement. When he attempted to fingerprint them, he made a shocking discovery: the ends of each finger had been surgically removed and sutured.

What the hell?

Inspecting the insides of their mouths, he saw that all their teeth had been removed, reducing their gums to misshapen masses of gray tissue. The zombie that had attempted to bite him had not been an isolated case. With a sickening feeling in his gut, he removed their shoes and peeled off their socks. The ends of their toes had been cut off and sutured with catgut.

No wonder they staggered around like Boris Karloff in elevator shoes. Someone went to pretty extreme lengths to make sure these things can't be identified.

Their flesh felt like shoe leather, which explained why their faces had been so inexpressive, besides the fact they were dead.

After returning the camera and fingerprint documents to his office, Jake seized the Chinese and black zombies by their wrists and dragged them into the waiting elevator. Possessing no desire to ride in the cramped elevator with two corpses, he thumbed the button for the basement and stepped out just before the door closed. He returned to his office and took a spare blanket from his bedroom closet, then took the stairs.

It was easy enough to cover the Caucasian zombie with the blanket, harder to sling the corpse over his shoulder and carry it to the alcove, where he dumped the thing without ceremony and watched it flop and thud its way to the basement below.

With all the assassins gathered together, he opened the large, curved hatch of the industrial garbage compactor. The weapons he had dropped down the chute rested atop garbage waiting to be crushed. As he understood it, when a certain weight of garbage had accumulated, the compactor automatically went to work. He loaded the corpses into the machine in the order in which he had put them down. They seemed far heavier now, as his muscles had grown fatigued.

With their arms and legs entangled, blank eyes staring at him, he closed the hatch and pressed the red button on the compactor's side. Issuing a great rumble, the compactor folded, crushed, and packed the human bones and flesh into a dense package that it forced deep into its bowels, ready for pickup.

One hour later, after sweeping and scrubbing the sawdust and liquefied brains from the walls and floors, Jake sat at his desk, with the Afterlife file uploaded again, and keyed a single word into the search engine: *voodoo*.

An hour after that, with the sun rising, he grabbed a round container and poured salt across each doorway of his office.

EIGHT

"Grandma! Grandma!"

Carmen Rodriguez awoke with a start, snapping her head up. She caught her breath. "What is it, Victor?"

The boy stood beside her bed. "Someone's trying to get in!"

Seeing the panic in her young grandson's eyes, she threw back her bedsheet and climbed out of bed, her nightgown sticking to her body. She snatched the wooden baseball bat from where she left it propped against her bedroom doorframe and rushed past the bathroom and the bedroom that Victor had shared with Louis.

Early morning light shone through the blinds in the kitchen and living room, and as she rounded the corner, her heart jumped in her chest. Through the front door, open six inches but held in place by the chain lock, she saw her other grandson, Louis, standing in the green hallway and staring at her with flat, expressionless eyes.

Dios mio!

She felt Victor clinging to her nightgown, the poor boy. Raising the bat, she said, "Louis, you get out of here, boy. I don't care if you are blood—you set one foot in this apartment, and I will do you some serious harm."

Louis kept looking at her with unblinking eyes, which zeroed in on Victor. A terrible moment passed, and then he stepped back from the door.

Carmen took a deep breath and exhaled. Louis wasn't the first boy who had tried to menace her only to back down. Just the first dead one. Why had he come home? Perhaps it had been a mistake for her to hire that private investigator. She hurried to the door, intending to close it again and throw the locks, but as her fleshy fingers closed around the knob, a long blade seemed to materialize out of nowhere, shearing the chain on the door in a shower of sparks.

"Grandma!"

Carmen heard the terror in Victor's voice. As she moved away, the door flew open and crashed into the far wall, and Louis stepped inside holding a deadly looking machete. She raised the bat again, and he mimicked her movement with the machete.

The last thing she heard as the long blade whistled down toward her eyes was Victor screaming.

NINE

Gary Brown and Frank Beck sat in the front seat of their unmarked car, observing the Shaft bar across 116th Street. The bar had closed at 4:00 a.m., and the Narcotics detectives arrived an hour later. Now streaks of pink outlined the buildings on either side of the street as the sun poised to emerge from the darkness. A homeless man dug through the contents of an orange metal trash can, and a pimp waited for his top girl to return from a "date," location unknown. The short Guatemalan wore a leather vest over his muscular torso and a beaded choker around his neck.

"Looks like someone's impatient for his breakfast money," Frank said as he pulled a plastic bag filled with white powder out of his jacket pocket. He sprinkled cocaine on the passenger-side dashboard.

"Haven't you had enough?" Gary said. Working the night shift, they both did their share of blow, but he liked to come down as the sun came up. Frank, on the other hand, never knew when to quit. Gary had calmed a panicked Frank's wired nerves more times than he cared to count, and on more than one occasion, he had called a doctor who catered to the fringe elements of society to treat his partner's overdoses in secret.

"Nah," Frank said, snorting two lines off the vinyl. "I'm just getting started."

I bet you are, Gary thought.

He held out the half straw. "You want?"

"No, thanks. I want to be straight for this."

Frank inhaled the coke deeper into his septum. "Suit yourself. It always gives me an edge on the opposition."

"You don't need an edge. You need to be cool."

Frank massaged the coke particles into his gums. "Whatever."

Gary's pulse quickened as he eyed the coke remaining on the dash. *Ah, what the hell.* "Give me that straw."

With a crooked grin, Gary did just that.

They got out of the car a few minutes later, and Gary inhaled the fresh morning air. Blue seeped into the sky, and behind them two garbage men emptied rubbish into their truck. The pimp had disappeared, fading in the light, but the homeless man lingered at the corner. As Frank joined him, Gary's eyes settled on a woman heading their way. Her fashionable clothes appeared as disheveled as her hair.

"Morning," Gary said with a knowing smile to the woman as her eyes met his.

Red faced, she turned her gaze toward the sidewalk and passed them without answering.

"I love when they have that *morning after* look," Gary said, and Frank chuckled. They watched the woman reach the corner, ignore the homeless man, and disappear from view.

The homeless man looked up, no doubt alerted by the aroma of her perfume.

Gary and Loraine had been divorced for almost two years. She had moved out to the island with their three kids, and he kept a place in Chelsea. He loved his kids and made sure Loraine had everything she needed to take care of them, which meant he had to be more resourceful in how he earned extra cash.

Fortunately, Frank had proven himself game for any scheme Gary thought up. They were partners on and off the clock and had each other's back. That didn't mean he considered Frank infallible. On the contrary, his partner's impulsive behavior made him a severe liability. Gary knew he had to keep a careful watch on the man's erratic behavior.

"Come on," Gary said.

They circled the corner bar to its side door, which Gary rapped on. The sun peered over the rooftops, casting light on the green leaves of the trees growing from the sidewalk.

The face of a dark-skinned teenage boy appeared in the door's window. He looked about fifteen to Gary and wore the dirty white uniform of a cleaner. He wasn't old enough to be working at a bar, let alone the night shift. The boy waved one hand sideways across his throat, indicating the bar had closed.

Gary rapped on the door again and shook his head.

Looking over his shoulder at some unseen person, the boy unlocked the door. "We're *closed*."

"Tell Papa Joe that he has company."

"Ain't no one here with that name."

"Tell him."

The boy held Gary's gaze, then closed the door and retreated from view.

A moment later, a tall man with a shaved head and a trimmed beard answered the door. He looked the detectives up and down.

"Don't make me take out my shield," Gary said. "I want to see Papa Joe. He'll want to see me, too. We need to discuss certain *baked goods*."

Shaved Head's eyes shifted from Gary to Frank, who said, "*Now*, eight ball."

Ah, shit, Gary thought. Too much blow always made Frank talk tough. He never knew how ridiculous he looked, all five feet of him.

The sentry closed the door and slipped into the shadows.

"Will you watch it with that shit?" Gary said.

"What? He was dicking us around, and now we're getting somewhere. Bite my head off—why don't you? That mope's just hired muscle."

"You think he doesn't have Joe's ear? You think they aren't gonna talk about the cops who were pricks? In case you haven't noticed, this city's running out of high-level dealers for us to freelance for."

In addition to the Machete Massacres, a number of drug lords had been assassinated or had simply disappeared during the last several months. At least three men Gary and Frank had done work for had ceased to exist. That made Papa Joe an extremely important man to them. But these hits did not point to a power grab; the drug lords' operations were not taken over by an outside force. Rather, the operations were being cut off at the knees. Cocaine, crack, heroin, and ecstasy had become increasingly rare—and therefore prohibitively expensive—commodities on the streets of Manhattan and its suburbs. And the distribution of Black Magic had reached epidemic proportions. All fingers pointed to the source of this new narcotic as the mastermind behind the shift of power.

A third man opened the door. Gary recognized him as Chess, Papa Joe's right-hand man.

Now we're getting somewhere. Maybe Frank had taken the proper approach after all.

"In," Chess said, nodding into the dark interior and stepping back.

Gary and Frank entered the bar.

Chess closed the door behind them and twisted the locks. The tall, muscular man faced them. "You come when Joe calls you. He didn't call."

Holding up his right hand as a cautionary sign, Gary said, "We were at the bakery earlier and picked up a loaf of bread for him." He opened his jacket, revealing a wrapped brick of cocaine. "I don't feel like keeping it at my place until Joe decides he wants a report."

Chess's eyes registered the key of coke, then looked past the detectives. "Put it behind the bar."

Gary glanced behind him at the bar, where the boy who had first answered the door mopped the floor. "Do I look like an errand boy? I'm putting this in Joe's hands and nowhere else."

Anger flared in Chess's eyes but not in his voice. "Joe's hands don't touch product. Ever."

Gary saw this was going nowhere. He took out the brick. "Then you take it and put it wherever you like. Just take us to Joe, so we can get out of here. It's been a long night."

Chess fixed him with a stare, then took the key and disappeared down a flight of stairs.

"Real diplomatic," Frank said with a bemused grin.

"I get tough when I have to. You get tough when you want to. There's a difference."

Chess returned a minute later. "This way."

They followed him downstairs past restrooms and a kitchen to the manager's office. Inside the spacious room, the second man who had answered the door stood in the corner. Bodyguard. A slim black woman in an elegant dress sat at a desk, running bills through a cash-counting machine. Chess sat on a leather sofa beside a heavyset man in his midforties with his hands folded over his wide belly.

"Have a seat, gentlemen," Papa Joe said.

As Gary and Frank sat in plush chairs facing the sofa, the bodyguard closed and locked the door behind them.

"You ever hear of calling ahead to make an appointment?" Papa Joe Morton had come of age as a teenager during the rise of crack cocaine in the 1980s. He had done a single stint in juvie for possession of narcotics with intent to sell, then had never been arrested again. He had worked his way up through the ranks of lower management, eventually taking the top spot with a series of canny business moves in the wake of 9/11 when law enforcement agencies concentrated their resources and efforts on counterterrorism.

He had weathered gang wars and internal strife, ruling his territory with an even hand. If anything, he had proven himself a soothing influence in a volatile business. He had no ambitions of moving in on other dealers' territories but tolerated no moves on his own. He owned Manhattan, plain and simple. Until now.

"Can't make a call like that when you change your number every day," Gary said.

"The price of doing business. How'd you know where to find me?"

"We make it our business to know where you are," Gary said.

"That makes you an asset. It also makes you dangerous."

Gary nodded at Chess. "Today it makes us valuable."

Chess grunted. "Looking at the two of you right now, you probably saved another key for yourself."

Gary spread his hands in a gesture of futility. "I guess you'll never know. Nevertheless, we shaved your losses tonight."

"True that. But it was still a bad night. We lost product, we lost people, and we lost a location."

Gary knew that despite his dislike for violence, Joe had already ordered the death of the bakery owner. Killing citizens who could put him in prison was necessary.

"Tell me about the crime scene," Joe said.

"Messy."

"Machetes?"

Gary nodded. "No weapons were left behind, but your people were dismembered."

"Kenny was a good man," Chess said. "We never had to worry about counts or product when he was on duty."

"This is a war," Joe said. "Good soldiers fall during wartime."

"This war's killing more than soldiers," Frank said. "It's killing business. For everyone."

"This Black Magic is bad news," Joe said in an agreeable tone. "Once a customer tries it, they don't want to touch the product I carry. When this is all over, we're going to have to build our operation up from the ground floor again."

"Or take over the Black Magic business," Frank said.

Gary's stomach tightened. He didn't like the idea of Frank suggesting business moves to Joe. It put him in a precarious position.

"No," Joe said.

Gary thought he had seen Chess nodding in response to Frank's comment. *Better keep my eye on these two*, he thought.

"I won't touch the Magic. It's worse than crack or angel dust or any other drug out there. I provide contraband to a steady customer base. They know what they're getting, and they know what they're getting themselves into. It's almost like a contract. I don't pretend that I'm doing God's work. I know what I am, and I can live with that. But Black Magic is worse than illegal; it's worse than immoral. It's an evil, soul-sucking product. I want it gone from my city. Hell, I want it gone from my *country*."

"I didn't know you were such a patriot," Gary said.

"You think drug dealers can't be patriots? Shit, I say the Pledge of

Allegiance when I take my boys to see the Yankees. You don't know anything about me. You just think you do. But I know a lot about you. I make that part of *my* business. For instance, you two *po*lice got your hands in a lot of fires. Leastways you did when those other fires were still burning."

Joe's revelation neither surprised nor alarmed Gary. "A man's got to make a living. Frank and I have never been exclusive agents."

"I'd call that a conflict of interest," Chess said, an edge creeping into his voice.

"This can be a complicated business," Gary said. "Nothing Frank and I have done has ever posed a threat to your operation."

"I know that," Joe said. "That's why you're both still alive. We know about every unauthorized bust and raid, every stickup you've made and every handout you've taken. Nothing goes on in this business—in this city—that I don't know about. Too bad for you that so many players have been taken down or out and I'm the only fire left in town. I think y'all are more exclusive than you realize."

He knows he's got us, Gary thought.

"Unless we make bank with this Black Magic outfit," Frank said.

Joe burst into laughter. "You're welcome to try; you're welcome to try. But there's a big difference between playing with fire and showering in gasoline."

"We're not looking to cut a deal with anyone outside the normal circle," Gary said. "We want these people put away."

"Putting away a drug dealer doesn't do any good. Powerful men continue to conduct business whether they're on the inside or the outside. You got to put these players *down*. Then we can all start making money again."

"It's not that easy. We don't even know who these players are."

"Shit, is that all that's stopping you? All you had to do is ask. I know who's running that outfit. It's my nephew, Prince Malachai. My sister's boy."

Gary's mind tracked Malachai's rap sheet. He'd been busted for slinging a number of times and had been a suspect in one homicide. "I thought Malachai worked for you."

"He did. But the boy was too ambitious, so I had to cut him loose. He took his crew with him. They laid low, working small time out of Brooklyn until a year ago. Then out of nowhere they started dealing Black Magic there and in Queens, and now they're moving into Manhattan. Wiser heads wanted me to take him out right away"—he glanced at Chess—"but I had a soft spot in my heart for the boy, what with him being family and all."

"Why don't you take him out now?" Frank said.

"It's too late for that. He knows me; he knows Chess. Knows our whole operation, which is why he's been so successful at breaking us down. He knows who and what to look out for. Why you think I'm living in the shadows? But he doesn't know you, and you say you got resources. A couple of crooked cops could get the job done."

"Where is he?"

Joe shrugged. "That's the one thing I don't know. We snatched one of his dealers off the street and tortured his ass for three days.

Motherfucker never said a word, never screamed, never even made a sound. He looked as dead when we grabbed him as he did when we dumped him." He smiled. "Well, almost as dead."

"Grab another one," Frank said.

"We've grabbed four of them. Same story. You ever seen these 'soldiers'? Malachai's messing with forces he shouldn't be."

Frank's voice assumed a mocking quality. "What are you saying?"

"They don't call it Black Magic for nothing."

TEN

Jake slept for two hours. His dreams never became intense enough to awaken him, but when he opened his eyes and took in his surroundings, the vague images of swampland, creepers, and snakes lingered in his mind like fading ghosts. He thought he remembered swallowing a mouthful of dirt, and he craved a cigarette for the first time in eleven months.

They'll be back, he thought, picturing his zombie assassins. *Whatever they were, more will come.*

He rose from his bed, and pain seized his lower spine and rocketed up his back. He unleashed an agonized scream and dropped to all fours, only to have the impact send another wave of pain ripping through his body.

Oh, Jesus Christ!

He had not experienced such intense physical distress since Cain had tortured him in an abandoned factory in Queens. But that had been in his mind, a form of mental torture that had only seemed real. The excruciating pain he experienced now was all too existent. He tried to stand but screamed again and pitched face forward to the floor

107

with tears in his eyes.

Ah, God . . . God, make it stop . . .

Jake allowed his breathing to normalize, then worked his way up onto his hands and knees again. He found it impossible to move without triggering the pain and surprised himself by whimpering like a wounded dog. In those moments, he knew that if for some reason he had to live with this pain forever, he would kill himself—even if it meant being subjected to Cain's vengeful torture for eternity.

He steeled his mind and crawled to the bathroom. Using the sink for leverage, he pulled himself into a standing position and pissed in the toilet. Wincing, he imagined his body as two cones, one perched upside down on top of the other, with their touching points representing his lower back. If either cone moved even a centimeter off point, pain racked his physical being.

After relieving himself, he sighed. Even ten seconds without the torturous pain eased his mind. But the mere act of zipping his jeans fly sent new tremors through his body, causing him to cry out. He collapsed into a heap on the bathroom floor, his legs dangling out of the cramped space.

Oh, God . . . Oh, God, what's happened?

The car wreck, he thought. *Whiplash or something.*

Crashing the Malibu had been an act of desperation that saved his life, but now he had to pay the price.

A pound of flesh . . .

Even when he remained still, the pain in his back throbbed, disorienting him. He had no idea how much time had passed before he motivated himself to get up and crawl again. He made it halfway to the bed when his quivering arms gave out and he collapsed yet again. Grimacing, he rocked back and forth on his back. What had he done to deserve such torment?

Don't answer that . . .

Jake lay on the floor in a fetal position, praying his body would recover. Hearing the door open and close in the reception area, he could not help but flinch. He gritted his teeth to keep from screaming in response to the spasm in his back.

He heard footsteps in his office.

Holy shit . . . Holy . . . fucking . . . shit!

He peered up at his bed, where he had left his Glock hidden beneath his pillow. Sweat beaded on his brow and stung his eyes. He had not expected the dead things to return in broad daylight.

Why not? This building was as deserted before business hours as it was in the middle of the night.

"Jake?" A female voice.

Carrie!

Carrie Scott worked for him as a bookkeeper, scheduler, and occasional receptionist. Three times a week she came in for two hours, and he called her his Person Friday. He had even used her on a couple of stakeouts.

"Carrie . . ." Speaking increased the pain.

"Are you okay, Jake?" Her voice sounded louder, and he knew she had her face close to the door now.

"No!" Spittle flew from his mouth, and he groaned. "Get in here!"

The door opened, and he heard heels clacking across the hardwood floor. He saw her shadow, then her legs, and he looked up. She towered five feet above him.

"Oh, my God! What the hell happened to you? Were you shot?"

He shook his head.

She crouched down on one knee, and he found himself focusing on the texture of her sheer black stockings. A dwarf with a perfectly proportioned body, so that she resembled a person of normal height who had shrunk, Carrie favored provocative Goth fashions. "What's wrong, then?"

He forced himself up on one elbow. "My back . . ."

"Well, I'm too small to lift you up and carry you to bed. You're going to have to do it yourself." Her voice took on a surprisingly maternal tone for a twenty-two-year-old grad student. "I'll do what I can, okay, sweetie?"

Jake nodded, grateful for a simple yes or no question.

Carrie stood and offered her hand, which he took. She wore black fingernail polish and a pewter bracelet with a grinning skull surrounded by a floral wreath. Her glossy black stacked platform boots added seven inches to her height. She pulled him up, and he set his weight on one knee, then managed to stumble the rest of the way to the bed and collapse onto the mattress with a protracted cry.

"Honey, what did you do to yourself?"

"I don't know," he said, gasping. "I just woke up this way . . ."

"Uh-huh." She looked him over. "I find that a little hard to believe. Something must have happened."

"I totaled the Malibu last night. The tow slip is on your desk."

"Oh, a car accident. And you waking up like this. What a coincidence."

"Save the sarcasm. Can't you see I'm dying here?"

"I think it's unattractive when a grown man cries."

"Then it's a good thing we're not screwing."

"I'm not going to tell Ripper what you just said because you're a pathetic cripple, and he won't care about that."

For the five months she had been working for him, Carrie had referred to her boyfriend, Ripper, in a manner reserved for groupies. Jake had never met Ripper, who Carrie described as a musician, but as far as he had been able to discern, the lothario was normal height. "Go to the Rolodex and look up Dr. Metivier. Tell him it's an emergency, but don't tell him what's wrong. I want him over here right away."

Carrie's Irish features formed a frown. "What kind of doctor makes house calls in this city?"

"Just call him."

Dr. Lawrence Metivier had a thriving medical practice, albeit one unknown to the Internal Revenue Service. Although he maintained a private practice with a limited number of patients in Amityville, Long Island, he made regular house calls to Brooklyn, Staten Island, Manhattan, and Queens. He drew the line at New Jersey.

Lawrence had several high-profile clients, most of them on the shadier side of the law: Mafioso, crooked cops, criminal defense lawyers, even politicians, men and women who had reason to keep certain medical needs off the record, which was how the doctor preferred to keep his income. Jake first learned about the unique medical services that Lawrence provided through Gary Brown. Lawrence treated drug overdoses, gunshot wounds, and stabbings with equal discretion. He had even falsified a death certificate or two.

Jake held none of this against the man and, lying facedown on the bed with his buttocks in the air, breathed a sigh of relief when he heard Larry enter and exchange pleasantries with Carrie, who showed him into the bedroom.

"Lying down on the job?" Larry said to Jake, then turned to Carrie. "Thank you, dear." He closed the door on her, giving them privacy.

"Har, har," Jake said.

Larry set his black bag down on the foot of Jake's bed. "The sad thing is, I've seen you look worse. Where does it hurt?"

"Back," Jake said, groaning. "Hips. Neck. Balls."

Larry pulled up a chair and sat, then looked Jake over. In return, Jake focused on the man's gleaming leather shoes and Italian slacks.

"I don't see any blood, so I take it nobody shot you in the back?"

Jake shook his head, the result being that he pressed his face against the mattress. "I totaled my car outside One PP last night."

"That was *you*? I saw the photo on the front page of the *Post*, but I didn't bother to read the caption. I just figured it was an incredibly stupid and inebriated crook turning himself in after suffering a guilty conscience. Jesus, man, what happened?"

"Doesn't matter. I walked away from that feeling fine. Then when

112

I got out of bed this morning . . ."

"Yeah, that's how it happens. Too bad you can't sue yourself for negligence. Well, I can't do much with you like that. You're going to have to stand up." Larry offered his arm, which Jake took, then swung his legs off the bed. "That's it."

Wincing, Jake staggered forward, then back, grabbing the bed's headboard for balance. His face contorted in ways he didn't know possible.

"Try to stand straight," Larry said.

Jake's head trembled with effort, and his eyes watered.

"Okay, okay. Don't kill yourself. Here's what I see: your left hip is two inches higher than your right hip. That's a hell of a lot of twisting and knotting going on inside your body. I'm going to give you a shot of morphine to ease the pain and prescribe some heavy-duty muscle relaxers, the kind you'll have to receive by special delivery, if you know what I mean. All you can do is stay off your back and wait for them to kick in. Your muscles have to relax in order for your spine to return to normal. This will pass as quickly as it started."

"How long will that take?"

"A minimum of four days. Then you'll need an MRI—"

"Screw that."

"What?"

"I can't wait a minimum of four days. Some people out there are trying to kill me. I need to be able to defend myself, and I need to be clear clearheaded."

Larry glanced at the window. "Is this something I need to be concerned about while I'm in here?"

Jake shook his head.

"Good. Well, I guess we can skip the morphine, then. With your history, I thought you'd consider that a silver lining. I can probably get you in for an MRI tomorrow—"

"Today."

"That's not possible, Jake."

"Today."

"Be reasonable."

"Did you hear what I said a minute ago?"

"Yes, but—"

"Then make it today."

"I'm not God, and you're not the president of the United States."

"How much am I paying you for this little visit?"

"Minus the injection? Five bills and we're even. But the meter's running."

"I'll double that. Just get me in now."

"You have insurance?"

Jake nodded.

Larry sighed. "All right, but you'll have to come out to the island. I know someone who will squeeze you in there."

"No problem. You can drive me."

"Only because I have to go that way anyway, but I'm not bringing you back."

Jake blew air out of his cheeks. "Now you can give me the damned shot."

"Thank God. If nothing else, it will make you more pleasant." Larry opened his bag, rumbled through its contents, and prepared a hypodermic needle, which he flicked with his finger and squirted into the air.

"Then you can help me get dressed."

"Christ. Be sure to leave your gun here."

"Fat chance."

"You know what MRI stands for? Magnetic resonance imaging. Also known as *N*MRI, as in *nuclear* magnetic resonance imaging. The scanner is so magnetic that when you're pinned down inside it, any metal objects in the room will be sucked into it with so much force that the object will tear through your head and into your brain. They'll make you check your belongings, but knowing you, you'll find a way to smuggle in your piece. I strongly advise against it."

"Whatever you say," Jake said.

"Help is on the way," Larry said right before injecting Jake's ass with the morphine.

The drug kicked in before Jake got into Larry's BMW. Numbness spread through his body, followed by tranquility.

"I thought you'd like that," Larry said.

For the first time in a year, Jake found himself thinking of cocaine.

Stop it, he commanded himself. He had to be careful every day, and he knew it was dangerous to lose control of himself even for an hour.

They took the Long Island Expressway past Hicksville and Old Westbury and Huntington to exit 49 South 110, Amityville.

Larry parked beside a three-story, modern-looking medical facility in a section of the lot reserved for physicians. "How about I just drop you off here?"

"Not a chance," Jake muttered.

Larry walked around the BMW and helped Jake out. "You know, I make house calls to special patients, of which you barely qualify, but I don't normally provide ambulance service."

"It does the soul good to walk an extra mile once in a while," Jake said, grimacing as they limped onto the sidewalk.

Larry supported his arm. "You couldn't last a mile. I'd have to carry you."

The MRI technician, a young Chinese woman with glasses and a pony-tail, led Jake into the magnetic resonance imaging room. Larry had cut out as soon as Jake had been registered, and a nurse had given Jake a hospital gown and disposable slippers and had shown him to a small locker room. Now he stood in the quiet room, gazing through the soft lighting at the mammoth MRI machine, which resembled a giant womb, complete with its own fallopian tube, a sliding table on which he was expected to lie. The machine was constructed of vacuum-formed plastic, giving it the appearance of NASA technology.

"Lie down on the table, please," the technician said.

Jake hobbled over to the giant donut in the middle of the room and positioned himself on the cool plastic table, his eyes focusing on the overhead ceiling panels.

The technician placed a plastic headset with foam earpieces on his head. "This is going to take about forty-five minutes. Are you claustrophobic?"

"No."

"Good. Some patients find this procedure very upsetting. It's a tight fit inside the scanner, and the noise is pretty fierce. The headset is so I can talk you through the process." She grabbed Jake's wrist and guided his right hand to a button a few inches below his hip. "That's a panic button. If for any reason you decide you can't take any more, press the button. I'll switch off the machine and pull you out. Do you understand?"

"Yes."

She retreated from his field of vision, and he listened to her footsteps recede. "Here we go."

He heard a hum and felt a vibration through the table, which carried him headfirst into the scanner. The room vanished from his view, replaced by the bright tube. It was impossible to determine the distance from his face to the top of the tube, but he guessed it to be about six inches.

I can handle this, he thought despite the disorientation he felt.

Then his shoulders entered the tube, and he felt the tube pressing his arms against his torso.

Tight fit is right. He felt like a nail driven into a cement block.

His heartbeat quickened, and he took a deep breath. It seemed to take forever for his entire body to enter the tube. Then the table stopped vibrating, and he heard his own breathing amplified.

Slow down.

"Are you okay?" Over the headset, the technician's voice sounded distant.

"Yes," he said, closing his eyes.

"You're going to hear a loud noise for two minutes," she said.

Swallowing, he waited.

A deafening roar emanated from the scanner, and he imagined a subway train running over him.

Jesus Christ!

His brain rattled inside his skull. He no longer heard his breathing because it was impossible to hear anything over the roar. He couldn't even construct a thought. The noise continued, and he had to open his eyes. Staring at the ceiling inches from his face, he pictured a construction worker manning a jackhammer on the other side and half expected the power tool to burst through the plastic and burrow between his eyes, splattering the tube with cartilage and gore.

Stop it.

The noise stopped, but his body continued to shake. His breathing came in tortured rasps.

"Are you okay?"

He calmed his breathing. "Yes . . ."

"This will last for six minutes."

Oh, God.

The roar resumed. Sweat formed on his brow. He felt the immense machine pressing against him from every direction.

Don't open your eyes, he told himself.

He opened them.

The bright ceiling seemed only four inches away now instead of six.

What the hell?

Perhaps he had misjudged its distance from him. The noise continued. He felt trapped inside—

A coffin!

Panic seized him. "Hello?"

He could not hear himself over the roar, nor could he be certain that he had even spoken.

"Hello?"

He raised his forearms so that his knuckles brushed across the coffin lid. He could not press his palms against the lid, but he managed to fold his arms over his chest for what little purpose that served. The ceiling pressed against his nose.

The panic button . . .

He worked his right arm down again, then felt along the side for the panic button. His fingers clawed at the heavy-duty plastic.

No button!

Then the lights flickered and died, enshrouding him in darkness. He heard a rhythmic sound over the scanner's roar: *thrum . . . thrum . . . thrum . . .*

He tapped the headset.

Drums!

The tube continued to shrink. He turned his head to the left, so the ceiling would not crush his nose. He tried to position his arms in such a way that he could press his palms against the surface, but the narrowing circumference prevented movement of any kind. He felt thick, sinewy snakes entangling his ankles. Tears filled his eyes, and he screamed for his life.

Sheryl!

The constricting scanner pinned his arms to his sides and crushed his ribs.

Jake felt light on his eyelids. Opening them, a blurry shape loomed overhead. Murky sounds.

Underwater?

Fire burned his nostrils, and the technician's face came into focus.

"What happened?" His throat felt hoarse. *From screaming*, he thought.

"You passed out," the technician said. "I don't understand. You had a panic attack, but you never pressed the button."

He took a deep breath. Panic attack? He didn't think so. Someone had attacked his mind . . . or his soul. But he had survived, goddamn it. "Couldn't find it . . ."

"I'm so sorry. Would you like a sedative?"

He considered the offer. The pleasant numbness provided by the morphine had begun to wear off. "Sure." *Why the hell not?*

ELEVEN

Scarecrows walked the Polo Grounds in broad daylight. The Washington Heights public housing projects occupied land that had once been Polo Grounds IV, the stadium which had served as home to the New York Giants, Yankees, and Mets. The four towers—surrounded by West 155th Street, Frederick Douglass Boulevard, and Harlem River Drive—contained 1,616 apartment units.

"Look at 'em go," Frank said from the passenger seat. "They're even uglier in the daytime."

"Frigging skells," Gary said behind the wheel. God, how he hated them. Downtown, the Black Magic dealers and druggies only came out at night, but here in the hood . . .

They had parked on 155th, which afforded them a clear view of the drug activity in the grassy lawns between the towers.

"Just looking at this depresses me," Frank said.

"I know what you mean."

"We gonna do this or what?"

"You bet."

They got out of the car and didn't bother to lock the doors. They crossed the wide street, ignoring the oncoming traffic, and vehicles slowed to allow them to pass. They carried themselves like the cops they were, and two hardened white faces around here meant one thing: NYPD. Birds chirped in the gray trees. The scarecrows showed no fear of the narcotics cops; they just moved around them and resumed their previous course.

Gary homed in on a trio of corner boys occupying a single park bench painted dark green and bolted to the asphalt. One boy sat on the bench. Another sat on the bench back with his sneakers on the bench. And the third stood on the patch of cement upon which the bench rested. Gary and Frank walked right up to the boys, who barely registered their presence.

They're lit, he thought, gazing at the emaciated boys' unblinking eyes.

Frank said, "Good afternoon, fellas. Maybe you can explain to us what you're doing here."

The corner boys ignored Frank.

He took out his shield. "I'd like to know what the fuck you're doing here."

Blank stares. Empty eyes. Silence.

Gary let loose an exaggerated sigh. "Okay, men. Which one of you is in charge?"

They stared past him.

Fuck. Gary felt his blood growing hot. "You," he said, pointing at the boy sitting on the bench. "You look comfortable. Stand up."

The boy ignored him,

"Son of a bitch!" He didn't want to punch the kid—God only knew what diseases they all had—but he couldn't help it. Before he could control himself, he had clocked the kid in the jaw.

"Yeah!" Frank said.

Oh, great. He knew he was out of control when his partner approved of his actions.

The kid looked at him for the first time, his eyes cold. That look sent a shiver of fear down Gary's spine. The kid didn't even rub his jaw. He just went back to staring across the yard.

Gary took out his handcuffs, which gleamed in the afternoon sunlight. "Okay, tough guy. Get on your feet and show me some ID, or we're taking you in."

No reaction.

Gary grabbed the kid's shirt and hauled him to his feet. He spun him around and shoved him forward onto the bench, planting his left knee in the small of the kid's back as he locked the bracelets around his wrists. The kid weighed even less than he had thought. Glancing sideways at the other two boys, he said, "Do I need to read him his rights?"

Ignoring him, they stared straight ahead with unblinking eyes.

"Come on," Gary said, jerking the kid toward the street. "Say good-bye to your playmates."

Frank surveyed the vacant expressions of the remaining boys, then spat on the cement.

The kid did not resist as Gary guided him through the yard. None of the scarecrows paid any attention to them. Crossing the street, Gary felt his anger lingering. He didn't care what people did to make money, but he had no patience for people who disrespected his authority. He intended to enjoy what this kid had coming to him. Frank opened the back door, and Gary shoved the kid inside. Then the two detectives got into the front.

"It gets creepier up here every day," Frank said. "I don't know how people live like this."

"You got that shit right." Gary started the engine and pulled into the oncoming traffic, which provoked a honking horn or two.

"It stinks in here," Frank said, lowering his window. "Don't you little hoppers ever bother to bathe?"

In the backseat, the kid did not answer. He just stared out the side window.

"These corner boys are creepier than their customers," Gary said. He had become accustomed to mindless drug fiends over the years, but something about these teenage dealers troubled him. He couldn't put his finger on it, but they possessed an apathy the likes of which he had never seen. They didn't care about anything.

Gary drove two miles uptown, then pulled over to a stretch of abandoned houses in a field of tall grass. He parked in a driveway and looked over his shoulder at the kid. "Do I ever feel sorry for you."

They got out and led the kid toward the cement porch of the house. No traffic appeared on the pocked street. They might as well have been in another country. The kid took the stairs one at a time, showing no fear. Frank opened the storm door, which swung on a creaky, rusted spring. Stepping inside, Gary noted the paint peeling on the walls. The house reeked of mildew.

"Down we go," Frank said, taking a flashlight out of his pocket and shining it into the dank blackness.

Gary didn't know why he grasped the kid's arm as he led him down the bare wooden steps. He didn't care if the kid got hurt or not, and he intended to hurt him anyway. Maybe that was it; he wanted the kid to know that any pain he incurred was *intentional*. Humidity rose from the cellar as the flashlight beam bounced around the gray cement walls. Dirty sunlight sliced through filth-encrusted windows.

"Nice," Frank said with admiration in his voice.

Gary positioned the kid before a rusted slop sink stained with layers of rotting gunk. "Don't move," he told the kid. He uncuffed one wrist, pulled the kid's free arm around a sewage line that ran from the ceiling to the floor, and snapped the cuffs again. Then he shrugged off his jacket and laid it over a workbench. Staring at the kid, he rolled up his sleeves. The kid paid no attention.

"I'm going to ask you a question. If you answer that question, you'll save us all a lot of time and yourself a lot of unnecessary suffering. Where can we find Prince Malachai?"

The kid stared into emptiness with equally empty eyes, and Frank grinned with anticipation.

Not nearly so pleased, Gary took a pair of black leather gloves out of his jacket pocket and pulled them on. Without saying anything, he stepped forward, seized the kid's hair, snapped his head forward, and threw a ferocious punch that connected with the kid's jaw. He heard the unmistakable sound of bone snapping, and the kid swung around the sewage line like a pole dancer and smashed one hip against the slop sink, all without uttering a single protest. He looked up at them, his jaw hanging loose on one side.

Gary shook his hand and flexed his fingers. "This isn't going to be easy."

"Enjoy the ride," Frank said, delivering a powerful kick at the boy's groin, which only managed to connect with his inner thigh.

The kid flew back, and the handcuffs snapped against the line.

Frustrated that he had missed, Frank pummeled the kid's sides, his fists blurring like pistons. He worked the kid over with all the fury of a little man suffering from an inferiority complex, unleashing years' worth of anger in a full-on assault. The kid took his beating like a punching bag, and Frank finally stepped back, winded.

"He didn't even blink," Gary said. "Not once."

"That's impossible," Frank said between tortured gasps.

Looking around, Gary spotted a rusted garden rake with a long wooden handle, which he retrieved. Standing before the kid with the rake clutched in both hands, he said, "Where's Malachai?"

The kid stared past him.

"Answer me, or I swear to Christ I'll go Abu Ghraib on your ass."

The kid kept staring past him.

That does it! Winding his arms, Gary swung the rake over his head, but the tool's metal teeth bit into a wooden beam in the ceiling. Grunting with anger at his clumsiness, Gary wrenched it free and swung the rake sideways. This time, the teeth bit into the kid's left side.

Still the kid didn't blink, and other than regaining his balance, he did not react to the blow.

Frank did a double take. "What the *fuck*?"

Gawking at the sight before him, Gary wiggled the rake back and forth, working it even deeper into the kid's side. Then he jerked the tool free, leaving twenty holes the width of a dime in the kid's shirt. No blood came out.

Frank pointed at the kid's legs. From beneath his shirt, what appeared to be sawdust poured along his jeans and onto his sneakers and the cement floor.

Gary twirled the rake like a baton, stopping it so that the teeth extended from his own mouth. "*Where's Malachai?*"

When the kid ignored him, Gary pivoted the rake at his face. The teeth tore into the kid's eyebrow, nose, and broken jaw at an angle.

"Scream, goddamn you!" Gary wrenched the rake, splitting the kid's face open with a dry tearing sound. Sawdust streamed out of the wide fissure, obscuring one eye.

"What the *fuck*?" Frank said again.

Gary watched the kid. Only it wasn't a kid. Christ, it wasn't even a *human being*.

Frank dashed to the basement corner, seized a shovel, and charged at the kid like a soldier brandishing a bayonet on the end of his rifle. He drove the shovel's blade into the kid's sternum, and it sounded like metal driving into gravel. Frank pulled the shovel out with a demented grin on his face and watched sawdust pour out in a torrent.

Thing's got to be about empty from the waist up, Gary thought.

"Holy shit," Frank said. "*Look* at this!"

Now what do we do with this . . . thing?

127

Frank swung the shovel over his head and buried it in the kid's, bifurcating it. Grayish pink fluid sprayed out of the new wound, and all at once, the kid toppled to the floor and did not move. Frank poked him with the shovel, with no response. The corpse might just as well have been a real scarecrow stuffed with sawdust rather than straw.

Stepping back, Frank discarded the shovel, which clanged on the floor. Then he massaged his temples. "Okay, okay. I know I'm not hallucinating. What the fuck was *that*?"

Gary shook his head. "I have no idea."

Frank took out a bag of blow, opened it, and fingered a blast up each nostril. Ever the codependent gentleman, he offered the bag to Gary. "You want a hit?"

Don't do it, Gary thought. "Fuck, yeah."

Gary snorted some coke up both nostrils at the same time, then handed the bag back to his partner.

"Now what do we do?" Frank said, his voice becoming a whine like it did whenever he snorted while already excited.

Gary considered their predicament. "Now we get a live one."

Jake caught the 2:20 p.m. Long Island Railroad from Amityville to Penn Station in Manhattan. The trip was scheduled to last one hour, with stops in Jamaica, Queens, and Flatbush Avenue in Brooklyn. He did not relish the thought of returning to the scene where this latest nightmare had started.

The morphine had worn off, leaving his back feeling like a train wreck, but the sedative he had been given made it possible not to care. Taking his seat on the train, he marveled at its plush seats, a far cry from the mass transit to which he was accustomed to as a Manhattan resident. A dozen passengers joined him in the car, with plenty of seating left, and the train glided out of the station. Jake watched the stores flash by, then attractive homes, and he saw kids playing softball in a manicured playground rather than in the street.

A different world, he thought, closing his eyes. Exhaustion claimed his weary body, but his mind would not allow sleep. He rocked gently from side to side, listening to the steady chug-chug of the train. His mind wrestled with the MRI photos the technician had shown him— sectioned images that showed his body turned inside out—and with what she had said: "I'm sorry, Mr. Helman, but the MRI shows that there's absolutely nothing wrong with your lower back physically. No herniated disc, no torn cartilage, no pinched nerve, no sprain."

How could that be? She had said there was nothing *physically* wrong with him, but he knew his symptoms were not psychosomatic.

Don't worry about it, he told himself. *Enjoy this sedative while it lasts. Just go along for the ride for now.*

The sound of the train sped up, but when he opened his eyes, the train seemed to be traveling at a consistent speed. Closing his eyes again, he tried to sleep, but he could not shake the lingering aftereffects of his unexplainable experience in the MRI scanner.

Thrum . . . thrum . . . thrum . . . THRUM!

His eyes snapped open. Concentrating, he heard the sound even though he was awake. *The steady rhythm of drumbeats.* The same sound he had heard inside the scanner. Turning in his seat despite the spasm of pain, he looked at his fellow passengers. Except for one young guy with dark hair, all of them were middle-class working stiffs, probably worried about the failing economy and how it would affect their families.

All because I took down Old Nick.

None of them showed any indication that they were troubled by an inexplicable drumbeat. He closed his eyes and tried to relax.

Thrum . . . thrum . . . thrum . . . THRUM!

The shrieking of metal against metal caused him to open his eyes again. The metallic scream sounded more like the New York City subway than an aboveground rail. The ceiling lights went off and failed to come back on, although sunlight streaming through the wide windows illuminated the interior.

Something did not feel right to Jake. He heard a door slide open and recoil behind him, and as he forced himself to turn around once more, he heard a woman's piercing scream.

Three Indian men had entered the car. At least he thought they were Indian. But there was no doubt in his mind that they brandished semiautomatic rifles. And as he narrowed his eyes, he saw that the emaciated-looking men wore blank expressions, their eyes unblinking. His body turned numb, except for the pain in his back.

They're looking for me!

Without warning, the lead dead thing lowered his AK-47 and triggered a burst of gunfire that decimated a woman's torso like canned tomatoes.

No!

Screams filled the car, and a passenger stood up. The second man fired a burst from his weapon, causing the passenger to dance with his arms spread wide before he dropped to the floor like a slaughtered cow.

Jake reached inside his jacket for the reassuring grip of his Glock, only to realize he had left it at the office on doctor's orders.

Shit out of luck . . .

Panic drove half a dozen passengers running past Jake to the opposite door. Before they could escape, the dead men mowed them down. Blood spattered the windows and seats and remaining passengers.

With the assassins almost upon him, Jake managed to stand and face them. "Stop! It's *me* you want. Let these people go."

The lead man shoved Jake, and Jake toppled onto his back in the aisle with a cry of debilitating pain. The killers continued to fire at the trapped passengers, filling the air with their agonized death cries until no one remained except Jake. Then the men laid their smoking weapons on the gore-drenched upholstery and drew machetes from their belts. They went to work, hacking off the limbs of their victims.

Rolling over onto his chest, Jake worked his way up onto his hands and knees, and a spray of hot vomit gushed from his mouth. His eyes teared up and his throat burned as he gazed at the startled passengers.

Oh no . . .

The good news was that everyone on the train was still alive and seated, with no evidence that undead hit men had been anywhere on the train. The ceiling lights shone down on blood-free seats. The bad news was that every man and woman aboard the car now stared at Jake with an equal measure of puzzlement and disgust.

What the hell is happening to me?

He had not dreamed the incident. Somehow he had suffered some sort of waking delusion, the big city equivalent of a desert-induced mirage. *Only with machine gun–wielding zombies who liked to clean up after themselves with machetes . . .*

Grabbing an empty seat beside him, he rose, stepped over the vomit as best he could, and limped to the door through which the assassins had entered, hoping to escape his embarrassment.

"Sorry," he said to no one in particular.

His hand closed around the stainless steel door handle, but the locked door would not budge.

Oh, great. Bowing his head against the door's glass pane, he counted to five, then turned around and returned to his seat.

Parked once more across the street from the Polo Grounds, Gary and Frank noted that a new corner boy had replaced the one they abducted. His gaunt features made his pronounced brow appear Neanderthal.

"Meet the new boss, same as the old boss," Frank said.

Gary scanned the front yard. Dozens of scarecrows sauntered across the asphalt. "The zombies are dealing Black Magic to the scarecrows. Prince Malachai is using zombies to push his shit."

"Saves on payroll," Frank said.

"Maybe the Magic turns the scarecrows into zombies."

"No doubt."

132

A silver Grand Cherokee pulled over to the curb closest to the projects. The new corner boss lumbered toward the vehicle.

"Bingo," Gary said. *Delivery time.*

The corner boss leaned inside the vehicle's open passenger window, then turned around and returned to his station. The Grand Cherokee pulled into traffic.

"How much you think that package is worth?"

Gary started the engine. "Not as much as the driver of that vehicle." He followed the Cherokee a couple of blocks before setting his portable siren on top of the roof of the car and activating it.

The Cherokee's driver immediately pulled over, and Gary motored the unmarked car into position behind it. A number of pedestrians glanced at them but kept walking. The detectives climbed out of the car at the same time and approached opposite sides of the Cherokee. Rap music blasting from the vehicle faded, and the driver regarded Gary from behind dark shades through the open window.

Gary held out his shield in his left hand, his right hand resting on the butt of his Glock.

"What's the problem, Officer?"

"*Detective.* Take off your sunglasses, please."

The man removed the sunglasses and held them in his right hand, visible on top of the steering wheel. He wore his hair in cornrows tight to his scalp.

"License and registration."

Rolling his eyes, the man reached inside the CD compartment for his wallet and handed his driver's license to Gary. *Leon Jennings.* Gary recognized the man by his street name GQ, one of Prince Malachai's chief lieutenants. GQ leaned across the seat and reached for the glove compartment. His body tensed when he saw Frank standing outside the passenger door. Recovering, he gave the registration to Gary, who barely glanced at it.

"Would you mind stepping out of the vehicle?"

GQ sighed. "Would you mind telling me what I did wrong?"

Gary remained deliberately impassive. "Get out of the car, GQ."

Weary anger flushed the drug dealer's eyes. "Man . . ."

"What's that?"

"Nothing." GQ opened the door and got out. He stood six feet two, just like his license said, and wore a sky blue muscle shirt.

"Turn around."

"For *what*?"

Frank circled the front of the Jeep. "For dropping off that package back there."

GQ sucked his teeth. "Man, I didn't drop off *nothing*."

"Our video camera begs to differ."

"How do you know what was in that package? Maybe it was just some Betty Crocker cake mix."

Frank stepped forward and took out his handcuffs. He looked comically small next to GQ, Gary thought. "Turn around so we can put these on, or we'll make you put them on yourself the hard way."

Shaking his head, GQ turned around. "This is bullshit."

Frank snapped on the cuffs.

"I know you guys. I've seen you around. I know your rep. How much to let me walk?"

Setting one hand on GQ's right shoulder and guiding him toward the unmarked car, Gary said, "Not today, Leon. This is city business."

"This is *bull*shit."

They took him to the same decrepit house.

"I don't see no precinct house," GQ said.

"You aren't going to, either," Frank said, leering into the backseat.

They guided him inside the house.

"Oh, man . . ."

In the basement, Gary saw GQ stiffen at the sight of the inanimate kid on the floor.

"Ah, shit."

"Don't pay him any mind," Gary said.

They led GQ to the other side of the basement, and Frank leveled his Glock at the man.

GQ closed his eyes, possibly in prayer.

"Yeah, this is not your lucky day," Frank said.

Gary unlocked the handcuffs. GQ gave him no trouble as he threaded the cuffs over a ceiling pipe and secured the captive's hands above his head.

"No begging," Gary said. "I like that."

"Oh, he'll beg," Frank said, holstering his weapon.

GQ regarded them with his eyes surrounded by white. "What do you want?"

Gary raised one finger to his lips. "Shhh . . ."

Frank picked up the shovel from the floor. "Don't say anything yet."

Sweat beaded on GQ's forehead and trickled down into his wincing eyes. "Oh, fuck . . ."

Frank swung the shovel sideways, like a baseball bat. The blade bit deep into GQ's left knee, shattering ligaments, cartilage, and bone.

GQ let out an agonized wail absorbed by the basement walls.

"This one bleeds," Frank said.

TWELVE

Although both the morphine and the sedative had worn off by the time Jake's train pulled into Penn Station and the crippling pain had returned to his back, he felt better just being in Manhattan. Limping through the enormous train terminal, he could not wait to reach the Seventh Avenue sidewalk, which faced Thirty-fourth Street. In the shadow of Madison Square Garden, he inhaled the rancid odors of garbage bags piled to a ridiculous height at the curb—the result of a sanitation workers' strike, now in its second week—and took out his cell phone. Men clad in rags surrounded him with outstretched hands, and he turned his back on them.

"Hello?" Larry answered on the second ring.

"What the hell was in that shot you gave me?" Jake said through clenched teeth.

"Morphine. Just like I told you. Why do you ask?"

"Because I had hallucinations you wouldn't believe inside that MRI machine."

"People sometimes react badly to those. I thought you were made of tougher stuff, though."

"I didn't have an emotional reaction to the machine, you son of a bitch. Something was in that shot. The same thing happened on the LIRR on the trip home."

Silence on the phone for a moment. "Did they give you anything at the clinic?"

"Yeah, a sedative of some kind."

"Pill or injection?"

"Another shot."

"Well, there you go. What did they give you?"

A wave of pain radiated from Jake's left hip. "I don't know. I didn't write it down."

"They must have given you paperwork."

"It wasn't the medication, Larry. They gave me that shot *after* I got out of the MRI. It couldn't have been a contributing factor to what happened inside the machine."

"Were the hallucinations the same in both instances?"

Jake bit his lip. *Damn it.* "No."

"Then your theory doesn't hold much water, does it? Let me ask you something: did you ever drop acid during your wilder, crazier days?"

Jake ran one hand over his sweaty face. "No. I never got high before I joined Homicide, and you know I was strictly into blow. I'm not suffering LSD flashbacks."

"What did the MRI show?"

Jake's stomach tightened. He didn't want to say. "The pictures were inconclusive."

"What do you mean? They either showed spinal injury or they didn't."

"They didn't show anything."

"So you made me drive you out to the island practically at gun-point, where you suffered some hallucinations, it turns out there's nothing wrong with you, and this is somehow *my* fault? I'm not in the habit of spiking my patients' treats. It's too expensive, for one thing. For another, despite the occupations of many of my patients, I do have ethics."

Jake took a deep breath and let out a slow sigh. "I have to get going. It's killing me to stand out here."

"Call me tomorrow."

"Right." Shutting down his phone, Jake limped between homeless people to the street corner and raised one hand in the air. "Taxi!"

A yellow cab materialized in front of him, followed by another. These days, few people could afford private transportation. He eased himself into the backseat of the sedan and swiped his credit card through the slot.

"Where to, mon?" a man with a Jamaican accent said.

Jake gave him the address, then turned on the TV recessed in the back of the front seat. Soap operas, game shows, and doom and gloom financial forecasts. On New York One News, an update on the Black Magic epidemic.

Dark days, he thought, holding back tears of pain as he bounced around inside the cab.

Staring out the window, sunlight highlighting the dirt on the glass, he felt alone. He had been alone since before Sheryl's murder. As desperate as he had been on the morning when he had inserted the barrel of his Glock inside his mouth, threatening to blow out his brains as his father had, he felt worse now. Because now he was afraid to die. Now he believed in some form of afterlife, and he feared the revenge that the demon Cain would take on his soul . . . forever. The angelic Abel had told his brother that Sheryl had purged Jake's energy of his sins, but Jake felt in no hurry to prove him right.

How had he landed in another fantastic situation? Seeing the scarecrows haunting the sidewalks, he knew the truth: he hadn't become embroiled in the situation; it was all around him in every neighborhood and on every street corner, like a plague.

Who could he turn to for help? Who would believe the unbelievable tale he had to tell?

No one.

Edgar parked in front of a Brooklyn apartment house in the middle of the block. A working-class neighborhood, feeling the pain of an uncaring economy. Groups of young men—he hesitated to call them boys; they hadn't known boyhood innocence for who knew how long—gathered at all four corners. Garbage stained the sidewalks, and potholes scarred the street.

"You okay?" Maria said.

"Yeah. I grew up around here. The place has changed a lot. I thought it would get better, but it's way worse than I remember."

"Brooklyn boy, huh? I had you pegged for the Bronx, like me."

"I spent some time on the Grand Concourse, but this was definitely my turf."

Getting out, he surveyed the houses on each side of the street. All of them looked the same to him: peeling paint, siding in need of repair, chipped concrete steps, graffiti scrawled on the walls facing driveways. Even the sky seemed gray here. They passed two RPM cars, an unmarked squad car, and a coroner's van. The mainstays of any homicide scene.

A PO holding a clipboard stood in an open doorway.

They showed their shields to him. "Detectives Hopkins and Vasquez," Edgar said. "Special Homicide."

Nodding, the recorder wrote down their names on his clipboard. "Second floor."

Edgar went inside first. He liked to walk through all doorways first, so that if anyone faced unexpected danger, it was him. Maria had complained that she wanted to take her share of risks, but he wouldn't hear of it. The world had changed for him when the Cipher had murdered Sheryl Helman. He knew Maria could handle herself, but he saw no reason to take unnecessary chances. Against his better instincts, he had grown to think of her almost as a younger sister more than a partner.

His vision adjusted to the darkness, and he climbed the creaking wooden stairs to the second floor, followed by Maria. They entered the open apartment, nodding to another PO and the pair of Detective Area Task Force detectives inside. He didn't know either of the men, something that occurred only when he was called to a crime scene outside Manhattan. But he recognized the dark stains on the apartment walls: blood.

"You Hopkins?" the Chinese man said.

Edgar nodded. "And Vasquez."

The man thumped his chest. "Chang."

The heavier set man raised his latex-gloved hands. "Manelli. I'd shake your hands, but . . ."

Edgar pulled on his own pair of gloves. "No sweat. What have we got?"

"Carmen Rodriguez and her grandson Victor. Both vics were dismembered."

Edgar swallowed, a rare reaction of discomfort. He took homicides in stride, like a professional. He never allowed them to eat him up inside like Jake had. But Edgar had been raised by his own grandmother, a Baptist, after his teenage mother had run off to L.A., never to be heard from again.

"Weapons?" Maria said.

Manelli gestured at a baseball bat. "Looks like they put up a fight. They weren't shot first; they were just hacked to pieces."

"Any drugs?"

"No. The lady was a churchgoer. The boy stayed out of trouble."

Edgar and Maria exchanged knowing glances, reading each other's mind.

"Yeah, we know," Manelli said. "Your Machete Massacres have only involved drug gangs, and these were civilians. But there's *another* grandson—Louis. Fifteen, sixteen years old. Corner boy. Landlord downstairs says the boy moved out a month ago, but he's seen him over on Flatbush Avenue slinging Black Magic."

Edgar stepped deeper into the apartment. A heavyset woman

lay on the floor, her flabby arms and bifurcated head scattered around her corpse. The corpse of a young boy in pajamas lay a few feet behind her. His torso was riddled with cut wounds, and his head and arms had also been chopped off. The rugs had soaked up blood like a giant tampon.

Edgar pointed at several fingers on the floor. "The grandmother took a machete in the head and went right down. She must have had the bat, because the boy put up a fight with his bare hands." Dozens of bloody footprints marred the floor. "Only one set of prints with sneakers. A single perp."

"The grandson?" Chang said.

"I'd look there first."

"Then that's what you should do," Manelli said.

Edgar cocked one eyebrow.

"No disrespect, but we were told to hand this over to you if it looked like your case."

"We're not going to get into jurisdictional shit, are we?"

"Not at all. Our captain said to give you any assistance we can. Just tell us what you need."

"Run this investigation as you would any other. Just keep us in the loop. If not me and Vasquez, then any of the other members of our task force. Go ahead and bring the other grandson in. We don't care who gets that collar. We're after whoever gave the order, not the button man."

"I'll call it in," Chang said, heading for the door.

"Hang on. I'll go with you," Manelli said. "I could use a cigarette."

With the DATF detectives gone, Maria started snooping around the apartment. "Think they already called it in before we got here?"

"Sure," Edgar said. "Wouldn't you?"

"You bet."

Edgar stared at the dead boy's head: eyes open and spattered with blood. *Almost the same age as Martin. What kind of monster would—?* He closed down the thought. Drug dealers committed some of the most heinous murders in the city. Entire families were massacred as payback for theft. The second grandson had probably not committed these murders but had more likely pissed off whoever did.

"Edgar?"

He turned toward Maria, who had moved into the living room and stood on the far side of a round coffee table. She held something in her right hand, and her face showed concern.

Stepping around the blood on the floor, he joined her and looked at the business card in her hand. He had seen it before. *Helman Investigations and Security.*

The taxi pulled over to the curb before Jake's building, and he spilled out of the vehicle, feeling very much like a flesh sack containing bones that no longer fit together. Crying out, he staggered in a half circle. Pedestrians on the sidewalk moved out of his way but continued walking, making no move to help him. Limping toward the front glass doors, he feared he would topple to the sidewalk and be unable to stand again.

After glancing at the entrance to Laurel Doniger's parlor, he found himself changing course. He grabbed the brass door handle, then leaned into the door with too much force. The door swung open, and he fell inside, tumbling down the steps. The bells on the door jingled, and a shadow glided into the room.

"Are you all right?" Laurel said, crossing the parlor.

He rocked back and forth. "No."

She knelt beside him and grasped his left wrist in her right hand. Staring into her bright blue eyes, he couldn't help but think that she sensed everything he felt at this moment, that she really *understood* him.

"Take my arm," she said. "I'll help you."

Getting to her feet, she helped him to his. Then she led him to the archway in the rear of her parlor. Through it he glimpsed a living room, a kitchen, and a bedroom, but she guided him into a wide bathroom. Hunched over like a cripple, he clutched the sink for support.

"Take off your clothes," Laurel said.

He reached for his shirt button, fumbled with it, then gave up, shaking his head.

So she undressed him, and minutes later, he stood naked before her, feeling no shame except for the way his spine wrapped around itself. She eased him onto the toilet lid, ran hot water in the tub, then took colored bottles from a shelf and poured oils into the steaming water. Finally, she helped him into the tub, and he gasped as the water scorched his flesh. Crouching beside the tub, she scooped water in her cupped hands and tossed it on his chest. The intense heat distracted him from the pain in his back. He didn't know why she was helping him, and he didn't care.

"This won't solve your problem," she said. "But it will relax your muscles, so I can go to work on them. Stay here while I wash these clothes. Meditate, if you know how. Put your mind at ease. You're safe here."

And then she was gone, and so were his clothes. He took several deep breaths. Even that hurt. When the water filled the tub to capacity, he used his feet to twist the knobs controlling the water flow. Sweat beaded his forehead. Steam cleansed his pores. His mind wandered.

Sheryl . . .

Laurel helped him, still naked, to the massage table in a side room. Jake needed her help to climb onto the towel-draped table mat. Hot oils splashed his back, and he felt the sensation of her hands working the liquid into his flesh. She kneaded his muscles like dough, and it felt good.

"You've been to a doctor," she said.

His eyes widened, and he stared at the cabinet before him. *Don't stop.*

"He found nothing wrong with you. In the strictest medical sense, this is understandable. In that respect, you're fine."

She didn't seem to require him to say anything, so he allowed her to continue.

"You're cursed. I feel it. Someone has put a hex on you. When I'm finished, you'll be fine, as if nothing had ever been wrong. It doesn't matter if you believe me now. You will when I'm done."

I want to believe you. Just make this pain go away!

Her fingers dug deep into his muscles. He imagined them piercing his body, as if his skin were nothing but hot water, and applying pressure directly to his muscles. He inhaled her perfume, felt her body heat. Before he knew it, his penis became erect, its head pressing against his stomach. No woman had touched him since Sheryl's murder. He didn't want to be touched now, but he needed it. She grasped his buttocks, then rubbed his thighs. He felt his testicles constrict. Then she returned her attention to the small of his back, where he felt her fist pressing into his discs.

"Roll over," she whispered.

Obeying, he felt no pain.

"Close your eyes."

He did, and she closed her hands around the shaft of his cock and stroked it until he came, which didn't take long. He felt her wiping him down, then heard her step from the room and close the door. He slept.

"Wake up."

Jake's eyes fluttered open. He saw Laurel standing before him, his clean clothes in her hands. Sitting up, he said, "What time is it?"

"Just after five."

He realized that he had sat up without experiencing pain. Looking down, he saw that she had covered him with a towel in his sleep. He felt fully rested, even though he had slept for only forty minutes. More important, he felt no pain. Glancing at her with bewilderment, he took in her bemused smile.

"You were cursed," she said. "I removed the curse."

He swallowed. "How?"

"I'm a healer as well as a sensitive. My abilities operate through touch. And I touched you all over."

His face turned red.

"Don't be embarrassed. I'm not accustomed to giving clients happy endings, but I could tell you needed that. It didn't take much work on my part."

Now he *really* felt embarrassed.

"See for yourself. Get off the table."

Hopping down, he caught the towel as it slid from his groin. He shifted his weight from foot to foot. *No pain!* "What kind of curse?"

"You're welcome."

He studied her eyes, looking for some sign of sarcasm. "Thank you."

"Vodou. Whether Haitian vodou or Louisiana vodou, sometimes known as New Orleans voodoo, I'm not sure. But I've removed the curse from your body. Your enemies will need to find a new method of attack now."

Jake didn't want to believe her or give her any credibility, but he had experienced enough in the last year to know there was no point in doubting anything. The supernatural *did* exist.

"I know you've already poured salt across the thresholds in your suite. This is a good first step—"

"How do you know that?" he said.

"I read people by touching them. I didn't just touch you; I massaged your entire body and got you off. And now I know everything about you. *Everything.* I know that the Cipher murdered your wife and you took revenge against him. I know that you carry part of her soul inside you. That Cain tortured you and that you've had three separate encounters with the undead in less than twenty-four hours."

Unbelievable, he thought. "Then you also know that you got me into this mess by sending Carmen Rodriguez to me in the first place."

"She needed help."

"You said the undead—"

"Zombies. Or *zonbies*, depending on the type of vodou."

"What's the difference?"

"None, really, since you've already discovered how to destroy them, no thanks to that disc locked up in your safe."

"Please stop doing that."

"The only reason to care what type of vodou is being used is so you can figure out how the zombies are being created and where your enemies are hiding."

"How can I figure out what type of magic is being used?"

"I can tell you. Just bring me the hand of one of those creatures."

Thinking of the bodies he had dumped down the incinerator shoot, he grunted. "*Now* you tell me." His cell phone rang, and she handed it to him. He recognized Edgar's number. "I have to take this."

Laurel laid his clothes on the table and left him alone in the room.

"Hello?"

"I've been calling you all day." Edgar sounded troubled.

"I know. It's been a crazy afternoon."

"Crazier than your night was?"

That's a good question. "If you're going to quantify everything . . ."

"It's all over the newspapers that you crashed your car into One PP."

"That's a bit of an exaggeration."

"I've seen the photos; it's no exaggeration. Are you all right?"

"Yeah, I'm fine."

"Where are you?"

He didn't like a quality he detected in Edgar's voice. "Not far from my office."

"I need to see you right away."

Jake considered his situation. "Okay. Can you meet me at the office in half an hour?"

"Sure."

"Come alone."

Edgar waited too long before answering. "All right."

Official business, Jake thought. "I'll see you then."

Buttoning his shirt, Jake stepped into Laurel's parlor. She sat in a chair with a high back, one shapely leg crossed over the other.

"I have to go," he said. "But I'll be back."

She offered him a slight smile. "I know you will."

THIRTEEN

Gary sat on a park bench, his back to the East River and Manhattan's FDR Drive, the mini-binoculars in his right hand trained on the top floor of The Octagon, Roosevelt Island's most luxurious apartment complex. Kids swam in The Octagon's swimming pool, and the sun turned burnt orange, readying its descent behind the building. Bicyclists, pedestrians, and dog walkers glided across the walkways close to the river.

The former New York Lunatic Asylum had been renovated for the Starbucks crowd: five hundred units in two modern wings flanked the eight-sided rotunda. According to the property's Web site, the building offered studio, one-, two-, and three-bedroom apartments to those who could afford them, and it housed more solar panels than any building in Manhattan. Gary could never afford to live in such luxury on a cop's salary, even with his extracurricular activities, which he regarded as simple moonlighting.

But a drug-dealing scumbag like Malachai has no problem paying the tab, he thought with bitterness. It was going to be a pleasure to take the shit bag out.

Frank's voice came over the receiver in his ear: "Anything happening?"

"Looks like our boy's getting some powerful head," he said into the transmitter in his jacket collar.

Malachi stood naked not far from the floor-to-ceiling windows in his fourteenth-floor apartment, baring his muscular frame for all the world to see, at least those possessing high-powered binoculars, while a woman kneeled on the floor with her back to the window, her head bobbing up and down on her lord and master.

"Maybe she can do me after I do *him*," Frank said.

"Stand by." It was the only way he could think of to shut his partner up.

Roosevelt Island, "the Big Apple's Little Apple," was too contained for his taste, too unreal, like a toy version of Manhattan. He found it unnatural that the island ran beneath the Queensboro Bridge. Who the hell could live underneath a bridge? Once prison grounds known as Blackwell's Island, Roosevelt Island claimed thirteen thousand people as residents.

After GQ had given up Malachai's location and dinner plans for the evening, Gary and Frank had stolen license plates off a parked Subaru and then affixed them to an SUV they signed out of the NYPD motor pool. They had driven to Astoria, then taken the Roosevelt Island Bridge to a parking lot across the street from The Octagon, and Gary had taken watch from the park bench while Frank had infiltrated The Octagon's underground parking facility.

"Look alive," Gary said as Malachi arched his back and faced the ceiling. "Mount Vesuvius just blew. I'm heading back to our wheels."

"Copy that."

Returning his binoculars to his jacket pocket, Gary stood and crossed the park. He wore a Yankees cap with the visor pulled low, so no one would be likely to remember his features. He circled the building to Main Street, where he waited for a bus to clear his path before he jogged over to the parking lot. Climbing into the SUV, he fastened his seat belt, started the engine, and waited for all hell to break loose.

Prince Malachai felt good even before Katrina went down on him. Business was way up, and money was rolling in. He had only to look around his crib to know that he had succeeded beyond his wildest dreams. And it had taken only one year, thanks to Katrina.

Daryl Havek had grown up in the South Bronx. He had been a smart kid, passing his classes with ease, but had been lazy when it came to schoolwork. He had graduated but just barely. And then his mother had sent him off to work for his uncle, Papa Joe, who had a lock on the Upper West Side of Manhattan.

Joe had four daughters, at least that he admitted to, by three different women, and he had taken Daryl under his wing and mentored him like the son he never had. *Uncle* Joe started him out on a corner, then put him in charge of another corner, then trusted him with making runs across the state, delivering large quantities of cocaine, crack, and heroin.

Within three years, Daryl had become one of the drug lord's most trusted lieutenants. Then he was busted for possession with the intent to sell. The judge sentenced him to four years, but he had walked after only thirteen months. A year had been long enough to harden him. He returned to Joe expecting big things, but Joe wanted him to take things slowly "to readjust to freedom," he had said. Daryl saw things differently: he wanted to be Joe's right-hand man, and he discovered that Chess, one of Joe's former top earners, had stepped into that role.

Bitter, Daryl had started to skim the money he earned for his uncle— a little at first, then a lot. He renamed himself Prince Malachai as a sign of disrespect to the king. When Joe figured things out, he cut Daryl out of the operation. But he hadn't killed him because they shared some of the same blood.

Because he's soft, Malachai thought.

Joe had spared his nephew's life on the condition that Daryl stay out of the business, at least in New York City. Malachai gave his word, never intending to keep it. He lay low for a few months, staying in touch with the men who had been in his crew, while recruiting new blood and staying in touch with contacts he'd made in prison.

And then he met Katrina. She was dancing up a storm in a night-club downtown, staring at him with wide eyes, shaking her hips in a manner he had never seen before—some kind of witch dance. Malachai had grown up around believers in voodoo and Santaria, but he had always scoffed at their faiths and rituals. He did not believe in the power of the Houngan priests or Mamba priestesses. Superstition dominated their version of Catholicism, and his mother had been a Baptist anyway.

But Katrina had beguiled him, luring him into her arms and her bed, and she had dominated *him*. Her body writhed like a snake, and he drank the hot blood from between her legs. They had sex all night long, and she had instinctively served his fantasies. Exhausted and panting, his chest covered with sweat and his cock covered with her menstrual blood, he had listened as she whispered into his ear schemes that filled him with inspiration.

He left her, promising to return but believing that he would not keep his word. Instead, he returned the very next night. If anything, her body had been even more demanding, her proposals even more enticing. And as she laid out her plans for him, he hung on her every word. She promised to transform the prince into a king and deliver Papa Joe's kingdom to him. The sexual excitement he felt for her gave way to stunned admiration when she showed him just what powers she possessed as the heads of various drug gangs met violent and bloody ends.

Standing nude at the floor-to-ceiling window, Malachai gazed out across the East River at Manhattan. He enjoyed the high-rise apartment on Roosevelt Island. He didn't give a shit about its "green" functions, only that it offered a life of spacious luxury. When he boarded the elevator and wealthy white neighbors viewed him with curiosity, he felt important. Powerful. But he always remained polite. No gangsta shit here. Every day he proved that these executives were no better than him, and he knew he made more money than any of them.

A reflection appeared in the window.

Katrina, he thought. Also nude. Turning, he saw her approach him. Creamy brown skin. Full breasts. Slim waist. Straightened hair. His cock stood at attention.

A smile played over her features as her gaze darted to his penis, then back at his eyes. As she stepped before him, she closed the fingers of her left hand around his shaft, and he felt her gold rings dimple his sensitive flesh.

With an appreciative smile, he set his hands on her shoulders and pushed her down to her knees.

"We'll be late for dinner," she said.

"We have time."

Returning his smile, she took him into her mouth.

Malachai sucked in his breath. He didn't like showing Katrina how good she made him feel, but the woman had a magic tongue. As she ran it over the head of his cock, she massaged his balls with one hand and stroked his shaft with the other.

Jesus, he thought as she brought him to the point of climax, then switched techniques, drawing out his pleasure to nearly unbearable extremes. The woman knew how to satisfy him. Sinking his fingers into her hair and thrusting himself deep into her mouth, he signaled his desire to come. She brought him to the threshold again, and this time she increased the speed of everything she did all at once, and his throbbing member ejaculated. Still she worked on him, draining him of his strength. He groaned as if he had been struck, a loud and cathartic sound that filled the white-walled apartment. *Shit, yeah!*

Katrina folded her legs beneath her and wiped his semen from his lips. Then she giggled, a teasing sound that made him want to fuck her.

The telephone built into the living room wall rang.

"That's Marcus," she said. "We can continue this later."

"Yeah," he said. *Thank God*. He knew he'd need to eat a full meal to summon the strength to take her on in bed tonight.

Marcus Jones stepped off The Octagon's elevator and strutted down the wide, sunlit corridor to Malachai's apartment. He didn't like the way the building made him feel out of place, but he understood that Roosevelt Island provided Malachai with a level of comfort and safety not available in Manhattan or the other boroughs of New York City. Katrina had chosen it well.

Katrina. He tried to keep an open mind about her, but her presence unsettled him. How could it not? The bitch was responsible for bringing Black Magic to New York City—*his* city—and for creating the zombies that pushed it.

Zombies.

The word summoned his fear. The creatures he had grown up watching in movies and video games. But these were not flesh-eating monsters created by some unknown force. They were pitiful, mindless slaves, almost like machines, created through some combination of witchcraft and voodoo, which Marcus only pretended to understand. Only Malachai avoided the damned things, a benefit of being the boss. Marcus had to deal with them on occasion, but he had delegated as much of that responsibility to GQ and others whenever possible. The undead creatures made for an obedient workforce, but they creeped him out to no end. He knew that Katrina was the real power behind them, that without her they would remain inanimate corpses. He also knew that she was the real power behind Malachai.

Marcus had been Malachai's chief lieutenant in Papa Joe's organization. He had observed the political machinations that took place while Malachai served his time in prison, and he had counseled his friend upon his release. He watched Malachai skim the profits from Joe's organization, socking away the cash for a rainy day, and when Joe drove Malachai from the business, Marcus was shocked that his friend was permitted to live. There was no question that the younger man would pursue his uncle's empire, and when Malachai asked him to join his fledgling gang, Marcus rolled the dice and took a chance.

What he had not counted on was Katrina: she had become Malachai's chief confidante and adviser, the role Marcus had envisioned for himself. He saw how things were between Katrina and Malachai, and he knew better than to make a play for her spot. He also knew better than to cross her. As long as he remained loyal and unquestioning, they would take good care of him. Problem was, he didn't want anyone to take care of him. He was no goddamned pet. But Malachai's empire was expanding, and Marcus knew he was better off going with the flow than against the river of blood that had already been spilled.

He rang the doorbell to Malachai's apartment and cooled his heels until Katrina opened the door. She wore a bright red dress that hugged her figure and gold earrings that matched the jewelry around her neck and wrists. As soon as he saw her, he blocked his thoughts, a protection he had developed soon after realizing she possessed powers. Offering her a smile, he said, "Wow, you look great."

"Thank you." She raised one cheek for him to kiss.

Casting a sideways glance at Malachai, who stood in the center of the apartment buttoning a hundred-dollar shirt, he planted a kiss on her smooth skin.

"Hey, watch that," Malachai said.

Marcus knew that Malachai intended the comment as both a joke and a serious warning to him. *Block your thoughts.* "Hey, hey, brah, how's it going?"

"You tell me."

Straight down to business. All right, my man. "I left Six Pack in the car, so we could talk."

Malachai sat on the white leather sofa and spread his arms. "So talk."

Marcus sat in the matching chair and waited for Katrina to sit next to Malachai before speaking, a sign of respect. She rarely spoke during business conversations, but Marcus knew that Malachai liked to have her beside him and in the loop. "A couple of knockos grabbed one of our . . . pieces of meat at the Polo Grounds."

Malachai raised his eyebrows. "Yeah?"

Marcus nodded.

Katrina slid one hand over Malachai's bicep, reassuring him.

"Did they take it into custody?"

"I don't think so, but the cops came back and snatched GQ."

Malachai sat up. "What? Son of a bitch! Do we know who these motherfuckers were?"

Marcus felt some satisfaction from the rise he'd gotten out of Malachai. The two of them and GQ had been close for years, and Marcus had been opposed to allowing any zombies to work during the daytime. He saw Katrina working overtime to keep her man calm. "Nah, we got no ID on them."

Malachai faced Katrina. "If the cops find out what those things of yours are—"

Slap the bitch, Marcus hoped, although he knew that would never happen.

Glancing at Marcus with a knowing look, Katrina slid her hands over Malachai's forearms. "They won't, baby. If our slaves get anywhere near a police station, they'll just stop functioning, and the arresting officers will suddenly have a dead dealer on their hands."

Malachai furrowed one brow. "A dead dealer filled with sawdust instead of blood, you mean. You think that's what happened?"

"Maybe. But I think we'd better skip dinner and go to my place, so I can find out for sure."

"What about GQ?" Marcus said.

Malachai gave him a confident look. "G wouldn't talk to five-oh any more than you or me would. If they got him, he'll stay cool. If he needs us, he'll call."

"What about his package?" Katrina said.

Both men looked at her. Marcus waited to answer until Malachai glanced in his direction. "He delivered it right before he got snatched up."

Malachai stood. "Good. No harm, no foul. Let's roll outta here."

Frank's fingers danced along the denim covering his thighs. He wore baggy jeans, loose around his hips, with the waistband of his boxers showing, and white sneakers with the tongues curling outward, just like the yos did on the street. He also wore an unbuttoned black shirt over a turtleneck, light enough to keep him from melting into a puddle of nervous perspiration but bulky enough to conceal the Glock tucked into the front of his jeans. He wore a black knit cap, sunglasses, and a fake mustache he had purchased at a costume store in Manhattan, just in case the security camera he failed to avoid captured his image. Anyone who passed close to him might notice that he had removed the lenses from the shades and had darkened his eyelids and the flesh around his eyes black.

Rap music escaped from a piss yellow Escalade parked near the building's parking garage elevator. He could not see the driver, but he knew who sat in the front seat: Laird Black, aka Six Pack, Prince Malachai's driver and bodyguard. Black had served eighteen months on Rikers Island and another twelve upstate in Sing Sing for shooting a man five times in the chest. The man had survived, then disappeared under mysterious circumstances.

"The wheelman's waiting," Frank whispered into the miniature radio clipped to his shirt collar.

"Copy that," Gary said, his voice tinny over the receiver in Frank's ear.

Frank stood in the cool shadow of a white cinder-block wall, his back pressed against another wall, with a clear view of the parking garage elevator. A wide column hid his body. Removing the sunglasses, he unrolled the knit cap into a ski mask with eyeholes but no opening for his mouth. Then he pulled on a pair of tight black leather racing gloves. No one who saw him would assume he was Caucasian.

With his hand resting on the Glock's grip, he shifted his weight from one foot to the other. Christ, he needed to do a line. But Gary had forbidden it. *Hypocrite.* Gary liked to indulge just as much as Frank did, but Frank didn't repress his habit just because he carried a shield. *Fuck that.* He worked hard, he played hard, and he lived hard. If it came down to it, he intended to die hard, too. *Come on. Come on. Come on.* He didn't mind moonlighting as Papa Joe's hit man; he just hated waiting. *Let's do this already and get high.*

The light next to the elevator glowed white.

"Someone's coming," he said into the radio transmitter.

"I'm in position," Gary said.

The elevator door opened, and Frank saw three people inside: Prince Malachai, dressed head to toe in white; Marcus Jones, his right hand; and a stunning woman who immediately caught Frank's attention. In her high-heeled boots, she stood almost as tall as Marcus. She wore her straightened hair long, so that it framed her high cheekbones, and her makeup shaded her wide eyes. Frank almost regretted that he had to kill her.

Marcus held the elevator door open with one hand, gesturing for Malachai and his companion to wait. Six Pack climbed out of the Escalade and opened the passenger door. The elevator's occupants filed toward the waiting vehicle, and the elevator door closed behind them. As Malachai guided the woman toward the door Six Pack held open,

Marcus opened the other front door.

With his Glock in hand, Frank walked straight toward the column separating them, then stepped around it, revealing himself as he raised the gun sideways in one hand like a gangsta. He saw realization spread across Marcus's features.

"Gun!" Marcus said.

Malachai looked to his right at the short man wearing the ski mask. Panic sped his heart rate, and with no thought for his own safety, he shoved Katrina inside the Escalade and slammed the door behind her. An instant later, a round struck the bulletproof window. Even as he heard the semiautomatic gunfire, hot metal grazed his left cheekbone.

Son of a bitch!

By the time he turned around, Marcus and Six Pack were returning fire. The window of a Mercedes behind the gunman shattered, and a car alarm filled the underground space in protest. The gunman continued firing, and Six Pack took a shot in his left shoulder. Marcus's shots struck their attacker in the chest, propelling him backwards.

The gunman fired again, this time striking Six Pack in the chest. As the driver crumpled to the ground, blood spilling over his fingers and across the cement, Malachai dropped to the ground and rolled under the Escalade. Hearing Katrina's screams inside the vehicle, he emerged on the other side of the SUV, below Marcus, who continued shooting. Malachai rapped on the window to show Katrina that he was okay.

If only I had a piece, he thought.

Then another SUV sped into the garage, tires squealing, and lurched to a stop between the gunman and Marcus and Malachai. The vehicle's passenger window was down, and the driver fired his own weapon in the drug dealers' direction.

"Get down!" Marcus said, and Malachai ducked for cover with him.

Malachai heard echoing footsteps and a car door slam; then the vehicle took off.

"You okay?" Marcus said.

"Yeah." Malachai looked down at the blood and grime covering him. "But these clothes are garbage now." He touched the gash on his cheek.

"You just got grazed," Marcus said.

"Payback is a bitch." *And her name is Katrina.*

Marcus circled the front of the SUV with Malachai right behind him. Six Pack lay on the ground, sucking air through a punctured lung.

"Motherfucker," Malachai said.

Marcus reached inside the Escalade and popped the hatch. "Let's get him in the truck. We can't leave him here."

Malachai nodded. *We can't take him to a doctor, either.*

Both men hauled Six Pack to his feet, which caused the wounded soldier to cry out. Katrina got out on the far side, where Malachai and Marcus had made their stand. As they guided their comrade to the open hatch, Katrina passed them.

"Who the hell were they?" Marcus said.

"I don't know, but that driver was a white dude."

"Cops?"

"Joe's got more than one on his payroll."

"That explains it. Little runt was wearing a vest. I know I hit him in the chest."

They loaded Six Pack into the back and closed the hatch.

"That's it for this truck, too," Marcus said. "He's going to bleed all over the interior." He rounded the Escalade, slid behind the wheel, and closed the door.

Seeing Katrina standing where the gunman had been, Malachai said, "Come on. We gotta get outta here before five-oh shows up."

"Just a minute," Katrina said, crouching low to the ground.

Malachai advanced on her. "I said, *come on*. We don't have time for you to play *CSI*." He saw her dabbing at blood on the cement with the fabric of her dress. "What are you *doing*? That dress set me back a G!"

Rising, Katrina offered him a knowing smile. "You'll thank me later."

FOURTEEN

When Jake entered his office, he found a note awaiting him on the reception desk.

Cobb salad in the fridge.
Hope you feel better, boss.
~Carrie

Devouring the salad in his office and washing it down with a Diet Coke, he still could not believe that Laurel had erased the excruciating pain he had felt all day simply by massaging him. *Not erased. Absorbed.* Her abilities disturbed him, and he had to wonder if she would prove to be an ally or yet another threat to his existence. She reminded him somehow of Kira Thorn, the deadliest woman he had ever met.

Waiting for Edgar to arrive, he cleaned and loaded his Glocks, Beretta, and blue steel .38 revolver. A buzzing sound caused him to look up at the security monitors. On one screen he saw Edgar standing outside the front doors. Reaching for the controls on the side of his desk, Jake pressed a switch and unlocked the doors. He watched Edgar cross the narrow lobby and summon an elevator. Once Edgar had boarded the elevator, Jake set his guns inside his side desk drawer, locked it, and then made his way through the suite to the front door, which he held open.

Edgar exited the elevator with a serious look on his face.

Uh-oh, Jake thought. The thought that NYPD would one day uncover some morsel of evidence that would prove he had executed the Cipher nagged him on a regular basis. He found it hard to imagine anything more humiliating than being handcuffed by his friend after they had worked so many cases together. He doubted Edgar would find that scenario very appealing, either. "Why so glum?"

"What's there to smile about? The economy's in the toilet, unemployment is skyrocketing, inflation's up, crime's up, and our remaining uniforms are threatening to strike over the layoffs."

"And you're in love."

Entering the suite, Edgar did not see the line of salt across the threshold on the floor. "That, too. You don't look bad for a guy who's lucky to have climbed out of his car alive."

Jake closed the door. As he twisted the locks, he heard Edgar's footsteps crossing the reception area. "I have an uncanny knack for survival."

He found him in the kitchen, rummaging through the refrigerator.

"You need to stock beer for your guests."

"This is a place of business, not a bed-and-breakfast. I don't have guests."

Edgar removed a soda, popped the can's tab, and took a gulp. "Let's talk shop."

Jake gestured to the next room. "You know your way around here. After you."

Inside the office, Edgar sat down in the chair facing the desk rather than on the sofa against the wall.

He does *mean business*, Jake thought as he sat behind his desk. "What brings you to my little corner of the island?"

Edgar picked up the replica Maltese Falcon statue that he had given Jake when Jake had obtained his PI's license. He weighed the heavy stone reproduction in his hand, then set it down. "Carmen Rodriguez."

Jake felt an involuntary twitch in his left eye. "What about her?" But his mind was already busy making connections. Edgar was here on business, and his business was homicide.

"She's dead."

Guilt compounded the shock Jake experienced. He hadn't even called Carmen to tell her he planned to take the case free of charge.

"So is her grandson Victor."

A second shock wave ripped through his gut. "Murdered?"

Edgar nodded. "And dismembered."

Synapses fired in Jake's brain. *The Machete Massacres.* "Jesus . . ."

"We found your business card in their apartment, so I went down to One PP and requisitioned the reports on your stunt last night. I know

Carmen Rodriguez hired you to find out if her older grandson is slinging, and you were nosing around when you got yourself into trouble."

"You ought to be a detective."

"This was obviously a drug-related massacre. I've put out an APB for Louis Rodriguez, but no one's been able to find him. What can you tell me about him?"

Jake held Edgar's gaze. He wanted to spill his guts about everything he knew and everything that had happened to him, but he knew that Edgar would never believe him. Who could blame him? Still, he had an idea. "I was planning to stake him out tonight. Why don't you come with me?"

Edgar narrowed his eyes. "Because I'm not a PI, and you're not a cop."

"But we both want to see the right thing done, right?"

"Right. So why don't you just tell me where you planned to look for this kid, and I'll be on my way?"

"There's something I'd rather show you in person than try to explain."

"I thought you were Mr. Independent Operator now. Why do you suddenly want backup?"

"Because my wheels got totaled. Come on. Let's get the band back together. If anything happens, I promise to let you handle everything."

"Then it really will be just like old times."

"Oh, shit, I'm hit!"

Frank had rolled up his T-shirt, revealing the Kevlar vest beneath it.

A single round had burrowed through the Velcro strap connecting the front and back portions of the vest and had found its way into his left armpit. Blood flowed from the wound, and chunks of gore-drenched deodorant dangled from his hair.

"Okay," Gary said as he sped onto the Roosevelt Island Bridge that would take them back to Astoria. "Take it off, so we can find out how bad it is."

Frank peeled off his button-down shirt, but when he tried to unfasten the Velcro with his left hand, pain shot through his arm. "It fucking hurts!"

Gary glanced in the mirror. "We can't stop here. We'll be busted for sure. Just sit tight until we get to Queens."

"Son of a bitch! I should have killed that asshole."

"Why didn't you?"

Because I was hurting for blow, Frank thought. "Marcus saw me approach the vehicle. I got off the first shot but not before he warned Six Pack and Malachai." He snorted an ugly-sounding guffaw. "At least I got Six Pack. That's one mope who won't be walking the streets anymore."

Gary eyed the pink sun setting on the far side of the city. "No sirens yet. At least we got away with it."

Frank slugged the glove compartment with his right fist. "God-damn it! Joe's going to have our asses!"

"Relax. We'll get another crack at Malachai."

"No way. You should have seen the look of fear on his face. He turned *white*. No way he's going to be where we can find him again."

"How do you feel now?"

"My back is on fire."

"The bullet must have exited there and got stuck in the back of your vest."

"I need some blow to dull the pain."

"Later."

Edgar parked his Plymouth on Montclair, and he and Jake sat drinking coffee as they observed the corner of Caton and the sun disappeared behind Flatbush Avenue. Jake felt nervous returning to the location where three zombie drug dealers and four zombie hit men had tried to extinguish his life less than twenty-four hours earlier.

When Edgar sees what's going on with his own eyes, he'll have to help me, he thought.

Unfortunately, he saw no signs of any dealers, living or dead.

"This where the Rodriguez kid slings?" Edgar said, his voice exhibiting skepticism.

"Yeah." Jake sipped his coffee. "I came out here last night after I dropped Dawn off at her apartment."

"I thought you said you didn't know if the kid was slinging or not?"

"I lied. He was here, with two other little hoppers. I got out to speak to him, and the corner boss pulled a gun on me. I got back in my car, and an SUV full of urban guerillas tried to wipe me off the face of the earth."

"So you led them straight to One PP and got your car killed."

"Something like that."

"And now you've brought me to the scene of the crime, so *I* can get killed."

"Relax." Jake nodded at the windshield. "You see any hoppers out there?"

"You must have scared them off with your heroic antics."

"Sarcasm doesn't become you."

"What becomes *you*, Jake?"

Jake rolled his eyes. "Oh, Christ. I suddenly remember why I resigned from the force."

"You resigned because of *me*?"

"Well, not *entirely*, but your constant nagging was definitely a contributing factor."

"Is that so? Because I bailed your white ass out of trouble more times than I can—"

"Oh, he's got to go and play the race card."

"You know what I miss about being cooped up in a car with you like this? *Nothing.*"

Jake burst into laughter, and so did Edgar.

"Motherfucker," they said at the same time.

"Dawn seems like a class act," Jake said when they had both settled down.

"You better believe it."

"You gonna let her get away?"

"I don't think so."

Jake raised his eyebrows. "Really?"

Edgar shrugged. "Hey, I'm getting old. Maybe I'm ready to settle down."

"Son, you *are* old. It's past time for you to settle down."

"Yeah, well, you're catching up to me. I know you've got feelings to work out, but maybe you should take a good look at Maria."

"I have looked. I like what I see. I'm just not ready to get back in the game yet."

Edgar narrowed his eyes, and Jake saw the scraggly hooker he had seen the night before approaching them.

"What is *that*?" Edgar said.

The hooker wore cowboy boots, short shorts, and a button-down red shirt tied below her breasts. She resembled a skeleton with a layer of dead skin stretched tight over her bones.

She looks even worse than she did last night, Jake thought.

"Scarecrows, scarecrows everywhere."

"I think she heard you," Jake said as the emaciated hooker veered toward them. *She's one of them. Or she will be soon.*

The hooker stopped outside Edgar's window and ran her gray tongue over cracked lips. Edgar shook his head, and she sauntered off.

"Jesus," he said. "Are we doing anything here?"

Jake considered the question. "No. He isn't going to show." *None of them are.* "I have another idea. Let's go back into the city."

"I didn't like doing Six Pack like that," Malachai said, sitting on the sofa in Katrina's apartment.

"You did the right thing," Marcus said, sitting beside him. "We couldn't take him to the hospital. The brother was gonna die. You just ended his suffering."

You mean he just covered his own ass, Katrina thought as she crossed the room. They had driven the Escalade to a junkyard, where Malachai had taken Marcus's handgun and capped Six Pack. Katrina had felt nothing watching Malachai's lieutenant perish. *They're all expendable. Even Malachai.*

"Where are you going?" Malachai said to her.

"I'm going to take care of business, baby," Katrina said. Then she opened her apartment's second bedroom door. Two planks, each one foot wide, ran from one end of the bedroom floor to the other, serving as a barricade across the doorway's bottom. Raising one leg high, she set her bare foot down on dirt, then entered the room, turned on the light, and closed the door. Two feet of soil covered the entire floor. Standing with her head close to the ceiling, she crossed the floor, feeling the cool, moist dirt squish up between her toes. It felt like being home on a summer day.

The only furniture in the room was a table hewn from the stump of a great oak tree bleached stone gray. Thick, petrified roots curled around the floor like the tentacles of an octopus. She kneeled at the table and lit the dozen candles that rose from glass holders on the wooden surface. Then she took her dress in both hands and tore off the area stained with blood. Centering one of the candles before her, she concentrated on the fabric and deposited it onto the yellow flame.

Closing her eyes, she began to chant, a low, moaning sound that defied any spoken language. She felt the center of her power, the core of her being. And with her eyes closed, she felt herself floating, her spirit self drifting. She felt the city below and around her. Felt herself drawn to the man whose blood burned before her. She inhaled his acrid fragrance, and when the world came into focus through her closed eyelids, she saw through the eyes of the little man who had attacked them, saw his partner, the white man who had driven his SUV into the parking garage, gun blazing, and had rescued his partner. They were still in that vehicle.

Partner.

Malachai had been correct. The would-be assassins were policemen.

Now Katrina would teach them *her* law.

Edgar parked the Plymouth on West Forty-fifth Street. Jake got out first, breathing in the stench of garbage rather than the aromas of restaurants, outdoor cafes, and gasoline that he associated with Hell's Kitchen. He felt oddly excited to be standing here again, even though it meant acknowledging his character flaws once more and owning up to the tragedies they had caused.

"Who lives here?" Edgar said, joining him outside the building.

"An old snitch of mine."

"I thought your snitches were *my* snitches."

Jake opened the door for him. "I did have a career before you, you know. This guy was my snitch when I was in SNAP with Gary Brown."

Edgar surveyed the names listed on the tenants' directory. "That was in Alphabet City."

"So I kept tabs on him."

"When was the last time you saw him?"

"Last year." He couldn't say the words without an edge creeping into his voice.

"Then he could be gone by now."

"Uh-uh." Jake pointed at the name Dilson, L. "He's still here."

"But he may not be home."

"Let's find out." Jake pressed the button for an apartment on the second floor. When no one responded to his call, he pushed another button.

This time, a woman's voice came over the speaker: "Yes?"

"Police, ma'am. We're responding to a complaint about another tenant. Please let us in."

"How do I know you're really police?"

Paranoid much? But he knew that people had good reason to be cautious these days. "You can come down and see our detectives' shields, if you like."

The woman did not reply.

Jake glanced at Edgar, who appeared unimpressed. Then the door buzzed, and Jake jerked it open.

As they entered the lobby and mounted the stairs, Edgar said, "You are *not* a cop."

"No, but you are."

"Yeah, well, *we* are not responding to any complaint."

"How's that choir practice going?"

On the second floor, a brunette woman stood in the open doorway to her apartment. Her features were drawn in, her eyes filled with fear, and she whispered to Jake, "Are you going to the third floor?"

"Yes, ma'am," Jake said. *Don't you want to see our shields?*

"Thank God. I've been complaining to the co-op board for months. They just say, 'Call the police.' What do they think, that I want to get killed? I'm glad they finally called you."

"What's the problem?" Edgar said.

"He blasts his rap music twenty-four hours a day. All kinds of thugs come and go at all hours, always to his apartment. Scarecrows, you know what I mean? Once I came home and caught him trying every doorknob on this floor. He didn't say a word to me, just went back upstairs and closed his door. I don't feel safe in my own apartment anymore. Please *do* something."

"We'll look into it," Jake said. "Don't you worry about a thing. Go inside now."

"Thank you." She closed the door, and they heard several locks turn.

"What kind of people do you associate with?" Edgar said as they moved to the next stairway.

"The lowest of the low. Notice who she spoke to first."

On the stairway leading to the third floor, the dull throb of rap music filled their ears, and they stopped talking.

At their destination, Jake pressed a doorbell and then banged on a gray metal door. "Police!"

The music stopped, and they heard frantic footsteps and shuffling inside. When the door opened, a skull with dead gray flesh and bulging eyes stared out at them.

Jake recoiled. The last time he had seen Lester "AK" Dilson, the small-time drug dealer pretending to be big-time, he had been well toned. Now he looked emaciated.

Black Magic, Jake thought.

AK appeared just as surprised by Jake's appearance. "I thought you said you was *police*."

"Show him your shield," Jake said to Edgar, who complied.

AK's eyes darted to Edgar's gold shield like a pair of scurrying cockroaches. Then they returned to Jake. "Whatchoo want?" His voice sounded like gravel.

"Just to talk to you. Inside."

"You got a warrant?"

Jake pushed the door open wider. "I don't need one. I'm not a cop anymore, remember?"

AK backed up, and Edgar followed Jake into the apartment and closed the door behind them.

The apartment was smaller than Jake remembered. Garbage littered the floor, and dirty dishes overflowed in the small kitchen's sink. The coffee table in the living room looked conspicuous because it was the one clean spot in the room, as if AK had just cleared it off. The place reeked of cigarette smoke.

Jake wanted to retch. "What happened to your maid?"

"Who you talking about?"

"That girl who was staying with you the last time I was here. Pretty blonde on her way down."

AK blinked at Jake, who felt a strange sadness. The wannabe gangsta's mind was so far gone he didn't even remember the young girl whose life he had no doubt ruined less than a year ago.

"Why don't you just tell me what you want, so you can get the fuck outta my crib?"

"Easy, Lester, easy. This won't take long. You still in the game?"

AK's face scrunched up, a mixture of disbelief and disgust. "You crazy? *What* game? You can't find no more coke or heroin in this town, just Magic. Anyone dealing the old-school shit gets dead."

"Why aren't you selling Magic?" *Because you're sure as hell using it.*

"You wouldn't understand." He looked at Edgar. "*Either* of you."

"Try us."

"You ever see the things slinging Magic? They're not *alive*."

You should qualify for employment soon enough. "What do you mean?"

"You want me to spell it out for you? All right, I will. They're motherfucking zombies."

The word on the street. How long before NYPD figures this out? "You're a very astute observer, Lester."

"Stop calling me that." His voice took on a hard quality that chilled Jake's blood.

"Don't threaten me. There's two of us, and you look like you only weigh a hundred pounds. I doubt you'd survive a good beat down."

AK focused on Edgar, as if trying to read him.

Jake snapped his fingers close to AK's face. "Hey, I'm the one talking to you. We need to do some business."

AK snorted. "What kind of business? You looking to buy some blow? I already told you there *isn't* any, so go shake down someone else."

Jake's chilled blood started heating up. He had wondered how long it would take before AK revealed to Edgar the nature of his relationship with Jake. "I don't want any blow. I don't do that anymore. What I need is information, just like in the old days, back on the Aves."

"What kind of information?"

"I'm looking for someone who deals Magic."

"Shit, you don't need me for that. They're all over the city. Just look for the dead guys pretending they're still alive."

"I'm looking for a particular hopper, but he's disappeared."

AK snatched a pack of Newports off the coffee table and lit a cigarette. "If your hopper's gone, he's gone. Ain't no finding him."

"These things can't go home to their families at night, so they have to be holed up somewhere."

AK sucked on his cigarette. "I thought I heard you say 'business.'"

Removing his wallet from his back pocket, Jake took out a twenty-dollar bill.

"You want me to drop a dime on the biggest, deadliest operation in this city for twenty bucks? You better learn your multiplication table fast."

Jake took out a fifty-dollar bill. "Seventy will buy you enough Magic to keep you going for a couple of days."

AK's eyes dilated at the sight of Jake's money. "That's what you think."

Jake knew he had him. "Take it or leave it."

AK started breathing faster. "What you planning to do at the front office?"

"None of your business."

A sigh that sounded more like a wheeze escaped from AK's lips. "Hunts Point. You want an abandoned factory on Garrison Avenue. But trust me: you won't be coming back."

Jake hid his elation at this revelation. AK reached for the bills in his hand, and he held the money beyond his reach. "Who's behind this operation?"

AK's lips parted, and his eyes turned wild. "You trying to get me killed?"

"You're doing a good enough job of that all by yourself."

"I don't know."

"Bullshit. You know the name of whoever squeezed you out of business. You want this money? Give us a name. You want to get high? *Then give us a name.*"

AK seemed to draw in on himself, shrinking, becoming even skinnier. "Malachai. You want Prince Malachai."

FIFTEEN

Gary parked the department's SUV in front of Frank's Bay Ridge, Brooklyn apartment building. Riding the elevator to the fifth floor of the immense pre–World War II building, Gary steadied his partner.

Inside the cluttered apartment, Frank made a beeline for his bedroom. Gary closed and locked the door. One minute later, Frank emerged sniffling with white powder under his nose. He appeared very much relieved, as if his gunshot wound didn't matter.

"Help yourself." Frank nodded at the bedroom.

"No, thanks." *One of us has to stay clearheaded.* "Let's go look at that wound in the kitchen. You're bleeding all over everything."

Frank looked down at the blood drops on the blue carpet. "Oh, fuck. I'm going to kill those cocksuckers for sure."

In the green and yellow kitchen, Gary flicked on the overhead light and pulled out a chair for Frank, who sat facing the chair's back. Gary dabbed at the exit wound below Gary's shoulder blade with a wet paper towel, which soaked up the blood from the penny-sized hole.

Frank groaned, snorted coke, then moaned.

You sick fuck, Gary thought. "I don't suppose you got any disinfectant in the house or gauze bandages?"

"What are you, kidding?"

"That's what I thought." Grabbing a bottle of Bacardi from the counter, Gary unscrewed the cap. *This is going to hurt you a lot more than it is me.* Without warning, he poured the alcohol over the wound.

Screaming, Frank wrapped his arms around the chair. "Oh, Jesus! Jesus Christ! I'm gonna kill those cocksuckers. That bitch, too."

Gary pressed a Band-Aid over the wound, and it immediately turned red. "Who was she?" He put another Band-Aid over the first one.

"Beats me. But she was a real looker. Malachai threw her into the truck and turned around to face the music. Who says chivalry's dead?"

And you still managed to miss him, Gary said. *I'm beginning to think I need a new partner in crime and law.* But what to do with the one he already had? "Turn around."

Frank rose and faced him.

Looking his partner in the eye, Gary poured rum over the entry wound.

Frank snorted coke and glared at his partner. "You're enjoying this," he said.

"That's where you're wrong." But he really did enjoy seeing Frank in pain.

"Okay, so I fucked up. Maybe you should have been down there with me. It was three against one, you know."

He's right. "I'm not blaming you. It was a difficult situation. Right now, we have to worry about stitching you up."

"You don't look like a seamstress."

Gary took out his cell phone. "You're an excellent judge of character."

"Who you gonna call?"

"Our friend, the doctor."

"Metivier? He costs a fortune. Who's gonna pay for that?"

Gary frowned. "I insist that we split the cost."

Frank beamed. "You're all heart, partner."

Gary's cell phone rang in his hand, startling him. Checking the display, he did not recognize the number. His stomach tightened. He never recognized the number when Papa Joe called him because Joe and his lieutenants used burners: disposable cell phones. "Hello?"

"I just saw a disturbing news report on TV," Joe said without identifying himself.

The uncomfortable feeling in Gary's stomach worsened. "There's never any good news these days."

"Ain't that the truth? There was a shoot-out in the parking garage of a luxury apartment building on Roosevelt Island called The Octagon. Maybe you know the one I'm talking about."

"I think I do."

"Security cameras recorded two vehicles leaving the scene. One of them was registered to an ex-con named Laird Black, whose street name is Six Pack. There's an APB out for him now."

"If the police are looking for this guy—"

"—then his boss will likely take him out of the game. Exactly what I was thinking. The most disturbing part of all this is that no bodies were found in that garage."

Gary ran one hand across his brow. "I guess things didn't go as the shooter had planned."

"One shooter? I thought there might have been two."

"You said there were two vehicles, right? One belonging to the target, the other to the shooter. I assume each car had its own driver."

"I'll call you right back." He hung up.

Gary powered down his phone and slid it into its holder. Then he held out his hand, and Frank took out his cell phone and handed it to him. A moment later, that phone rang, and a different number appeared on the display. "Yeah?"

"Sounds like a real botched job," a new voice said.

Chess, Papa Joe's right hand. "I have to agree."

"That royal pain in the ass knows he's in trouble now. If he was hard to find before, he'll be impossible to find now."

"I understand."

"I wouldn't be surprised to hear that there's a million-dollar bounty on his head."

Oh, shit! "That would turn the five boroughs into one big shooting gallery."

"It is what it is." The line went dead.

Gary handed the phone back to Frank, who said, "What?"

"Papa Joe just put out a million-dollar bounty on Malachai's head."

Frank raised his eyebrows. "*What*? Jesus!"

"Joe's running scared. He knows that Malachai knows who sent us after him. That means Malachai's gunning for Joe."

Frank shrugged. "He always was. It was just a matter of time."

Gary's mind raced. "We need to find Malachai again and take him out."

"You won't catch me arguing about collecting a million-dollar bounty."

"No, we need to take him out and forget about the bounty."

"You're crazy."

"Joe and Malachai are the only drug lords left in this city. We work for Joe. If Malachai does him, we're out of work."

"Unless we take out Joe for Malachai," Frank said in an ice-cold voice.

Gary stared at his partner. *What are you thinking in that coked-up brain of yours, little man? You just spent the last hour telling me you'd kill Malachai for free.* "We know Joe. We can deal with him. As I see it, no one can trust Malachai. Switching teams would be a big mistake."

"Yeah, whatever. I need some more blow."

Gary refrained from shaking his head as his partner headed to the bedroom.

A minute later, he heard Frank screaming for his life.

Frank strolled into his bedroom, where he kept his stash hidden in a bureau drawer. Sometimes Gary really pissed him off. They were partners, which meant Frank had a say in what they did whether Gary had seniority in the department or not.

Opening his favorite drawer, he removed the bag of cocaine and the plate with his works. He spooned coke onto the plate, chopped it with a razor blade, and snorted two lines with a half straw. Damn, that was good shit! Massaging residual powder into his gums, he considered that if the street situation continued on its current path, pretty soon coke would become completely impossible to find in New York. He could only fly on what they'd stolen from the bakery for so long.

Fuck it. I'll fly to Miami if I have to. Hell, if it came down to it, he'd join Miami PD and drive around town in a cool car like Don Johnson on *Miami Vice.* To hell with New York. Manhattan was crawling with zombies and scarecrows anyway.

While waiting for his bloodstream to absorb the coke, his ears clogged up as if the air pressure on the fifth floor had changed. He swallowed and heard a popping sound as his ears cleared. Then he heard a strange, rhythmic sound.

My heart? No—drumbeats!

Then his guts knotted up, expanded, and writhed. Pain spread through his body like white-hot fire, and he screamed.

Gary bolted into the bedroom and froze in the doorway. Frank stood over the bureau, a plate of cocaine on the wooden surface beneath him. He gripped his stomach in both hands, his face turning beet red.

"Frank?"

Frank looked in his direction. Gary had never seen such fear up close. Then Frank's stomach heaved, and he turned back to the bureau, vomiting a stream of chunky white fluid, like spoiled milk, at the mirror.

Gary's eyes widened. *Oh, my God!* He looked at the plate of cocaine again. How much of that had Frank snorted?

Frank projectile vomited again. This time blood splashed over the mirror and plate of coke, turning the white substances uneven shades of pink.

"Jesus!" Gary said as Frank fell backwards onto the carpet and writhed on the floor, red, white, and pink fluids streaming from his nostrils and mouth.

What the hell do I do? Gary thought. *He's overdosing! Do I call an ambulance? It will probably be too late. Do I just leave him here to die?* The idea certainly had its merits.

Frank's eyes turned to him, pleading for help.

Gary took a step forward, still uncertain what course of action to take. Frank's neck appeared as thick as his entire head, and his body turned spastic, arms and legs flopping around as if he lay upon the most powerful vibrating bed ever constructed, his hips humping the air. Frank opened his mouth wide, and Gary heard an unnatural sound, something not human: a hiss. And then Frank's tongue, swollen and covered with white paste, protruded from his mouth. Only it wasn't a tongue.

Oh, dear God in heaven . . .

The head of a great albino snake emerged from Frank's mouth. Its eyes and skin were pure white, like the cocaine Frank had been snorting, but streaked with Frank's blood, which appeared bright red on the serpentine palette. The snake rose from Frank's corpse, coiling its body beneath it, hissing at Gary, its white tongue flicking in and out of its mouth, and its blood-soaked eyes staring at him.

A snake made out of cocaine, Gary thought, incredulous. He took a step backwards, afraid to turn his back on the creature, and reached for the butt of his Glock.

The snake shot forward, launching itself at Gary, a line of white streaking through the air. Gary saw its jaws open wide, and he groped the thick, scaly body with both hands. But the snake buried its fangs into his cheek even as he pulled on it. He felt a jolt of pain, and then his cheek turned numb. Crying out, he stumbled backwards and landed on the floor. His hands closed into fists, the snake seeming to evaporate, and cocaine poured into his face and over his shirt. Gary sat up in a panic and saw the white powder scattered over his torso. The creature had crumbled into its original state!

With a cry of disgust, he leapt to his feet, no longer caring about Frank or Papa Joe or Prince Malachai. He cared about only one thing: survival. Sprinting across the room, he hurled open the front door and charged into the hallway. He raced for the elevator, heart pounding.

What the hell's wrong with me?

Sticky sweat formed on his forehead as the elevator opened.

Oh, Christ, I'm high! The snake must have injected him with liquid cocaine rather than venom. But how much? *Enough to overdose like Frank?* Boarding the elevator, he stabbed the button for the first floor and tried to regulate his breathing as the elevator began its slow descent. Hearing a rubbing sound, he looked up at the elevator's ceiling. *What the hell is that?*

Not a rubbing sound.

Drumbeats. Who was playing drums? The drumbeats reverberated through his entire body. *Ah, shit. What now?* He reached out for the wall with one hand, steadying himself. He wanted to vomit, but the image of Frank painting the mirror with his projectile barf turned him off to the idea. Was a magic cocaine snake trying to chew its way free of his body? *God, I hope not.* He made up his mind to do everything he could to keep that from happening.

The elevator door opened, and he raced across the lobby. Through the glass lobby front, he saw that the sky had turned black. Flinging the door open, he ran outside, glad to be free of Frank's house of horrors. Jesus Christ, what had caused all this to happen? The drumbeats continued to pound in his head and rattle his ribs. He bolted down the sidewalk, scanning Fourth Avenue for the unmarked police SUV. His clothes felt soaked with sweat.

Heart . . . racing . . . no good . . .

He slowed to a stop, his SUV only yards ahead.

Can I make it?

His body did not respond to his mental commands.

Oh, God. I'm going to die right here in Bay Ridge. Not even in Manahttan.

His stomach felt even worse. Something inside him was . . . growing. He staggered to the car and doubled over its hatch. Cars passed him in the darkness.

"Oh, *Go-aaaaaaaaaaaaaaaaaaargh*!"

Gary rolled over onto his back. Staring up at the black sky, with his elbows pressed against the metal, his hands opened and closed, his fingers digging into his palms. The mass in his body seemed to be expanding in different directions, like tree roots.

Or like a nest of snakes . . .

The drumbeat in his head came at a steady rhythm—

Thrum . . . thrum . . . thrum . . . THRUM!

—while his heart jackhammered at a much faster rate. Tendrils of agony continued to blossom through his body, spreading like weeds.

It isn't fair, he thought. What had he done to deserve such an indescribable fate? He knew the answer, and thoughts raced through his mind.

I've lied to the people I love. Stolen from criminals. Accepted money from other criminals. Committed murder. Betrayed my shield. Sold my soul for drugs.

His stomach shook, and pain crawled up his throat and through his colon.

"Fuuuuuuuuuuuuck!"

He thrashed from side to side, then rolled his face against the glass and vomited all over the hatch. Solid matter hurled out of his mouth and rained down on the rear windshield wiper. He gasped in horror at the black and gray chunks mixed in with his blood.

Realization dawned on him like a ton of bricks. *Tumors . . . cancer!*

Then his stomach heaved again, and something solid obstructed his windpipe. Gary tried to expel whatever it was, but pain ripped through his ass, causing his body to go spastic. What looked like a thick tree branch covered in fat slithered out of his mouth. Dripping blood, it curled and uncurled like a tentacle. Still he could not breathe. Worse, he felt the tentacle throbbing in his throat and through his sternum to his belly. Another tentacle ruptured through his sphincter, sending shock waves of pain through his body like broken glass.

Pounding on the SUV, he tried to force the cancer out of his body. In his mind he compared the experience to what he imagined it must be like to give birth through one's mouth or ass. The upper tumor grew out of his mouth, filling it. He bit down on it with all his strength, his teeth penetrating the vile surface. Acid filled his mouth and leaked between his teeth, and the end of the tumor splattered before him.

This did nothing to ease his breathing, though; the rest of the tumor remained lodged in his throat. Then it snaked through his mouth, impossibly wide, and snapped his jaws apart. He screamed through his nostrils as the corners of his mouth tore open and the thicker portion of the tumor telescoped out of his head.

By the time the lower tentacle had burst through his anus, spilling blood and feces down his legs, his right hand had already closed over the butt of his Glock. With tears filling his eyes and the drumbeat filling his ears, he clicked off the gun's safety, pressed the barrel against his temple, and squeezed the trigger.

SIXTEEN

No sooner had Jake and Edgar settled into the Plymouth's front seat than AK emerged from the building and scurried down the sidewalk. Neither Jake nor Edgar said anything. They didn't have to; they both knew that AK had run off to score some Black Magic.

"So that's who you used to get your shit from."

Jake took a deep breath. "It seems like a lifetime ago."

"You miss it?"

"No more than I do Homicide. For me, the coke and corpses went together."

Shaking his head, Edgar started the engine. "I knew you were fucking up, but I never said anything. I'm sorry."

"Don't worry about it. I wouldn't have listened to you anyway. Or to Sheryl. I needed to hit bottom to open my eyes."

Edgar pulled into traffic, then took the FDR north to the Willis Avenue Bridge and Bruckner Boulevard to Barretto Street. During the twenty-minute drive, Jake watched Manhattan transform into the

South Bronx. The lit windows of hundreds of buildings illuminated the cloudy sky.

"What was all that talk about zombies?"

Jake had been waiting for the question, but that didn't make him any more ready to answer it. "You remember a movie called *The Serpent and the Rainbow*?"

"Yeaaaaah. Paul Winfield, right?"

"I guess so."

"What do you mean, you 'guess so'? Paul Winfield played Martin Luther King Jr. on TV. He starred in *Sounder* and appeared in *Damnation Alley* and *The Wrath of Khan*. And he was in *The Serpent and the Rainbow*."

"Okay, whatever you say. Anyway, *The Serpent and the Rainbow* was a fictional movie based on a true-life book."

"About zombies?"

"The guy who wrote the book used several case histories to try to prove that Haitian witch doctors used poisons to put people into a trance that lasted for years. The regular population mistook these trance cases for zombies."

"Okay. So what? Are you trying to tell me that Black Magic comes from Haiti and is turning people into zombies?"

"Something like that."

"Get the fuck out of here."

"You've seen the scarecrows. They're all over the city."

"Yeah, they're zombies, all right."

"No, they're transitional cases, like AK. The real zombies are the ones slinging the Black Magic."

"Get. The. Fuck. Out. Of. Here."

"Just for the sake of argument, let's say that Black Magic is screwing with people's minds and bodies. At some point it turns them into mindless things that do whatever they're told."

"Told by whom?"

"According to AK, this Prince Malachai."

Edgar blew air out of his cheeks. "His real name's Daryl Havek. Papa Joe's nephew.

His mama is Joe's sister; that's how he got into Joe's operation. He did time at Rikers on a possession charge. When he got out, he started calling himself Prince Malachai, and Joe pushed him out of the organization. His name has popped up more than once since we formed this Black Magic Task Force."

"So he really could be the brains behind this operation?"

"Could he be the mastermind behind this drug war? Sure, why not. Could he be importing some drug from Haiti that turns people into zombies? Fuck you."

They turned onto Garrison Avenue and prowled the deserted neighborhood located on a peninsula of the South Bronx and bordered by the Bruckner Expressway, Bronx River, and East River. Arson and abandonment had scarred the area, and over half the population lived below the poverty line.

"Look at this place," Edgar said as the Plymouth crept past bright murals and rusted-out cars without tires. "Two years ago this was a struggling neighborhood, but I would have given it half a chance of surviving."

"That was before the economic collapse," Jake said, feeling a familiar pall of guilt.

"No hookers or drug dealers," Edgar said. "Scary."

"The question is, what scared them?" After another block of desolate, abandoned buildings, Jake said, "Pull over and kill the headlights."

Edgar followed Jake's instructions. "Now what?"

Jake scanned the empty buildings, silhouetted like giant tombstones. "Let's get out and walk."

"Did I say 'fuck you' earlier? Because I meant it."

Jake flipped the switch on the ceiling dome light to off so it would not turn on when they opened their doors. "What's wrong? You're not frightened of some nonexistent zombies, are you?"

"I don't believe your snitch that Black Magic is being manufactured up here. Where I come from, big-time drug dealers kill to protect their business. God knows what you're getting me into."

"This could be the biggest bust of your career." Jake opened his door, got out, and closed the door with a gentle touch that still produced an echo. Edgar did the same. They felt a cross breeze from the East and Bronx rivers.

"They should raze this whole place," Edgar said in a sad tone.

"You're so serious in your old age."

They moved onto the cracked sidewalk and walked side by side up Garrison Avenue. Between Edgar's suit and Jake's complexion, they felt like easy targets.

Two blocks later, they peered around the corner of a sandstone building at an industrial complex with a chain-link fence around it. Windows on the bottom two floors of a building resembling a fortress fallen into ruin glowed yellow in the night. A rusted sign with peeling paint above the front door said Tower Steel.

Speak of the devil, Jake thought.

"That plant closed a year ago," Edgar whispered.

"Then why is smoke rising from the chimney?" Thick, choking clouds of black smoke rose from the smokestack, almost invisible against the night sky. Jake nodded at a silhouetted figure standing near the entrance. "Whatever's going on inside is important enough to warrant posting a guard outside."

"He's not moving."

"But he is standing."

"Fuck you."

Jake studied the building. "Look at that open window on the second floor. The roof of that toolshed is practically beneath it."

Edgar stared at the darkness behind the building. "We don't know what's back there."

"Only one way to find out."

Backing up the way they had come, they walked a block toward the car, then crossed Garrison, heading away from the building. They circled a block in the opposite direction, passing silent buildings with lit windows.

"See, people do live here."

"Doesn't make it any less creepy," Edgar said. "No industry, no jobs, no *families*. You want to know where the junkies are, look no farther."

They walked back to Garrison in silence, studying the shadows and darkness for any sign of movement. Jake was glad when they reached the avenue because the streetlights provided ample illumination. Newspapers blew across potholes as they crossed the street, approaching the building from the other side of the block. With their backs close to the brick walls they passed, they jogged over to an abandoned gas station with no pumps left. Peering around the corner, they studied the rubble-strewn rear of the steel plant. Another sentry, standing in a pool of light, guarded a back door above four metal steps.

That's one of them, Jake thought. "Let's follow this fence separating the properties."

"I don't have a warrant."

"You don't need one. We're just going to look around."

Crouching low to the ground, they entered the dark backyard of the abandoned building and crept between tall weeds and plants to the fence that ran alongside the steel plant's property. Their feet crushed grass fragments, and Jake caught the branch of a thornbush on one sleeve. They passed the sentry, and the darkness thickened around them as they reached the large metal shed.

"That guy wasn't blinking," Edgar said.

"Like he was in a trance?"

"Shut up."

Ten feet of dirt and cracked cement separated the fence from the shed. A rotted construction vehicle beside the shed reached almost to the structure's roof.

"That's a corrugated roof," Edgar said. "There's no way that guard isn't going to hear us up there even if we tiptoe."

"You're right. Wait here."

Before Edgar could protest, Jake vaulted over the four-foot fence and scrambled to the corner. He could almost hear his friend's frustration. Peeking around the corner, he saw a glassy-eyed Hispanic man. His own eyes dropped to a garden hoe lying on the ground. He looked over his shoulder and saw Edgar poised to follow the fence back to a point from which he could observe him tussling with the undead guard. Jake didn't want that. With his right hand, he gestured for Edgar to stay put. Frowning, Edgar settled into position.

Jake searched the ground until he found an egg-sized rock. Glancing around the corner again, he surveyed the terrain on the far side of the building and calculated the distance. Then he wound up his arm and sent the rock soaring over the dead guard's head. The rock struck the cracked asphalt leading to an industrial hangar, and the guard made a robotic turn in the direction of the scraping sound.

Jake sprinted forward, trying to make as little noise as possible. But as his fingers closed around the hoe's wooden handle, the dead thing turned in his direction. Jake swung the hoe high into the air and brought its metal blade down into the zombie's head with such force that the handle snapped in two.

The undead guard teetered left, tottered right, then collapsed in a heap. Grayish light flickered around the hoe's blade, and a soul rose into the night.

I'm becoming an expert at this, Jake thought before rounding the corner again. He beckoned a relieved-looking Edgar forward and climbed the dead construction vehicle. Rust bit into his hands as he mounted the roof of the vehicle's cab. He offered Edgar his hand. They stood on top of the cab, fully exposed in the night air.

"What happened?" Edgar said.

"It was lights out for Gracie," Jake said, cherry-picking the facts.

The good news was that the edge of the shed's slanted roof reached a foot below their elevation. The bad news was that it was five feet away. If either of them failed to reach the roof, they would land on several metal receptacles below.

"What are you waiting for?" Edgar said.

"Why don't you go first? You have longer legs."

Sighing, Edgar stepped to the very edge of the cab's roof. He counted to three, then jumped into the air, kicking off with his right leg. His left leg caught the roof with a shaking crash, and he touched down on his outstretched fingers, his right foot hanging in space. Looking over his shoulder at Jake, he set his right foot down, stood, and took two steps backwards. Then he extended his right hand.

Jake stared at Edgar's hand, unsure if he could reach it. Standing where Edgar had, he took a deep breath and launched himself forward. The front half of his left foot landed on the roof's edge, followed by his right foot, but the impact of his landing reversed his momentum. Before his fingers could reach the roof, he felt himself springing back in the direction from which he had jumped.

Edgar seized his collar and jerked him forward. "I can't take you anywhere," he said.

Regaining his balance, Jake stood up. "Just keeping you on your toes."

They clambered up the roof's slight incline to where light spilled out of the open window.

"It looked a lot closer down on the ground," Jake said.

Edgar planted his feet on the roof with his back to the wall, then crouched low with his fingers interlaced. "I hope you haven't stepped in any dog shit today."

"Just this case," Jake said. Setting his right foot between Edgar's hands, he stepped up at the same time Edgar gave him a boost, then scrambled up the wall. His hands slapped the concrete window ledge, and he pulled himself up.

Peering through the window, he looked down at the metal floor of a catwalk six feet wide, illuminated by lights in the ceiling high above. Beyond the catwalk he saw nothing. Raising himself up on his hands, he swung one leg inside, then the other. As far as he could tell, the catwalk ran all around the interior and no sentries patrolled it. He felt intense heat rising from below and heard equipment rumbling.

My, oh my, what have we uncovered?

Turning back to the window, he held out his hand to Edgar, who grabbed it with both of his and walked up the building's side.

"You've gained weight," Jake whispered.

"It's all that Creole cooking I'm eating."

"I hope you go on a diet before the wedding." Jake lay facedown and wormed his way toward the edge of the catwalk, and Edgar did the same thing. Gazing over its edge, he realized that the second-floor windows were more like third-floor windows because the catwalk stood thirty feet above the sunken floor level. Between motionless conveyer belts and useless machinery, he estimated he saw at least fifty figures at work, their movements mechanical and tireless. The perfect workforce.

Zombies. He sensed Edgar tensing up beside him.

"What the hell are they doing?"

Jake tried to follow the production line's progression. Two zombies stood by a huge furnace, taking turns shoveling ashes from its glowing interior. They deposited the ashes in a metal bin as wide as a Dumpster and as deep as a bathtub. Four zombies used metal scoops to fill large buckets with the ashes, which they dumped into a second bin, where the ashes cooled. Four more zombies moved the cooled ashes to a vat, where they added the ashes to a substance Jake could not see. Here, two zombies stirred and cooked the concoction. Using buckets, two other zombies poured the concoction into glass molds, where the thick liquid formed gray bricks.

Black Magic.

Farther down the line, more zombies wrapped the bricks in plastic, while still more loaded them onto a flatbed dolly.

"This is it," Jake said to Edgar. "This is where they process the shit that's destroying the city."

Edgar said nothing at first. He stared at the emaciated figures toiling below. Jake recognized the look on his face: shock.

"Edgar?"

Edgar turned to him. "What the hell *are* those things?"

Jake swallowed. "You need me to spell it out for you?"

"They're not in any trance. They're fucking corpses. What the hell have you gotten me into?"

"I haven't gotten you into anything. You're a cop, remember? A member of the Black Magic Task Force. Well, here's your Black Magic. You going to do your job or pretend you didn't see this?"

Edgar returned his attention to the operation below. After a minute, he nodded at a spot across the plant's interior. "Those guys are alive."

Following Edgar's sight line, Jake spied two young black men relaxing in an alcove across the factory floor. One stood with his arms folded, a pistol sticking out of his waistband, while the other sat in a tipped-back chair, his feet crossed on the card table before him. Smoking reefer, they traded jokes and laughter and paid little attention to the creatures under their supervision.

"Overseers," Jake said.

"But overseeing what?"

Turning to his left, Jake's vision of the factory was obstructed by the industrial furnace. "I want to see what's at the other end. I want to know what they're putting *into* that furnace." He backed up to the far wall and rotated his body counterclockwise. Then he crawled along the catwalk, commando style, followed by Edgar.

Once they had passed the furnace, Jake worked his way to the edge of the platform again. He saw at least a dozen naked zombies standing in line. They looked worse than the others he had seen so far—the skin pulled over their skulls had turned purplish gray; bones protruded through flesh; gums were visible through rotted away lips; and clumps of hair had fallen out. Staring at the line of still creatures, he imagined toppling them like dominos. A metal stairway descending from the catwalk like a fire escape prevented him from seeing whatever was happening at the front of the line.

I need to know, he thought, realizing that very line of thinking had gotten him into a great deal of trouble in the past.

Motioning to Edgar, he resumed crawling. As he passed the wide metal stairs, he moved faster, his elbows growing sore. His high-top sneakers dug into the metal grooves on the catwalk for traction. Once clear of the stairs, a wide air duct obstructed his view. He reached the end of the catwalk, and the duct still blocked his view. *Damn it.* Then he saw a metal ladder bolted to the cinder-block wall. *Now we're talking.*

Facing Edgar once more, he nodded at the ladder and looked back. Edgar gave him the finger.

Winking, Jake crawled to the opening in the catwalk through which the ladder descended. The walls of the square shaft melted into darkness, with bright light at the bottom, where a doorway faced the main floor. Jake gripped the ladder in both hands, then swung his legs over the edge, taking no chances that would permit anyone below to see him. He maneuvered his feet onto the rungs and climbed down the ladder.

Halfway down the shaft, he felt darkness closing over him. Looking up, he saw Edgar descending. As he reached the light below, he stepped off the ladder, pressing his back against one wall to keep from being seen. Edgar dropped to the ground with his back against the opposite wall.

With great caution, they peeked around the doorway. At the front of the line leading to the furnace, the zombies shed their clothing and deposited them into bins on wheels. Zombie workers retrieved the bins, which they pushed to the furnace. They threw the filthy garments into the flame, feeding it. The naked zombies stood without any sense of shame, their genital areas rotting like the rest of their bodies. Zombies lay upon four out of six cafeteria-style tables. The two standing at the front of the line—a man and a woman—filed toward the remaining tables and laid down on them. Two clothed zombies stood on either side of each table. Men, women, teenagers, black, white, Asian, Hispanic—they all held machetes.

Then, all at once, they raised their machetes and buried them in the limbs of their fellow creatures. The machetes continued to rise and fall, hacking away at the zombies, which failed to react to the blows. The butchers hacked hands away from forearms, forearms away from biceps, chests from stomachs, legs from hips, shins from thighs, and feet from shins. Finally, they split the heads open like coconuts.

Jake squinted as released souls rose into the air and faded away.

"Jesus Christ," Edgar said, oblivious to the soul activity.

The butchers tossed the body parts into wheelbarrows, then carted them over to the furnace, where the attendants used pitchforks to throw the parts into the hungry flames.

Good God, Jake thought. *Black Magic creates zombies, and zombies are used to create Black Magic!* Scarecrows were the junkie equivalent of cannibals.

Then high-intensity light shone down on him and Edgar, exposing them.

SEVENTEEN

Pressing his back against the shaft wall, Jake squinted at the flashlight aimed at them from above. He could not see the face of the figure holding the light, but he heard the man's voice loud and clear: "I was right! There *is* someone here!"

Jake heard a gunshot, and one of the ladder rungs disintegrated into wood chips. The sound of the gunshot ricocheted around the shaft, right behind the bullet. Jake turned his face to the wall, shielding it. As soon as he heard the round strike the floor, he threw himself at the doorway, where he collided with Edgar.

They burst free as their assailant fired a second shot and stood facing the dozen machete-wielding zombies stationed at the tables, where another half dozen zombies waited to meet their demise. With their instruments raised, the machete zombies turned their decomposing faces to Jake and Edgar, who froze in midstep.

"Take them down!" The voice above echoed throughout the factory.

Jake and Edgar looked up at the catwalk behind them. The overseer who had been standing on the other side of the factory now stood at the railing, a pistol in one hand. Turning back to the zombies, who moved in their direction, they looked at each other and drew their Glocks.

"Go for their heads," Jake said.

"Of course."

Jake spun on one heel and squeezed off a shot at the overseer. The round struck the man's hip, shattering it, and he fell down screaming. Beside him, Edgar fired his first shot.

Flickering blue light caught Jake's attention, and he turned back in time to see a soul rise from a toppling body. Jake brought his gun to bear on the advancing horde. Taking careful aim, he fired at the head of a zombie that had locked its eyes on him. A bullet hole appeared in the creature's forehead, and brain juice blew out the back of its skull. The dead man's soul rose even as his body fell.

These souls are trapped in their bodies, Jake thought. Just like Old Nick had imprisoned souls in a secret chamber in the Tower.

The zombies showed no sign of concern as their fellow undead creatures hit the ground and stopped moving. They continued coming, and Jake and Edgar kept shooting. The air filled with gun smoke, and the ground deepened with rotten flesh. Machetes clattered on the floor. Escaping souls flickered like the camera flashes of paparazzi at a red carpet affair, but only Jake saw them. *My gift.*

With the first wave of zombies dispatched, those lying on tables sat up. They were in worse shape than the others, which Jake concluded was the reason they had been deemed disposable. *They passed their expiration date.*

Glancing at the pile of flesh on the floor, Jake remembered Laurel's instructions to him. "Cover me," he said to Edgar. Then he jammed the hot Glock into its shoulder holster and approached the mound.

"What the hell are you doing?" Edgar shot one of the sitting zombies in the head as it prepared to slide off the table. As the body fell over, others touched their rotting feet to the floor.

"No time to explain!" Jake seized a machete from the fingers of one of the zombies on the floor. The creature now looked unreal, like a mannequin or Halloween prop, especially with its abbreviated, sutured fingers. Raising the machete high in the air, he brought it down with all his strength. The steel blade severed the zombie's hand from its wrist, spilling sawdust. As Jake reached for the hand, he registered bodies dropping around him, almost keeping a beat with Edgar's gunshots. His body shuddered as his fingers closed around the dry, leathery body part. Then he heard Edgar's gun slide back.

"I'm out!" Edgar said.

Stuffing the hand into his inside jacket pocket with the open wrist facing up, Jake heard the familiar sound of a magazine dropping on the floor. He glanced over his shoulder and saw the shadow of a figure fall over the flesh pile.

Reload fast, partner.

Jake turned and stood at the same time. He did not have time to drop the machete and pull his gun, so he squeezed the machete's wooden handle and came face-to-face with features he recognized, shadowed by a hoodie. Louis Rodriguez, who he gathered had murdered his grandmother and younger brother, stood two feet from him.

Bastard! He swung the machete over his head.

Louis raised his right arm in a defensive move, and the machete in his hand deflected Jake's blade. Then Louis's left hand shot out and grabbed Jake's right wrist. The zombie twisted Jake's arm. Groaning, Jake released the machete, which clattered on the floor. Now Louis swung his machete. Jake caught the zombie's wrist before the machete reached its intended target—his head. They stood struggling, Jake's arms trembling, Louis showing no emotion at all. Then Louis braced his right foot against Jake's chest and kicked him, and Jake landed on top of the unmoving zombies on the floor.

They can fight! That means they can think. They're more than programmed machines.

Swinging the machete over his head, Louis charged at him faster than Jake had expected.

Feeling faces and limbs pressed against his back, Jake drew his Glock and prayed he had time to aim before the zombie brought the machete down. As he raised the weapon, he heard a gunshot. Before he could squeeze the trigger, Louis's forehead exploded in a shower of liquid brain that rained down on him. Jake clamped his eyes and mouth shut and looked away, feeling the rotten juice on his cheeks.

The zombie landed on top of him, and when Jake looked back, he stared into the undead thing's dry eyes. Liquid brain continued to pour over him. Louis's eyes did not change as his soul escaped its prison and faded.

"Don't just lie there. Get your ass up!"

Jake shoved Louis's corpse off him and leapt to his feet, grateful to be off the pile on the floor. Edgar had finished off the table zombies, but a score of the things had surrounded them.

Before he could join in the melee, Jake wiped the brain juice from his face onto his jacket sleeve in disgust. Then he opened fire. Shifting his aim from left to right, he turned his body so that his back met Edgar's. Bracing their shoulder blades against each other's, they let loose with semiautomatic gunfire. Jake succeeded in dropping four of the things before his gun barrel slid into the locked position.

"Reloading!" He ejected the Glock's magazine, fished another from his jacket pocket, and slapped it into the Glock's grip. The undead force had gained significant ground, and he saw the gray of their eyes. Squeezing the trigger, he held it in the depressed position. The gun barked in his hands, spitting empty shells and spewing smoke as he laid down a blanket of gunfire.

Zombie heads snapped back, eyes exploded, and liberated souls rose. The creatures he hadn't destroyed stumbled over the carcasses of those he had. He supposed that he had matched Edgar's body count. Then his gun locked again. So did Edgar's. Another dozen zombies charged at them.

"Shit!" Edgar said.

"Run!"

They spun in opposite directions, and Jake ran past the furnace, where a pair of zombies reached out to claw at him. Without missing a beat, he pounded one's head with the Glock's butt, knocking it against the furnace but not inside it.

Damn it.

Feeling bodies all around him, he dared to peek over his shoulder and saw half a dozen zombies sprinting after him like track stars, none of them breaking a sweat or breathing heavy.

Or breathing at all.

Jake picked up his pace, but with the Glock in his right hand, he had difficulty pumping both arms. Feeling fingers tickling his collar, he stomped one foot on an invisible brake and dropped to the floor in a protective ball. The creature that had been reaching for him flipped over him, and the other zombies swarmed past him. Springing to his feet, he ejected the magazine onto the floor and slapped another in its place.

My last one . . .

He stepped forward and aimed the Glock at the zombie on the floor. His first shot blew its face away. The second sheared off the top of its skull. As he watched the flickering soul rise, he saw the other zombies turning to face him. Gunshots rang out behind him.

Come on, Edgar . . .

Taking careful aim, he fired two shots, the first a clean hit, the second a complete miss. He fired again, taking out his second target.

Five shots gone already. I can't keep this up.

Breaking into a run again, he veered right, circumventing the remaining three zombies pursuing him. He made for the metal stairway leading to the catwalk he and Edgar had passed earlier. As he climbed the metal stairs, he heard the zombies right behind him. Gripping the metal railing with his left hand, he turned and pressed his Glock's barrel against the forehead of a zombie within arm's reach and squeezed the trigger.

The brain juice blown out the back of the zombie's head coated the face of the next closest creature. The blinded zombie tripped over the unmoving corpse before it, and the zombie bringing up the rear stumbled over its predecessor. With their heads in such close proximity, Jake put a bullet in each skull.

Eight rounds fired. Five left . . .

He heard a steady burst of gunfire in the distance. Scanning the factory, he saw no sign of Edgar, just four more machete-wielding zombies running in his direction. "Edgar!"

Another staccato of gunfire.

Goddamn it! Charging up the stairs, he thought, *I won't leave him behind.*

Halfway up, his heart skipped a beat as the overseer he had shot in the hip limped into view, a trembling sneer on his face as he raised his pistol. Jake froze. He had sworn never to kill another human being again. Eyes locking on the barrel of the overseer's gun, he brought up his Glock.

"Drop it!"

The overseer pivoted on his good leg and swung his gun in the direction of Edgar, who had climbed back up the shaft.

Jake lowered his aim and fired first. Blood erupted from the overseer's right hip, and he went down screaming. Hearing clanging footsteps behind him, Jake took the stairs two at a time and met Edgar at the top. He only had to look at Edgar's fearful expression to know that an army of zombies pursued him.

With his Glock in one hand, Edgar stepped on the overseer's wrist and plucked the gun from his hand. He turned around and saw a tide of zombies swarming up the stairs, three wide.

The overseer said, "You're dead, you motherfuckers!"

Jake looked down at the man writhing on the floor. Then he holstered his weapon. "Pick him up."

Edgar raised his eyebrows, glanced at the advancing creatures, then holstered his Glock and pocketed the other gun. They encircled the overseer with their arms.

"What the hell do you think you're doing?" the overseer said, fear evident in his squealing voice.

Jake grimaced as they lifted him. "Giving you some face time with your employees. I think they want to unionize."

They waited until the closest zombies were four steps below them, then pitched the overseer at them with their combined strength. The man struck them at chest level, knocking them back. The front row of zombies fell into the second row, which fell into the third row, which fell into the fourth. All the undead creatures fell backwards, the overseer screaming the whole time.

Jake and Edgar traded looks, then ran for the window they had sneaked in through. Jake climbed out first, breathing in the night air and leaping onto the corrugated roof below with an echoing thud. He caught his balance as Edgar landed beside him, and they slid down to the roof's edge and jumped onto the roof of the construction vehicle waiting below.

"Promise me something," Edgar said as they drew their guns.

"What's that?" They scrambled down the vehicle's side.

"If you make it out of here and I don't, I want your word that you'll keep an eye on Martin."

They sprinted around the building's corner, forgetting discretion.

Jake could not believe what Edgar had just said. "We're both getting out of here."

"Your word!"

"All right, all right, I promise!"

They reached the front driveway and came to the locked gates topped with coiled razor wire. Veering left, they vaulted over the lower four-foot fence. Jake passed Edgar as they circled the abandoned gas station. They had to pass the factory's front gates to reach Edgar's car, and as they did, the final twelve zombies poured out of the factory and charged the gates, rattling them.

Jake looked at the corner across the street. The car was two blocks to its right. As he calculated how long it would take to reach it, the other overseer emerged from the factory's front door, a set of keys jingling in one hand.

"Son of a bitch," Edgar said.

Jake raised his Glock, took careful aim, and fired at the man's hand. Instead, he hit his thigh, and the man dropped to all fours.

Just as good, Jake thought.

"Take the keys!" the overseer said. "Unlock the gate!"

A single zombie lurched forward, bent over, and took the keys.

Jake's eyes widened. "Come on!"

They sprinted to the corner. As they rounded it, they almost collided with a skeletal figure with bulging eyes.

Edgar pressed the barrel of his Glock against the cadaverous-looking man's forehead.

Jake closed his fingers over his partner's gun hand. "No! He isn't one of them. He's just a scarecrow."

"Today," Edgar said.

They heard the gates swing open behind them and turned to see the zombies racing into the street. Edgar lowered his Glock and they took off, shoes pounding cracked sidewalk as they passed empty storefronts. Seeing Edgar's car a block ahead, Jake looked over his shoulder. The zombies sped forward, their faces impassive.

Jake's left foot caught in a gaping hole in the sidewalk, and he soared through the air, impacted concrete, and rolled. His Glock slid across the sidewalk. Edgar helped him to his feet. With his left knee throbbing, Jake retrieved his gun and started running again. By the time they reached the Plymouth, their breathing had become ragged.

"Do you want me to drive?" Jake said.

"Fuck you!" Edgar unlocked the car with a remote control, and they climbed inside. As Edgar locked the doors and turned the ignition, Jake secured his seat belt.

"Hang on," Edgar said, and the car rocketed forward.

Jake massaged his injured knee, and his fingers came away dripping with blood. Glancing at the side mirror, he saw that the zombies had run into the street and were chasing them down Garrison Avenue. He watched them shrink as Edgar floored the gas.

"Zombies," Edgar said in disbelief as they raced back to Manhattan.

"Fucking, real-life zombies!"

"Be glad they didn't have guns," Jake said. He kept looking at the mirror, expecting an army of SUVs to appear on the horizon behind them.

"You *knew* what they were. You knew what we'd find out here."

"I did know what they are, but I didn't know what we'd find."

"Why the hell didn't you warn me?"

Jake faced him. "Would you have believed me?"

Edgar's silence provided the answer. Finally, he said, "I have to call this in."

"What will you say?"

"I won't report the zombies, just that stockpile of Black Magic."

"If you don't report the zombies, anyone walking in there could get taken by surprise."

"A SNAP unit will be armed . . ."

"We left those two overseers alive. Trust me—the zombies are relocating the drugs right now. That warehouse will be deserted again in minutes."

"With all the bodies we left behind? Not likely."

"This will blow up in your face."

"We should go back and blow up that *building*."

"Now you're making sense."

Edgar looked at him. "The scary thing is, I don't know if you're joking or not."

Neither do I.

"Those things are all over the city. Walking right out in the open. Pushing Magic. No wonder they stink so bad."

Jake considered their next move. "If we want to stop this, we have to go after upper management."

"Malachai."

"I'd like you to get me everything you can dig up on him."

Edgar snorted. "Oh, really? And risk screwing myself in the department? No way I'm letting you drag me down to your level."

"Malachai needs to go down first and fast. This has to be done outside the department."

"It sounds to me like you're talking about murder."

I don't do that anymore. "No. I think we should frame him for something else so he goes away for a long time. Maybe someone will do him in prison. Or maybe we uncover his location and give that information to Papa Joe. Let him worry about it."

"You're crazy."

"Are you aware of any laws against creating a zombie labor force? Because I see a lot of wiggle room there for any defendant. Besides, if the department screws you, you really can become my partner again. Wasn't tonight fun?"

"Fuck you. I saved your ass three times."

"Who's counting?"

"I am. Why the hell did you chop off that hand?"

Jake didn't want to tell Edgar about Laurel yet. "I just thought we might need evidence someday. Something the CSU boys can work on if it comes down to that." Sometimes his own lies impressed him.

"What are you going to do in the meantime, sleep with it under your pillow?"

"That's not a bad idea. I could use the extra buck."

"Especially with your client dead." Edgar's cell phone issued a series of beeps. He checked the display and answered it. "Go ahead, Maria."

Maria. Jake felt glad that he had insisted on Edgar coming alone. There was no need to drag her into this. He listened to her loud, excited voice coming from the phone.

"What?" Edgar sounded dumbfounded. Maria continued to buzz like a bee. "I'm on my way in from the Bronx right now. I can be there in half an hour or so." Maria's buzzing calmed. "Right. Right. See you soon." He handed the phone to Jake for him to power it down.

"Trouble?"

"Brown and Beck are both dead. From the looks of it, Beck over-dosed in his apartment, and Brown blew his brains out on the street near his car."

Jake felt the blood drain from his face. He recalled how strung out Gary had appeared at One PP, and he could not help remembering the morning after his own fall from grace when he had tasted his gun barrel.

"I'm going to drop you off and report to the scene. This is going to be one long assed night for me."

Not for me, Jake thought. *I'm crashing as soon as I get inside my office.*

Edgar let Jake off in front of his building and sped toward the FDR Drive. Jake gazed at Laurel's storefront, debating whether or not to wake her and give her the zombie's hand.

It can wait, he decided, looking up and down the street at shadowy couples shuffling along, then at the Tower. At least he couldn't blame his current situation on Tower's corporate royalty.

Taking out his keys, he unlocked the front door, passed through the vestibule, and punched in his security code. Traces of salt remained scattered at each threshold. His footsteps echoed in the lobby as he crossed the polished floor. He tried to focus on the elevator, but the stairway kept drawing his attention, and he felt a slight numbness in his knees and fingertips.

Fear, he thought. How many of those things had he and Edgar put down? Scores of them, close to a hundred. And they had kept coming after them.

How many of them are there? And how the hell had a street punk like Malachai discovered how to create his undead army and Black Magic? He thumbed the call button and the elevator door slid open. Boarding the elevator, he pressed the button for his floor, and the door closed once more.

So tired. It had been an exhausting twenty-four hours. He just wanted to crawl into bed and stop thinking. But what had happened to Gary and Frank? They had been assigned to the same task force as Edgar and Maria, investigating Black Magic and the Machete Massacres. Had they stumbled onto Malachai's operation as well? He knew them to be opportunists at best and criminals at worst. Perhaps they had attempted to blackmail the drug dealer . . .

The elevator door opened, and he stared at the dark hallway, a single light illuminating the path to his front door.

Nope. No zombies here.

Had the salt deterred them, or had they simply not returned for him? He contemplated relocating until he had dealt with this situation. Running to his door, he jammed his keys into their respective locks. Inside the reception area, he flicked on the lights, slammed the door, and entered a second code into this alarm pad.

He peeled off his jacket, took a Diet Coke from the refrigerator, and entered his office. He flipped on the light switch, crossed the office to the safe, crouched down, and manipulated the combination dials. The heavy door swung open, and, anxious to rid himself of his extra five fingers, he removed the severed hand and shoved it into the lower compartment.

Then he felt a peculiar sensation: a breeze on the back of his neck, almost too slight to notice. Rising, he faced the window behind his desk and became aware of the traffic sounds outside, louder than usual for this time of night. He crept toward the desk and stared at the blinds. Certain that he had closed and locked the window before leaving the office, he narrowed his eyes. The blinds moved ever so much. And a shadow moved over the blinds.

With his heart racing, Jake turned around just as the source of that shadow lunged at him: not a zombie but a scarecrow with snarling features. Jake flinched as AK raised a knife and drove the long blade down toward him with deadly precision. Jake managed to snare AK's wrist, slowing the knife's descent. He reached for his Glock, then realized he needed both hands to take the knife away, so he seized AK's forearm in a two-on-one hold.

AK surprised him by setting his other hand around the knife's handle, doubling the power and momentum behind its trajectory. Caught off guard, Jake fell back and sprawled across the desktop. AK leaned over him, putting all his weight behind the knife.

Sweat beaded on Jake's forehead and stung his eyes as the blade inched closer and closer to his face. The metal tip went out of focus, and AK drove it straight into Jake's left eye.

EIGHTEEN

Jake screamed in agony as the long blade penetrated his eyeball. He continued to resist AK's momentum with both hands, which saved his life. The blade's tip cut into the nerves behind his eye, which multiplied the searing pain. As AK leaned his body against the knife, Jake focused his undamaged eye on AK's knuckles, six inches above his face.

The blade disappeared from the peripheral vision of his right eye, and AK's face trembled with effort, sweat beading on his brow and saliva dripping from his yellow teeth. The drug addict looked as bad as the zombies, and Jake supposed that his former snitch and shakedown victim would become a dead thing in another day or two. He already reeked like death.

AK released his grip on the knife handle with his left hand and seized Jake's throat. Then he twisted the knife back and forth, rotating the blade clockwise and counterclockwise, churning Jake's ruptured eyeball in its socket.

The intense pain Jake experienced radiated from his butchered nerves. He knew there was no saving that eye, but after everything he had faced and conquered in his life, he did not intend to lie down and die for a foe as inconsequential as AK without putting up a fight. Taking an immense chance, he released AK's wrist with his right hand, which he closed into a fist, and pounded the side of his attacker's head.

AK twisted his head away, and when he looked back at Jake, he removed his left hand from around Jake's throat and tried to claw at Jake's remaining eye.

No! Not that eye, too!

Desperation drove Jake into frantic action. Putting all his weight on the back of his head, he bridged on his neck and turned his face away, protecting his surviving eye from AK's rancid fingers. The movement caused AK's knife to scrape against fresh nerves, and he screamed again.

Upside down, his right eye glimpsed an object that had been knocked over in the struggle: the Maltese Falcon reproduction that Edgar had given him. He grabbed for the stone bird but discovered that his depth perception had been crippled. His hand floundered around the reproduction until his fingers finally closed around its neck. Turning back toward AK—which drove the blade even deeper into his eye socket—he swung the statue over his head and brought it crashing down on top of AK's, braining the man with a terrific cracking sound.

AK turned rigid, his eyes rolled up, and blood erupted from his oily scalp as he collapsed to the floor, leaving the knife protruding from Jake's eye.

Whimpering, Jake sat up, his right hand hovering around the blade, but he was afraid to touch it. Summoning his courage, he gripped the knife's handle. Even that little bit of movement sent shock waves of pain through his brain. He sucked in his breath and jerked the knife out of his head, praying that his eyeball remained intact but knowing that could not possibly be the case.

The knife came free without the ruptured eyeball skewered on its end like a shish kebab, and Jake immediately cupped his left hand over the socket. Clear liquid oozed out between his fingers, followed by clear jelly, then blood that seeped into the other fluids.

Looking down at AK's corpse, blood spooling on the Oriental rug, he kicked the dead man in the ribs. "You piece of shit!" He kicked the corpse again.

Still holding the knife, he resisted the temptation to stab AK in the chest until nothing remained of it.

Instead, he dropped the knife on the rug and staggered into the bathroom. Clicking on the light, he stepped before the sink and gazed in horror at his face. AK's knife had turned Jake's eyelid into a miniature mouth through which his head threatened to vomit the remains of his decimated eyeball. The blood-water-jelly mixture continued to ooze out of the two slits in his lid, carrying with it chunks of the white of his eye, which resembled pieces of a hard-boiled egg. His face collapsed into a defeated expression, and tears rolled out of his right eye. Covering his left eye again, he gritted his teeth, his face scarlet as he wept.

How the hell did I get myself into this?

Wiping snot from his nose, he washed his hands in the sink one at a time.

It doesn't matter. I'll make Malachai pay for this.

Jake popped four Tylenols into his mouth and washed them down with Diet Coke. In his bedroom, he snatched a pair of clean underwear from his top bureau drawer. Balling it in his left hand, he pressed the fabric against his eye, producing a fresh wave of pain and an extended groan. Then he picked up his cell phone and pressed autodial.

"Yeah?" Edgar said on the other end.

Pain throbbed in Jake's head. "Where are you?"

"I'm almost on the Fifty-ninth Street Bridge."

"I need you to turn around and come back here."

"I take it you're drinking again or worse."

I could use a stiff drink. Or something better. "This is no joke. But it is a matter of life and death. I can't say more over the phone."

Seconds passed before Edgar answered. "I'm on my way."

Returning to his office, Jake sank onto the sofa. The entire left side of his head ached. What had Malachai's people promised AK in exchange for his services?

As much Black Magic as one junkie could possibly want. *Enough to make him climb a fire escape and through a fourth-story window.*

Ever on the case, Jake stood and made his way over to the corpse on the floor. Crouching, so as not to get blood on his knees, he searched AK's pockets. His right hand came out clutching plastic packs of black powder. He estimated he held ten little bags.

Maybe two hundred bucks on the street, he thought. *That's all my*

life is worth to them

He shoved the bags back into AK's pocket, then removed his hand. A single bag lay centered in his palm. He focused on the fine black powder.

What if I snorted one line, just to kill the pain in my eye? That might even give me some insight into what this shit is doing to people . . .

He closed his fingers over the bag, feeling its texture.

No! Not a chance. Don't even think about it.

He shoved the bag into AK's pocket with the rest, then picked up the knife and carried it into the bathroom, where he rinsed little pieces of himself off the blade. Returning to the office, he stored the knife in his safe. No telling when that might come in handy. Then he settled into the chair behind his desk, stared at the security monitors, and waited.

Ten minutes later, Jake buzzed Edgar into the building and waited for him in the suite's doorway.

Edgar stepped off the elevator and strode in his direction. "What the hell happened?" he said, nodding at the underwear Jake clutched against his eye.

In response, Jake gestured to his office.

"This better be good." Edgar crossed the reception area to the open office doorway and came to a sudden stop.

Jake joined him, and they stared down at AK's corpse together.

Edgar said nothing until he located the bloodied weapon Jake had used to crush AK's skull like an eggshell. "Don't expect me to get you a replacement."

"The zombies couldn't get in here because of the salt, so they sent someone who was still alive. A scarecrow. I bet AK couldn't wait to spill his guts when he went out to score."

Edgar cocked an eyebrow at him. "Salt?"

"Yeah, they can't cross any doorway that's protected by salt. It's some ancient voodoo superstition. I guess I forgot to tell you that."

"So if you had taken salt with us to the Point, we could have poured it on each doorway, and they couldn't have chased us?"

"Good point. Of course, I would have had to explain everything to you then, and I needed you to see things with your own eyes." Jake lowered the wadded underwear, revealing his wound to Edgar, who recoiled. "Seeing is believing."

"Jesus!"

"AK managed to get in one good lick before I bird brained him."

Leaning closer, Edgar inspected the injury, his lips peeled back in a grimace.

"That look on your face isn't making me feel any better."

"You have to go to an emergency room."

"Yeah, that's near the top of my to-do list. But I don't want to leave a corpse in here. I do have office help."

"You don't seem very concerned about"—he gestured with his hand—"this . . ."

"There's no saving this eye, and since I'm not bleeding to death, I can afford to prioritize my crises."

"You still carrying that hand on you?"

Shaking his head, Jake pointed at the safe.

"Then let's get out of here. Give me an extra key and your alarm codes. I'll take you to Saint Vincent's, then come back here and deal with this stiff."

"What are you going to do with him?"

"I don't know yet."

Edgar pulled over in front of Saint Vincent's emergency room on Eleventh Street and Seventh Avenue, an unhappy look on his face. "You took a gypsy cab here after some punk tried to rob you and stabbed you in the eye. You only called me to tell me what happened."

"Understood. Are you going straight back to my office?"

"No. I'm going to need some tools."

Jake let that statement stand by itself. "Thanks," he said, opening the car door.

"Stay alive."

"You, too."

Edgar drove off, and Jake sauntered into the emergency room, where he saw scarecrows, homeless people, and generally miserable-looking individuals sitting with impatient scowls on their faces. He gathered that many of them had already been here for a long time. Passing the security guard, his underwear still pressed against his eye, he scrawled his name on a sign-in sheet on a clipboard and stood before a heavyset woman seated behind a glass partition.

Looking up at him with disinterested eyes, the woman said, "Can I help you?"

"I've been stabbed in my eye, and I need immediate attention."

"Please have a seat, and we'll call you in a few minutes."

"There are no seats."

"I'm sorry, sir."

Fuck this. "I said, I've been stabbed in the eye, and I need immediate attention." Removing his balled-up underwear, he revealed his wound to the woman and leaned against the glass despite the pain.

The woman turned white at the sight of the nasty stain he left on her partition.

"Excuse me, sir." The voice came from behind Jake. *The security guard.*

Rather than deal with another tool of the medical system, he closed his good eye and collapsed onto the floor.

"Oh, shit!" someone said in the waiting area.

"Call some orderlies!" the guard said to the woman behind the glass. *That's more like it.*

The orderlies rushed Jake into an examining room.

"He got stabbed in the eye," one of them said, "and he just passed out in the waiting area."

The physician, an Indian man, examined Jake's lacerated eyelid. "Can you open your eye?"

"No," Jake said, the smelling salts that he hadn't really needed still burning his nostrils. "There's nothing left in there to repair anyway."

"How do you know?"

"Because I saw pieces of white on the sidewalk and on the knife of the scarecrow who attacked me."

Reaching forward and leaning close, the physician used his thumb and forefinger to force Jake's eyelid open. "This is going to hurt . . ."

No shit. Jake screamed, but the physician took his time inspecting Jake's ruptured organ.

"Did you take anything for the pain?"

Just four Tylenols. "No," he said, gasping. *Load me up, boys.*

"I'm afraid you're right. That eye is going to have to come out. The procedure is called enucleation surgery and involves disconnecting muscles from your damaged eye."

"Great. Can I have some drugs now?"

"You'll be under anesthesia soon enough."

Damn. Jake grabbed the doctor's nearest wrist. "Do whatever you have to do. Just make sure that whoever does the job takes the right one out, and by the 'right one,' I mean the left one. I don't want any screwups; do you understand? I can't afford to lose both eyes."

The physician offered him a sympathetic smile. "I understand your concern. It's normal in this situation. The nurses and surgeons will take numerous precautions so that no mistakes occur. Frankly, looking at this particular injury, there is very little possibility of error." He turned to the orderlies. "Take him to prep."

They wheeled Jake out of the examining room.

Jake had never undergone surgery before. Lying on his back in the operating room, he watched in fascination as the nurses made preparations on behalf of the surgeons. Their blue surgical scrubs and gleaming silver equipment made him feel as if he had been taken aboard an alien spaceship. More personnel filed into the operating chamber. A male nurse hooked his arm up to an IV.

"What's that?"

"Your anesthesia."

Thank Christ.

A short man with glasses stepped forward. "Mr. Helman, I'm Dr. Fisher. You're in excellent hands, if I say so myself."

"Just don't fuck up my good eye by mistake, or I'll hire someone to fuck up yours."

The doctor blinked. "I promise. You'll be out in another minute. While you're unconscious, the anesthesiologist will snake a breathing tube down your throat. When you wake up in a couple of hours, you'll feel sore there as well."

Jake's vision turned blurry, and Dr. Fisher's voice grew distant. He wondered how Edgar was faring with his cleanup operation, then forgot all about him. "More drugs . . ."

NINETEEN

For the first time he could remember, Papa Joe tasted fear. Not fear of dying—that came with the business he had chosen or that had chosen him. No, he feared losing those things that meant the most to him: his position in the world, his family, and the respect of those who knew the streets. At forty-four, he'd enjoyed a good, long run, six of them at the top of the heap. He knew it was inevitable that someone would dethrone him; he just hated that it was going to be his nephew, Daryl, who he refused to call Malachai, let alone Prince Malachai.

In the last three months, his six chief competitors had all been slain or had vanished, which amounted to the same thing. In the short term, his own business increased several times over, which meant good times.

But a month ago, someone had targeted his crews for assassination. Corner after corner fell, and there wasn't a damned thing he could do about it. He had to give Daryl props: when the boy moved, he moved *large*. Joe had lost so many men to drive-by shootings and Machete Massacres that many of his surviving people had retired from the business. They hadn't defected to other operations, because no other gangs existed besides Daryl's, and Daryl wasn't recruiting, at least not from the ranks of the living.

Joe didn't know what Daryl's soldiers were—brainwashed, enslaved by drugs, hypnotized—he just knew that they were unfalteringly obedient and endlessly replaceable. Some people on the street called them zombies, and Joe didn't disbelieve them. Daryl's woman was known to be a Mamba, a voodoo priestess. Joe had never even contemplated selling Black Magic because he believed it was more than a deadly drug; he believed it was truly *evil*.

He never thought he'd see the day when the hard drugs of his era—cocaine, heroin, and crack—were replaced by something even more addictive and dangerous, but that day had come. The streets he knew would never be the same. The city he loved was bound to die a horrible death only to be reborn as something incomprehensible and wicked.

With his ranks thinned and Daryl impossible to find, Joe had ordered the white drug cops Gary Brown and Frank Beck to trace his nephew and assassinate him. He found it ironic that he had been forced to turn to cops to save his operation, but Brown and Beck were the most corrupt cops he had ever met. They were worse criminals than his ilk because they pretended to be something they weren't: law enforcers. Joe and his fellows were straight up about what they were all about: power and money. The only protection they provided came in the form of extortion. The real parasites on society were Brown and Beck, not the drug lords and dealers who believed in the simple philosophy of supply and demand. And now, less than twenty-four hours after receiving their marching orders, they were dead. Goddamn, those white boys had proven to be a disappointment.

Chess knocked on the open door of Joe's office. "Wagon's all loaded, boss."

Looking around the office, Joe sighed. This had been one of his favorite fronts. "Do me a favor. Close that safe door."

Chess glanced inside the safe. "But it's empty."

Joe had just cleared it out. "I know that and you know it. But Daryl doesn't know it, and the cops don't know it. Let whoever comes snooping around waste some time, manpower, and money for nothing. Can't you just see their faces?"

Laughing, Chess closed the door and threw the lever.

Joe stood up. "All right, brah. Let's close this joint down. We had some good times in this club, didn't we?"

"True that, true that."

Chuckling, Joe led the way out of the office and down the stairs.

They left through the front door. Joe didn't believe in skulking through alleyways or sneaking out fire exits. A caravan of three SUVs idled at the curb, waiting for them, and the sky had begun to lighten with dawn's approach. Joe looked up and down 112th Street. Deliverymen unloaded magazines and produce from their trucks, and whores checked their watches. A few scarecrows lingered here and there but no zombies.

Good. Joe hated zombies.

Chess opened the back door of the middle SUV, and Joe climbed in and sat down beside WMD, who sat with an AK-47 stashed between his legs, pointed at the floor. Chess closed the door and got into the front next to K-Man.

"Okay, fellas," Joe said, "there's no time for sentimentality. Let's clear the fuck out of here."

"Ready, chief."

The voice had come from a cell phone, set on speaker, clipped to the sun visor above K-Man's head. The driver reached up and clicked the phone off. The lead SUV pulled into the street, followed by the main vehicle and then a team bringing up the rear. They stayed in tight formation, obeying the speed limit, and took Seventh Avenue to Dr. Martin Luther King Jr. Boulevard, then merged onto the Triborough Bridge toward Queens. Manhattan vanished behind them. Joe would miss the old girl.

"Play some Miles," Joe said as the sun rose into the sky and cast golden light on the water below.

Chess located Miles Davis on the SUV's MP3 player, and jazz-funk came over the speakers, bringing a smile to Joe's lips. They took the Grand Central Parkway east toward LaGuardia Airport and then the Van Wyck Expressway toward Kennedy Airport.

"Take your time," Joe said to K-Man. "We don't want no *po*lice pulling us over." Gentle laughter filled the vehicle. "That would get pretty messy."

The caravan got off the Belt Parkway east onto the Nassau Expressway.

Chess looked over his shoulder. "Hey, Joe, what's the difference between a corner boy and a ho?"

"The ho washes her crack and sells it again, son."

They all laughed, having heard and repeated the joke many times.

WMD turned to his boss. "There were eight cooties on a ho's ass. Four of them were smoking reefer. What were the other four doing?"

"Sniffing crack," Joe said, provoking another round of cackling.

The Nassau Expressway became Rockaway Boulevard.

Almost home, Joe thought. Then they boarded the Rockaway Expressway. *Just forty minutes to leave a lifetime behind.* Far Rockaway was one of the four neighborhoods occupying the Rockaway Peninsula in Queens. It had been a Jewish neighborhood before becoming largely African American. Driving along Central Avenue, Joe gazed at foreclosed homes covered in graffiti. He had lived here as a boy and had enjoyed the beach. Now scarecrows stalked the sidewalks, but he saw no zombies. *They haven't come this far out yet.*

K-Man drove parallel to the beach, and Joe looked at the boats on the North Atlantic. He regretted that he had never learned to swim.

Plenty of time for that now, he thought.

They passed a housing project on the beach, and he studied an empty playground.

Is that where Shana plays?

After a few more minutes, the caravan pulled alongside the curb of a weather-beaten Dutch Colonial home that had been a converted two-family house when Joe bought it. He turned it back into a single-family house for Toni and Shana, his common-law wife and daughter.

They both lived under Toni's maiden name, Robbins, but he paid their bills and sent Toni money every week. He visited them at least once a month but preferred the excitement of the city. He kept them out here for their own protection, so Shana could live as normal a life as possible.

All eight occupants of the three vehicles got out. Joe's most trusted men. Chess and K-Man fetched Joe's bags.

Toni appeared in the doorway as the men approached the peeling porch. She wore a white dress and a brave smile. At thirty, she looked more fit than women five years her junior.

Cupping her face in his hands, Joe said, "You look good, girl."

She smiled despite the tears in her eyes. "It's good to see you."

"Aw, you'll be sick of looking at my fat ass soon enough."

She laughed. "I don't think so. Come inside."

They walked inside arm in arm, followed by Joe's army. Toni had packed two suitcases, which stood waiting at the bottom of the staircase.

"That's all you packed?" Joe said.

"That's all I need. I'm looking forward to leaving all this behind. I only want you."

Joe believed her. "Go on upstairs and wake my daughter. I'll be up to see her in a minute."

She walked up the stairs, and Joe faced his men. "Hand me that bag, Chess."

Chess passed a leather bag to Joe.

He set it on the glass coffee table and popped its tabs. "I want to thank all of you for sticking with me these last few months. I know it's been rough. I know some of you wanted to run and didn't. I know others of you want to stay and fight still. But it's time for me to step down and for us to go our separate ways. Chess has my blessing to keep the organization going if that's what he wants. And if he's smart enough not to want that, then the offer is open to each one of you. Work it out among yourselves. What happens to this city's trade in the future isn't my concern. I'm done with it.

"But I've got something for y'all, a parting gift. Call it severance pay." Reaching into the bag, he removed several bulging manila envelopes with names scrawled on them. "A working Joe could live on what's in these envelopes for four years. I know you ain't working stiffs, but if you pace yourselves, you could make it for two."

The men laughed, and Joe handed out the envelopes.

"I'll be leaving out of here tonight," Joe said. "Chess and K-Man and WMD are going to see me off. The rest of you are free to leave now. We're not employer and employees anymore. We're not even business associates. We're just old friends with common memories."

One of the men, a runner named Jackson, gave a loud snort. "Fuck that, Joe. We all stayin'. What's a few more hours of servitude?"

The other men nodded in agreement.

"I appreciate that," Joe said. "Make yourselves comfortable. I told Toni to stock the fridge with Heineken and malt liquor, and that woman has never let me down. Chess, you'll find menus in the kitchen. Let's order up some pizzas as soon as a joint opens."

"You got it, boss man."

"Now if you'll excuse me, I'm going upstairs to say hello to my little girl. Y'all stay alert down here."

Joe opened the door to Shana's room and saw his six-year-old daughter on the bed, rubbing sleep from her eyes, Toni beside her.

"Daddy!"

His heart filled with warmth, and he knew he really was ready to leave the business behind. "Hey there, pumpkin. Come give your daddy a hug."

Shana jumped up and ran across the mattress. Joe opened his arms, and she flew into them. He squeezed her tight.

"I missed you so much," Shana said.

"I missed you, too, baby girl." Over her shoulder, he saw Toni shedding tears of joy.

"But you know what? I'm never going to leave you or Mommy again."

"Mommy says we're going to fly on an airplane!"

"Two of them," Joe said. Everything was going to be all right. *Better* than all right.

Then he heard glass breaking downstairs and machine guns with silencers firing.

Chess came back from the kitchen armed to the teeth with Heinekens, which he distributed to his men. *His* men. He had worked too hard for too long to just walk away from the empire he had helped Joe build. He had always expected to inherit the kingdom, and now was his chance, regardless of Malachai's designs.

Fuck that traitor and his supernatural bullshit.

"What's the plan, Chess?" Jackson said.

Chess held up a bottle opener and started prying off the metal caps on the bottles held by his men. "First we see Joe off safely. He's earned that much. Then we take back our streets. To do that, we need an army. So we gotta start recruiting little shorties. I know that ain't Joe's way, but this ain't Joe's business anymore. Once he leaves town, we don't worry about what he likes or doesn't like."

Chess raised his bottle in a toast, and the six men touched their bottles to his.

Then the windows on either side of the front door exploded, and gray-faced assassins opened fire. Chess watched in startled horror as his men—some of the most ruthless killers he had ever known—danced the jitterbug as gunfire riddled their bodies. None of them even got off a shot, including him.

Toni screamed, and Joe shoved Shana into her arms.

"Wait here," he said, drawing his .32 from his waistband. Downstairs, the gunfire had stopped.

"No! *No!*" Toni was hysterical, which caused Shana to scream.

Now they know where we are for sure. He loved her with all his heart, but she lacked street instincts. *Stupid bitch can't help herself, I guess.*

Joe strode to the door and opened it. He saw six of Malachai's soldiers storming upstairs. *Six bullets, six of them. Not very good odds. I can't exactly go Tony Montana on their asses.* Popping his head back inside, he closed the door and pushed in the doorknob's feeble lock. Then he turned to Toni with a hopeless look on his face.

"No," she said, tears streaming down her cheeks as Joe crossed the room. "It isn't fair. It isn't fair. We were so close . . ."

Joe raised the .32 and shot her in the head at point-blank range, the gunshot reverberating against the walls. Toni collapsed to the floor, and Shana rolled screaming from her arms. The things in the hall pounded on the door, and Shana ran to her closet and pressed herself against the wall.

Joe advanced on her. "It's okay. This won't hurt. You're going to see Mommy real soon . . ."

She looked at him with petrified eyes. Before he could fire, the door crashed open and the zombies stood there, clutching AK-47s.

No! I have to spare my little girl—

The zombies fired their weapons, which had been reset to semiautomatic. Single rounds from each gun blazed across Joe's torso, ripping his flesh. He felt their impact but no pain. Shock, he knew. He would feel it soon enough. In the meantime, his gun fell from his hand, and he crumpled to the floor in a bloody heap.

The soldiers filed into the room and circled him, guns aimed at him.

An army, he thought. Staring up at them, he knew the whispers were true: Daryl's thugs were dead. Robots made of flesh. Zombies. He saw nothing in their eyes as they looked into his. Turning his head left, he saw Shana frozen with terror in the closet. Turning right, he saw his .32. He had meant to shoot Shana first to spare her a terrible death, then blow his own brains out. But he could not reach the gun because he could not move his arms. A horrible sucking sound clawed its way free of his chest.

Punctured lung, he decided.

"Stand back," said a familiar voice. The zombies standing at his feet parted like the Red Sea, and Marcus Jones, Daryl's chief lieutenant, strode into the room. Ascertaining that Joe had been immobilized, he called out, "It's all clear."

A second living being entered the room. Tall and muscular, with a conceited gleam in his eyes. His nephew, Daryl.

"Good job, Marcus," Daryl said as he leaned over Joe. "Hey, Uncle. Whazzup?"

Joe coughed up blood that tasted like bile. "Go to hell."

Daryl raised his eyebrows. "You first."

"You . . . little . . . shit . . ."

Daryl's face scrunched up into an angry mask, and he kicked Joe in his groin.

Grimacing, Joe squeezed his eyes shut.

"I'm not little anymore, and I'm not shit. But you look very small now, and you *are* shit. You're through and I beat you. There's no retirement for Papa Joe, no hiding in obscurity. I won't let that happen."

Joe's eyes flicked to the closet. He just wanted to see Shana one more time before he died. But Daryl jerked his head in that direction as well and saw the little girl, too frightened to move.

No! Why had he given her up? He should have known better.

A smile spread across Daryl's features. "Well, what have we here?" Taking a step forward, he extended one hand. "Come here, girl. Don't be afraid. I won't hurt you. We're blood, you and I. This man killed your mommy, but I won't let him hurt you."

Confusion clouded Shana's eyes.

Oh, God, please no, Joe thought. *Run!* But he knew she could never escape them.

"Bring her to me," Daryl said.

Marcus moved to the closet. He snatched one of Shana's little arms and dragged her into the room. She screamed and tried to resist.

"Let her go," Joe said, pleading.

"Is that what you want, Uncle?"

Joe nodded.

"Then say my name. My *proper* name."

"M-m-malachai." Joe could barely hear himself over his sucking wound. "Prince Malachai."

Daryl smiled. "Very good." He faced Marcus. "You do her."

Without hesitation, Marcus drew a pistol from his belt and aimed it at the little girl's forehead.

No! Joe thought.

"No!" said a female voice.

For a moment, Joe thought that Shana had uttered the word. But this voice belonged to a woman. *Toni—?*

A woman entered the room. Beautiful and black, with long straight hair. Joe recognized her: Daryl's woman, the Mamba. *Katrina.*

"What are you doing?" Daryl said, his displeasure evident. "I told you to wait in the car."

"Put that gun away," Katrina said to Marcus, ignoring Daryl.

Marcus turned to Daryl for guidance, an impatient look on his face.

Interesting dynamic, Joe thought.

Daryl spun the woman around by her bicep. "You don't tell my people what to do—you hear me?"

"Then *you* tell him to put that gun away."

"She's a witness!"

"Tell him to put the gun away."

Joe thought his nephew wanted to bitch slap her. Instead, he threw up his arms and told Marcus, "Put the gun away."

"Are you kidding me?" Marcus said. "She saw everything, including our faces!"

Katrina cocked her head at Daryl, as if to say, *See what I mean?*

Daryl took a step closer to Marcus while Katrina watched. "Who gives the orders around here?"

"You do," Marcus said.

Sure, you do, Joe thought. *This bitch has you completely pussy whipped, boy.* He wanted to laugh, but his chest ached too much.

"Then the girl lives."

Katrina kneeled before Shana and cupped the little girl's face with her hands.

Joe grimaced. *Get your hands off my daughter, you witch!*

"Everything will be okay, honey," Katrina said. "No one is going to hurt you. Do you understand?"

Shana nodded.

"Come on. Let's go downstairs." Standing once more, Katrina extended one hand.

Tears filled Joe's eyes, blurring his vision. *Don't do it!*

Shana took Katrina's hand, and without looking back at Joe, she followed her out of the room and down the stairs.

Joe's heart constricted. *That about does it.*

Daryl stepped closer to Joe and kneeled beside him. "I promise you I *will* kill her before I leave this house."

"Sure, you will," Joe said, forcing a wet laugh from his lungs that caused Daryl's face to darken with anger. "Your woman looks good in a dress, but she's wearing the pants."

Holding his right hand out to Marcus, Daryl said, "Give me a machete."

Marcus took a machete from the belt of one of the zombies and set its wooden handle into Daryl's waiting palm. Gripping the handle, Daryl positioned the machete's blade against Joe's throat.

"I beat you, old man." He raised the machete high in the air.

Joe refused to close his eyes, and the blade whistled down. He felt the impact, hot blood filling his mouth and spattering his face, and the last thing he saw was Daryl leaning on the machete with both hands.

TWENTY

Jake opened his lone eye to the sight of a nurse taking his temperature with a digital thermometer under his arm. He blinked several times, getting his bearings.

A hospital room. Private, at least. Nighttime.

But he did not know why he was here. Reaching back into the recesses of his mind, he wondered if he had been brought here after crashing into the barrier outside One PP.

No, a lot's happened since then.

His throat ached, which triggered a memory. Someone had said something to him about a breathing tube recently. The blinds over the window were drawn. He looked from side to side, and dull pain filled the left side of his head.

"Don't do that," the middle-aged black woman said. "You'll only hurt yourself."

What am I doing here?

He touched a thick pressure pad covering his left eye, causing a tidal wave of pain that ricocheted around his skull.

My eye . . .

Memories seeped into his conscious brain. AK had stabbed him in the eye, and Edgar had brought him here for emergency surgery.

My eye is gone!

In his mind he saw one hundred zombies processing Black Magic. He swallowed. "Time?"

"It's 2:00 a.m.," the nurse said. "You've been out cold in here for two hours."

He swallowed again. "Bathroom?"

"You can use the bathroom. It's right over there." She pointed across the room. "Let me help you get out of bed." She lowered the metal rail and took Jake by his bicep.

Still wearing a hospital gown, he swung his legs over the bed. "Groggy . . ."

"That's just the anesthesia. It's perfectly normal." She helped him to the bathroom and turned on the light for him. "Do you need any help?"

He shook his head and entered the bathroom, then closed the door. Facing the mirror, he focused his good eye on the pressure pad covering his other eye and vowed to get revenge against Malachai, despite his previous vow to never again take a human life. After all, he had already broken that promise defending himself against AK.

An eye for an eye.

He opened the door after relieving himself, and the nurse helped him climb back into bed. His head swam in the darkness. "Salt . . ."

"What?" she said.

He fell asleep.

Jake was eating scrambled eggs and toast when a dark-complexioned man of uncertain ethnicity entered. The doctor wore a blue shirt with his sleeves rolled up and a tie but no coat. Sunlight flooded the room through the blinds.

"Good morning. I'm Dr. Rash." He picked up Jake's chart and studied it. "How do you feel?"

"My eye hurts. My *missing* eye."

The doctor studied him through his glasses. "That isn't your imagination. Your brain will continue to send signals to the muscles in your eye socket for the rest of your life. When you turn your right eye to look around, the muscles in your left socket will turn as well. Eventually, your muscles will adjust, and you'll feel no pain. But for now, you must take painkillers and try not to move your good eye more than necessary."

"What kind of painkillers?"

"Tylenol, Motrin . . ."

Damn. "What happens next?"

"A specialist will see you before lunch to ensure that you're fine to go home; then we'll discharge you. We'll provide you with a healing gel and a saline flush for your eyelid. Your eye socket will be sore for about five days. Take Tylenol as needed. In three or four days, you'll develop a shiner around the outside of the socket. Expect some discoloration for maybe ten days. In a week, you'll come back for a postsurgical exam."

Just like that, Jake thought. "Then what?"

"For the time being, you'll wear an eye patch or a plastic cup over your eye. Your choice. Some patients prefer dark wraparound glasses. In a few weeks, you'll be fitted for a glass eye. You can also apply for therapeutic cloning, although the waiting period can be extremely long unless you're selected for an experimental program."

Jake snorted. "I won't be cloning my eye."

"Why not? It will be healthier than the one you have now and a perfect match. Cutting-edge medical technology will allow you to live your life exactly as you did before."

Jake stared at the doctor. "No offense, but I'm not interested in living with any organs incubated in a petri dish."

"Are you religious?"

Jake considered the question. "Not the way you mean. But I do believe there's a natural order to the universe that Old Nick was not meant to change." Just mentioning Tower's nickname caused Jake to recall the replacement eyeball the billionaire had received before his death. *No, thank you.*

Dr. Rash smiled. "Well, you have plenty of time to think it over. You don't need to make such an important decision now. Can I have the nurse get you anything?"

"More drugs."

"Well, well, well. If it isn't Dr. Cyclops."

With his head propped against a pillow, Jake mustered a smile.

"Edgar!" Maria's voice registered shock at her partner's joke.

"That's Edgar for you," Jake said. "Always making fun of other people's misfortunes. What do you do for an encore? Kick a crutch out from under someone with a broken leg?"

"I can't let you feel sorry for yourself," Edgar said.

Maria's face showed real concern. "How do you feel, Jake?"

"Doped up. Unfortunately, it's wearing off."

"When do you go home?"

"I was supposed to get a final checkup an hour ago."

"Just like that?"

He nodded. "It was a simple enough operation. I just want to get out of here and chow down on a Blimpie with everything on it. I'm starving."

Maria's eyes widened with dismay. "A Blimpie?"

"A large one, with the bread soaking up that special Blimpie sauce."

Maria crossed herself. "*Dios mio.*"

"I told you he was okay," Edgar said. "He always ate like that."

Jake twisted his back, trying to get comfortable. "Thank you both for coming. Are you going to stick around and give me a lift home in a real unmarked police car?"

Edgar clucked his tongue. "No time for that, buddy. We just got a call from Far Rockaway PD. Someone whacked Papa Joe and his old lady. From the sound of things, the perps took out everyone left in his crew."

Jake felt a familiar tightening in his stomach. "Machetes?"

"I'm really not at liberty to say," Edgar said in a slow cadence. "But we'll likely be at the beach all day. I figured I'd check in on you and let you know I took care of that errand for you last night."

"Thanks." He wanted to know what Edgar had done with AK's body, but he couldn't ask him in front of Maria. Edgar had obviously only stopped by to tell him about Papa Joe's murder. "Call me later?"

"You bet. Get some rest. Stay out of trouble. Maybe you shouldn't go into the office for a few days until you get used to operating with one lens."

"We'll see."

Edgar nodded at the door. "Let's go, Maria. Dead bodies await us."

Maria gave Jake's arm a gentle squeeze. "Take care of yourself."

"Thanks." He found himself admiring her ass with his remaining eye as they left.

Papa Joe has left the planet, and a prince has become king.

Jake exited Saint Vincent's after 1:00 p.m. with a white plastic bag containing eye pads, a plastic eye cup, and medication. No drugs, though.

Just as well. I need to stay alert. It was fun while it lasted.

But the fun had stopped. As he walked down Eleventh Street, he found himself looking over his shoulder and scanning the shadows ahead. Scarecrows, no zombies. Hungry eyes, not vacant expressions. His altered depth perception only added to his sense of paranoia. Worse, he had gone to the hospital unarmed, and now he felt naked without a weapon.

I have to stop doing that.

He took a taxi to Twenty-third Street. Facing Laurel's storefront, he felt tempted to walk into her parlor to ask her for help. But he really wanted to get into the security of his own space and make sure Edgar had disposed of any evidence that AK had been in his suite. *Security?* He laughed out loud. So what if pedestrians on the street thought him insane? He rode the elevator to the fourth floor. Skipping the stairs was becoming a habit. He crossed the sunlit hallway to his door, which he unlocked. Inside the reception area, he discovered that Edgar had not reset the alarm even though Jake had given him the code. Careless. He passed the kitchen, his attention on the closed door ahead of him.

"Jake?"

His heart recoiled in his chest as his entire body flinched. He recognized Carrie's voice but without his left eye had walked right past the kitchen without seeing her. And she sounded so *close*. As he spun to his left, she came into view, and when she saw the pressure pad over his eye, she jumped and cried out, which caused Jake to flinch a second time.

"Son of a *bitch*!"

"I'm sorry!" Carrie fanned herself with one hand. "What happened to your eye?"

Willing his heart to slow down, Jake gasped. "It's gone. It doesn't matter why."

"What? Jesus! Are you all right?"

"I will be in a minute. What are you doing here today?"

"Getting a head start on your quarterly income tax filings."

Death and taxes, Jake thought. "Oh, right. Thanks. I have work to do, so I'll need a little privacy."

"Do you want me to leave?"

"You know what? I think you'd better. In fact, I'd like you to take next week off."

"But I've got so much—"

"Let me rephrase it without any bullshit. People are trying to kill me. That makes this office as dangerous for you as it is for me."

"Dangerous?"

Setting his hand on the back of her neck, he guided her into the reception area. She felt so tiny, like a child. "Very. And I don't want anything bad to happen to you. I'll let you know when it's safe to come back."

"Do you want me to call Ripper to come over here?"

"Thank you. But I don't think your boyfriend can help me with this."

"I don't know. He's got a bad temper and a real mean streak."

"Then why are you with him?"

"Oh, he's got a sweet side, too."

Jake took out his wallet. "Let me pay you in advance for next week. You'll be absent with pay."

Carrie raised one hand. "No. Thank you. I don't want money I haven't earned. Call me when you want me to come back. Call me if you want me to send Ripper to watch your back. Call me if there's anything I can do to help you with whatever trouble you're in."

Jake smiled. He liked Carrie. Holding out a fifty, he said, "Then at least take this. Buy Ripper a nice dinner."

She smiled back. "Okay. Thanks, Jake. Take care of yourself."

"You, too." He watched her leave. *Good things come in small packages.*

After the front door closed, he went into his office, sat down, and booted up his computer. He spent half an hour checking news headlines and his e-mail. His eye grew tired, so he took a break, then popped some Tylenols for the pain. He went to the safe and took out the Afterlife laptop. Reviewing the zombies and voodoo sections, he came to a conclusion: those areas were far less comprehensive than others in the file, as if someone had deliberately left out research. But who?

Not Old Nick. He spent millions of dollars on that research.

Jake studied the names of the researchers: Dr. Donna Bidel, Ramera Evans, Professor Blake Carlton, and Javier Soueza. One of them hadn't earned his or her fee.

Or one of them held back information.

His fingers danced over the keyboard. Because he didn't need to look at the keys, he felt like he had found something in his life that hadn't changed because of his new disability. He Googled each member of the team. Dr. Bidel had died of heart failure four years earlier. Professor Carlton had fallen to his death from the top floor of his San Jose condo three years ago; he had not left a suicide note. And Javier Soueza had died from a brain aneurism two years ago. Following this pattern, Jake fully expected to discover that Ramera Evans had died under mysterious circumstances one year ago, but he found no reference to any such person.

Curiouser and curiouser.

Three out of four researchers responsible for a portion of Old Nick's big research project had met with sudden deaths. Had Tower ordered them killed to protect his secrets? Jake would not put it past the old man. If so, had Ramera Evans's body simply not been discovered, or had she gone into hiding to escape the fate of her colleagues? Or was she responsible for the deaths?

The bells on the front door to Laurel's parlor jingled. Jake stepped down the stairs as Laurel appeared in the shadowy doorway leading to her quarters.

"What happened to your eye?" she said with apparent alarm.

"I used it to stop a knife from entering my brain last night."

Her eyes widened. "Who did this?"

"You tell me."

"Give me your hand," she said, offering him hers.

"Will this one do?" Reaching into his pocket, he took out the severed hand, wrapped in red fabric. "I always wondered when that handkerchief would come in handy."

With no sign of disgust, Laurel accepted the hand and carried it over to the round table in the middle of the room. She sat down and unwrapped the handkerchief, revealing the yellowish gray hand, its fingers uncurled. Her own hands rested flat on the tablecloth, as if she was afraid to touch the hand by accident. "Please sit down. You're making me nervous."

Pulling out the chair opposite Laurel, Jake sat. "Show me some of that magic."

Sensing the sarcasm in his voice, she glanced at him. "Still doubting me?"

"Not your ability. I know you really removed that curse from me—or whatever it was."

"Then you just doubt my intentions?"

"You like to play things close to the vest."

"But you do want me to read this hand and provide you with some answers?" Just a touch of sarcasm.

"Yes, please."

Returning her attention to the hand, she took a deep breath, then shook her hands in the air as though limbering up. Pumping a small amount of sanitizer into her hands, she rubbed them together. Then she slid her left palm out beneath the back of the severed hand and closed the fingers of her right hand around the dead flesh.

Jake studied her features, searching for a reaction.

Massaging the hand, Laurel leaned forward, cocking her head as if listening to a distant voice. Her eyes grew unfocused and glossy, trancelike. Then she blinked, looked down at the hand, and separated her hands from it. She pumped more sanitizer on her hands. "This hand belongs to a zonbi. Zonbies are Creole—Louisiana vodou."

"What's the difference between them and regular zombies?" *Regular zombies?*

"A vodou Houngan is a priest, a Mamba a priestess. They're religious figures, with no more power than a Catholic priest or a Jewish rabbi. But a bokor is a vodou sorcerer or sorceress. The majority of men and women claiming to be bokors are scam artists. A true bokor has forged an alliance with a demon. When a bokor creates a zonbi, the creature's soul remains in its body, acting as a receiver for its master's commands. The bokor communicates with its slaves mentally, as if they're its physical appendages. The spirit, or soul, is trapped inside the body unless the body's brain is destroyed."

"Why the brain?"

"Because the source of thought is the source of the soul."

"And when the brain liquefies . . ."

"It still retains the soul."

"And if a brain is destroyed . . ."

"The soul escapes."

"This city is crawling with these zonbies. Are you telling me that every one of them is walking around with its soul trapped inside?"

"Yes. They're unwilling slaves, with no ability to resist the orders they're given. But inside each one of those corpses is a soul screaming to get out."

Oh, Jesus. "Is there a way to set all their souls free without having to destroy their brains individually?"

"Certainly. All you have to do is kill their master."

Jake digested this information. It went down surprisingly easy. "With what, a silver bullet?"

She gave him a look that suggested she was humoring him. "Any bullet will do. Bokors are still human beings."

Rising, Jake drew his Glock and aimed it at Laurel's head.

Although she appeared to maintain her cool demeanor, what little color she had drained from her face. "What do you think you're doing?"

Jake focused his aim on her forehead. "Whatever it takes, lady."

"You're making a serious mistake."

"I'm prone to that."

"You don't want innocent blood on your hands."

"Did you ever work for Nicholas Tower?"

"No."

"Who are you? *What* are you?"

"I'm no bokor. I have nothing to do with Black Magic or the zonbies distributing it."

Staring into her eyes, he wished he could squeeze the gun's trigger and end this nightmare, but he believed everything she said. Lowering the Glock, he said, "If I find out you're lying, I know where to find you."

Then he holstered the gun and exited the parlor.

TWENTY-ONE

Sitting behind the wheel of the black SUV he had rented, Jake watched the mailman stuff envelopes into the mailbox of the two-story house on 168th Street in Jamaica, Queens, not far from Sutphin Boulevard. Residents of multiple ethnicities passed his temporary vehicle. Once predominantly African American, the neighborhood had seen a large influx of West Indians, Asians, and Puerto Ricans in recent years.

As the postman moved on to the next house, Jake slipped on the pair of wraparound sunglasses he had purchased earlier. They obscured the pressure pad over his left eye socket but also cut down the vision in his right eye. He snatched the narrow CD mailer that he had addressed to Occupant from beside him and hopped out of the SUV. Crossing the busy street at a quick pace, he locked his vehicle with a remote control. On the sidewalk, he opened the metal gate and approached the house, which had gray composite siding.

Not exactly a mansion but expensive enough in this city, especially for a woman with no discernible income source.

He mounted the concrete steps, and as he reached for the lid of the black metal mailbox, he heard the steel front door unlock. Popping the lid, he snatched out the mail and used it to cover the cardboard CD mailer. The door swung open, and a black woman in her midforties stood there, attractive for her age, with a long, curly black wig. Judging by her toned biceps, she worked out on a regular basis.

A woman of leisure.

Alice Morton's startled expression faded into one of disdain.

Jake handed her the stack of junk mail with the CD mailer on the bottom. "Here's your mail, Mrs. Morton."

She hesitated, clearly caught off guard by his use of her name, then took the mail from him. "I don't use that name anymore."

"Oh, right. Sorry, Mrs. Reid." Jake had no trouble projecting his old cop persona.

"It's miss. Detective . . . ?"

"Brown."

"Do you mind if I see some ID?"

"Not at all." Jake took out his wallet and handed her the business card Gary had given him at One PP.

Holding the card in her free hand, she scanned the information on it. "What can I do for you on this sunny October day, Detective Brown?"

"I'm afraid I come bearing bad news. Don't shoot the messenger." He waited for a reaction but got none. "Your brother Joe is dead. He was murdered early this morning."

She didn't bat an eye. "I know. One of your people already called me. I guess you didn't get the memo."

I guess you aren't too broken up by the news. "Did they also tell you that your son murdered him?"

She froze.

That got a rise out of her.

"No, they didn't. Because it isn't true."

"How do you know that?"

"Because Daryl loved his uncle."

"Even after Joe threw him out of the family business?"

"There is no family business. Whatever Joe does, he does on his own."

"That's funny, because with Joe out of the way, Daryl's the city's biggest drug kingpin. Everyone in the NYPD and FBI knows it. You'd better get used to seeing strange faces around here. Word is Malachai ordered two cops killed. We're going to do whatever it takes to bring him down, even if that means going through you."

"I'm calling my lawyer," the woman said, waving Gary's card at Jake.

"That's premature, but you'll need that lawyer soon enough."

She closed the door in his face and locked it.

Charming family, Jake thought as he returned to the rental SUV. After setting the black radio receiver on the dashboard, he inserted a miniature speaker into his ear and waited. The listening device inside the CD mailer transmitted the bass of a rap song. Then the music cut off.

That's it. Call your boy.

"Hello, Daryl?"

I wish I could hear the other side of this conversation.

"I don't care what you call yourself. I'm your mother, and I'm going to call you by the name I gave you." A pause. "Never mind that.

You've got big trouble. A man in a blue suit was just here doing a survey. He said my favorite family TV show was canceled. Also said two cop shows were canceled."

Jake waited in suspense.

"How could you be so stupid? Didn't Joe and I teach you anything?"

Son of a bitch.

"I don't care what Katrina said. How many times have I told you that bitch is bad news? She's just using your ass."

Katrina. A new name for the file. Jake had suspected that Malachai's bokor had been behind the two detectives' deaths, and now he was sure of it.

"What are we going to do about these cops?"

Good question. And she had dropped her coded language.

"Gary Brown. Yeah, Gary Brown. That's what his card says. Detective, Narcotics. He isn't from credit card fraud."

Jake snorted.

"I don't want no motherfucking cops sniffing around my motherfucking house; that's why."

Come on. Come on.

"I need to see you."

That a girl!

"No, not this weekend. Tonight. Where you gonna be at?"

Repeat the location. Repeat the location . . .

"Send a car for me."

Shit. Nothing ever came easy.

"Because I don't want to take the subway or a cab into the city."

Not specific enough.

"Just have someone here by nine sharp." Then she snapped her phone closed.

Sighing, Jake removed the earpiece. Malachai's mother planned to meet him somewhere in the city, and someone was picking her up at 9:00 p.m. Plenty of time for him to switch vehicles.

Sitting at the dining room table in Katrina's apartment, Malachai shut off his phone and stared at it.

"What is it?" Marcus said from across the table.

"My mother says a cop just came to see her."

Katrina served them each a bottle of cold beer and sat down.

"So? She'd better get used to it. We're big time now."

Malachai turned the cell phone end over end in the palm of his hand. "She said the cops know we had those two pigs killed."

Marcus raised his eyebrows, then glanced in Katrina's direction. "I thought you said they would never know it was murder."

"They never will," Katrina said in an even tone. "Whoever this cop is, he's guessing or bluffing."

"Why would anyone bluff about that? One of those pigs OD'd, and the other blew his brains out. How could they know we had anything to do with either one of them?"

"They don't know a thing." She looked at Malachai. "I don't suppose your mother got this guy's name?"

Malachai nodded. "Gary Brown."

Katrina narrowed her eyes. "That's the name of one of the two cops I killed. The one with the stomach cancer. Baby, somebody is fucking around with your mother."

"And that means they're fucking around with *you*," Marcus said.

Malachai stared at each of them in turn. "A fake cop."

"Or a private eye," Katrina said.

"Wait a minute," Marcus said. "A scarecrow came by my crib last night. He was a small-time coke dealer I supplied before all of this here. He told me this ex-cop who used to shake him down for cash and coke gave him a beat down because he wanted to know where you were at."

Malachai closed his fingers into a fist around the cell phone. "What ex-cop?"

"He said the name, but I don't remember."

"What did you do?"

"I gave him a handful of Magic and told him there'd be more if he took the guy out."

"Was the name Jake Helman?"

Marcus shrugged. "Yeah, I think so."

Malachai turned to Katrina, whose face hardened.

"You shouldn't have done that," she said.

Marcus looked at her in disbelief, trying to keep his anger in check. "Say *what*?"

Katrina drummed her long fingernails on the tabletop. "You have no idea what plans we have for Helman."

Marcus looked at Malachai for support. Seeing none, he turned back to Katrina. "You're right; I don't know. Because I never heard of this cracker before, and you don't tell me shit."

Staring into his eyes, Katrina said in a tight voice, "We tell you what you need to know."

"Who are *you*? I was in this organization long before you. I'm Malachai's right-hand man. I don't need your say-so to make a move."

"Well, you didn't serve him very well, then, did you? Because I'm the one who put him on top."

"Your voodoo shit can only go so far. This is New York, not Haiti."

Katrina opened her mouth to speak, but Malachai raised his hand. "Enough. I need both of y'all, and I don't need to be listening to this shit right now. You want to take someone out, you run it by me. Period."

"Maybe we shouldn't go out tonight," Marcus said. "Maybe we should keep staying low."

Malachai shook his head. "Nah, nah. Fuck that. We're going out for the whole world to see where we stand now. If Helman's dead, he can't touch us. If he's alive, he doesn't know shit, and we still get what we want out of him. Have a car pick up my moms and bring her to us."

Jake returned to Alice Morton's house in a fresh change of clothes and a black Monte Carlo at 8:30 p.m., half an hour before her scheduled pickup. Having ditched the sunglasses when the sun went down, he wore a baseball cap pulled low over his eye and pressure pad. At 8:40, Edgar called his cell phone, which Jake set on speaker. "Talk to me."

"How's your eye?"

"The one in my head or the one in the medical waste Dumpster at Saint Vincent's?"

"The one that's keeping your head from being completely empty."

"That one's fine. A little tired, but it's getting the job done. What's new on your end?"

"Papa Joe and his entire crew were shot, then hacked apart with machetes. Medical examiner's going to have a hell of a time putting all these pieces together."

"Any witnesses?"

"One, but she isn't talking. Joe's little girl. I don't know why they let her live, but she's in deep shock."

I wonder if she'll live with her aunt Alice. "When are you coming back to the city?"

"Couple of hours. We're getting dinner with the Rockaway detectives, then dealing with a mountain of paperwork. What's up?"

"I might have a lead on our runaway prince."

"He's wanted for questioning. You see him—call me. Understand?"

"Why? So you can tip him off, and he can skate circles around us?"

"That's my job. That's the law. That's the way it's going to be."

By the book. "Okay, okay."

"Maria's coming. I'll call you later."

"Right." Jake felt relieved to have Edgar for backup, so he ignored any frustration he felt at being hamstrung by the legal system.

An hour later, a white SUV pulled up to Alice's house.

Half an hour late. Good help is hard to find. Unless Malachai wanted to show his moms who the boss is.

Jake took out his Canon digital camera and set it to high-def video mode with night vision. He recorded a bulky black man with baggy jeans, a red shirt, and a cap getting out on the passenger side and strutting to Alice's front door. The man pressed the doorbell and waited. When Alice came out, dressed to the nines in a black dress with sparkles, she said something to the man, who snatched the hat off his head, making Jake laugh. The man escorted Alice to the vehicle and opened the back door for her. After she got in, he climbed into the front, and the SUV took off.

Jake zoomed in on the license plate, then set the camera aside and followed.

They took the Triborough Bridge to Harlem River Drive. Jake's hands tightened on the steering wheel. With his altered depth perception, driving at night felt like an entirely new experience. He kept squinting, which sent pain lancing through the nerves in his left eye socket.

Switching lanes, he dropped back, switched lanes again, came forward. He was sure the driver of the SUV had no idea he was being followed. On 125th Street, a block away from the Apollo Theater, the SUV pulled in front of a nightclub called Caribbean. The bodyguard got out, opened the door for Alice, and walked her inside. The SUV idled at the curb.

Meaning she's coming right back out.

Twenty minutes later, she did. Jake could not read her expression.

The bodyguard helped her into the waiting vehicle and got in himself. Then the SUV pulled into traffic, and Jake faced a decision. If Malachai was not inside, and Alice had simply been given another rendezvous point, he would be unable to relocate the SUV.

Damn, damn, damn.

He drummed his fingers on the steering wheel. Then he located a parking spot for the Monte Carlo. From the bag at his side, he took out a canister of styling mousse and sculpted his hair into a slick shape that he hoped would serve as an adequate disguise in case anyone he knew saw him. At least his strawberry blond hair appeared darker. Hopefully the pressure pad over his eye altered his features enough. Next question: *Do I take my Glock or not?* These days, nightclubs often employed metal detectors to stem violence.

But that fat boy got in. He couldn't imagine the bodyguard wasn't strapped. *Which means Malachai really is King Shit around here.*

Jake stowed the gun under the seat and got out. As he crossed 125th Street, the sound of calypso music grew louder. Inside the lobby, he paid a twenty-dollar admission fee and walked right in. No metal detector. *Damn it.*

The club's interior swallowed all unnecessary light, and Jake appreciated the darkness. The four-man band onstage performed for two dozen men and women dancing on the floor. About twenty small tables surrounded the dance floor, and another forty tables were on the upper level. Jake knew that Malachai would not be sitting at a small table. On the night of his ascension to the throne, he would have a large entourage with him.

But he wasn't be in a private room. He'll want everyone to see him, to know that he's celebrating his victory.

Malachai wasn't hard to find. Jake zeroed in on a large table in the back, around which sat ten people. Dressed in white, Malachai was the center of attention. Bottles of Dom Pérignon protruded from buckets of ice, and laughter rose above the music.

The king's big night.

A beautiful woman with long, wavy hair and light-colored skin sat next to Malachai, whispering into his ear. She wore a beige dress and plenty of gold.

Katrina? Alice had mentioned her by name. Jake believed Katrina was an alias used by Ramera Evans, the missing member of Old Nick's voodoo research team.

As he stepped closer to the table, but not close enough to alarm any bodyguards paying attention, his heart skipped a beat. His head turned numb, and his testicles shrank inside his scrotum. He did not know if Katrina and Ramera were the same person, but he did know Katrina under another name.

Dawn Du Pre.

The woman Edgar hoped to marry.

TWENTY-TWO

Jake stood paralyzed in the nightclub, a constant flow of bodies circumnavigating him. He fished in his pocket for his cell phone and brought it out. Training the camera lens on the celebratory table, he zoomed in on Malachai and Dawn and touched the record icon. A body passed before him and he looked up, half expecting to see one of Malachai's thugs. Instead, a tall man wearing a suit moved around him. Looking down at the screen, he saw Malachai and Dawn snuggling and laughing.

On top of the world, Ma.

And then Dawn looked straight at the camera.

Jake's blood turned cold, and he snapped his head back, making eye contact with her.

Bad move.

Praying that she did not recognize him, he slapped the phone closed, moved deeper into the crowd, then returned to the entrance. He recalled having dinner with Edgar, Maria, and Dawn and driving

Dawn home before he staked out Louis Rodriguez and the other two zonbies in Brooklyn.

As he exited the nightclub, anger seethed inside him. Somehow Dawn—no, he wouldn't call her that; Dawn was a fictional creation, a façade constructed to deceive Edgar. Maybe her real name was Ramera Evans and maybe it wasn't, but Katrina fit her well. She had insinuated herself into Edgar's life and seduced him into falling in love with her. Just as she had made Malachai fall in love with her.

Why?

In Malachai's case, the answer was easy: power. She was the woman behind the man. But Edgar was just a cop. A civil servant.

As Jake grabbed the Monte Carlo's door handle, he froze. *A cop working in the Black Magic Task Force.* A tremendous source of information. Katrina wasn't just using Edgar; she was abusing his integrity as a cop.

Sliding behind the wheel, he looked into the rearview mirror, then retrieved his Glock. He did not intend to part with it again. Laying the weapon on the seat beside him, he closed the door and gunned the car's engine.

Jake drove downtown with no specific destination in mind. He wanted to do some research on Dawn Du Pre and contrast that with the little bit of information he had found on Ramera Evans. A search on Katrina, without a last name, would be hopeless. He didn't want to return to his office suite or even Laurel's parlor. Salt or no salt, that building was unsafe for him. He drove over to Astor Place, where he knew of a twenty-four hour Internet café, and parked within sight of the café's wide window. Opening the glove compartment, he took out a container of Tylenol and popped four tablets into his hand.

Inside the café, he bought a large black coffee and made himself comfortable. He fed the Tylenols into his mouth like quarters into a parking meter and washed them down with hot caffeine. The place was largely empty except for a handful of college students, and he wondered how soon this business would be unable to meet the demands of Manhattan commercial real estate and join all of the others that had closed.

Sitting before a computer, he started with Ramera Evans. What had he missed in his first search? He knew he had to go farther back.

It took him less than ten minutes to discover the first nugget of information. Forty minutes after that, he called Edgar.

Jake stood at the railing of the Carl Schurz Park walkway overlooking the East River. He had come here often with Sheryl and had returned on a regular basis after her murder. It was easier than visiting her grave in the cemetery off the Long Island Expressway, though he managed to get out there at least once a month.

Marc Gorman, the Cipher, had murdered Sheryl less than three hundred yards from where he now stood, underneath a stone viaduct close to Gracie Mansion, the mayor's official residence. Jake tried to shut out the memories, but he never succeeded. He had seen Sheryl's bloodstains on the ground beneath the viaduct, and he had seen the image of her terrified face tattooed onto Gorman's chest right before he had executed the serial killer.

Jake had been in an insane bind then, just as he found himself now. He didn't know how to tell Edgar that Dawn was behind the horrors that had infected their city. Gazing across the river at Roosevelt Island, he shuddered in the night breeze. But at least he felt safe here, standing in the circle of illumination provided by the overhead streetlight. A garbage scow chugged across the dark water below, and couples walked hand in hand along the stone walkway behind him. A three-quarters moon gleamed in the clear night sky.

The sound of footsteps rose above that of waves crashing against the retaining wall, and Jake turned to see Edgar approaching him from the direction of the stone steps that curved down to street level. Edgar had unbuttoned his collar and loosened his tie, and he carried his blazer over one shoulder.

"Dr. Helman, I presume?" He sagged onto the dark green bench before Jake. "Why all the cloak-and-dagger?"

"It's a good idea to stay on the move when a drug lord has an army of zonbies hunting for you."

"I guess it does. Zonbies?"

"The accurate term for this particular breed of undead slave."

"According to whom?"

"I have my sources."

"Yeah, well, I'm up to my chin in this crap, so I think I'm entitled to know who these sources are so I can make up my own mind whether or not to believe any intel they provide. My life is on the line, too."

Jake had expected no less, but he had long ago promised himself that he would never reveal that he possessed Old Nick's Afterlife research. "You're right. Well, there's the Internet, of course."

"Great."

"And there's this woman I know. Sort of a psychic."

"Even better. Did you find her through the Psychic Friends Network?"

"Look, we're dealing with a lot of unknowns here. A lot of stuff that has its roots in the supernatural."

"Old wives' tales, you mean."

"Somewhat. But what you have to realize is that these folktales and superstitions stem from reality. People with little or no scientific knowledge created them to explain what they couldn't understand otherwise. It's the same thing with religion. Sure, there's a lot of fantasy and nonsense involved, but at the core is something that fundamentally exists."

Edgar mustered a patronizing smile. "I'm not arguing, Jake. Last night I blew away a few dozen dead people who were stumbling around like extras in a George Romero movie. I saw them with my own eyes. I had their rotting flesh on my clothes and in my hair when I got home. So I know they're real, and I know they're all over this city. You and I are the only ones who know what they are, and we have to do something on our own to stop all this. I just don't want to fuck around with any comic book bullshit. How do we stop them? We can't hunt down every one of them and blow their brains out. There's too many of them for that. And with the way Black Magic is spreading through the city, there's more every day."

Edgar had made it impossible for him to set up his revelation. *It has to be now.* "My psychic lady friend says there's a way to stop them all at once."

"I hope it doesn't involve a nuclear bomb, because that's just stupid, not to mention counterproductive."

"No, nothing like that. The zonbies are under the control of a bokor— a voodoo sorcerer or sorceress with actual powers bestowed by a demon."

Edgar clapped. "So now we're dealing with demons."

"They exist. So do angels. Just not the way that our traditions and cultures have indoctrinated us to view them."

Edgar raised his eyebrows. "I've seen recovering alcoholics become Jesus freaks, but I had no idea you'd joined the flock."

"I haven't. I don't subscribe to any religion. Like I said, organized religions are based on fantasy. But most of them contain germs of truth, too. Demons and angels do exist, and when my source tells me that a true voodoo witch receives her powers from a demon, I believe her."

"Have you ever seen a demon?"

Jake stared at his friend. *Don't make me answer that.*

Edgar narrowed his eyes. *"Have* you?"

Jake swallowed.

"Son of a bitch!" Edgar leapt to his feet. "How the hell can I put my life in your hands if you're delusional? Demons, witches, voodoo . . ."

"Don't forget angels," Jake said. *And ghosts.* But he didn't dare tell Edgar about the Soul Searchers who had haunted Old Nick's tower. "Are they any harder to believe in than zonbies?"

"I don't know!" Edgar pulled his hair with both hands. "Aaaargh!

Why did you pull me into this?"

Jake folded his arms across his chest. "If anything, you were involved before I was." *And on a much deeper level than you realize.*

"I know. I know. But Maria is on the task force, too, and I don't see her gunning down zombies."

"Zonbies."

"Whatever!"

"Gary Brown and Frank Beck were on the task force, too."

Edgar recoiled as if realization had slapped him upside his head. "Oh, my God. You're saying their deaths—"

"—were murder. This isn't about zonbies. It's about voodoo. Black Magic."

"Why Gary and Frank?"

"Don't pretend you don't know how dirty they were. They worked for drug lords and moonlighted as cops, not the other way around. Malachai probably ordered his bokor to take them out because Papa Joe had them looking for Malachai."

"So, what, this bokor put a spell on them?"

"A curse. She did the same thing to me. I spent half a day hallucinating and hearing drums in my head."

"Now that I believe. How do you know this bokor—if there is a bokor—is a she?"

"I'm getting to that. It was the day after I escaped the first zonbi hit team by flipping my wheels outside One PP. She sent another team to my building, and then she screwed with my head."

"Why didn't she kill you like she did Gary and Frank?"

"I don't know. I haven't figured that out yet. For some reason she wanted me out of commission but not dead."

"There's always got to be some fucked-up shit with you, doesn't there?"

"It's what makes me special."

Edgar sighed. "So tell me what our end game is. What do we have to do to put these things down as quickly as possible?"

"We have to kill the bokor."

Edgar stared at him. "Murder."

Jake shrugged. "She's their brain. Without her, they're just a bunch of rotting corpses."

"And if we arrest her?"

"On what charges? Who will believe us? And even if they put her away, she can still work her magic wherever she is. She can continue to reanimate the dead, and she can come after you and me. There's no other way. She has to go."

"What if your 'psychic lady friend' is wrong about all this? What if you're wrong? Are you really willing to chance killing an innocent woman?"

And spend eternity in the Dark Realm, suffering at Cain's hands? Not really. "She isn't innocent. She's killed God only knows how many people, and she's destroying this entire city."

"How do you know this bokor's a woman?"

"Like you said, I'm always deep in shit. But I'm also a good private eye. I know how to do my legwork, and I've seen her with Malachai."

"Who is she?"

Jake hesitated. *Here we go.* "You know her."

Edgar knitted his eyebrows together. "*I* know her?"

"That's right. You're in this a hell of a lot worse than I am."

"Jesus Christ, don't spend all night dancing around the head of a pin. Give me a name."

"You'll think I'm crazy."

"Trust me. I already do."

"You're my best friend. I mean that."

Edgar took a step closer, impatience sketched across his face. "Jake . . ."

"Her name is Ramera Evans."

Edgar's simmering anger evaporated. "That means nothing to me. You're barking up the wrong fire hydrant, brother."

"Malachai and his people know her as Katrina. You know her as Dawn Du Pre."

For a moment, the lack of any reaction at all by Edgar made Jake think his friend hadn't heard him. Then Edgar chuckled, and the chuckle blossomed into hysterical laughter. He held up his hand, gesturing for Jake not to speak. "Oh, Jake. I don't know what to do with you. Are you back on the sauce or the blow? Or have you even moved on to Magic?"

"Even if I was frying my brains again, it wouldn't change what happened to us last night."

Edgar's expression and voice turned dead serious. "No, it wouldn't. But at least then I could forget about what you just said."

Jake took out his cell phone, cued up the video feature, and offered it to Edgar. "I'm sorry."

Edgar cast a wary look at the cell phone in Jake's hand, then took it from him. Jake watched Edgar's expression as the video played. The blue light from the small screen highlighted his features as they registered disbelief, then shock. Then the footage stopped.

"Play it again," he said.

Jake took the phone, reset the playback, and handed it back to him. "Again, I'm sorry."

"When did you shoot this?"

"Just a couple of hours ago. I told you I had a lead on Malachai. I bugged his mother, then followed her to Caribbean on 125th."

Edgar's voice turned as cold as the ice in a glass of vodka on the rocks. "What else do you know?"

"Ramera Evans was born in the Bronx. She was an only child. When she was eight years old, her parents were butchered by drug dealers after they called the cops on a bunch of corner boys. They were murdered in their apartment. She was there, but she hid in the closet. I'm guessing that's why Papa Joe's little girl was allowed to live."

Edgar's jaw tightened, and his eyes grew shiny.

"She went to live with her maternal grandmother, Louise Du Pre, in New Orleans. Grandma must have been a good woman, because Ramera went to Tulane University on a full scholarship. She majored in history and world religion and wrote a book called *The Dark Art of Voodoo*, considered the definitive history of voodoo." *And Old Nick hired Ramera to serve on his voodoo research team*, a detail Edgar didn't need to know.

"Then Hurricane Katrina hit New Orleans, and Grandma Du Pre drowned in her own living room. Sometime after that, Ramera ceased to exist. No payroll records, no income tax records, no credit card records." *Because Old Nick financed her reinvention of herself.*

284

"Based on her rental information, Dawn Du Pre moved here ten months ago." *Probably right after Old Nick's death when the coast was clear for her to operate without detection.* "There are no records of her existence prior to that and no records of an income source now. She doesn't own a PR firm, and if she freelances, her clients pay her cash."

Edgar's expression remained stoic. "Anything else?"

"That's all there is."

Edgar gave him a slight nod. "Thanks. I owe you one." He turned to leave.

Jake grabbed his arm. "Hey, wait a minute. Where are you going?"

"To find that bitch and see what she has to say for herself." He said it matter-of-factly, as if the answer was obvious. *"Alone."*

"She and Malachai will kill you without giving it a second thought."

"If it comes to that, I'll do whatever needs to be done. It might as well be by my hand, right?" Edgar started walking.

Jake fell into step with him. "I'm going with you."

"I don't want you with me on this."

"Why not?"

"Because you'll just mess things up, like you did with the Cipher."

Jake froze. "What's that supposed to mean?"

Edgar turned to him. "It means you fucked up. Just like you always fuck up. And as usual, I covered your ass."

Jake's mouth opened, but no words came out. He remembered when Edgar had called to tell him that Kira Thorn had provided an alibi for him on the night Marc Gorman was executed in his own apartment.

"The building across the street from Gorman's had a fancy new

HD security camera in its lobby. You can take a frame grab from that footage and blow it up twenty times over without any loss in resolution. It showed Gorman leave his building, then you enter it, then him return, and you leave. Guess who got dead in the meantime?"

Jake felt himself turning numb. *I always thought he suspected, but he knew the entire time.* "What happened to the footage?"

"What do you think? I destroyed the source file. Nobody else saw it."

"You never said anything . . ."

"Neither did you, so I let it be. Hey, I loved Sheryl. I'm glad you did that fucker. But I took a big chance covering for you. I knew that as long as you didn't get caught some other way, my secret was safe."

"I'd have done the same for you."

"I know that. But this isn't the whole story, is it?"

Oh, shit, Jake thought.

"Kira Thorn. Your supervisor at Tower International. Why did she come into the station and provide an alibi for you?"

Jake took a deep breath. He had hoped this moment would never arrive. "Because she wanted to have me killed, so I couldn't reveal any of the dirt I uncovered on the company." *No need to complicate matters by telling him the Cipher worked for Tower.*

Edgar's eyes registered a glimmer of surprise. "What happened to her?"

Jake said nothing.

Edgar jabbed a finger at the space separating them. "I can understand what you did to the Cipher, but this executive? You went too far."

"It was self-defense." *You see, Kira transformed into this giant spider monster and tried to eat me alive . . .*

"I'd like to believe that's true, but I'm going to take care of business my way tonight, and I don't want you anywhere around me. Maybe you can be *my* alibi. Don't follow me. I mean it."

Jake watched Edgar disappear into the night.

TWENTY-THREE

Katrina entered her apartment building at a brisk pace, aware that Malachai's driver, Forty-five, watched her every step from his Jeep. It hadn't been easy to convince Malachai to let her visit her "sister," whom she claimed lived in the building instead of herself, but she had been persistent. It was imperative that she return to the apartment where Dawn Du Pre lived. She was certain she had seen Jake Helman at the nightclub, and she was just as certain that he had seen her and taken her photograph with his cell phone camera. And then he had hightailed it outside. Had she mentioned this to Malachai, especially after Jake's name had just come up at the apartment she maintained as Katrina, he would have done something stupid. And she needed Jake alive.

But she also knew that Jake would tell Edgar she had been Malachai's companion at the club. Edgar had proven a useful source of police information the last couple of months, but she knew him to be a righteous man capable of righteous anger, and she could not afford for that anger to be directed at her. He was a good man and a wonderful lover—

much better than Malachai—but he had outlasted his usefulness.

"Good evening, Miss Du Pre," said the doorman, who rose from his station at the lobby counter.

"Hello, Randy."

She boarded the elevator, and as the door closed, she saw Forty-five staring at her from the Jeep idling at the curb. She felt better as soon as she no longer saw him, because that meant he no longer saw her. The game she had played between Malachai and all his soldiers and with Edgar had proved exhausting. As much as she would miss Edgar, she looked forward to a simpler approach to her business. It was much easier to lie to one man than two, and soon she wouldn't need to lie at all.

As the elevator rose, her mind drifted back to this morning when her zonbies had eliminated Papa Joe and his crew. The little girl whose life she had spared—Joe's daughter—had affected her more than she had at first realized. Those wide brown eyes had reached into her soul, something she did not allow people to do. Of course, the girl's own soul had been damaged after seeing both her parents murdered, as Katrina's had been scarred by the killings of her mother and father so long ago.

Following those murders, a double funeral for her parents was held in the Bronx. Her mother's mother, Grandma Louise, had come to New York, and *Ramera* understood that she would be returning with the old woman to live with her. Grandma Louise had been a tall, friendly woman who did what she could to make her granddaughter feel at home in the old New Orleans house, which Ramera thought smelled like rotting wood.

Grandma Louise had frequent visitors: several old ladies who liked to get together once a week without fail. They wore bonnets and long skirts and jewelry, just as the slaves of old had done. They whooped and hollered and smoked cigars, which disgusted Ramera.

"Whatchoo going to do with that girl child?" one of Louise's friends said one day.

Louise looked down at Ramera and said, "I'm gonna teach her some of that ol' black magic."

All the women laughed.

But Louise had been sincere, and she schooled Ramera in the ways of vodou. Ramera viewed the rituals as traditions and approached them from a scholarly point of view in college. Her book *The Dark Art of Voodoo* brought her to the attention of Nicholas Tower. It was while working as one of his research members that Hurricane Katrina had claimed Grandma Louise's life. Bitterness at the lack of government response to the crisis consumed Ramera's soul, and she learned to embrace that bitterness. Just a few years later, she understood true power and wielded it like a weapon.

Stepping off the elevator, she strode to her front door and inserted her key into the lock. She enjoyed living here and enjoyed her time as Dawn Du Pre, away from Malachai and the brutal world into which she had immersed herself. Entering the apartment, she flicked on the hallway light, then closed and locked the door. She entered the living room and kneeled before a round glass table upon which stood a thick purple candle. It was the only vodou artifact she had permitted Dawn to possess, and it appeared to be decorative.

She struck a wooden match and lit the candle's wick, then rose and went into the bathroom. From a shelf in the medicine cabinet she took out a small plastic bag. Using tweezers, she removed one of the curly black hairs collected in the bag, which she had removed from a pillow on her bed. One of Edgar's hairs. She took the hair into the living room and deposited it into the candle's flame.

Then she kneeled on the floor once more and, reaching deep into her soul, chanted in the ancient tongue she had discovered while doing research for Nicholas Tower. The language was an odd mixture of French, Spanish, African, and Native American tongues. As the guttural sounds rose from within her, she pictured Edgar's face and body. She became aroused as she chanted:

Take this one,
Chain his soul,
Transform his body
Into his prison!

"You've got a lot of explaining to do," Edgar said behind her, startling her so much that she jumped to her feet with one hand over her heart.

After leaving Jake alone at the Carl Schurz Park walkway, Edgar had run full speed to his car, which he had parked outside the park entrance, one of the benefits of being a cop. Keying the ignition, he raced to Central Park, crossing over to the West Side, then uptown along the West Side Highway. His head throbbed with the stunning revelation that Dawn had been cheating on him with the city's new drug kingpin; that she had most likely been using information she had gleaned from him to assist Malachai in his conquest of the drug trade; and that, if Jake was right, she was the driving force behind the plague of undead slaves infecting Manhattan.

Impossible, he thought. He accepted that Dawn had played him in some Machiavellian chess game but not that she was somehow capable of resurrecting fatally overdosed junkies as zombies.

Not zombies. Zonbies.

Jake had managed to surprise and impress him. His former partner had always been a schemer, too smart and too reckless for his own good. It had not been a huge decision for Edgar to destroy the digital file of Jake entering and exiting Marc Gorman's building. In his opinion, serial killers deserved death, and Jake had spared the state and city untold expense in what would have amounted to a sensational trial.

But Kira Thorn's sudden disappearance troubled him. He and Maria had sat with Kira when she had vouched for Jake's whereabouts the day of Gorman's murder, and nothing about her demeanor suggested she was capable of ordering a hit on Jake. Then again, he had slept with Dawn—had fallen in love with her—and had never suspected that she could possibly be entangled with Malachai and Black Magic.

Damn it! He pounded the steering wheel's rim. How could he have been so wrong?

Parking in front of Caribbean, he ran inside and paid the admission fee rather than advertise that a cop was on the premises. There was no telling if someone would alert Malachai or whether or not Edgar would need to conceal his identity. He circled the club's interior three times before concluding that Malachai and Dawn had already left.

Maybe Jake scared them off without realizing it.

He knew of just one place to look for Dawn: at her apartment. She had given him a copy of her keys on their one-month anniversary. Now he stood before her, the living room filling with the burning candle's sweet scent. She had been chanting in a language he did not recognize. *Vodou?*

"Edgar!" Dawn said, her surprise palpable.

He appraised her dress. Blatantly sexual, not sophisticated at all. "That's a different look for you."

Her expression turned pensive. "Did Jake speak to you?"

Edgar drew his Glock from its holster. "What do you think?"

She swallowed. "Then there's no need to play games."

"I never played games with you. I loved you. I guess I still do. It's pretty funny, isn't it? A guy my age getting his heart broken."

"I'm sure you've broken plenty of hearts. Your son's mother's, for one."

"Don't ever talk about my son or his mother. Put them out of your mind right now."

She offered a nod of concession. "For what it's worth, I do care about you."

"I never figured you for a drug dealer's whore."

"I'm not Malachai's whore. He's mine. So are you."

He tightened his grip on the Glock. "Keep talking, lady. It isn't helping your case."

"What case? Are you planning to arrest me, lover? On what

charge—infidelity? I didn't realize that was a legal offense, and we're not even married."

"We might have been."

Mocking laughter escaped her lips. "Oh, did you plan on proposing to me? How sweet. No, thank you. I grew up in poverty and never plan to go down that road again. Your salary couldn't pay for my wardrobe budget."

Edgar felt his skin turning hot. "So you're all about the money, huh? Maybe you should have slept with Gary Brown or Frank Beck instead of killing them."

Dawn took a step forward. "I didn't know who they were when I met you. And I knew that you were close to Jake."

Edgar could not mask his surprise. "Jake?"

She took another step closer. "That's right. You were my way to reach him."

"What do you want with Jake?"

She stood before him with the barrel of his gun pressed between her breasts. "That's for me to know and you to find out, darling. If you can." Her eyes flicked down to his gun. "Are you going to pull the trigger or talk me to death?"

With his free hand, he reached into his pocket and took out his handcuffs, which he tossed onto the table behind her. The metal clinked on the glass. "Put those on."

She smiled. "One for the road, huh? You're on." Turning, she slinked back to the table. With deliberate exaggeration, she bent over, giving him an unobstructed view of the contours of her ass. Looking over her shoulder at him, she stood up with the handcuffs dangling from one finger. "Are we going into the bedroom, or do you want to take me right here?"

"I wouldn't put my dick in you again if you were the last woman on Earth."

She allowed the handcuffs to slip from her finger, and they clattered on the carpet. "That's what you think, boyfriend. You'll do anything I tell you to."

Edgar heard his heart beat in his chest.

What the hell?

No, not his heartbeat and not in his chest. Drumbeats in his head. What had Jake said about hearing them? "I'm not your puppet. You can't whip me."

"You think? Stick that gun in your mouth."

"Go to hell."

No longer smiling, she burrowed her eyes into his. "Do it."

Edgar's arm bent at the elbow, aiming his Glock at the ceiling. Then he raised his elbow to the level of his shoulder.

I didn't do that!

His forearm shook as he resisted whatever force commanded his body, his muscles aching. Sweat formed on his brow from the strain. The gun inched closer to his face. Using his left hand, he seized the wrist of his gun hand and tried to push it away. Unfortunately, he was right-handed. Staring down the Glock's barrel, he felt the muscles in his face twitch and jump. Releasing his wrist, he grabbed for the gun and tried to wrest it free from his other hand. No good: his right hand would not relinquish its hold on the weapon, which kissed his lips.

"Open your mouth," Dawn said.

Glancing at her with bulging eyes, Edgar felt panic as his mouth opened through no effort of his own.

"Good boy."

He felt the metal scraping over his teeth, the barrel pressing against the roof of his mouth.

"Now get down on your knees."

He sank to his knees on the carpet, praying the impact would not trigger the gun.

Dawn moved closer to him, a hungry look in her eyes, and he experienced a rare emotion: naked fear. She caressed his cheek with one hand. "Do you see how easily I can control you? Just as easily as I do Malachai and my zonbies. It would be so easy to make you kill yourself but not so easy to explain how a dead cop got in my living room. Multiple identities or not, between Jake and Maria, I have no doubt I'd have to leave the city, and I've worked too hard to make it mine. So I'm going to let you live, darling."

Edgar gagged on his gun.

Dawn inhaled deeply. "Smell that fragrance. Change is in the air."

Pitching forward, Edgar supported himself on his left hand. With his gun still jammed in his mouth, he choked back vomit.

Jake pulled over to the corner of 104th Street, half a block behind Edgar's

Plymouth. Across the street from Katrina's building, the skeletal structure of the unfinished skyscraper rose into the night. He had returned to Caribbean first but had not seen Edgar or any of Malachai's crew. He queried the bouncer and the box office woman, but they just shrugged. Either they didn't remember seeing Edgar, or they did not want to give him up to Jake. Reaching for the car door handle, he froze. A woman exited the condominium.

Katrina.

She took her time, walking with great poise and confidence. Jake waited to see if Edgar would emerge from somewhere in the darkness and confront her. Instead, Katrina circled the front of Edgar's car and stopped at the driver's-side door.

Jake ducked behind the wheel just as she looked in his direction. His heart thundered in his chest, and he reached for his pistol grip. Then she aimed a remote control at the car, and its lights flickered on with an electronic chirp. She opened the door and got in, and a few moments later, he heard the engine rev up. Katrina drove away, and he did not know whether to follow her or search for Edgar.

Damn it all to hell!

He leapt out of the Monte Carlo and locked it with his remote control as he raced to the building. Inside, he ran his finger down the names in the directory until he found Du Pre, D beside 5-C. Then he slipped on his wraparound shades, threw open the inside door, and ran toward the doorman's station. A man with an alarmed expression got to his feet.

"Hey, did you see that broad who just left here?"

The doorman raised his eyebrows. "Yeah . . ."

"She just fell down getting into a cab and broke her ankle on the sidewalk! She sent me in here to get you."

"Oh, God . . ." The doorman raced around his station.

"Come on. Hurry!" Jumping in place, Jake beckoned the man forward. The doorman ran past him, and Jake watched him go outside. Then Jake ran to the elevator and pressed the call button. The door opened immediately because Katrina had just gotten off it.

As he boarded the elevator, the doorman ran back into the lobby, a flustered look on his face. "Hey!"

Jake thumbed the button for the sixth floor as the doorman sprinted for the elevator. The door closed, and he heard the man slam into the door. On the sixth floor, he ran down a carpeted hallway, searching for the emergency exit. Then he took the gray stairs two at a time down one floor. As he closed his hand around the knob, he prayed the door would open. It did, and he ran full speed down the hallway to Katrina's apartment.

The door was locked. He rang the buzzer and pounded on the door. Stepping back, he aimed a powerful kick at the door's lock. A powerful shock wave reverberated through his heel all the way up to his empty eye socket, but the door did not open. He tried again, harder this time despite the pain, and the door burst open.

Staggering inside, he whipped off his sunglasses and drew his Glock, even though Katrina had already left. He closed the broken door and inhaled a sweet scent. Sweeping the perimeter, he entered the living room and saw men's clothing on the floor. He recognized the slacks and jacket as Edgar's. But something was wrong: the clothes were arranged facedown, as if Edgar had collapsed on the floor and vanished, his gun near his empty sleeve.

"Edgar?"

Jake checked the bedroom and bathroom, both empty. Returning to the living room, he kneeled before the table and squinted at the burning candle. A single black feather lay on the table's surface. He picked it up and inspected it. Just an ordinary bird feather but something that could be used in some vodou ritual. Setting it down, he blew out the candle's flame. Then he noticed a business card tucked into the candle holder. Plucking it out with two fingers, he saw it was his own card, which he had given to Katrina—Dawn—the night he met her. Without thinking about it, he pocketed the card.

Then he heard a deep croaking sound.

Jerking his head toward the floor, he saw a shape moving beneath Edgar's blazer. He rose, aiming the Glock at the great lump working its way toward the shirt collar beneath the jacket. It appeared to be the length of a cat, but its movements were all wrong for a four-legged animal. Crouching low, he reached forward with tentative fingers and yanked the collar and jacket away.

The black eyes of a raven stared back at him.

Oh, Jesus Christ.

TWENTY-FOUR

Jake looked at the raven in disbelief. *Edgar?*

His mind reeled. *No, oh, God, no . . .*

The raven blinked and quivered.

It's in shock. "Oh, Edgar . . ."

He pulled the shirt down, covering the bird, then gently gathered Edgar's clothes in his arms.

The raven made a low croaking sound.

Jake holstered his Glock and retrieved Edgar's gun, which he jammed into the folds of the bunched-up blazer. Stepping toward the door, he turned back and ran to the table, then snatched the feather. He raced out of the apartment to the stairwell and managed to open the door.

Only four floors to go, he thought, descending the stairs.

Inside the clothing, the raven croaked again.

Not a bird. Edgar. Somehow that bitch turned him into a fucking raven!

He felt the raven trembling in his arms and hoped it would not die of fright or shock. He did not run down the stairs for fear of slipping and crushing his precious cargo.

Oh, God, oh, God, oh, God.

One minute later, he peered out the door leading into the lobby just as the doorman escorted two uniformed police officers to the elevator.

Observe and report.

As soon as he heard the elevator door close, Jake slipped on his wraparound shades. He swung the door open with his foot and hurried into the lobby.

"Holy shit!" the doorman said.

Jake ignored the doorman, who looked at the elevator for support, then tried to head Jake off.

"Hey, what the hell do you have there?"

Jake pulled Edgar's Glock free of the blazer. "Do yourself a favor: be smart and stay the fuck out of my way."

The doorman's eyes widened, and he raised his hands in a placating gesture. "Okay, okay. Whatever you say. The cops are on their way to the sixth floor. Hurry up and leave before they come down, so there won't be any trouble."

Jake turned and ran for the door, concealing Edgar's gun again. Outside, he hurried to the Monte Carlo. He unlocked the doors and laid the bundle of clothing in the backseat.

"Just don't peck my eye out if you get loose," he said, closing the door. Then he ran around to the front of the car, hopped behind the wheel, and keyed the ignition.

Leaving the horrors of New York behind, Jake drove to New Jersey and checked into a Motel 6. After locking the motel room's door, he unfolded Edgar's clothes over the desk, allowing the raven a modicum of freedom. The bird was enormous: two feet in length from beak to shiny black tail feathers. It darted away from him on its claws, flapping its wings in protest.

He doesn't know how to fly, Jake thought. *Good. That will make it easier to bundle him up in the morning.*

He didn't know what birds ate, and since he had no intention of running out to a store this late, it didn't matter. Reaching into his pocket, he pulled out the candy bar he had bought in the motel office. Tearing the wrapper open, he twisted the candy bar in two. He took a bite out of one half, then broke the other half into little bits of chocolate and caramel and nuts and sprinkled them over the desktop. "What's mine is yours."

The raven pecked at the crumbs.

He filled the bathroom sink with water and left the door open.

With the lights on, he climbed into bed and fell asleep with a loaded Glock in each hand.

In the middle of the night, Jake felt something sharp digging into his chest. Springing awake, he sat up, the startled raven flapping its wings in a flurry of frantic motion as it descended to the floor.

Oh, Jesus, he thought.

It had been looking right at him. What was it thinking? Was it capable of human thought? Did it have Edgar's memories?

Lying back on the bed, he closed his eyes.

While I pondered, weak and dreary . . .

The next morning, Jake left Edgar inside the car while he went into a gigantic pet store to shop for necessities. The bird seemed to have grown accustomed to his presence, and Jake supposed it had retained at least some vestigial memories of their friendship. He located a large, circular cage with a cover, bird feed, and a water bottle that clipped onto the cage's side.

On his way out of the store, he felt his leg vibrating. With his free hand, he took out his cell phone and was not surprised to see Detective Vasquez flashing on the display. Squeezing the phone between his head and shoulder, he also took out his remote control and unlocked the car doors from a distance.

"Hi, Maria." He tried to feign blissful ignorance.

"Jake, do you know where Edgar is?"

"No. What's up?"

"He was supposed to clock in two hours ago, and he's not here. Nobody's heard from him, and he doesn't answer his cell phone."

In truth, Jake had turned Edgar's phone off earlier this morning because Maria wouldn't stop calling. He found her loyalty touching, but he needed to concentrate on his own crises. "I haven't seen him since you guys visited me in the hospital. But I'm sure he's okay. Try not to worry, and have him give me a call when he shows up."

"Okay. Thanks."

Opening the driver's-side door, he peered in at the giant black bird on the backseat. He tossed the bag of supplies onto the passenger seat, climbed in, and said, "You hear that? They miss you at work."

Then he started the engine and headed back to Manhattan.

Jake parked in his regular garage a block away from his building on Twenty-second Street. Carrying the covered birdcage in one hand, its base almost scraping the concrete, he scanned the crowded sidewalk for any signs of danger. So many New Yorkers walked to work to save money now that his eye barely absorbed the faces and clothes around him.

A scarecrow with bulging eyes cut a swath through the crowd, homing in on him. "I'll carry that for you for a dollah," he said.

Jake gave the man a hard look that sent him scampering for another mark. An uneasy feeling gripped his stomach as he neared his building. *The perfect place for an ambush.*

Passing the building's entrance, he entered Laurel's parlor and saw her sitting at the round table, surrounded not by tarot cards and a crystal ball but facing a laptop and an old-fashioned adding machine.

"I hope you're not planning to point a gun at me again."

"Not today." He set the birdcage on top of the table and pulled back the cover. "Meet my partner—*ex*-partner—Detective Edgar Hopkins of the Special Homicide Task Force, currently assigned to the Black Magic Task Force."

Laurel studied Edgar's eyes and beak. "I assume this isn't the feathered version of a K-9 dog?"

Jake shook his head. "Until last night, Edgar was as human as you or me. It turns out he was closer to the bokor behind these zonbies than either he or I realized. She did this to him. Her birth name is Ramera Evans, but she also goes by Dawn Du Pre and Katrina. Do any of those names mean anything to you?"

Still staring at the raven, Laurel said, "I'm afraid not."

Jake reached into his pocket and took out the black feather he had snatched from Katrina's table. "I found this in the same room as the bird next to a burning candle and Edgar's empty clothes."

Now she looked up. "What color was the candle?"

"Purple."

"What did it smell like?"

"I don't really remember. Pungent, I guess. I blew out the flame." He sat down in the chair opposite her, the birdcage between them. "She had this, too." He slid his business card across the table. "I gave it to her myself."

Laurel picked up the card and turned it over in one hand without looking at it. "This is what she used to curse you. To a true bokor, a business card is the modern equivalent of a voodoo doll. It's a representation of you. Just a little bit of oil from your fingertips would make this an ideal transmitter for a curse."

Son of a bitch, Jake thought. When would he learn to stay away from corporate totems?

"She probably had something similar that belonged to your friend here."

"They were sleeping together." He couldn't bring himself to call them lovers.

"A hair, probably. Something with his genetic code."

That old DNA devil . . .

"I'll tell you this much: she didn't want either of you dead, or she would have killed both of you. She's that powerful."

"How powerful are *you*? Can you make him like he was?"

She looked into his eyes. "I'm sorry. Only the witch who cast this spell can reverse it. I wouldn't even know where to start. I've never seen an actual case of transmogrification before."

Great. "So I need to kill her to stop the zonbies, but I need her alive to make Edgar normal again?"

Laurel nodded.

"I guess my agenda is set, then."

"How will you convince her to reverse the spell?"

"I'm not sure, but I can be pretty persuasive when I need to be. Listen, I know I have brass balls, but can you watch him for a few days while I do what needs to be done?" He nodded at the raven. "I can't take him with me, and you're the only one who knows his situation. I can't . . . trust anyone else."

"Of course. Eventually you'll need to take him to this Katrina."

"I know." Jake stood. "Thank you." He wiggled one finger between the cage's thin metal bars. "Be good, Edgar. Stay away from any more bad women." He crossed the parlor to the stairs, then turned back. "There's always the possibility that I won't be back."

"I understand. Take care of yourself."

Nodding, he left them alone.

In his suite, Jake pulled out two large bags from his closet, one of them a long Army duffel bag. He packed a week's worth of clothing and other supplies, including all the guns and ammunition he owned.

As he left the building, he glanced up at the Tower a block away. It no longer seemed like the sole symbol of supernatural evil in New York City.

Walking back to the garage, he processed the information Laurel had provided him. *Why doesn't Katrina want me or Edgar dead? She certainly didn't show Gary Brown and Frank Beck any mercy. Does this mean that the zonbies who chased me over the Brooklyn Bridge acted independently of her? What about the hit squad that broke into the building later that night?*

Loading his arsenal into the Monte Carlo's trunk, he formulated a plan of attack. He needed to buy some additional supplies, and then he intended to find a place to park the car and rest until sunset.

Jake decided to start on Montclair Street, near Flatbush Avenue, because that was where this colossal mess had started for him. Killing the car's headlights, he parked with the corner of Caton in sight. Three fresh faces had replaced Louis and his partners in undead crime. Well, not *fresh* faces, exactly. Two young African American men and a Chinese girl in her late teens. All three wore hoodies and stood as still as statues when not serving customers. Scarecrows skulked the sidewalks, made their buys, then melted into the shadows. No other people dared to walk the street.

An entire neighborhood destroyed by Black Magic, Jake thought.

The prostitute he had seen twice before rounded the corner. When she did not beg the zonbies for drugs, he knew that she had crossed over. She circled the block, her bones sliding beneath her skin, and Jake supposed she had been "promoted" to lookout status. The second time around, she made a beeline in his direction.

Keep walking, you skank.

But she walked right up to his window. With no other choice, he lowered the window. She set her skeletal hands atop the door and leaned forward, staring at him with bulging eyes and running her purplish gray tongue over cracked lips.

Jake wanted to vomit. Easing his Glock off the seat beside him, he said, "Suck on this," and blew her soul out the back of her head. Even with the silencer affixed to the gun, the muzzle flash blinded him for a moment, and he did not see her strike the lopsided sidewalk.

The zonbies on the corner turned their heads toward him in unison, so he threw the car into gear and floored the gas. The Monte Carlo lurched forward. He waited until he was closer to the curb, then switched on his high beams, blinding the dead things. Their faces appeared like skulls in the intense white light.

Stopping just shy of the curb, Jake jumped out of the car and pulled the scoped Remington from the cradle he had created for it between the front seats. Standing behind the car for cover, he aimed the sleek black rifle at the farthest corner boy and squeezed the trigger. A bullet hole appeared in his head, and he fell backwards to the sidewalk. A moment later, his soul rose and faded.

The other man and the Chinese girl drew their handguns at the same time. Jake took out the man, but the girl surprised him by charging around the car at him, her pistol leading her like a heat-seeking missile.

Jake's heart thumped in his chest. He didn't have time to aim the cumbersome rifle at her, so he waited until she was almost on top of him, and then he slammed the rifle's butt into her face, smashing bone and cartilage. Her legs flew out from under her, and she crashed to the asphalt. Stepping on the wrist of her gun hand, Jake aimed the rifle at her with calm precision and fired a round through her forehead, blowing brain slime out the back of her head. She stopped moving, and her soul flickered up and faded.

Without missing a beat, Jake scooped up her pistol and tossed the Remington into the car and popped the trunk. He threw her handgun into the trunk, then collected those of her companions as well. He had already decided not to use Edgar's Glock, so as not to implicate him in any of this, so the more firepower he obtained the better.

He removed two glass liquor bottles filled with gasoline and dish detergent from the trunk, which he closed, and set the bottles on top of it. As he lit the cloth fuse on the first bottle, the black SUV that had chased him over the Brooklyn Bridge raced around the corner, its tires screeching. Touching the unlit fuse to the one already burning, he walked into the street and spread his arms wide.

The SUV bore down on him, and he hurled the first Molotov cocktail at the oncoming vehicle's windshield. The bottle shattered and splattered the chemical mixture across the glass, and an instant later, blue flames danced across the windshield. The SUV stopped beside him, and he threw the second cocktail through the rolled-down window before the zonbies inside could fire their automatic weapons. The chemicals ignited, transforming the interior into an incendiary hell. Fire consumed the occupants, which continued to move without making a sound. Two of them fired their AK-47s, and Jake ducked behind the SUV's hatch as the Monte Carlo's windows exploded across the sidewalk.

Hearing one of the SUV's doors open, he ran around the vehicle, crouching low to the ground, and came up behind a zombie staggering around in a ball of fire. Presumably blinded by fire, the zombie fired his AK-47 in random blasts. As Jake approached the burning figure, he felt intense heat on his back from the vehicle burning beside him and on his face from the zombie hunting for him. Aiming his Glock at the smoldering and blackened head, he squeezed the trigger, and the zombie pitched forward to the asphalt.

Maneuvering around the crackling flames, Jake kicked the AK-47 aside. He didn't bother to watch the dead thing's soul rise through the blue flames. Facing the SUV, he saw that the figures inside had stopped moving. He knew he could not free their souls; hopefully the fire would accomplish that.

Turning back to his car, he glimpsed the fires reflected in the darkened windows of abandoned buildings. Then he discerned silhouettes separating from shadowed doorways and alleys. Half a dozen figures crawled out of the darkness on their hands and knees, their desperate countenances ghostly in the firelight. They did not care about the twin bonfires or the man in their midst holding a machine gun. They only cared about taking free Black Magic off the corpses on the ground.

Seven down, Jake thought. *But these six look half dead already. They probably will be dead by sunrise, and then they'll rise again.* He felt tempted to shoot them now and spare himself a return trip, but he couldn't kill them in cold blood. *I'll do that when* their *blood is cold.*

He got into his damaged car, popped four Tylenols, and drove back to Manhattan.

It's going to be a long night.

Jake circled the Polo Grounds twice before parking in an illegal spot with a clear view of zonbies dealing Black Magic from a park bench located between two enormous housing projects. He saw no police and knew that the housing cops could not contend with the level of crime occurring now. Scores of scarecrows traversed the walkways. Jake didn't see a single healthy human being in the vicinity.

Leaving his car, he penetrated the parkway, scanning the haunted faces around him. Once upon a time, his white features would have elicited automatic suspicion among junkies and dealers alike, but neither zonbies nor scarecrows paid any attention to him now.

A line of scarecrows twenty deep extended from the park bench. Three zonbies sat on the bench, the one in the middle sitting high on its back. He seemed to be the supervisor. The zonbie on his left collected cash, and the one on his right dispensed packets of Black Magic.

Jake walked straight to the bench and drew his Glock.

"Hey, get back on line!" a woman with a strangled voice said behind him.

The zonbies stared at him with dead eyes.

Jake fired a round into the supervisor's head at point-blank range. The kid fell backwards off the bench, and his soul rose. Jake shot the second zonbie in the head as the third drew his own Glock. Jake swung his Glock in that zonbie's direction and fired first. The zonbie's head absorbed the hit, and he fired a shot into the crowd behind Jake.

Someone screamed as the scarecrows scattered in all directions.

With his Glock held loosely at his side, Jake returned to his car. He heard the scarecrows stampeding to the corpses he had left on the ground.

Three down with twenty soon to replace them, he thought. *I need to kill Katrina fast.*

His cell phone rang as he got into the car. Checking the display, he took the call. "Hi, Maria. What's new?"

"Edgar's been missing for twenty-four hours now, so Missing Persons is taking over the case. I'm being shut out. The only way I'm allowed to help is from my desk. Can you believe that shit?"

He started the engine. "Has anyone spoken to Joyce?"

"Yeah, she and Martin are worried sick. Everyone knows this isn't like Edgar."

He pulled into traffic. "What can I do to help?"

"Well, you're a PI, right? You must know a thing or two about finding missing people." She lowered her voice. "And you're a free agent, so the department can't interfere with your operation."

"I'll do everything possible to help you find him," he said as he sped through a red light.

Jake drove downtown to Battery Park located on the southern tip of Manhattan. He saw a crowd gathered near the waterfront, mostly white people in casual attire.

Yuppie scarecrows, he thought as he pulled over to the curb. *Black Magic doesn't discriminate.*

He got out of the car with the AK-47 held in both hands, and as he approached the crowd, he raised it over his head and fired a burst into the air that sent panic-stricken scarecrows scattering. He approached the trio of white-faced zonbies with his machine gun lowered.

With their baseball caps backwards on their heads, they stared at him with dull, lifeless eyes. One pulled a revolver from his waistband, and Jake blasted all three of them, strafing their chests. As their bodies jerked on the ground, sawdust pouring out of their wounds, Jake fired a short burst into each of their heads, decimating them. He continued to fire until the AK-47 made a clicking sound.

The zonbies stopped moving, and Jake returned to the car, where he checked the luminous clock.

Almost midnight. Plenty of time to make more stops.

TWENTY-FIVE

Peering through her Toyota's windshield, Maria approached the caravan of RMP cars, unmarked detective units, and other assorted emergency response vehicles with a growing sense of unease. Multicolored strobe lights illuminated the Grant Street neighborhood like a rock concert, silhouetting the uniformed POs who stood interspersed along the yellow tape that surrounded the crime scene.

As the last detective called in, she had to park almost a block away, and she checked her hair and makeup before getting out. Ordinarily she didn't worry about such things, but ordinarily she wasn't awakened by a phone call from Night Watch Command in the middle of the night ordering her to a triple homicide site. Answering the call, she had feared that Edgar's body had turned up somewhere and felt relieved to learn that three hoppers had been killed instead. Without time for a shower, she had pulled her curly hair into a ponytail and dressed in jeans and a short-sleeved sweater.

As she followed the sidewalk to the crime scene, she saw light blue breaking up the gray sky and sunlight outlining the brick-faced apartment buildings on either side of the street.

Nothing like a little dawn to show the city's garbage, she thought, wondering when the sanitation workers' strike would end. She flashed her gold shield at a sleepy-eyed PO and ducked beneath the crime scene tape.

"The cavalry has arrived," Bernie Reinhardt said, holding a Styrofoam cup of coffee in one hand. His eyelids drooped as much as his blond mustache.

"You're the primary?" Maria said.

"Thanks for the vote of confidence. The department's suffering an extreme shortage of murder police tonight. Since I'm on your Black Magic Task Force, they pressed me into service until you could get here."

Maria looked at the Crime Scene Unit members photographing three corpses on the sidewalk. Teenage boys, from the looks of them. "Why the shortage?"

"There were seven similar incidents tonight in Manhattan and Brooklyn. Someone's finally declared war on whoever's running Black Magic."

"A rival gang?"

Bernie nodded. "Twenty-four stiffs in groups of three. With our current manpower shortage, the bosses are looking at a hell of a lot of OT."

"Maybe this is payback for our Machete Massacres."

"I'd hazard a guess Prince Malachai is learning that leadership is overrated right about now. Come on. I've got something to show your expert eyes."

He led her over to the nearest corpse, a sixteen-year-old boy with cornrows tight to his scalp. A bullet hole in the center of his forehead resembled a third eye.

"Look at his hands."

Crouching low to the ground, Maria studied the boy's gun hand. All his fingers lacked third joints, and their ends had been sewn shut with black thread. She looked at the other hand and saw the same thing.

Bernie crouched beside her. With the pointer finger and thumb of his free hand, he separated the dead boy's cracked lips, revealing mangled gray gums. "No fingertips, no teeth, no identification. Same thing with the other two and all the bodies at the other crime scenes."

Maria looked at Bernie in disbelief, then took out a pair of latex gloves, snapped them on, and duckwalked to the corpse's feet. Seizing the ankle of one leg, she pulled off the sneaker and sock covering the boy's foot and recoiled. *No toes, either!* Leaving the sock and shoe beside the foot, she rose.

"Someone went to a hell of a lot of trouble to make it hard for us to identify these guys," Bernie said.

"There's no blood. If the killers messed with these corpses after killing the vics, they did it somewhere else and dumped them here."

"This is a known drug corner. Odds are these kids worked it. If your theory is right, they were abducted, executed, mutilated, and returned here. Why go through all that trouble? Why not just kill them and run?"

"To send a message."

"Okay, I'll give you that. But why sew the ends of their finger stubs?"

Maria shuddered despite the rising sun. "What kind of monsters are we dealing with?" *And what the hell happened to Edgar?*

As Malachai walked through the abandoned Long Island City factory, Marcus felt the walls closing in on them. They had come so far in the last year since Mal had hooked up with Katrina, and now, just when they had reached the pinnacle, they stood to lose everything, all because of one man. Corpses littered the industrial floor, each with at least one bullet hole in its head. Another dozen bodies lay unmoving upon the tables set up near the furnace. Worse, the packing area for the drugs was empty.

"How many?" Malachai said.

Marcus did not like giving his boss bad news. "Twenty-four here, another thirty between eight of our spots in Manhattan and Brooklyn. We got hit hard. He's dismantling our entire operation."

Forty-five stood watch in the doorway behind them, his arms folded across his man boobs.

"How much Magic did he get?"

"At least twenty bricks." He saw the anger building in Malachai's face. It showed in his eyes and in the way he kept drawing in his lips.

"How the hell did he find this location?"

"He probably waited until sunrise, then followed some of our dealers back here. Papa Joe would have done the same thing if he'd figured out what our workers are. I told you, we need to house those things in a separate area, keep the factory workers and the sellers separate, just like in the old days."

"Damn it!" Malachai kicked over a stainless steel cart used to transport the kilos of Black Magic. "Okay, first things first. You need to find us a new location, so we can set up shop. Look for something in Brooklyn this time, somewhere around Prospect Avenue. Make sure you find a secondary location nearby where these things can go at the end of the night. I'm going to have Katrina send every fucking zonbie we have after Helman. He has to go down today."

Marcus blinked at his commander. "You mean in *daylight*?"

"That's right. Helman probably thinks he's safe in the daytime. We're going to keep him on his toes 24-7. Sooner or later, he'll fuck up, and then he's ours. I think I'll turn him onto a little Magic, then flay him alive. Let him walk around without his skin and his soul screaming for help in a skull full of mush."

"But other people will see our"—he hated using the word—"*slaves* for what they really are."

"I don't care." Malachai's lower lip quivered with anger. "I want Helman dead."

Marcus couldn't believe what he was hearing. The zonbies were supposed to be their dirty secret. Look what had already happened in the Polo Grounds. "This will be bad for business. Can't Katrina just do him like she did those two cops?"

"Nah, she can't reach him. Some 'psychic interference' bullshit I don't understand."

"Then let's do this thing ourselves. Helman dropped so many of those things that the city's meat wagon picked a bunch of them up before we could." He had hoped for a better opportunity to release that piece of information.

Malachai snorted like a bull, and Marcus anticipated another outburst. "When it rains it motherfucking pours, doesn't it? The cops won't know what to make of those bodies, even when they cut them open."

"You send those things out into the daylight, where people can see them, and they'll figure it out. You'll destroy everything we've got faster than Helman can."

Malachai opened and closed his fists. Marcus knew he needed to hit something. *Someone.* Instead, he unleashed a primal scream.

Marcus lowered his voice. "I think we need to lay low with this supernatural shit. It's getting out of control. We've already wiped out the competition, so let's go back to selling what we used to: coke, heroin, crack. Put this Black Magic on the back burner." He had to be careful suggesting a course of action that contradicted Katrina's plans.

"He's right," Katrina said.

Marcus flinched. *Oh, shit.* He turned to see Katrina gliding past Forty-five in a short lime green dress that hugged her curves and showed off her long legs. *I am?* He couldn't recall her ever agreeing with his advice.

"I thought I told you to wait in the car," Malachai said.

Marcus liked that Malachai believed he was in charge of Katrina. It struck him as humorous that his boss didn't even realize he was pussy whipped.

"I wanted to see the damage for myself," Katrina said with no rebuttal from Malachai as she looked around the abandoned factory.

"Those things need to fight better," Malachai said.

"It's not that easy. I can program them all with general reactions, but if you want me to actually pull their strings, I can only do it one at a time." She cast a sideways glance at Marcus, who felt a chill run down his spine. "With the other drug operations out of business, we need to expand our horizons. It's time to start selling the more traditional products again. Put people on the street in the daytime, pushing the old-school shit, and let the zombies own the night."

Marcus saw what Katrina was doing. She wasn't looking to curb the use of voodoo in their organization; she just wanted more money. She had only pretended to go along with his suggestion to appear cooperative. *Think of something else . . .*

"People cost money," Malachai said. "People can give us up to the cops. People try to take down the boss. That's what you told me when you sold me on this shit in the first place, and you were right."

Katrina stepped closer to Malachai.

Work your magic, lady, Marcus thought.

"My strategy worked. You're the power in this city now, not Papa Joe. But we need to diversify. It makes sense economically, and by owning the entire drug market, you'll keep our enemies from rebuilding their operations. A wider variety of drugs will also keep the cops from concentrating solely on Black Magic, and the longer we keep that on the down low the better."

Marcus saw the wheels in Malachai's brain turning. A smile spread across his boss's lips. *I knew it.* When it came to Katrina, Malachai had become predictable, a true weakness.

Malachai stroked Katrina's long hair. "I like it. But what about Helman? We can't let him continue to cut us off at the knees."

Katrina smiled. "Don't worry. I have plans for Helman."

Maria and Bernie sat facing Lieutenant Mauceri in his glass-faced office in the Detective Bureau Manhattan on East Twenty-first Street. Maria sipped orange juice through a straw while Bernie worked on another coffee. Wearing a wrinkled vest, Mauceri had rolled up his sleeves.

You're doing a heckuva job, L.T., Maria thought, still resenting that she had been excluded from the investigation into Edgar's disappearance.

"Cards on the table," Mauceri said. "We got thirty DOAs in three boroughs, and there's no question they're linked. Each stiff was mutilated in an identical manner. Since the vics all appear to have been hoppers, this points to the biggest drug war this city's ever seen. And since the head of the Black Magic Task Force is MIA and this department is operating with a skeleton crew, the chief of detectives has authorized me to absorb what's left of BMTF into Homicide. Welcome aboard, Reinhardt. For the time being, you're murder police."

"Do I have any say in this?" Bernie said.

"None at all."

"In that case, I'm happy to be here."

"You'll liaison with Gang Prevention. This is their mess as much as it is ours." Mauceri pointed at them. "It only makes sense to partner you two up."

"I already have a partner," Maria said in an arch tone. "No offense, Bernie."

Bernie sipped his coffee, "None taken."

Mauceri kept his cool. "I don't see your partner anywhere, Vasquez. Produce him."

"Assign me to assist Missing Persons, and I will."

"Not happening. I need you here, and I'm not letting go of you. And if you have any notion of conducting a personal investigation on your own time, forget it. There's no room in your life for any other cases. Since you and Reinhardt are the only BMTF members still around, I'm making you jointly responsible for all these murders. That's thirty names in the Green Book."

Maria's eyes widened. "L.T., you can't do that!"

"Can't I? I just did. The primaries for each set of three murders will do the legwork on their respective cases, but they're answering to you. This whole bag of shit is yours."

"I'm too inexperienced. I'm a third grade gold shield . . ."

"Bullshit. Edgar mentored you for a year, and he's the best we've got, God help him. You're no rookie, and fortunately for you, Reinhardt's a seasoned pro. Aren't you, Reinhardt?"

Bernie pushed his glasses up the bridge of his nose. "I'm a seasoned pro."

"For now, you'll work out of Detective Hopkins's desk."

For the first time, Bernie's expression registered emotion as he glanced at Maria with something akin to terror in his eyes.

"Now both of you get over to the ME's office. I understand Walsh has some eye-opening information for you."

Maria stood, and Bernie did the same. She opened her mouth to speak. But Mauceri waved her on. "Run along. I've got to requisition uniforms and plainclothes cops to help out with this workload."

Maria led Bernie to Edgar's desk in the bull pen.

"I'm sorry about this, Maria."

"Don't be. It's not your fault. Just do me a favor." She gestured at a framed photo of Edgar and Martin. "Leave his stuff up. You're going back to Gang Prevention when this is over anyway."

"No problem. I only need the back of a chair for my jacket and one drawer for my lunch and gun."

"Thanks. Shall we go?"

He offered a slight smile. "Lead the way."

Jake laid a bouquet of lilies on Sheryl's grave in the cemetery off the LIE.

Maybe for the last time, he thought, gazing at Sheryl's marker.

He had checked into a fleabag hotel with an hourly rate and slept for three hours. Standing before the bathroom mirror, he stared at his closed left eyelid. The swollen muscles behind it made it appear as if his eye was still there. Then he forced himself to pull his lower lid out and apply the flush and healing ointment. After checking out of the hotel, he went to a pharmacy and bought his first eye patch, which he now wore.

Looking around the cemetery to make certain no one stood within listening range, he spoke in a low and tentative voice. "I could use some help, babe. Edgar was the only one I've been able to turn to since . . .

the Cipher, and now he's gone. I have to save him just like I did you, and I don't think I can do it alone."

Taking a deep breath, he waited for a reaction.

The clouds in the sky did not part. A shaft of golden sunlight did not fall upon him. No choir of angels sang. The gentle breeze that blew his hair into his eye remained consistent.

Jake sighed. Abel had warned him that he would never see Sheryl again unless he ascended to the Realm of Light, a situation that became more in doubt whenever he killed a living person, even in self-defense.

Fuck you, AK.

"What about you, Abel? You didn't exactly rule out another meeting between us. I'm freeing souls, just like before. What makes this any different than last time? Tower had thirteen souls. Katrina has hundreds."

Nothing.

Jake supposed the souls of drug addicts didn't rate very high on heaven's list of priorities.

"You owe me!"

No response.

Alone as usual, he thought. Then his cell phone vibrated in his pocket, and he checked its display. *Just the call I've been expecting.* Pressing the phone against one ear, he gazed across the cemetery at the Manhattan skyline in the distance. "Yeah, talk to me."

The silence on the other end seemed interminable. "I want my drugs."

"Sorry. You have the wrong number. I'm no drug dealer. You must want some lowlife, murderous scumbag."

The breathing on the other end grew louder. "I want *my* drugs, cracker."

"Oh, you mean those twenty keys of Black Magic? Be more specific, sport."

The breathing on the other end came in short, angry bursts. "When can we meet?"

"As it happens, I'm free for lunch. What do you say we meet someplace public?"

A pause. "Name the time and place."

Jake had just the place in mind.

Maria and Bernie walked down the long corridor on the fourth floor of the City of New York Office of Medical Examiner.

"I need a shower," Maria said.

"That makes two of us." Bernie pushed open the swinging door leading into Autopsy Room C and followed her inside.

Assistant Medical Examiner Samuel Walsh stood in the middle of the room, poised to cut into the skull of a male corpse with a bone saw. A dozen metal autopsy tables surrounded him, each home to a corpse. A young woman in a smock and face mask assisted him.

"I've never seen it so crowded in here," Maria said.

"Standing room only," Bernie said.

Walsh turned at the sound of their voices and killed the bone saw. "Ah, the cavalry has arrived." He handed the bone saw to the woman. "Why don't you take a break, Janet?"

"Thanks," the woman said, nodding. As she passed Maria and Bernie, she removed her face mask, revealing tired features.

"You're not the only ones feeling the budget crunch," Walsh said, joining them. "We're shorthanded and overworked, too."

Maria looked around at the corpses, most of them male. All of them had mutilated stumps rather than toes, with identification tags strapped around their ankles. "Business is booming."

"Death is a growth market. These are all yours. There's more in Room B and Room D . . ."

Bernie walked over to a table and pointed at the gray corpse upon it. "*This* just came in last night?"

"Actually, it came in just a few hours ago."

Bernie gestured at the Y incision that divided the dead man's torso. "And you already autopsied it? Wham, bam, thank you, Sam."

Walsh smiled. "As much as I like to believe that I'm a model of efficiency, I can't take credit for that. It came in self-autopsied. Or, rather, self-*embalmed*. They all did."

Maria gaped at the dead bodies. Every one of them had a Y incision. "What the hell are you talking about?"

Walsh motioned for them to follow him over to the table occupied by the corpse he and his assistant had been working on. The body's chest had been peeled back in three sections of flesh, revealing a dry rib cage.

"These bodies have no blood. Their organs were removed and soaked in a cleansing solution, which makes it all but impossible for us to determine the causes of death, then returned to their proper arrangement. The bodies were packed with sawdust, which acts as a fill-in agent, and sewn back up. I'd hazard a guess that the fingers, toes, and gums were mutilated at the same time."

Bernie said, "Forgive me for stating the obvious, Doc, but it's pretty apparent to me that there was only one cause of death: a bullet to the brain."

Walsh jabbed the air in a gleeful manner. "You're wrong! They were all shot in the head *after* they were embalmed."

"Fuck you," Maria said. Then she covered her mouth with one hand. "Oh. Sorry. That just slipped out."

"That's okay. You sounded just like Edgar. Sorry to hear the news, by the way."

"Thank you. I'm still pulling for him."

Staring at the bullet hole in the corpse's head, Bernie rubbed his forehead. "Any theory as to why all this occurred?"

Walsh snorted. "That's your job. I'm just telling you what we have on our hands."

"We need to tie these stiffs to Malachai," Maria said. "And then we need to tie Edgar's disappearance to him."

"Why is that?" Bernie said.

"Because if we do, the bosses can't keep me from working Edgar's case."

TWENTY-SIX

Jake sat in the back of Viand, a Greek diner on the corner of Eighty-sixth Street and Second Avenue. He and Sheryl had lunched here often. With his back to the wall, he had a perfect view of the entire restaurant, and no one could sneak up on him.

He ordered lunch, then waited for his dates to arrive. A few minutes later, three men walked parallel to the windows, their backs to him. He recognized Malachai, Marcus, and their fat bodyguard from two nights earlier at Caribbean. The drug dealers approached the diner's entrance and peered inside. Perhaps because they saw the diner's narrow dimensions, Malachai and Marcus left Fat Boy stationed outside the door and entered. They strode between patrons eating at the counter and in the booths opposite it, making their way toward Jake. Jake sipped his half glass of ice water.

"You Helman?" Malachai said.

"That's right." Jake gestured at the seats opposite him.

Marcus sat next to the window, leaving Malachai to sit across from Jake.

"I never met a real private dick before," Malachai said. "You don't look like one."

"You mean I don't look like detectives on TV?"

"Yeah, you know, *Magnum, P.I.* and shit. You're no Tom Selleck."

"I was a lot prettier before one of your scarecrows stabbed me in the eye."

"I don't know anything about that." Malachai turned to Marcus. "You know anything about that?"

Before Marcus could answer, a server set down Jake's lunch: a turkey burger deluxe with melted Swiss cheese, fries, and a Diet Coke with lemon. Flipping open his order book, the server said, "What can I get for you today, gentlemen?"

Watching Jake slap ketchup onto his burger and fries, Malachai said, "We're not hungry."

Marcus handed the server a twenty-dollar bill. The man thanked him and left.

"It's funny," Jake said, biting into his burger, "but you two look *exactly* like drug dealers do on TV."

Malachai's face darkened. "Where's my product?"

"Someplace safe," Jake said, chewing.

"What do you want for it?"

Chewing, Jake considered the question. "I don't know. What's it worth to you? A million dollars?"

"Is that your price?"

"Not necessarily, but it's as good a place as any to start."

"What else you want?"

Jake swallowed. "I want your girlfriend to lift the curse she put on my ex-partner."

Malachai's left eye twitched at the mention of his girlfriend. "This ex-partner of yours a dick, too?"

"No, he's a cop. You two have a lot in common. For one, he's in charge of the Black Magic Task Force."

Malachai turned silent for a moment. "I don't know nothing about no cop. The drugs are mine. You deal with me on that. You want something from my woman, you deal with her. Separate deals."

Jake gulped his soda and set the glass down. "Good, because I flushed your shit down the sewer, where it belongs."

Malachai slapped the table, causing Jake's plate to rattle, then touched Jake's table knife. "I should stab your other eye out."

Jake picked up his burger again. "I think I'm going to get that a lot. Cut the shit, Daryl. You're not going to do anything to me, and neither is your boy here."

Malachai narrowed his eyes. "What makes you so sure?"

"Because Katrina wants me alive for some reason."

"Katrina doesn't call the shots. I do."

"Okay. Whatever you say."

"What kind of curse did she put on your friend?"

"If you don't already know, I'm not saying. He's safer that way."

"Why'd she curse him?"

"I'm not sure. I guess because she was fucking him behind your back, just like she was fucking you behind his, and he learned the truth. She must have wanted him out of the way, but she cared for him too much to kill him like she did Brown and Beck."

With his eyes appearing ready to pop out of his skull, Malachai leapt out of his seat.

As a precautionary measure, Jake dropped his hand to his Glock, hidden inside a newspaper folded on his bench.

Marcus stood and set his hand on Malachai's shoulder. "Not here, not now. Later. Let's just do what we came here to do and get out."

Glowering at Jake, Malachai sat down again, and so did Marcus. Malachai leaned forward and spoke through quivering lips. "You're lying."

"Katrina's real name is Ramera Evans. Edgar knew her as Dawn Du Pre, a publicist." Jake took out a business card on which he had scrawled Dawn's address. "She has a second apartment not far from here on 105th. You can probably see it when you step outside. That's where she fucked Edgar, and that's where she cursed him. See for yourself. She's playing you."

The anger on Malachai's face had gone from a simmer to a boil. Jake waited for the explosion to come.

Marcus leaned over and whispered into Malachai's ear.

Malachai nodded. "Katrina knows what you want from her. Now here's what she wants from you: it's called Afterlife."

Jake's body turned rigid. His mouth fell open, and his throat went dry. He had underestimated Katrina's ambitions. It made sense: she had worked for Old Nick and had withheld some of her research, which was why Afterlife lacked concrete details about voodoo. She had murdered her fellow researchers to protect her secret and had moved to Manhattan sometime after Tower's death, reducing the chances of her activities being discovered. She wanted more than money; she wanted power.

Just like Old Nick.

Malachai grinned at seeing the shocked expression on Jake's face, but Jake doubted the drug kingpin possessed a clue about Afterlife's significance.

Rising again, Malachai tossed a piece of paper onto the table. "Katrina says for you to call that number at 9:00 p.m. sharp, and she'll tell you where to meet us."

Jake glanced at the cell phone number written on the paper.

As Malachai and Marcus stepped into the aisle, Malachai turned back with an insincere smile on his lips. "When I see you again? *With my bare hands.*" He offered a demented grin.

Watching them leave, Jake pocketed the piece of paper.

Afterlife.

He pushed the remainder of his food aside.

Shit.

"Go up Second Avenue," Malachai said from the backseat.

"You got it, chief," Forty-five said.

Marcus turned around in the front seat and looked over his shoulder. "What are we doing?" Like he didn't know.

"Relax," Malachai said. "I just want to check out that building, like the dick said."

"Don't listen to him. He's just trying to get inside your head, throw you off your game."

"It won't take but a couple of minutes, son."

Marcus turned around without say anything, careful that his body language didn't telegraph his disapproval. He knew better.

This is bullshit, he thought. But he had to wonder if Katrina was playing all of them.

"What are we doing here?" Bernie said as he followed Maria into Dawn Du Pre's apartment. The doorman had given her the keys to the apartment when she showed her shield and claimed to be part of the investigation into Edgar's and Dawn's disappearances.

"Dawn Du Pre is Edgar's girlfriend. Edgar signed the ledger downstairs at 2300 hours on the night he disappeared. I know he had his own set of keys, so he had no trouble getting in here. According to Missing Persons, the doorman who worked that night says Dawn came home just a few minutes before Edgar showed up, but Edgar wanted to surprise her. Approximately twenty minutes later, Dawn left. Edgar never did. But a Caucasian male ran into the lobby from outside and claimed Dawn had fallen down and hurt herself. Guess what the doorman found?"

Bernie stood near the door, his hands stuffed in his pockets, making it clear he was just along for the ride. "No sign of Dawn?"

"Don't let anyone ever tell you that you're no detective." Circling the table in the living room, she leaned forward and sniffed a purple candle centered on it. Frowning, she faced her companion. "So the doorman calls 911, and no sooner do they go upstairs than our Caucasian male runs out the emergency exit with what appears to be a bundle of clothes in his arms. The doorman tries to stop him, and the guy pulls a gun on his ass and tells him to step off."

"Was our Unidentified Caucasian Male missing an eye?"

Maria gave him a small smile. "I don't know. He was wearing sunglasses."

"At night?"

"Go figure. After the UCM takes off, the POs discover that someone broke into Dawn's apartment—and Edgar wasn't in here. Somewhere between 2300 and 2400 hours, my partner disappeared from this building. And so did his car."

Bernie glanced at the ceiling. "What are you suggesting?"

"I don't have a clue. But I'm not giving up until I get some answers."

Marcus followed Malachai into the building's vestibule, where Malachai pointed at the directory. "Du Pre, D."

"Stay cool, Mal," Marcus said. "Forty-five says this is where Katrina's sister lives."

As Malachai strode into the lobby, the doorman looked up from a newspaper spread across his workstation.

"Can I help you, gentlemen?"

Malachai held out his cell phone for the doorman to see. "You know her?"

The doorman looked at the image on the phone's screen, then back at Malachai. "Sir, I'm not really allowed to discuss tenants in the building with strangers . . ."

"*Is this Dawn Du Pre*? Yes or no."

The doorman's expression became constipated. "Yes, it is. But that's all I can say."

Oh, shit, Marcus thought.

Malachai glanced at the elevator doors. "When was the last time she was here?"

"I swear I don't know. I just work the day shift when people are at work. She's the subject of a missing person's case. There are police upstairs in her apartment right now."

Malachai and Marcus looked at each other, then exited the building.

"I'm going to kill that bitch," Malachai said as they climbed into their ride.

The elevator door opened, and Maria and Bernie got off.

"I got drafted by Homicide and a rogue missing person's case all in one day," Bernie said. "I don't know if my heart can handle the excitement."

As they passed the doorman, he raised one hand, like a kid in grade school. "Um, Officers? I mean, Detectives?"

Maria and Bernie exchanged looks.

"Yes?" Maria said.

The doorman looked around the lobby, as if trying to maintain discretion. "Two men were just here. African American gentlemen. They were looking for Miss Du Pre."

Maria felt her blood pumping faster.

"They seemed rather agitated. They showed me a photo of her taken on a cell phone and seemed surprised when I told them that yes, the photo was a picture of Miss Du Pre."

With her voice tightening, Maria said, "How long ago?"

The doorman seemed surprised by the question. "Sixty seconds?"

Maria bolted for the doors, flung one open, and ran to the curb. Looking left and right, she saw no sign of anyone suspicious on the sidewalk.

No, no, no, no, no!

Bernie appeared in the doorway, and as she ran back to the building, he held the door open for her. She marched to the doorman's station. "Did they give you their names?"

"No, I got the impression they didn't want me to know who they were."

"Describe them."

Bernie joined her side as the doorman described the two men who had intimidated him.

Malachai, she thought. "You need to get a security camera in here!"

"But I don't own the building. I just work here."

"It was Malachai," she said to Bernie. "I know it was."

Malachai entered Katrina's apartment alone. Assuring Marcus that he wouldn't kill her until they agreed they had milked her for every benefit they could, he sent his chief lieutenant and Forty-five on their way. But they didn't tell him what to do any more than Katrina did. He was his own man, and he made his own decisions. He would give the bitch one chance to explain herself, and if that explanation failed to satisfy him, he would kill her with his bare hands.

"Hey, baby," Katrina said in a silky voice, materializing in a bedroom doorway. She wore a sheer black top over midnight lingerie. "How did it go? Did you deliver the message?"

"I'm no messenger boy," Malachai said.

"Of course not. You're the motherfucking king of New York." She walked toward him, hips swaying and lips parted. "Did you give him the message?"

"Yeah, I gave it to him." Maybe he would fuck her one more time and then kill her.

"What did he say?"

He said you were rolling in the mud with a pig behind my back. "He talked a lot of shit and said he'd call you at nine. He also said he dumped our drugs."

She draped her arms around his taut neck. "We'll make more Black Magic. We'll make more zonbies."

Then she kissed him on the mouth, pushing her tongue against his, and grinded her pelvis against him. He felt his cock hardening against her and his gun pressing against his hip. He didn't know which weapon to use.

Before he could decide, she drove the long blade of a dagger between his ribs and into his heart.

"L.T.!"

Lieutenant Mauceri turned in the men's room doorway, a startled expression on his face as Maria intercepted him. "Yeah, Vasquez?"

"I want to issue an APB on Prince Malachai," Maria said between gasping breaths.

"What for?"

"He was involved in Edgar's disappearance; I know it."

Mauceri's expression hardened. "I told you to stay away from that case, Detective. You're supposed to be working two and a half homicides involving three hundred missing fingers, three hundred missing toes, and I don't know how many missing teeth. I should think that would be more than enough to keep you occupied."

Bernie joined them, coffee in hand.

"The Mutilation Murders are connected to the Machete Massacres, and the Machete Massacres are linked to Malachai. The doorman at Dawn Du Pre's building says Malachai was there looking for her today."

"That's circumstantial as hell. Isn't Malachai already wanted for questioning for the Papa Joe murders?"

"Yeah, 'for questioning,' but we can't find him. He's gone

underground. That's why I want the APB."

Mauceri managed to shake his face without shaking his whole head. "No deal. You don't have enough. All you'll do is scare him off." He turned to Bernie. "Is this how you try to impress your new boss? I heard you were a by-the-numbers kind of guy. I don't need another freethinker around here."

Bernie shrugged. "Sorry."

"Bring something more concrete, and you can have your APB, Vasquez." Mauceri entered the men's room.

Maria followed him. "If I get him into the box, I'll get what we need to convict him."

With his hand frozen on his zipper, Mauceri said, "It doesn't work that way. You think he's tied to all these headline crimes? If he's that big, we can't afford to risk letting him off on any technicalities."

"*Please*, L.T. Edgar could be alive somewhere. Malachai is all we've got."

Mauceri met her gaze. "You know, I think every cop should be given one opportunity to take a chance and bend the rules, throwing all caution to the wind and jeopardizing their careers. Do you want this that bad?"

"Fuckin' A."

"All right. Have it your way. Issue an APB. But *only* question Malachai about Papa Joe and Edgar. Don't you dare taint whatever leads we develop on the Machete Massacres and the Mutilation Murders."

With her eyes tearing up, Maria exhaled. "Whatever you say. Thank you, Lieutenant."

"You can thank me by finding Edgar alive."

"Yes, sir."

"Now get out of here and let me piss in peace."

Katrina knew she was taking a risk by sending Malachai to meet with Jake, but she couldn't do it herself and obviously couldn't send a zonbie in her place. As soon as she saw Malachai's eyes, she knew that Jake had sown the seeds of dissent in his brain. So she picked up the dagger from its hiding place behind a vase of flowers and plunged it into her lover's heart.

Malachai's eyes went wide, and his mouth fell open. He reached for the blade protruding from his chest but hesitated as if afraid to touch it. With blood gushing out of the wound, he looked at Katrina's face, and she flashed her best smile at him. Then he pitched face forward, the impact driving the blade even deeper into his heart.

Katrina felt no remorse. She had found Malachai vulgar and impatient and a bad lay and the manner in which he spoke to her distasteful. She had looked forward to killing him for quite some time. But timing was crucial, and she believed she had waited until the perfect moment. Rolling him over onto his back, she gave little thought to the growing puddle of blood on the floor. With the fortune she had amassed, she would leave this shit hole soon enough.

Malachai gaped at her, his face spattered with his own blood. "Bitch . . ."

Katrina stood straddling his chest, so that he had no choice but to gaze at her body. Then she made a face that was half smile and half sneer. "It was all me, Mal. Or should I call you Daryl?"

She crouched on top of him, feeling his hot blood lick her thighs. "My ideas. My powers. My success." She rubbed her crotch against his, teasing him. "You were nothing but my instrument, a method to realize my goals."

She pulled the dagger out of his heart, and his chest made a sucking sound.

"You'd be nowhere without me. And look at you now." Staring him in the eye, she ran her tongue over the blade, licking his blood from it. She grabbed his hair and pulled his head up, then pressed the dagger against his throat.

"*Bitch*," she said.

She slit his throat, and he gagged on his own blood. She watched him die, then dragged him by the ankles across the floor to the door of her special room. Opening the door, she measured his body, which she knew so well, with her eyes. Then she slid his body around so his head faced the wooden boards in the doorway that prevented the soil from spilling out. It took a lot of work, but she managed to push and pull him onto the dirt. And then she rolled him into the fresh grave that she had dug an hour earlier.

As he stared up at her with dead eyes, she pitched a shovelful of dirt into his face. In a short while, she had buried him and patted the dirt down with the shovel's blade. Then she stripped off her lingerie, so that she stood completely nude, and set her bongo drums on top of the layer of dirt that covered him. Kneeling over the grave, she beat the drums with her hands, creating a familiar rhythm. Her head rolled on her neck, her eyes half closed with pleasure, and she felt tremors rippling through her body.

The earth beneath her began to move, and she turned moist between her legs.

TWENTY-SEVEN

Forty-five steered the SUV around the Brooklyn block for the third time.

"I like it," Marcus said as they rolled along Forty-fourth Street and parked before one of several boarded-up buildings.

"I'm hungry," Forty-five said. "Can we get some Mickey D's? I need some Chicken McNuggets."

You need a bowl of lettuce without any dressing, Marcus thought. "After we check this place out. I don't want to hear any shit if Malachai calls."

"You right about that, but what makes you think he's gonna call? He didn't pick up when you called to tell him we found this new spot. He and Katrina are probably knocking boots."

I hope you're right, Marcus thought. He wanted Katrina out of the picture, preferably dead, but not now when everything was so insane. The bitch made Malachai crazy, but she also knew how to calm him down. "After this building."

Forty-five sighed. "Awright."

They got out of the SUV, and Forty-five locked the door with his remote control. The sun descended behind the apartment building, so they took flashlights with them. They looked up and down the street and saw a few black and Hispanic faces regarding them with curiosity.

Future customers, Marcus thought as he mounted the cracked concrete steps leading to the building's front door. Seizing the graffiti-covered plywood behind the cross board in both hands, he pushed and the plywood fell against the door with no resistance.

"Someone's been here already."

Forty-five shrugged. "So? Kids, maybe. Or junkies. No matter."

Marcus slid the plywood aside, revealing the broken panes of glass in the front door. He opened the door and stepped between the boards, entering the vestibule, where he faced an inner door with a hole where its knob should have been.

Forty-five looked at the empty space between the planks. "You're playing, right?" Together they removed one of the remaining boards, and Forty-five joined Marcus in the vestibule. Without discussion, they drew their guns and entered the building's darkened lobby. Forty-five carried a silver version of the weapon he had been named after.

Marcus gagged. The place reeked of human waste.

"God*damn*," Forty-five said.

"Shut up."

Their flashlight beams crisscrossed each other at the stairs, which they climbed. A hallway window on the second floor glowed with fading sunlight, outlining the metal railing at the top. Forty-five's heavy footsteps echoed around them.

Fucking Horton Hears a Crackhead, Marcus thought, listening to his corpulent companion's heavy breathing.

At the top of the stairs, he gasped as a creature with dead white features stepped into his flashlight beam. Before he knew it, Forty-five's gun appeared inches away from his face. The creature opened its jaws, and Marcus saw two rows of yellow teeth. Marcus swatted Forty-five's gun away with his Glock. "It's just a scarecrow! What are you trying to do, blind me or make me deaf?"

Moaning, the creature turned away, and the darkness swallowed it.

"*Sowry*," Forty-five said.

They crossed the hallway, which reeked of Black Magic. Flickering light escaped from the space between an open door and its frame. Raising their guns, they looked inside. Half a dozen naked men and women sat and laid on the floor, firing up glass pipes. They resembled animated skeletons, and a pair of children played in filth. Somewhere in the darkness, an infant cried.

"This ain't right," Forty-five said, his whisper still echoing.

None of the scarecrows reacted to his voice.

"Neither is turning our dead people into slaves, but you're still wearing that chain, aren't you?"

Forty-five glanced at the gleaming gold chain hanging from his neck, as if he had forgotten it was there. "Right . . ."

"Then stop your crying and let's go." But he felt sick to his stomach. *It's just the smell . . .*

They opened another door and gazed into an empty apartment. And then another and another after that.

"There's plenty of room in here for our sellers," Marcus said. "Let's go get those McNuggets now."

Forty-five made a face. "I lost my appetite."

As they turned back in the stairway's direction, they heard the echoing sound of wood striking the lobby floor, followed by dozens of hurried footsteps.

Jake tried the door to Laurel's place, but it was locked, so he rapped on it several times. Light shone through the red curtain in the window that hid the parlor's interior from the world outside.

A minute later, Laurel opened the door with a surprised look on her face. Her eyes settled on his eye patch.

"You should have known I was coming," Jake said, raising a brown paper bag. "I brought Chinese."

She opened the door. "I'm glad to see you're still alive. I had my doubts. Edgar and I have been watching the news. You've been busy."

He stepped past her, and she closed the door. "That's me: always a busy social calendar."

She followed him to the round table. "The city's recovered dozens of bodies."

"That will keep them busy at the medical examiner's office," he said, setting the food down on the table. "Where's Edgar?"

"This way." She lifted the bag and took him into her living room, where a sofa and a coffee table faced a TV.

Perched on the swing in his upright cage, Edgar crowed at Jake, his legs shifting from side to side on the swing. Seeing him again swelled Jake's chest. Jesus, what an insane situation!

Laurel went into the kitchen and returned with two plates. "Do you want some wine? Oh—no. I'm sorry."

Jake studied her. "That's okay."

"Your secrets are safe with me." She served the food. "To what do we owe this honor? Shouldn't you be out exterminating zonbies?"

He sat beside her on the sofa. "The last time I had scores to settle, I ate alone in a restaurant my wife and I used to frequent. I thought it might be nice to have some company this time."

"What's happening tonight?"

"I know who all the players are and what they're after. First I'm going to make Katrina restore Edgar; then I'm going to put a permanent stop to her zonbies."

"Afterlife?"

"It's scary how you do that."

"That disc contains deadly information, Jake. Apocalyptic, even. You can't turn it over to her, even to bring Edgar back." Laurel looked at the raven. "He's alive. His soul remains in his body. Share that information, and there will be repercussions that you and I can't imagine."

"Would you like me to share it with you?"

Her lips parted, her eyes opened with sudden temptation, and her body stiffened, like a recovering addict just offered a fix. "Once, maybe. But not now."

"I'm glad to hear it."

"You should destroy that disc."

"I'll consider it." Opening a fortune cookie, he plucked out the piece of paper. "'Loyalty is its own reward.'" He laughed.

Marcus ran to the stairway with Forty-five pounding the hallway floor behind him. Flashlight beams danced on the walls below, and he prayed the intruders were cops. Peering over the railing, he saw a small army of zonbies, armed with machetes, running up the stairs. The dead things spotted them.

"Aw, nah!" Forty-five said, his deep, flabby voice squealing.

"I don't think they're here to move in early."

"What the hell did *we* do?"

Good question. Marcus moved sideways to the top of the stairs. "Get your fat ass over here."

"No, let's get the fuck out of here!"

"We stand a better chance of picking them off right here."

"Ah, shit." Stepping beside Marcus, Forty-five pulled back his gun's slide.

The zonbies stormed upstairs, and the drug dealers opened fire on them. The semiautomatic gunfire slowed the ghoulish creatures down but stopped none of them.

Marcus shouted to be heard over the deafening noise. "Their heads! Their heads!"

"I'm trying!"

Marcus felt a hot shell casing from Forty-five's gun strike his left eye. Blinking fast to regain full vision, he glimpsed sparks below as a round struck a machete blade. *Worthless piece of shit!*

"I'm out!" Forty-five said, his silver gun clicking in his hand.

"So reload!"

"I can't! I don't have any more ammo!"

Seeing the advancing horde less than ten steps below, Marcus stopped firing long enough to plant his feet and hurl Forty-five down the stairs. The bodyguard screamed as he collided with the lead zonbies, and Marcus watched the mass of bodies tumble down into the darkness. Forty-five's screams turned shrill and gurgling.

Turning, Marcus ran to the Black Magic den and saw the scarecrows inside huddled together in fear. Opening the door wider, so the zonbies would see them, he sprinted to the next apartment, slammed that door shut, and pressed the doorknob's feeble button lock. Breathing heavy, he searched the apartment with his flashlight and discovered a chair with a broken seat in the kitchen. He ran back to the front door and wedged the chair beneath the knob.

That ought to hold them.

He ran into the living room, where dim moonlight shone through grime-encrusted windows. Jamming his Glock into his waistband, he twisted the brass window locks and braced his palms against the frame. Even before he opened the window, his heart sank. Up close, with his vision adjusting to the darkness, he saw the black bars that covered the windows from the outside. With his heart pounding in his chest, he forced the window up and seized each bar in his hands. All of them held.

In the hallway outside the apartment, fists pounded on the door.

Jake opened the door to his suite, flicked on the lights, and carried Edgar's cage into the reception area. Ignoring the mail that had collected on the floor, he went into his office and opened the safe. He considered copying Afterlife to his laptop's hard drive but rejected the notion.

If I don't survive the night, then two copies will exist to threaten humanity.

He ejected the original DVD and relocked the safe. Crossing the office, he sat behind his chair and turned the disc over in his hand.

So much horror over one damned research project.

But Afterlife was more than a research project: the file contained all of mankind's knowledge and theories on the supernatural, religion, and mythology, cross-referenced and indexed.

Tilting back in his chair, he opened the blinds and gazed out the window at the Tower. *You sure knew how to cause trouble, old man.*

He glanced at his cell phone: 8:55 p.m.

Edgar cocked his head at him.

"It's going to be a hell of a night," Jake told the raven. Four minutes later, he located the telephone number he had stored in his phone's memory and pressed autodial.

On the other end, Katrina answered after the second ring. "Hello, Jake. It's a relief to hear your voice again."

Staring at Edgar, Jake said, "I can't say the same thing, *Dawn*. But I have been looking forward to this call."

"So have I. You want Edgar returned to normal, and I want Afterlife. The exchange will be tonight at eleven." She told him where to meet her. "Needless to say, come alone."

"That's how I roll. Why not make it midnight?"

Her words tumbled out faster. "I have to let you go. I'm in the middle of something." She hung up.

With his flashlight and Glock both aimed at the front door, Marcus inched toward the banging. "Forty-five? Hey, I'm sorry about that, brother. I guess I just panicked."

The blade of a machete chopped through the door, and Marcus jumped off the floor. A second machete blade appeared, and the first one withdrew. Then a third blade hacked its way into view.

Marcus took a step backwards. *Oh, Jesus, no!*

Pivoting on one foot, he ran into the only bedroom. Aiming the flashlight, he saw the door had been removed. Around the corner, the front door crashed open. He fled to the bedroom windows and saw that they too had bars.

Footsteps stomped down the hall. Facing the direction of the noise, he switched off his flashlight and tightened his grip on the Glock. Beams of light sliced through the darkness. Some of them separated from the others and divided the bedroom, pinning him like a deer in headlights. He knew better than to fire blindly.

Let them get closer. Go for their heads.

The flashlights grew nearer, brighter, blinding him. He clicked on his own flashlight, and the silhouettes before him lit into zonbies. Dead eyes sunk within skullish heads regarded him with distant stares. Raising his gun, he fired at one of the dead things and hit it in the forehead. Dropping it to the floor.

Marcus grinned. *Take that, you stinking piece of meat!*

He aimed at the next zonbie. The thing grinned at him, revealing discolored gums.

He had been around a hundred of these things, and not one of them had ever shown the slightest degree of emotion.

Grinning even wider at his obvious discomfort, the male zonbie spoke, its voice hoarse and raspy and unmistakably *female*. "This is your judgment day, Marcus."

Katrina!

"Payback is a bitch."

"So are you," Marcus said, shooting the zombie in the head. The thing toppled to the floor.

Katrina's voice continued from the next zonbie's mouth. "I can do this all night long."

"So can I." Marcus aimed at the zonbie before him, and the slide of his gun locked back. *Son of a bitch!*

"It doesn't look that way."

Marcus squeezed the trigger over and over with the same result each time. Tears formed in his eyes. "You bitch . . ."

"Life's a bitch," the zonbie said in Katrina's voice. "And then you die."

"No . . ."

The crowd of zonbies in the room flowed around the talking zonbie like water, their machetes raised high in the air.

Over the sounds made by metal blades cutting into his body, Marcus thought he heard Katrina laughing.

TWENTY-EIGHT

Jake drove up Second Avenue, Dawn Du Pre's building rising from the darkness in the distance on his right. When he reached the building, he turned left at the intersection and circled the opposite block. A plywood fence surrounded the half of the block facing the apartment building, and on the other side of the fence, the skeletal structure of the unfinished high-rise rose from its foundation fifty feet below. Parking the dented, scarred, and shattered Monte Carlo along the curb facing the fence, Jake switched off the engine. When he had confronted Old Nick and Kira Thorn in the Tower, a storm had raged outside. Tonight the sky was clear and black, pinpricked with stars.

Opening his door and easing the birdcage out with both hands, he said to the raven, "Come on. Let's go save the world. Or at least this city." *Or your soul, buddy.*

He stood up holding the cage in one hand. Looking around the quiet neighborhood, he removed a container of salt from the backseat and poured the remainder of its contents over the car door's threshold.

Just in case I make it out of there in a hurry.

He tossed the container back into the car and closed the door. With half the windows shot out, he saw no point in locking the vehicle. Stepping onto the sidewalk, he whistled the tune to "Moondance," which had been Sheryl's favorite song. He circled the fence, searching for an opening.

At last he found a gate fabricated from the same material, so it blended into the fence. A chain with a padlock on its end lay coiled on the sidewalk. Pulling the gate open, Jake faced a covered gangway that led into the structure. The streetlights on the sidewalk illuminated the girders and crossbeams, but no light reached the structure's interior despite the lack of walls.

Taking a deep breath, he traversed the gangway. He looked over the railing and saw lights far below.

Not lights. Torches. So far down that no one else sees them.

At the end of the gangway, he stepped onto a metal floor. Switching on his flashlight, he saw a caged construction elevator. He pulled the gate open, stepped inside, and pulled it shut. The gate rattled like a grocery cart.

"Now we're both in a cage," he said to Edgar.

The raven cawed.

Scrutinizing the elevator's controls, Jake threw a lever so it aligned with a Down arrow. A motor hummed to life, and the elevator descended into darkness. A breeze blew in Jake's face, and his stomach felt queasy. He counted four floors, then saw the foundation come into view. Wondering if the elevator would stop on its own or if he would kill himself in a crash, he waited until he had almost reached the ground before flipping the lever into its Off position just to be safe.

He pushed the gate open and hopped down two feet onto the cement. Stepping forward, he imagined the space before him as a luxury condo's parking garage.

If it ever gets finished.

A series of work lights affixed to support beams provided enough illumination for him to see where he was going without the use of his flashlight, which he slid into a jeans pocket. He approached the burning torches at the foundation's far end, the smells of cement and plaster and other construction materials filling his nostrils. Glancing down at Edgar, he maintained an even pace.

Nearing the torches, he saw Katrina standing in the distance, wearing a tight white dress that emphasized her figure and made her skin appear darker. She had lashed the torches to steel girders.

As they got closer to her, Edgar made a sound that Jake had not heard from the raven before: a low, fearful croak.

"It's okay. Don't be afraid." *I'm afraid enough for both of us.* Jake stopped ten feet away from her. He did not set the birdcage down.

Katrina held a laptop with a handle. "Good, you came alone."

"Don't men usually do whatever you say?"

A hint of a smile. "Yes. Especially those who have drunk my menstrual blood without knowing it. An old vodou recipe."

He gestured at her dress. "White doesn't suit you. You seduced Edgar to get to me?"

She nodded. "When Tower died and Kira Thorn disappeared, I

cast a spell to locate Afterlife. When I found out whose safe protected it and I discovered your former relationship to the Tower, I decided to set up shop here in the city."

"Why didn't you come after me instead of Edgar?"

"I'm an expert researcher, remember? I knew your wife had been murdered and that you had thrown yourself into your work. Your relationship with Edgar seemed to be the only one you made an effort to maintain, so I chose him. When I finally met you at dinner and saw you with Maria, I considered that maybe I'd underestimated myself. I'm pretty sure I could have had you. No problem, though: everything went according to plan, and Edgar was a fine lay."

Jake felt anger radiating from his soul. *Stay cool, Jake. Stay focused.* "One minute you tried to kill me, the next you wanted me alive. That's confusing to a guy like me."

"I never wanted you dead. I came here for you and what you stole from Tower. You caused my Brooklyn zonbies to go after you when you invaded their turf. They're programmed to carry out basic functions, one of them being self-preservation. I didn't even know they tried to kill you until I read about it in the papers. But I did send the second crew to your building after you drove me home. Their orders were to torture you until you opened the safe so they could steal the disc."

"And then they wouldn't have killed me?"

She offered an apologetic smile. "I said I didn't *want* you dead. I didn't say I wouldn't hesitate to kill you if it served my best interest."

"Why the machetes?"

"What is this, *Meet the Press*? Machetes are easy to come by, and I wanted to ensure that my enemies didn't resurrect their soldiers. The last thing I needed was for zonbies to come after *me*."

"You threw my back out and caused me to hallucinate."

"Physical pain to keep you out of my hair and emotional distress so you'd beg me to make it stop. I wanted to trade you peace of mind for Afterlife then, but you found a way to beat my curse. Since we're playing twenty questions, why don't you tell me how you did it?"

"It's a trade secret."

"We'd make an interesting pair, if only we could trust each other."

"What about Malachai?"

"He and his crew are dead. I had no choice after you turned him against me."

Malachai is dead, Jake thought. *Good, now I don't have to worry about him.* "You shouldn't have sent him to deliver that message."

"I didn't want to risk meeting you face-to-face. You're more unpredictable than I expected. You might have killed me or kidnapped me and tortured me until I agreed to transmogrify Edgar again."

"You could have just called me; I'm listed in the phone book."

"You made that impossible when you stole our supply of Black Magic. Malachai was out of his mind with anger. I needed to make him feel proactive about settling his score with you or kill him. So I sent him to you, knowing that I'd still have to kill him eventually. You can't blame a girl for trying to have her man and eat him, too. It doesn't matter; he served his purpose, just like Edgar did. I can rebuild my drug operation with very little effort. With Afterlife, I can do almost anything in time."

"What secret sauce makes your zonbies tick?"

Katrina seemed to enjoy his attention. "Trade secret."

"According to my source, a true bokor gets her power from a demon."

"Hmm. Your 'source.' I wondered how you were so effective against me when I went out of my way to keep the really useful information about voodoo out of Afterlife. I thought maybe you'd used something else in Afterlife against me. I guess you're not such a loner after all. Isn't there a psychic on the ground floor of your building? I should pay her a visit one day for a little girl talk."

Careful, Jake thought. "Can I watch?"

"Let's see how tonight goes first."

"That suits me just fine. We were discussing your demon friend . . ."

She pursed her lips. "We call them Loa, the spirits of our vodou religion. The Petro Loa are aggressive and warlike. While conducting research for Nicholas Tower, I discovered a secret method of summoning the demon spirit Kalfu, who is a Petro Loa. Naturally, I kept this information to myself. I dreamed of one day revenging myself upon the drug dealers who murdered my parents in the Bronx. It was a silly schoolgirl fantasy, one that I've never been able to realize because I don't know who the killers were. Hopefully I can remedy that with Afterlife. But when my grandmother, who raised me and instructed me in the ways of vodou, drowned in her own home because our government wouldn't extend a hand to save its own people—the descendents of the slaves who built this country—I performed this ritual and summoned Kalfu to visit me.

"He didn't appear naked in a pentagram or in a burst of flame. I saw him on the street a few days after I'd made my sacrifice in his name. He was beautiful—boyish and feminine at the same time. As soon as he spoke to me, I knew my prayers had been answered. I took him home and made love to him. I'd never experienced such love. Then he raped me. It was brutal. Ugly. *Painful.* I don't know how I survived that night. It took weeks for the scratches and bite marks to heal, and I still have scars. When he left, he said, 'You're pregnant now. Call me when you've given birth.' And then he laughed at me, humiliating me even more than when he tore me open.

"It turned out he was right: I *was* pregnant. I had no job, no family for support, just Nicholas Tower's money. That was enough. I carried the baby to term and gave birth to a beautiful baby boy in a house I'd bought in Westchester. I named him Romero after my father. He filled my life with a joy I'd never known. But when I took him home, I remembered what Kalfu had said. So I summoned my god.

"He appeared in my bed when I went into my room. His skin was red and covered with runny sores. 'Let me see the child,' he said.

"I raised my son in my arms for his father to admire. 'Isn't he beautiful?'

"Kalfu laughed, a sound that degraded me. 'Do you love him above all else?'

"'Yes,' I said.

"'Then kill him now in front of me, and I will grant you the powers you seek. Wring the life out of his frail body, and you shall know the secrets of life and death, which you may use as you see fit.'

"I looked at my baby, Romero, with his soft skin and closed eyes. He weighed only six pounds. I caressed his hair and kissed his cheeks. And then I strangled the life from him and offered his corpse to Kalfu. Laughing, the demon raped me again, streaking my body with my own blood. I screamed, then cried, then passed out from the agony in my orifices. When I regained consciousness, Kalfu and Romero were both gone, and I could barely move. I didn't leave my house for two weeks until my wounds healed. During that time, I suffered feverish dreams, and in those dreams, Kalfu instructed me in the ways of true vodou." She smiled, her teeth white in the firelight. "For that, I love him to this day."

Jake felt sick to his stomach. He was no stranger to human-demon couplings; he had witnessed Kira Thorn fondling Cain and attempting to straddle him. But Kira had revealed herself to be a monster, genetically engineered in Tower's laboratories and programmed to lust after power. Katrina was all too human and had sacrificed her own baby to his father in return for the secrets of necromancy. And she craved even more.

Sensing his disgust, Katrina stopped smiling. "Don't look at me like that, just because I have the guts to walk where others are afraid to tread. I've brought this city to its knees. Not Papa Joe, not Malachai. *Me.* A so-called bitch."

"I don't need to hear any more. I don't think I can stomach it. I'm here to make a trade."

Katrina reached out with one hand. "Then give me Afterlife."

Jake grunted. "First, make Edgar normal again—with no side effects. I want him the way he was, the way he's supposed to be."

"Just like a man. Satisfy me first; then I'll satisfy you."

Jake drew his Glock from its shoulder holster and aimed it at her. He had learned a thing or two about high-pressure negotiating from Old Nick. "We seem to have reached an impasse."

"Shoot me and Edgar will never lose those wings and tail feathers. I'm the only person who can change him back."

"If I give you Afterlife now, you have no incentive to keep your end of the bargain. You'll checkmate me, and Edgar and I will end up dead."

A feint smile of admiration returned to her lips. "You're half right. I like Edgar just the way he is."

"Which leaves me six feet under."

"Not necessarily. Maybe I'll turn you into a field mouse and watch Edgar eat you alive."

"Not if I kill you now, sweetheart. At least I'll finish your zonbies and put an end to your vodou."

"I sacrificed my baby to get where I am. Are you willing to sacrifice Edgar to shut me down?"

Jake swallowed. *I don't know.*

Then a vicious smell overwhelmed him, an odor he hadn't smelled in over a year since his days in Homicide: the stench of a rotting corpse. Before he could react, muscular arms encircled his chest, pinning his arms to his side and squeezing the breath from him. The birdcage and Glock clattered on the cement, and the birdcage rolled with Edgar shrieking.

No!

Katrina had tricked him. She had only run off at the mouth to give her undead slave time to sneak up on him. And now she stood perfectly poised and unconcerned with any threat he might have posed, a look of amusement on her face.

Jake struggled in his oppressor's steel grip but could not shake the creature loose. None of Katrina's other zonbies had reeked like this. Unable to breathe, he twisted his head around and gaped at Malachai's dead face. Unlike the other zonbies, Malachai had not undergone any kind of preservation. He smelled and looked like death, and as his purplish lips pulled back into a snarl, revealing a full set of teeth, Jake saw hatred blazing in his eyes.

Hearing a stutter of footsteps, Jake snapped his head around in time to see Katrina seize the birdcage and dash back to her spot. Renewing his efforts to break free of Malachai's crushing hold on him, he lunged at her. With his oxygen cut off, he heard his brain throbbing in his skull and feared he would lose consciousness.

"Let him breathe," Katrina said, her eyes gleaming from the torchlight.

Malachai loosened his grip just enough for Jake to suck in some air.

"You'll have to forgive Malachai for being overzealous. He isn't a zonbie but a *zombie*. With the right knowledge, there are numerous ways to resurrect the dead. He remains a slave to my will, but I've allowed him to retain a certain amount of ambition. It's impossible for him to move against me, so you're his sole reason for 'living.' He doesn't like you very much. When he's finished with you and I'm finished with him, the police will discover what appear to be the corpses of two men who killed each other. I want his body identified. I want there to be no doubt on the streets about who's running this city now."

Arching his back, Jake gasped for more air and saw Katrina raise the cage high enough to stare at Edgar. Admiring her handiwork, she unlatched the cage with her free hand, groped for the quivering bird, which pecked at her hand, and allowed the cage to fall to the ground so she could restrain the panicked raven with both hands.

"No!" Jake's voice rose into the night.

As Edgar flapped his wings, Katrina closed the fingers of her right hand around his neck and extended both arms, as if offering a sacrifice.

Edgar stopped croaking, and his wings stilled.

"Give me Afterlife, or I'll break his neck and use him for a feather duster. I won't lie to you: there's no saving yourself. But at least Edgar will live."

Staring at the raven in Katrina's hands, Jake couldn't help but imagine her baby. He sagged in Malachai's rancid arms and bowed his head. "All right. You win. Afterlife is yours."

"Damn you. Where is it?"

"I taped it to the bottom of the birdcage."

Katrina set one foot on top of the birdcage and spun it around so that the jewel case taped to its bottom came into view. She looked up with disbelief spreading across her face. "That disc contains the most awesome secrets in the history of mankind and you hid it underneath *bird shit*?"

Kneeling on the ground with one hand still gripping Edgar's neck, she tore the tape from the jewel case, which landed on the cement, and removed the DVD. Opening the tray of her laptop, she inserted the disc and raised the screen. She watched the program boot up, the screen's blue glow illuminating her anticipation. Her face transformed into a flesh-and-blood realization of rapture as she paged through Afterlife's contents.

Folding his arms beneath Malachai's, Jake reached inside his left sleeve and pulled out the dagger that he had hidden there. He drove AK's weapon, which had skewered his eye, into Malachai's thigh with no effect. Yanking the useless dagger free, he held on to it for comfort as congealed blood oozed out of Malachai's leg like jelly.

Katrina rose, holding Edgar by his neck. The bird beat his wings to prevent being choked. "You're unpredictable, but so am I." She flung Edgar over her head, and he took to the air, soaring into the night and disappearing from view.

Jake screamed, a painful cry that petered out to a strangled gasp. He could never save Edgar now. All his actions over the last twenty hours had amounted to nothing, and Katrina possessed Afterlife. "Edgar . . ."

Katrina regarded him with cool eyes. "Kill him."

Malachai resumed his crushing hold, and Jake thought his ribs would snap.

"You don't mind if I stay and watch, do you, Jake? I like to watch."

With the wind knocked out of him, Jake could not answer.

Malachai leaned back, lifting Jake's legs off the ground. Unable to leverage himself, Jake struggled like a beached fish. Watching the fight, Katrina picked up her laptop. Jake flailed his arms, unable to make use of the dagger. He pitched his head forward, then threw it back into Malachai's face as hard as he could. Malachai did not react, but Jake felt the zombie's nose flatten out.

Jake rocked forward and slammed his head back again, sending pain through his skull and empty eye socket. He repeated this again and again. The pain of impact lessened, and he heard squishing sounds behind him. Lukewarm fluid ran down the back of his neck. Katrina's face screwed up in surprise, and Malachai increased the intensity of his hold. Jake's vision darkened, and he felt his consciousness slipping away.

One . . . more . . . time!

Throwing his head back once more, he heard a soggy sound and felt a skull caving in. He prayed it wasn't his and felt reassured when Malachai tipped forward and released him. Jake fell on his hands and knees but dragged Malachai with him. Through the pain, he realized that his head and Malachai's had merged together. Bracing his left hand against Malachai's chest, he twisted his body sideways and stepped aside. After a great ripping sound, his head came free. Malachai staggered in a half circle, muscles dripping off his brittle skull.

Stunned, Jake shook his head. Wasting no time, he lunged forward and swung the dagger at the blinded zombie. The blade drove into Malachai's temple with a deep crunch, and Jake realized his foe's body was already in a state of decomposition.

Malachai reached up for the hilt protruding from the side of his head, his body jerking from side to side. His fingers closed around the handle, then slipped away, and he collapsed in a heap on the ground. A dark sphere rose from the shell and faded.

Jake grabbed the back of his head. His hand came away dripping flesh that resembled cooked fat. *Malachai's face.*

As Katrina backed away, Jake's eyes settled on his gun. She sprinted in the opposite direction, running for the construction elevator. Jake scooped up the gun and ran after her, but the pain in his head slowed him down, and he even fell to one knee before resuming the foot chase.

Katrina threw herself into the elevator and slammed the cage door behind her. A moment later, as Jake caught up, the elevator's motor coughed to life and the elevator rose. Jake slowed to a stop beneath the elevator and watched its ascent.

Following the sound of the motor, he aimed his Glock at the greasy metal and fired at it repeatedly. The muzzle fire flashing from the Glock's barrel did little to soothe his headache. Rounds sparked against the motor, and shell casings collected on the ground. Black smoke spewed out of the motor, which sputtered to a stop. Looking up, Jake saw the elevator had stopped as well.

Seconds later, the cage door swung open, and Katrina stood at its edge. Measuring the distance to the ladder alongside the elevator, she jumped the four feet with one arm clutching the laptop. Jake watched in awe as her lead foot landed on one ladder rung and her free hand caught another with the grace of a dancer.

Holstering his smoking gun, Jake ran to the ladder and climbed after her. Twenty feet up, with his head throbbing, he saw her dress flapping around her. Then something dark obscured his view.

The laptop!

Flattening himself against the ladder, face turned down and left arm protecting his crown, he braced for the impact. A flat side of the laptop slammed into his forearm, fracturing it from wrist to elbow. Screaming, he wrapped his right arm around a rung so he would not release it. The laptop continued its descent, then shattered into pieces on the ground. He knew that if he investigated, he would find no sign of Afterlife and Katrina would evade him. Wincing, he looked up again.

She had vanished.

Without hesitation, he resumed climbing, every pull of his left arm reducing him to whimpers. He had to prevent Katrina from escaping. He needed to hear from her lips that she could not bring Edgar back, and then she needed to die. He scaled the ladder, feeling his injured arm swell up like Popeye's. Fifty feet from the foundation at ground level, he stopped.

Why would she go any higher than this?

He looked down just in time to glimpse a flash of white disappearing onto the fourth floor of the construction site, ten feet below him.

Tricked me, he thought as he climbed back down. Now he had to make the same leap she had, without the use of his left arm to grab the girder for support. Pushing off with his right hand and foot, he crossed the chasm, his left foot reaching the ledge. He pitched forward, rolled, and came up in a crouch.

Now what? This floor of the unfinished building stretched into total darkness. If he turned on his flashlight, she'd know his location. He edged forward into the darkness, his arm aching even more now that he had stopped climbing. Hearing a slight scuffling sound, he pivoted to see Katrina's silhouette darting from behind a girder. With great speed, she leapt off the edge and seized one rung in both hands and scrambled up the ladder. Jake mimicked her move, aware that he had only one good hand with which to grab the ladder. His hand passed between rungs in the darkness, and the impact of him crashing face-first into the ladder almost propelled him backwards into empty space.

Tilting his head back, he saw his quarry had almost reached the gantry that would lead her to the plywood fence and the sidewalk beyond it. Draping his left arm around the ladder, he reached for his Glock, doubting that a one-eyed man in extreme pain could hit a target, even at this close range and from his angle.

Katrina's hands touched the gantry, and then she screamed, a sound that chilled and surprised Jake. Her hair billowed around her head. She pounded on the gantry and kicked at nothing. Then she fell.

Jake saw it in slow motion: her hands clawing at empty space. As she tipped backwards so that she plummeted headfirst, Jake noticed a black shape perched on the gantry's edge.

Edgar!

But if the raven had not flown away, then the bokor must not die; she needed to return Edgar to normal. On reflex, as Katrina pirouetted to certain death, Jake seized the rung with his right hand and snared her wrist with his left.

This is going to hurt . . .

He hated being right at the worst times. Katrina's body jerked Jake's fractured arm, forcing him to scream again. Her legs swung past her head so that she became upright again, but the front of her body crashed into the ladder with a reverberating thud. The pain that traveled the length of Jake's left arm and back was so intense that he thought the bones in his arm would split in two, and he screamed through clenched teeth.

Katrina swung her free arm up and clutched Jake's wrist, which only intensified his pain, and he already clung to the ladder for dear life.

He made eye contact with Katrina, whose panic-stricken face bled from several deep gashes inflicted on her by Edgar. "Help me . . ."

Jake's face heated with strain. "Promise me you'll change Edgar back."

"I . . . swear it . . ."

He believed her, but he didn't know if he could save her. "Grab the ladder, so you can let go of my arm."

She kicked in the air. "I can't . . ."

And then Jake heard the flapping of wings as Edgar came in for the kill. The raven's claws raked Katrina's face, and he pecked at her eyes, wings still flapping.

Jake's heart leapt in his chest. "Edgar, no!"

Katrina sacrificed herself to the great god of gravity, and as she plunged through the air, Jake saw that her gaping left eye socket lacked an eyeball. As the raven spread its wings and circled the space above her, Katrina continued to claw at empty air, a look of disbelief on her face. Then darkness swallowed her features, and she flattened out on the foundation below.

Edgar . . .

Holding tight to the ladder, Jake found he could no longer use his left hand at all. He had no choice but to step onto a rung and shoot his hand up to a higher rung. With tremendous effort, he reached the gantry and saw the shiny Afterlife disc lying near the edge, its surface smeared with red lipstick where Katrina had held it in her mouth. Too exhausted to pull himself onto the gantry, he rested for a moment, gathering his remaining strength, then threw one leg over the metal walkway and rolled onto it, chest heaving.

Edgar lighted onto the edge, his black beak open wide to accommodate the ruptured orb he had ripped from Katrina's head. Bloody muscles dangled from the eyeball. With perfect balance, he spat the eye over the edge.

Jake closed his eye and swallowed, measuring the extent of his failure. Edgar would never be human again, but at least the zonbies had been destroyed. Opening his eye, he took in the clear night sky, then raised his throbbing left arm so he could see his watch. Midnight, the witching hour. Grimacing, he held back laughter and tears at the same time.

Edgar just blinked at him and cawed at the darkness.

EPILOGUE

Jake parked the battered Monte Carlo on a residential street in Jackson Heights. Surveying the row houses, brownstones, and two-family homes, he switched off the engine and gathered his thoughts. Sunlight glared off the car's dirty windshield. He saw teenage boys loitering on stoops, glancing at corners where zonbies had probably dealt Black Magic only the night before.

This morning the TV news shows had devoted all their airtime to the sensational events rocking the city: twenty-four hours after thirty embalmed corpses were discovered at drug spots around the city with bullet holes in their heads, another sixty had been discovered without bullet holes but also without fingertips, toes, or teeth.

Mayor Madigan announced his intention to arrange for mass viewings of the bodies to help with identification, and Governor Santucci assigned emergency funds to the city, so NYPD could rehire the thousands of cops who had been laid off. Both politicians vowed to take the city back from the vicious drug lords who had committed such heinous acts. According to police commissioner Bryant, "massive amounts" of the deadly narcotic known as Black Magic had already been confiscated.

Jake smiled to himself, knowing that his former colleagues in blue had taken into custody only the small amounts of drugs carried on the persons of Malachai's undead soldiers, now dead. He also knew that a certain amount of Black Magic would find its way back onto the streets and that in another day or two—hell, maybe even tonight—neighborhood hoppers would take to the corners, dispensing their customary contraband.

Getting out of the damaged car, he mounted the steps of a white house and rang the doorbell.

A black woman with hair tight to her scalp opened the door. She wore business casual slacks and a blouse, and her weary expression grew animated at the sight of him. "Jake . . ." Joyce embraced him, then pulled back. "What happened to your *eye?*"

"It's a long story. I'm still getting used to the patch. Can I see Martin?"

"Yes, thanks for coming by." Stepping back from the door, she allowed Jake to enter the hallway and then her living room. Martin sat slumped on the sofa, watching news.

"Hi, Martin."

"Jake!" Martin ran into Jake's arms, then looked up at him with hopeful eyes. "Do you know where my dad is?"

Jake offered a weak smile. "I wish I did. Let's sit down."

Joyce joined them on the sofa.

"Don't ask me how, but I know that your father is alive. Call it a sixth sense that partners develop over time."

"Is he hurt?"

Jake considered the question. "I don't think so. But I don't think he's able to contact anyone, either."

"All they're talking about on the news is this drug war," Joyce said. "It sounds like they're devoting all their resources to fighting these animals behind Black Magic."

"You're right. I don't think the police will find him. But *I* will. I promise you, I'll do everything in my power to find him and bring him home."

Joyce's eyes teared up. "I believe you."

"If either of you ever needs anything—and I mean *anything*—you call me first. Don't hesitate to pick up the phone or come by my office."

"Thank you, Jake."

"If I get tied up on a case and you don't hear from me, don't think I've forgotten about you or Edgar. I'm making this the number one priority in my life."

Martin bowed his head, hiding his tears, and Jake eased his hurt arm around the boy's shoulders.

Maria and Bernie stood on the construction site's foundation between two corpses, surrounded by uniformed officers and Crime Scene Unit members. The male corpse appeared bloated and discolored, the female broken and bloody.

"That's Dawn Du Pre," Maria said in a flat tone.

Bernie sipped his coffee. "What was she doing with Malachai?" They had identified the drug dealer through the driver's license in his wallet.

"We know he was looking for her. Maybe she witnessed whatever happened to Edgar, and he wanted to make sure she wouldn't talk."

"Neither one of them is talking now." Bernie gestured at the wire birdcage lying on its side. "What do you make of this?"

"I have no idea. It must be unrelated."

"I'm sorry. I know they were your only leads."

Maria looked at Dawn's smashed remains. How strange that they had enjoyed dinner together less than a week ago, and now Dawn was dead and Edgar was missing. "No, I have one more."

Laurel was feeding Edgar at the round table in her parlor when Jake entered with his arm in a sling.

"I bet no one ever lets me rent a car again."

"He's not eating much," Laurel said.

"Maybe we should try steak. Edgar liked meat."

"Ravens eat small mice. I'm sure he can handle some steak."

"Stick him back in the cage for me, will you?"

"You should let me keep him here." She eased Edgar into the cage. "At least you'll know someone will always be here to watch him."

Jake sat opposite her. "Maybe I'll let you bird sit from time to time."

"You know where to find me."

Jake studied her oval-shaped face. *So much mystery behind those eyes.* "I did a little research on you."

"You mean you're investigating me?" She seemed amused.

"It's what I do."

"What did you discover?"

"Would you be surprised if I found anything?"

"Yes."

"No birth date. No records of education, employment, or taxes. As far as the United States government is concerned, you don't even exist. Whoever you are and whatever you've done, you've managed to cover your tracks completely."

A trace of a smile appeared on her lips. "It's what I do."

Standing, he lifted Edgar's cage from the table. "Maybe I'd like some references before I let you watch my bird."

"I'm sure you'll keep looking."

"It's what I do."

Sitting at his desk, with Edgar hopping around getting his bearings, Jake turned the Afterlife disc, still smeared with Katrina's lipstick, over in one hand. Laurel continued to press him to destroy it, but as long as there was a chance that information on the disc could lead to a solution to Edgar's dilemma, he needed to hang on to it, regardless of the danger.

His intercom buzzed. "Detective Vasquez is here to see you."

"Send her in, Carrie."

He had been expecting this visit. Leaning back in his seat, he watched Maria enter. "Hi, Maria."

Her eyes darted to the raven, which croaked at the sight of her and jumped onto the coffee table. "I didn't know you had a pet."

"Birds of a feather," Jake said. Something about her expression told him that the raven had unnerved her.

"Prince Malachai is dead. So is Dawn. We found them together at a construction site near Dawn's building."

Jake controlled every muscle in his face, giving Maria nothing to read. "Did they kill each other?"

"It's unlikely. His head was smashed in and her body broken into a hundred pieces."

"Do you think whoever killed them is responsible for Edgar's disappearance?"

"That's a distinct possibility, isn't it? The night Edgar disappeared, he and Dawn were both in her apartment. She came out; he didn't. Then a Caucasian male in his early to midthirties ran out of the building and pulled a gun on the doorman. Where were you that night?"

Jake didn't blink. "I checked into a hotel in New Jersey."

"Only *after* the incident reported by the doorman. I checked your credit card activity."

She's good, Jake thought. "Am I a suspect in Edgar's disappearance?"

"Let's just say that in my book, you're definitely a person of interest. Edgar's cell phone records show that you two were in frequent contact during the time leading to his disappearance. What I want to know is, did you suck him into an investigation of yours, or did he suck you into a rogue investigation he was running on Malachai?"

"I'm sorry, but you're on the wrong track. I'm glad to help you look for Edgar, but I had nothing to do with his disappearance."

Setting her palms down on his desk, she leaned forward. "Bullshit. You're in this up to your eyeball, and I know it. I think we're going to see a lot of each other from now on."

Jake said nothing. She would have taken any flippant remark by him as a challenge.

Turning to leave, she glanced at the raven and said, "Oh, and by the way—we found an empty birdcage at the scene of this double homicide. Do you have a receipt for that bird?"

Jake shook his head. "No, he just flew in through the window one day, and I decided to keep him. You're not going to report me to Animal Control, are you?"

"And lay down a paper trail establishing grounds for harassment? Not a chance. But I will be seeing you around, so keep breaking those rules."

"It's what I do."

After she left, Edgar flew onto the desk. Jake raised his good arm level with his chest, and Edgar hopped onto it.

"When will my life ever get easier?"

The raven didn't answer him.

Glancing out the window at the Tower, Jake thought, *Nevermore.*

THE JAKE HELMAN FILES
PERSONAL DEMONS
BY GREGORY LAMBERSON

Jake Helman, an elite member of the New York Special Homicide Task Force, faces what every cop dreads—an elusive serial killer. While investigating a series of bloodletting sacrifice rituals executed by an ominous perpetrator known as The Cipher, Jake refuses to submit to a drug test and resigns from the police department. Tower International, a controversial genetic engineering company, employs him as their director of security.

While battling an addiction to cocaine, Jake enters his new high-pressure position in the private sector. What he encounters behind the closed doors of this sinister operation is beyond the realm of human imagination. Too horrible to contemplate, the experimentation is pure madness, the outcome a hell where only pain and terror reside. Nicholas Tower is not the hero flaunted on the cover of Time magazine. Beneath the polished exterior of this frontiersman on the cutting edge of science is a corporate executive surrounded by the creations of his deranged mind.

As Jake delves deeper into the hidden sphere of this frightening laboratory, his discoveries elicit more than condemnation for unethical practices performed for the good of mankind. Sequestered in rooms veiled in secrecy is the worst crime the world will ever see—the theft of the human soul.

ISBN# 978-160542072-1
Mass Market Paperback / Horror
US $7.95 / CDN $8.95
AVAILABLE NOW
www.slimeguy.com

JOHNNY GRUESOME

GREGORY LAMBERSON

The upstate village of Red Hill is about to learn the meaning of fear.

Johnny Grissom, nicknamed "Johnny Gruesome" by his high school classmates, is a heavy-metal hellion who loves to party, watch horror movies, and get into fights. His best friend, Eric, admires him, and his girlfriend, Karen, loves him.

One winter night, Johnny's car, the Death Mobile, is discovered submerged beneath the icy surface of Willow Creek, with Johnny's waterlogged corpse inside. The residents of Red Hill believe that Johnny's death was accidental.

Then the murders begin—horrible acts of violent vengeance that hint at a deepening mystery and terror yet to come. A headless body is discovered at the high school. A priest is forced to confront his own misdeeds. And a mortician encounters the impossible.

One by one, Johnny's enemies meet a grisly demise, as the sound of a car engine and maniacal laughter fill the night. The students at Red Hill High School fear for their lives—especially Johnny's closest friends, who harbor a dark secret.

If people thought Johnny had a bad attitude when he was alive, wait until they encounter him when he's dead!

Johnny Gruesome is a valentine to E.C. Comics, Marvel's *Tomb of Dracula*, and such gory 1980s splatter flicks as *Re-Animator* and *Return of the Living Dead*. The novel is a horror fan's nightmare come true!

ISBN# 978-193475545-7
Trade Paperback / Horror
US $15.95 / CDN $17.95
AVAILABLE NOW
www.slimeguy.com

THE FRENZY WAY

GREGORY LAMBERSON

In every hardened cop's worst dreams there lurks a nightmare waiting to become reality. Captain Mace has encountered his. When a string of raped and dismembered corpses appears throughout New York, the investigation draws Mace into an interactive plot that plays like a horror movie. Taking the lead role in this chilling story may be the challenge of his career, testing his skills and his stamina, but even a superhero would find the series of terrifying crime scenarios daunting.

Unlike anything Mace has experienced, every blood-spattered scene filled with body parts and partially eaten human remains looks like an animal's dining room strewn with rotting leftovers. Only Satanic legends and tales from the dark side of spiritual oblivion resemble the mayhem this beast has created in his frenzy. In the wake of each attack is the haunting premonition of another murdering onslaught.

As Mace follows this crimson trail of madness, he must accept the inevitable conclusion. Whoever—or whatever—is responsible for this terror does not intend to stop, and it's up to him to put an end to the chaotic reign of a perpetrator whom, until now, he's met only in the annals of mythology. The mere mention of the word would send New York into a panic: *werewolf.*

ISBN# 978-160542099-8
Trade Paperback / Horror
US $15.95 / CDN $17.95
AVAILABLE NOW
www.slimeguy.com

wormfood

jeff jacobson

Arch Stanton has a bad job that's about to get a hell of a lot worse.

He's sixteen, scrawny, and dirt poor. He has an almost supernatural ability with firearms, but it may not be enough to survive the weekend.

Welcome to Whitewood, California, an isolated small town in northern California, a place full of bad manners and even worse hygiene. Money is tight, jobs are scarce, and bitter rivalries have simmered just under the surface for years.

Fat Ernst runs the local bar and grill. He'd stomp on his own mother for a chance at easy money, and when he forces Arch to do some truly dirty work, all hell breaks loose.

Fat Ernst's customers find themselves being infected by vicious, wormlike parasites and dying in unspeakable agony. As events spiral out of control, decades of hatred boil over into three days of rapidly escalating carnage. Will anyone in this town escape . . . before they're eaten alive?

ISBN# 978-160542101-8

Trade Paperback / Horrible Horror

US $15.95 / CDN $17.95

AVAILABLE NOW

LIZ WOLFE

If it's not one thing, it's a MURDER

Twenty-two years of marriage have given Skye Donovan a life of structure and predictability. When she discovers some women's underwear—not hers—however, she begins to suspect her husband is fooling around. And she's right, he is. But she's wrong about who the underwear belongs to. Not her husband's girlfriend, but her husband. And then she walks in on her husband . . . and his boyfriend.

Skye finds herself confronting another new reality. She needs to start life over. She needs to find a job, a place to live, break the news to her teenaged daughter and—yikes—start dating again. At least she has her best friend to help her through it all.

Not.

Corpses are turning up. And her best friend is the prime suspect.

As Skye tries to prove her friend's innocence, her own life is further complicated by a handsome detective, a sexy writer, a pagan wedding, her friend's unexpected pregnancy, and a new career. Could it get any crazier? In a word, yes. She not only must exonerate her friend, but do so before the murderer strikes even closer to home . . .

ISBN# 978-193383639-3

Mass Market Paperback / Mystery

US $7.95 / CDN $8.95

AVAILABLE NOW

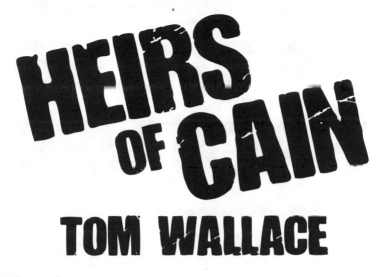

HEIRS OF CAIN

TOM WALLACE

Fallen angels.

The last words of a dying man. To the local cops, the words are meaningless.
But legendary assassin Cain knows exactly what they mean.

A hit is in the works.

And the target is big.

In 1971, five U.S. soldiers trained as assassins landed in North Vietnam to
complete a deadly mission under the watchful eye of Cain, a man feared by the
Vietnamese on both sides of the DMZ. Today, joining forces with his old boss
General Lucas White, Cain soon learns that Seneca, a former ally, has been hired
to kill the president of the United States and three top leaders in the Middle East.

Against a ticking clock, Cain must hunt down his former ally. But an even
deadlier betrayal could sabotage his mission—and cost him his life.

From the dark jungles of Vietnam to the midnight shadows of Central Park,
Heirs of Cain takes its readers on a thrilling ride they won't soon forget.

ISBN# 978-160542102-5
Mass Market Paperback / Thriller
US $7.95 / CDN $8.95
AVAILABLE NOW

STRESS FRACTURE

D·P· LYLE

Dub Walker, expert in evidence evaluation, crime scene analysis, and criminal psychology, has seen everything throughout his career—over a hundred cases of foul play and countless bloody remains of victims of rape, torture, and unthinkable mutilation. He's sure he's seen it all . . . until now.

When Dub's close friend Sheriff Mike Savage falls victim to a brutal serial killer terrorizing the county, he is dragged into the investigation. The killer—at times calm, cold, and calculating and at others maniacal and out of control—is like no other Dub has encountered. With widely divergent personalities, the killer taunts, threatens, and outmaneuvers Dub at every turn.

While hunting this maniacal predator, Dub uncovers a deadly conspiracy—one driven by unrestrained greed and corruption. Will he be able to stop the conspirators—and the killer—in their bloody tracks?

ISBN# 978-160542134-6
Hardcover / Thriller
US $24.95 / CDN $27.95
AVAILABLE NOW

MEDALLION
P R E S S

Be in the know on the latest
Medallion Press news by becoming a Medallion Press
Insider!

<u>As an Insider you'll receive:</u>

· Our FREE expanded monthly newsletter, giving you more insight
into Medallion Press

· Advanced press releases and breaking news

· Greater access to all your favorite Medallion authors

Joining is easy. Just visit our Web site at
<u>www.medallionpress.com</u> and click on the Medallion Press
Insider tab.

medallionpress.com

MEDALLION
P R E S S

Want to know what's going on with
your favorite author or what new releases
are coming from Medallion Press?

Now you can receive breaking news,
updates, and more from Medallion Press
straight to your cell phone, e-mail, instant messenger, or Facebook!

Sign up now at www.twitter.com/MedallionPress to stay on top of all
the happenings in and
around Medallion Press.

For more information
about other great titles from
Medallion Press, visit

m e d a l l i o n p r e s s . c o m